Offense combats offense, Murray-Ku had once said.

Cego waited for another of Bertoth's punches and let it nearly take his head off, before weaving to the side and slamming his shin into the boy's hefty thigh.

Usually, a leg kick like that would slow an opponent down, give them some pause. Bertoth didn't miss a step. He met Cego's eyes, smiled, and continued his onslaught.

Dodge, leg kick. Dodge, leg kick. Cego repeated the sequence several times, finally feeling some momentum. But Bertoth didn't appear to be slowing. The northerner's legs were like tree trunks.

Don't stop what's working, Murray's voice reminded him again. *Don't let up. Do damage until they figure out a way to defend.*

Cego kept chopping at Bertoth's leg. Same combo, same defense, same kick.

Finally, he felt something give. Bertoth wobbled slightly and Cego moved in with a low kick to finish the job.

But Cego didn't get the reaction he wanted. Instead, Bertoth dropped levels, caught his foot, and smirked again.

The Myrkonian raised his hand to elevate Cego's leg and jerked him forward. Cego blinked as Bertoth's skull careened toward his, the boy's considerable body weight fully behind it.

The lights went out.

Praise for
THE COMBAT CODES

"With surprising depth and touching relationships, this debut packs a punch and sets up a fascinating foundation for the rest of the series. Great for fans of Will Wight."

—*Library Journal* (starred review)

"Darwin skillfully deploys his expertise in this impressive debut and series launch.... [He's] adept at making blow-by-blow descriptions of bouts vivid and engaging.... This is a perfect setup for the next volume and will especially appeal to fans of Pierce Brown's Red Rising series." —*Publishers Weekly*

"This dark tale of martial arts and ancient Codes in a fallen world will captivate readers who crave action." —*Kirkus*

"Brutal and relentless. *The Combat Codes* is that rare book that fully satisfies me as an action fan."

—Fonda Lee, author of *Jade City*

"A vividly realized tale both focused and sprawling. It's a book about warriors written by a master of the martial arts, and the mastery shows." —Evan Winter, author of *The Rage of Dragons*

"This book kicks ass—literally and literarily!"

—Richard Swan, author of *The Justice of Kings*

"If Mike Tyson wrote a sci-fi novel (and could write like he threw a right hook), it would read a little like *The Combat Codes*. Bare-knuckle brilliance."

—Jackson Ford, author of *The Girl Who Could Move Sh*t with Her Mind*

"*The Combat Codes* is combat as it was meant to be written: raw but elegant, a blend of the poet's wordsmithing and the martial art master's technical expertise. A fantastic reading experience."

—Moses Ose Utomi, author of *The Lies of the Ajungo*

"A well-paced sci-fi brimming with action, brutality, thoughtfulness, and heart. From ruthless underworld to storm-harried, glistening academy, every fight is clear and visceral, and I couldn't help but be ensnared by the mystery and tension woven throughout."

—H. M. Long, author of *Hall of Smoke*

"*The Combat Codes* is a perfectly balanced cocktail of high-octane action, enthralling mystery, and genuine heart. A gritty, fully realized world sets the stage for lovable (and hateable) characters, heart-pounding action, and twists that literally had my jaw dropping."

—M. J. Kuhn, author of *Among Thieves*

"A great read for any fan of realistic martial arts fiction. The integration of a compelling sci-fi/fantasy plot and true-to-life martial arts action makes for a unique story that any student of warfare is sure to enjoy."

—Ryan Hall, UFC fighter

"A fantastic read that takes you along the martial arts' path of self-discovery. The storyline, training, fights, and philosophy in the book made it highly enjoyable. Whether you are a martial artist, a fan, or just an SFF reader, this book will be a lot of fun."

—Kenny Florian, MMA commentator and ex-UFC fighter

By Alexander Darwin

THE COMBAT CODES

The Combat Codes
Grievar's Blood
Blacklight Born

GRIEVAR'S BLOOD

THE COMBAT CODES: BOOK TWO

ALEXANDER DARWIN

orbitbooks.net

Copyright © 2020 by Alexander Darwin
Excerpt from *Blacklight Born* copyright © 2021 by Alexander Darwin
Excerpt from *Infinity Gate* copyright © 2023 by Mike Carey

Cover design by Lauren Panepinto
Cover art by Peter Bollinger
Cover copyright © 2023 by Hachette Book Group, Inc.
Author photograph by Jeanette Fuller

Orbit
Hachette Book Group
1290 Avenue of the Americas
New York, NY 10104
orbitbooks.net

First Orbit Edition: December 2023
Originally published by Insight Forge Press in January 2020

Orbit is an imprint of Hachette Book Group.
The Orbit name and logo are trademarks of Little, Brown Book Group Limited.

The publisher is not responsible for websites (or their content) that are not owned by the publisher.

The Hachette Speakers Bureau provides a wide range of authors for speaking events. To find out more, go to hachettespeakersbureau.com or email HachetteSpeakers@hbgusa.com.

Orbit books may be purchased in bulk for business, educational, or promotional use. For information, please contact your local bookseller or the Hachette Book Group Special Markets Department at special.markets@hbgusa.com.

Library of Congress Cataloging-in-Publication Data
Names: Darwin, Alexander, author.
Title: Grievar's blood / Alexander Darwin.
Description: First Orbit edition. | New York : Orbit, 2023. |
    Series: The Combat Codes ; book 2
Identifiers: LCCN 2023017243 | ISBN 9780316493239 (trade paperback) |
    ISBN 9780316493345 (ebook)
Subjects: LCGFT: Science fiction. | Novels.
Classification: LCC PS3604.A794 G75 2023 | DDC 813/.6—dc23/eng/20230414
LC record available at https://lccn.loc.gov/2023017243

ISBNs: 9780316493239 (trade paperback), 9780316493345 (ebook)

Printed in the United States of America

LSC-C

Printing 1, 2023

*To my girls, N & J & C, who keep me
writing and not writing.*

CHAPTER I

Ghosts

The Grievar who does not serve will be lost. All martial prowess shall be acquired for the purpose of serving the greater good of society, standing in the Circle in the stead of lord or nation. The Grievar who strays from the path of servitude will quickly find themselves stumbling in the thicket, tripped up by vice and lure.

Passage One, Ninth Precept of the Combat Codes

The eerie rays of the blackshift blanketed the Underground, sending most Deep folk homeward. Servicers, planters, and diggers trudged back to their hovels, ready to sleep and begin again at the rise of the rubellium dawn.

Some Deep folk did not return home for blackshift. Some gambled and drank away their meager wages at the all-night Circles, where gaudy lights and raucous cheers advertised blood and glory. Some bit-rich patrons spent their nights within the Courtesan Houses, under the hazy fog of honey-sweet perfumes and intoxicating neurogens.

Some did not have a home to return to.

A bottle clashed to the hard pavement, reflecting the neon glow of an overhead bar sign. The big man's head rocked to the side, his eyes rolling back in his skull.

A street urchin scrunched his nose as he rifled through the unconscious man's pockets. He reached in close, getting a whiff of the sour ale and crusted bits of vat-meat entangled in the man's wiry beard.

The kid's dirt-covered fingers pinched something hard: a square onyx piece. He smiled and pulled away.

"Big Grievar..." the boy whispered. "You be stinkin'."

Suddenly, a gnarled root of a hand latched on to the kid's wrist. A single piercing yellow eye shone out from the cowl of a cloak.

"Agh!" the urchin gasped, dropping the onyx bit and turning tail into the alley's shadows.

The big man moaned. He looked down at the onyx before hurling it after the kid.

"Take the darkin' thing!" the man shouted. "Buy me another drink while you're busy thieving my bits!"

He stumbled to his feet and used the wall to steady himself, before pulling down his trousers and releasing his bladder.

"Darkin' kids..." he muttered as the sound of his spray echoed in the back alley.

Another shadow joined the man's on the brick wall beneath the neon lights.

"Come back for more, thief?" the man growled. "Think I'm so slow I won't rattle your head this time?"

He pulled his pants up and turned around. It was not the street kid standing in front of him. His eyes widened.

"Hello, Murray."

Murray zipped his trousers up, uncaring that he was standing in a puddle of his own piss. He stared at the old man in the alleyway.

Farmer.

"Don't care if you're a darkin' ghost, give a man some privacy while he takes a piss next time." Murray slurred the words, still feeling the drink in him.

He staggered away from the neon glow of the bar sign, toward the darkness of the alley where the Underground's sweepers pushed discarded trash.

He began to dig through a pile while the old man stood silently and watched.

"Think you know something about me?" Murray turned and spat as he tossed aside a chewed-up fruit husk.

The ghost was still there.

"Wherever the dark you been, don't care," Murray said.

Farmer returned Murray's stare. He raised a hand to his mouth and barked a wet cough.

The old man looked frail, wasted away.

"I know I look like shit, but you've got me beat," Murray said as he turned and set back to digging through the trash heap.

He tossed a corroded can into the shadows, and a swarm of bats fluttered from their roost toward the cavern ceiling thousands of feet above.

"There we go!" Murray yelled as he dug his hand into the refuse down to the elbow and pulled out the black onyx bit.

Farmer stared at him, unmoving.

"I'm going to get a drink," Murray said as he brushed past the old man, stepping back under the neon light and into the dingy bar beyond it.

Murray walked straight to the counter and slammed the onyx bit onto it.

"Same stuff."

The Grunt barkeep sniffed the air before sliding an ale to Murray. "You smell like a Deep rat nest."

"Don't tell me you care, Tlik." Murray downed half the glass and slouched forward to watch the blurry SystemView feed set above.

A cloak brushed against his arm. Farmer sat beside him, the old man's eyes tracking Murray from beneath his cowl.

"Don't darkin' judge me, ghost," Murray said. "I know where you've been. I know what you've done."

Farmer didn't say anything; he sat there. Just like the way he used to fight.

Farmer had trained Murray along with the rest of the Citadel's veteran Grievar Knights. The man would wait for the slightest opening and give nothing before. And then it'd be over.

"You don't think I know what you're doing?" Murray yelled as he stood, towering above both the barkeep and Farmer. "You think I give a shit you've come back from the dead?"

"Settle down, Pearson," the Grunt said wearily. "Don't want to have to ask you to leave again. Why don't you take that table over in the corner?"

Murray grabbed his ale and stalked across the dim room, nearly empty besides a pair of hawkers dealing at the far end of the bar. He threw his bulk into a seat at the corner table and called back. "Two more, Tlik."

Farmer drifted across the floor and sat beside Murray. He pulled the cowl from his head.

Though Murray certainly wasn't a specimen of health, he couldn't help but frown, looking at his old coach. This was the man who had trained Murray, taught him nearly all he knew, acted a father to him.

Farmer's cheekbones seemed to want to burst from his ashen skin. The burning eyes Murray remembered were now dulled, like candles starved for air.

"What was it like?" Murray asked. "Being in there."

"You've trained in the Sim." Farmer's voice was parched, barely a whisper. "You know what these machinations are like."

"I've trained in the Sim, but I've not lived more than a decade of my life in it." Dormant anger bubbled up within Murray. "I've not stepped into the darkness, floating there in some tube, letting the Bit-Minders have their way with my path."

Farmer broke into a spasm of coughing. He took a sip of the ale Tlik had placed on the table to calm the fit.

"It seems a long time I was gone, but within the darkness, it was only a heartbeat," Farmer said. "To me, it was only yesterday when I was at the Citadel in my prime, leading the Knights alongside Memnon."

"How...how the dark did you get out?" Murray asked, downing another ale, not knowing if he wanted to know the answer.

"The Cradle where I trained the brood," Farmer said. "The Bit-Minders deemed it to be a flawed environment. They told me it was unlikely to turn out champions, as the program was designed for. And so, they released me from my service."

Murray's grip tightened on his glass. "I know. One of them, thing named Zero, told me as much. I paid him a visit at the Codex Surface-side. He said the Daimyo planned on deleting the program, getting rid of the kids hooked up to it still."

Farmer nodded. "This is true."

Murray's jaw clenched, the anger bubbling up again. "Always the same. Treating these kids like things to be bought and sold, tossed out when they aren't needed. And you, right in the middle of it. I used to admire you. I used to—"

"I accept my fault," Farmer said. "My intentions were to help guide the kids within the Cradle, teach them the Codes so that they might be more than killing machines. But I was misguided in what I could do in such a place. I did not understand what little effect my nurturing would have when the Minders were in control of the environment."

"Maybe death would have been best for them," Murray growled. "Better than floating in a tube, getting used by all."

"Perhaps," Farmer whispered.

"Why did you come here?" Murray was weary. He stood, wanting to get out, away from this ghost.

The old man hacked again. "Murray, I'm working for one of the lords down here—"

Murray slammed his empty glass down on the table, shattering it. "You're a darkin' merc now, working for some soap-eater? Farmer, the greatest coach to grace the Citadel, now wiping some lord's ass?"

"And you?" Farmer asked, staring up at Murray's swaying body. "I came to see you because I heard you'd come Deep. I know why you came down here, Murray. But look at yourself. You're a mess."

"Forget me," Murray whispered, staring off into the shadows of the bar. "Dark it all. I'm done with it."

He began to walk toward the door.

"Murray!" Farmer barked after him. "The path still lies before you. The Codes are still within you."

Murray didn't turn around.

CHAPTER 2

The Name Choice

When a Grievar begins their martial journey, they must seek to tame their wildness in order to achieve seamless technique. However, once a level of mastery has been achieved, the fighter must rekindle the chaotic nature of their being to remain unpredictable against trained opponents.

Passage Two, One Hundred Eighth
Precept of the Combat Codes

The beat of the drums reverberated in Cego's skull as he stood on his toes to get a better view.

"They be coming," Knees said from beside him; the Venturian was at least a head taller than Cego and able to peer over the crowd.

Cego felt a strong hand on his shoulder. Joba, his behemoth of a friend, was peering down at him. Joba pointed up to his own shoulder, where Abel was serenely perched.

"Cego, come here," little Abel yelled over the din of the crowd in his enthusiastic manner. "I see it all from here—wonderful!"

"Umm...are you sure, Joba?" Cego asked sheepishly. "I don't want to weigh you down or anything."

The huge boy smiled silently and reached down with one hand to scoop Cego up with ease, plopping him on his other shoulder across from Abel and well above the crowd.

From his new vantage, Cego could see the Myrkonian march.

Throngs of the long-bearded Grievar marched over the entry bridge of the Citadel, striding to the beat of their fight drums. They were stout, proud, and nearly naked despite the chill in the air. The Northmen chanted to match the percussion of the drums, their deep baritone voices carrying through the outer grounds.

Cego looked toward the center of the formation, where several men hefted a platform atop their shoulders with a pair of wide drums set atop it. Two boys stood in front of the drums and landed punches, elbows, kicks, and even head butts against the leathery skins in a percussive rhythm.

"Wonderful!" Abel exclaimed again from Joba's other shoulder.

Cego couldn't help but smile. Abel was right to be amazed; the way the two boys moved congruously, fighting the drums in front of them, was a feat of precision and timing.

The formation of near two hundred Myrkonians approached Cego's perch. He could see they were all heavily fluxed, even the boys, swirling tattoos moving across their bodies with the rhythm of the march.

"Dozer would be enjoying this," Knees shouted from below. "The drums, people hitting things, naked folk all around him..."

Cego chuckled. His friend Dozer had had some unfortunate disciplinary troubles at the end of last semester; the big kid was caught red-handed in the professors' meal quarters, halfway through feasting on their rations for the entire week. As punishment, Dozer had been cut from coming out today to watch the march.

"Sol also would have enjoyed," Abel said with a frown on his face.

Cego's thoughts drifted to his other missing teammate: Solara Halberd. The fiery-haired girl likely would have been citing a plethora of facts about the Myrkonians. Cego felt the pit in his stomach and shook his head.

He turned his attention back to the procession. Across the throng of Myrkonians, he could see the high stands set up for the Citadel's faculty and council. He could make out the high commander's broad, straight-backed figure, and though he couldn't see Memnon's face, Cego was dead sure the man wasn't smiling.

Beside the Grievar council, set higher up, were the ceremonial chairs of Ezo's Daimyo Governance. Some of the ornate thrones were empty, but at least a few of the Daimyo representation had come to welcome the Myrkonians to the Citadel.

Cego was jarred from his thoughts as silence enveloped the grounds. The drums had suddenly stopped, along with the procession. The Northmen now stood directly below the Citadel's council members.

A thickly muscled giant of a Grievar, his red beard tied in tassels, stepped out of formation. Tattoos swirled across his naked body, icy blues and blacks coursing his arms and legs, as if one could see his arteries pumping blood.

"He be as wide as I am tall," Knees muttered from below.

"Agh!" the man bellowed as he struck his bare chest several times. The entire contingent of Myrkonians behind him followed suit, screaming in unison.

The man advanced toward the council stand, keeping his blue eyes locked on to Commander Memnon. He lifted a hand in front of his face, as if displaying it, as he removed several black rings from his fingers.

The Northman suddenly grabbed his middle finger with his opposite hand and wrenched it violently backward, cracking it at the joint. The man then proceeded to snap each of the fingers on one of his hands, followed by two fingers on his second hand.

Commander Memnon stood from his chair as he watched the bizarre spectacle.

The Northman finally spoke, his accent thick and his voice booming. "Ye Ezonians have welcomed us here, to your home. I give ye seven of me fingers. For ye be taking seven of me boys under your wing."

From within the Myrkonian procession, seven boys came forward to stand beside the giant man. Cego recognized two of the boys as those who had been striking the drums during the march.

"My name is Tharsis Bertoth," the man continued. "But where we hail from, names is not important. We Myrkonians are all of the ice blood, born from the Frost Mother. My boys standing here, they'll eat your foods, sleep up high in your wooden beds, and hear your fancy southern words. My boys, they'll fight and bleed for ye in the Circle. But they'll not bend the knee to ye. Or to your Daimyo lords up there. None of us will, ever."

Tharsis directed his icy stare toward the Daimyo politiks in the high stands.

Commander Memnon waited for Tharsis to pause before responding. "Tharsis Bertoth, you and your people are welcome within our Citadel's walls. We embrace you fighting men of the North as our brothers and your brood as our own. I can assure you we'll treat your boys with honor and respect, and teach them our ways to become better fighters for the return to their northern home."

The response seemed to satisfy the giant man. A smile cut across his bearded face. "Now that the arse-kissing be done, let's have some fun, eh?"

Memnon looked down at the man, wariness in his eyes. "What have you in mind, Tharsis?"

"Well, we'll be needing some fists flying to get things started. And my men need their bellies full of drink."

"Of course," Memnon responded, obviously prepared. He waved his hand and several Grunt servicers moved into sight from below the partitions, each pulling a wagon full of barrels. The Grunts unloaded the barrels in front of the Myrkonians and screwed a spout into the top of each.

"Enough of our famed Highwinder Ale to fill all your men three times over," Memnon said. "And, as far as combat, we have one of our Knights ready to face your champion of choice."

Tharsis lifted a barrel over his head and took a long swig, dark froth covering his beard. He wiped his face with his broken hand, the fingers dangling. "Eh... but we all be here for the brood. That's what this be about, growing the next of blood to be right-standing Grievar. I say we put one of each of our boys up in the Circle."

Memnon seemed surprised. "I understand your sentiment, but we really haven't prepared any of our students for combat right here, right now."

"You're saying here, at Ezo's famed Lyceum, no boy be ready to stand and fight? What're they doing all this time, knitting scarves for their matties?"

The chorus of Northmen laughed loudly.

"Enough." Cego had heard Memnon like this before: put to a challenge and unlikely to back down. "I was simply saying we'd prepared a Grievar Knight from our team on this occasion. As is the practice for any exhibition bout when we have visiting dignitaries. But of course our students are more than ready for any of your boys."

"Ah, that's what I like to hear!" the big Myrkonian yelled. "Now I'll show ye how we in the North choose which of our boys be takin' to the Circle!"

Tharsis turned to his fellow Northmen and raised his hands to the air. "We from the frost are one. We from the frost choose as one. Raise your voices and let the Frost Mother's wish be heard!"

The contingent of Myrkonians bellowed all at once—but different names. To Cego, it sounded like a chaotic chorus, indecipherable what name anyone was yelling. The Myrkonians came to a crescendo, each man trying to bellow his name choice as loud as possible, before the chaos receded. Cego could now make out only two names being called, a back-and-forth volley between two groups of Myrkonians. Finally, all the Northmen were yelling one name in unison, a deep rumbling that seemed to shake the ground.

"Rhodan Bertoth!"

One of the drumming boys stepped forward from his companions. He bore a striking resemblance to Tharsis Bertoth. Though the boy didn't have a beard yet like his father, his hair hung in long tassels down his back, and the majority of his body was already fluxed with tattoos.

"I take to the Circle, with the Frost Mother beneath me!" the boy yelled, meeting his father's eyes.

Memnon turned to Callen Albright, the Scout commander at his side, and whispered something in his ear. The two appeared to be in discussion for several moments.

"I wouldn't be the one wanting to fight that boy, on these grounds in front of the entire Lyceum," Knees said. "Though, if Dozer were here, no doubt he'd be running up there right now to take it."

"It would be a great honor to be chosen to represent our whole school," Abel chimed in from Joba's other shoulder, to which the huge boy nodded in agreement.

Chatter began to spread throughout the crowd of Lyceum students, wondering who would be chosen to fight Rhodan Bertoth.

Commander Memnon held his hand to the air, and the chatter died. "In respect for our guests from the North, we've decided to honor their own custom of name choice. We've brought them here, to the Citadel, and their boys will be taking on many of our customs during the next semester, so it only seems right that we do the same."

The crowd buzzed again.

Memnon held his hand up. "And we'll be choosing only from

our pool of Level One to Level Four students, who are of similar age to Rhodan. It would be unfair if one of our older, more experienced students stood in against him."

Cego saw Tharsis snort at that mention as a wry smile rose on the younger Bertoth's lips.

"So, let's get this going," Memnon said to the students in attendance. "On my mark, raise your voice with your name choice to represent the Lyceum on this day."

Cego's mind flashed with possibilities. Of course, a Level Three or Level Four student would be preferable, given Level Ones were too young and inexperienced, and anyone from his own Level Two class didn't likely stand a chance against the burly Myrkonian boy. Cego looked to his teammates, and they all seemed to be doing the same calculations.

Memnon raised his hand and a chorus of student voices took to the air.

But unlike the Myrkonians' name choice, there was nearly no discord among the Lyceum students. They had already reached the same pitch. The same name. A name that rang loudly across the Citadel's grounds, like a bell being struck.

Cego.

*   *   *

"Cego of the Deep, Level Two, step forward toward the Circle," High Commander Memnon said.

Cego looked at his companions from up on big Joba's shoulder. They returned his wide-eyed stare; though, they did not look so surprised. In fact, Cego realized, both Knees and Abel had called out his name along with the vast majority of the Lyceum students who surrounded them. Of course, Joba hadn't said a word, but as he hefted Cego off his shoulder and placed him gently on the ground, the huge boy nodded his head in agreement.

"Looks like you be getting yourself into it again, my friend." Knees slapped Cego's shoulder.

"But...why?" Cego asked, feeling dazed and a little sick to the stomach.

"You know why they be choosing you," Knees responded. "After what happened last year during the challenges, you be something of a legend here."

Of course, Cego knew why he'd been chosen. For the entire first semester, the school had been abuzz about the now infamous *phenomenon* that had occurred during a match last year. *Doragūn*, they had begun to call him. A word in ancient Tikretian to describe the unique serpentine flux that had been burned onto Cego's arm that day. It was a day Cego had tried to forget; he'd become an incarnation of combat, sending a fellow student badly injured to the medward and another nearly to the grave.

Still, why hadn't they picked a Level Three or Level Four student to fight the Myrkonian boy? There were plenty who had far superior combat skills to Cego. In fact, in some of the intralevel challenges over the past semester, those very students had bested him in the practice Circles. He wasn't even close to the top of his class leaderboard this year; that spot was held firmly by the mysterious boy Kōri Shimo.

"I can't...What if someone else takes my place?" Cego asked helplessly.

"Doesn't work that way, my friend," Knees said as he started to prod Cego forward into the crowd. "They all called your name. Memnon spoke your name. High commander of the Citadel called you. No turning back now, unless you want to skip out on the Lyceum like your man Murray."

Cego started to protest but realized Knees was right. There was no turning back now. He started to push his way through the crowd. Students recognized him as he walked past, patting his back and calling his name.

A strong hand grabbed his shoulder just as he was almost through to the clearing. Gryfin Thurgood.

"Cego." The broad-shouldered purelight boy met his eyes. "Do your thing. We may fight for position during the semester, but on this one, we're all behind you."

Those were the first words Gryfin had said to Cego since the boy had been released from the medward. Cego nodded and moved into the open square.

The Grunts had dragged out a plain auralite Circle, the least reactive of any of the elements. Several bluelight spectrals were hovering over the surface of the steel like bees buzzing a calasynth poppy.

Rhodan Bertoth crouched within the Circle, shaking his head and whipping his long braids back and forth. He touched one hand to the stone below him and looked up at Cego as he approached.

The northern boy was bigger than he'd appeared from a distance. At least as wide as Dozer, with thickly muscled legs that looked like they were made for explosive movement. His tattoos shimmered with frosty blues and whites across his pale skin as he shifted his weight from one foot to the other.

A chill ran through Cego's body. He felt weary. Alone, despite the friends he knew he had in the crowd. Cego felt something missing, a pit in his stomach since last year, even before Murray or Sol had left.

Cego removed his light cloak and dropped it to the floor outside the Circle. At least he was already wearing his blue Level Two second skin. And he'd stretched his body when he'd woken, as was his ritual. Not too bad for prep, but Cego certainly hadn't been expecting to fight in front of the entire school, council, and foreign delegation, for the honor of his nation, at the drop of a bit.

He stepped within the Circle and felt the faint hum of auralite, the hairs on the back of his neck standing. As expected, Cego's left arm began to buzz.

It was a strange feeling: almost like his entire arm was vibrating, though when he looked down, nothing was moving. Also unmoving was the Doragūn flux tattoo that had been burned into Cego's arm during the phenomenon last year. For weeks, the serpentine flux had pulsed with vibrant energy, up and down Cego's arm, as if it were a separate entity from the rest of his body. But eventually, the flux had faded. It had become dull and lifeless. The dragon now remained dormant; it just gave Cego a strange buzz when he stepped within a Circle.

Cego took a deep breath as he watched the spectrals rise to the center of the Circle, condensing to focus their light on the combatants.

Bertoth bellowed and charged like a wild tusker just released on its captors. The boy's hands and feet exploded off the ground to drive him forward.

Cego barely managed to dive away, launching into a shoulder roll on the hard surface. He immediately regretted the decision. Darkin' stone. Cego was used to fighting on the more forgiving canvas in the Lyceum's practice Circles.

Bertoth whirled around and sprang toward Cego again, this time launching a flying punch. The boy was sharp. Cego barely turned his jaw to roll with the strike as the Myrkonian followed with a thudding hook to the body.

Cego covered up to block two quick shots to the head as he retreated on his heels. He'd faced opponents like Bertoth before, those constantly attacking, leaving no room for any counters.

Offense combats offense, Murray-Ku had once said.

Cego waited for another of Bertoth's punches and let it nearly take his head off, before weaving to the side and slamming his shin into the boy's hefty thigh.

Usually, a leg kick like that would slow an opponent down, give them some pause. Bertoth didn't miss a step. He met Cego's eyes, smiled, and continued his onslaught.

Dodge, leg kick. Dodge, leg kick. Cego repeated the sequence several times, finally feeling some momentum. But Bertoth didn't appear to be slowing. The northerner's legs were like tree trunks.

Don't stop what's working, Murray's voice reminded him again. *Don't let up. Do damage until they figure out a way to defend.*

Cego kept chopping at Bertoth's leg. Same combo, same defense, same kick.

Finally, he felt something give. Bertoth wobbled slightly and Cego moved in with a low kick to finish the job.

But Cego didn't get the reaction he wanted. Instead, Bertoth dropped levels, caught his foot, and smirked again.

The Myrkonian raised his hand to elevate Cego's leg and jerked him forward. Cego blinked as Bertoth's skull careened toward his, the boy's considerable body weight fully behind it.

The lights went out.

*   *   *

The high commander of the Citadel was shaking.

Memnon wore a heavy cloak to conceal the tremors, but his teeth chattered and sweat poured from his brow. The overcast spring sky hung above the festivities like a grey curtain.

"Not sure why they thought Murray's boy would be able to take on that northern beast," Dakar Pugilio slurred from beside Memnon, flask in hand as always. Memnon sat beside two of his lieutenant commanders, Dakar and Callen Albright, as they watched the Northmen consume another barrel of ale.

"They'd been taken by the brat's little show at the challenges last year," Albright sneered. "Now they'll realize what imbeciles they were to be impressed by some lacklight. The Bertoth boy made him look untrained."

Memnon wiped the sweat from his brow with a gloved hand. "Cego did all right, just was overpowered," he said weakly.

Dakar turned to Memnon. "High Commander? You doin' all right? You look like me after putting down too much street food in the Peddler District."

Memnon steadied himself to stop his jaw from quaking. "Yes, Dakar. I'm fine. Just caught something airborne, likely."

"Albion Memnon," Dakar said, slapping the high commander on the shoulder. "Sick! Now, there's something new. Don't think in all the time we served together I saw you less than splendid a single day."

As drunk as Dakar was, the commander of PublicJustice was right. Memnon was lying.

"Look at those barbarians," Callen Albright whispered in disgust as they watched one particularly large Northman shower his head with golden ale. "Can you remind me again why we're even considering letting their sort into the Lyceum?"

"They look all right to me," Dakar responded as he watched the Myrkonians below. "Right Grievar there. They know how to fight. They know how to drink. Who'd you like, Albright? Some more sniveling cowards to join our ranks like what you turned up so far leading Scouts?"

"Just because these brutes are strong doesn't mean they'll do us any good as Knights," Callen spoke rapidly. "Especially if they don't know how to keep to regulation and rule. Who is to say their brood will even decide to come on as Knights if they graduate? The only thing these Northmen are known for beyond drinking themselves stupid is their fierce tribal loyalty. I predict they deplete our resources before heading back to the Ice swollen with the secrets they've stolen."

"I've spoken with Tharsis," Memnon said flatly. "We've made a pact, and I trust the man to honor it."

"Honor is for fools," Callen muttered.

"What did you say, Commander Callen?" Memnon turned toward the wiry man sitting beside him.

"Nothing." Callen backed down, as usual. "Just that I don't trust them."

"Whether you trust them doesn't matter," Memnon said. "We'll honor our side of the bargain. We'll house and train their boys. Whether they stay or not, of course, is up to them, but I hope our system will reveal the opportunities they'll have here in Ezo that would not be available back north."

Memnon slumped in his chair, trying to catch his breath. What he'd give right now just for one dose. One single pill to kill the splitting headache, stop these darkin' shakes.

"Which means shut your mouth!" Dakar suddenly stood redfaced as he looked down at Callen. "Don't think I heard the words that came from your weasel face? You dare call my friend and our leader a fool?"

"I said nothing of the sort." Callen eyed Dakar. "I merely said we shouldn't put our resources into something that isn't a sure bet."

"If that's the case, maybe we shouldn't be putting no resources into you!" Dakar swigged from his flask and spat. "Don't think I've seen the little luxuries you've been expensing to Citadel? Trips to the Adar Hills, now, what's that for? Scouting some big leads out where the vines grow plentiful, you little shit?"

"My sources told me there was a talented boy from the Hills—"

"Enough!" Memnon tried to raise his voice but ended up in a coughing spasm. "Stop the bickering between you two."

Memnon just needed silence to relieve his splitting headache.

"If it's okay with you, High Commander," Dakar said, "I'll go head down and do some drinkin' with those untidy barbarians."

Dakar glared at Callen.

Memnon waved him off and watched as his lumbering commander stumbled down toward the festivities below.

"What's the real play here, High Commander?" Callen turned to him. "You know as well as I that those boys won't be staying aboard our teams after they graduate. Now that the idiot is gone, you can tell me the reality of the situation."

Memnon breathed deeply as he tried to steady his hand. "I wasn't lying. I do hope the Myrkonian boys who attend the Lyceum see the wealth of knowledge and opportunity we offer here, and perhaps consider staying on board as Knights…"

"And?" Callen prompted.

"And…Governance has given the go for this," Memnon said.

"Ah, as I thought," Callen said. "They think this will allow us to make a move north?"

Memnon nodded. "If we show goodwill to the Myrkonians, take in their kids, perhaps they'll take a few of ours in the future. And perhaps with that diplomacy, Governance can get eyes on their mines. Create some opportunity for trade. Or even set up some high-profile fights."

Callen smirked. "I knew something was going on. I'm surprised they didn't loop me in; I could certainly be helpful in a delicate situation like this."

"You're looped in when you need to be, Callen," Memnon said flatly. The high commander suddenly felt bile rising in his throat. The meager scraps he'd downed this morning making a plea to escape.

"I'm going to head back to quarters…" Memnon muttered, standing as he felt his stomach turn. "I'll see you later."

"Okay," Callen said, crossing his legs.

Memnon was already several paces down the stairs when Callen called out to him.

"Oh, High Commander?" the Scouts leader chimed.

Memnon turned, holding his breath, doing everything he could to prevent himself from hurling on the stands.

"Yes?"

"Are you absolutely sure you're feeling all right?" Callen asked. "Dakar was right for once. You do look quite…shaken up."

"Yes, I'm fine," Memnon said as he wheeled around and strode down the stands as straight-backed as he could manage.

He couldn't show weakness in front of that weasel. Callen served his purpose, but Memnon had no illusions; the commander of the Scouts had been eyeing his position for the past few years.

Memnon made it to the bottom of the stands, turned the corner, and ducked behind the steel girders. He vomited ferociously, wiped his lips, and stood face-to-face with a burly Northman.

"Nice." The bearded fellow grinned. "Just cleared some space for more ale myself!"

The Myrkonian slapped Memnon on the shoulder and stumbled back toward the ongoing party.

Memnon took the long path back to the Citadel to avoid prying eyes. He'd done this to himself. But it was necessary. Too many years on those neuros. Memnon had thought the enhancers had kept him whole, made his body a finely tuned fighting machine. But they'd clouded his mind, little by little, until he didn't even notice the path he was on.

And now, finally off the stuff, Memnon was paying the price he deserved.

The high commander threw up again, this time in a trimmed bush just outside the entrance to the Knight Tower. He wiped his lips, sighed, and began the long climb up the stairs to his quarters.

*   *   *

"I believe I have missed you," a voice said.

Cego opened his eyes to a barrage of light and a piercing headache. A pale, angular face hovered above him, veins streaking it, with two curious pitch-black eyes.

Xenalia.

"What do you mean, you *believe* you've missed me?" Cego asked, his voice hoarse. "Do you miss me or not miss me?"

"Such strange questions as always from you Grievar," Xenalia replied as she replaced the cloth on Cego's forehead with a fresh cold one. "You haven't been brought into my medward for quite some time. Since the incident of last year. And so, I believe I do miss you, although I cannot be sure, because the emotion of missing someone is foreign to me still."

Xenalia's flood of fast-paced words, strung together with barely any breathing room, served only to exacerbate Cego's headache. He closed his eyes again and took a deep breath. "Xenalia. Missing someone is...is like..."

Cego thought of Sol. Where was she right now? Was she thinking of the team back at the Citadel, wherever she'd gone?

He thought of Murray-Ku and the gruff Grievar's small home in the immigrant district, where the smell of sponge bread wafted through open windows and the rain drummed on the tin rooftops.

Cego thought of the old master, Farmer. The man who had taught him nearly everything he knew, who'd raised him from birth. But the old master was a man that Cego had never really known at all: a simulation, a vision projected onto the darkness of Cego's psyche. Cego thought of his brothers, Sam and Silas, the two boys he'd grown up with on his island home. Sam, his younger brother, had been carefree and known to avoid training by escaping to the black sand beach and the craggy nooks by the cliffs. And Silas, his older brother, had been focused only on winning, always ruthlessly beating them in the Circle with that curved smile etched on his face.

But Murray had revealed to Cego last year that the island, the place he'd grown up on along with his brothers, was a simulation, a training program the Bit-Minders had developed called the Cradle. Cego and his brothers had been born in vats, suspended in the Cradle, living their lives in some shadow world of the Bit-Minders.

Cego had been convinced that his brothers were a part of that simulation as well, like Farmer, until the morning the entire Lyceum had been gathered in the common ground. They'd watched the greatest Grievar Knight of all time, Artemis Halberd, die at the hands of an unknown fighter. Cego had been the only one to recognize the opponent. Silas. He had no doubt it had been his older brother standing over Artemis Halberd's lifeless body that day in the Kirothian Circle. Which meant that his younger brother, Sam, could also be here, in the real world, somewhere out there.

A piercing pain split Cego's skull as his mind raced toward the abyss.

"Missing someone hurts?" Xenalia broke the long silence. "You just seemed to be in deep thought about the concept of missing a person, and it looked to cause you physical pain. Your brow furrowed and your jaw clenched, which catalyzed the pain receptors near the base of your skull."

Cego breathed deeply and opened his eyes again. "Yes, missing someone hurts."

"Well, I would say I did not miss you very much, Cego," Xenalia said without an ounce of humor. "Although I thought of you from time to time, doing so never caused me physical pain. I did receive a strange feeling near my abdomen, although that could be due to faulty digestion of some of the new food the Lyceum's sizzlers have put into the rationing."

Cego smiled. No matter how chaotic the world outside was, he always found some comfort in the ever-truthful words of his cleric friend. Xenalia was unlike any Daimyo he'd ever met. In fact, she was really the only Daimyo Cego had ever met.

"So, what's the damage this time?" Cego asked, somewhat amused that he'd asked Xenalia the same thing so many times since starting school at the Lyceum.

"Broken nose, of course," the cleric started as she loaded up a syringe. "More specifically, a severely fractured nasal bone, crushed frontal sinus, and a damaged ethmoid plate. It is quite interesting how you Grievar have an extra layer of cartilage in your nasal cavity, called the octonial cartilage, that we Daimyo do not possess."

Cego couldn't follow what Xenalia was saying, but he nodded his head as usual. "Um...so, is that good?"

"Sorry, I have digressed," Xenalia said as she deftly punched the syringe into Cego's right arm. "You had a few fractured ribs as well, and a severely bruised clavicle bone. I am assuming from the front roll."

Cego was surprised. Xenalia had never mentioned anything about his fights before. She'd always done a fantastic job healing him, but Cego assumed she never even knew exactly how he'd been hurt in the first place.

"You saw my fight with the Myrkonian?" Cego asked.

"Yes, well, I did. I certainly have no interest whatsoever in watching Grievar bludgeon each other for the sake of…Let us see, why do you Grievar fight again? National or personal dispute resolution, mercenary bit-work, blood ritual, just to name a few reasons. In this case, I believe you were involved in a foreign delegation exhibition match. Although I do believe the Myrkonian—"

"Xenalia, you're going off the rails again," Cego interrupted. "I was just asking if you were out there in the courtyard, watching me get my face bashed in."

"Apologies," Xenalia said. "No, I was not out there, but I did hear a commotion outside the medward. I went to investigate and found most of the sweepers forsaking their duties to watch the local SystemView feed in the main corridor. I was surprised to see you up on the feed. *Getting your face bashed in*, as you put it."

"Yeah." Cego thought back to his bout with Rhodan Bertoth. "I wasn't trying to do that, I promise. I just felt…strange out there."

"Please describe the symptoms more expansively," Xenalia said.

Cego had felt alone in the Circle. That pit in his stomach. Something missing, beyond his friends who had left him. He knew he couldn't say that to Xenalia, though; she wouldn't understand.

"Well, my left arm has still been tingling whenever I step into the Circle."

Xenalia widened her jet-black eyes. After the incident last year, the little cleric had taken a deep, almost obsessive interest in Cego's strange new dragon flux. He regretted mentioning it immediately, given one of the reasons he hadn't visited the medward for so long was because Xenalia would never let him leave, because she was busy studying him.

Xenalia summoned her little red spectral, beckoning it with a hand wave to descend from a fixture overhead. It hovered just over Cego's arm and the dormant design on it.

"Do you feel anything right now?" the cleric asked.

"It feels a bit warm," Cego said.

"Yes, that is normal," Xenalia replied as she turned to examine a bedside monitor jumbled with numbers and squiggly lines. "This rubellium spectral often imparts a feeling of heat, especially close up, though it is not actually giving off any real heat. The light it gives off is absorbed through your retinas, and your neural network communicates and simulates the feeling of heat."

"Do you also feel the heat, then?" Cego asked.

"Yes, to a lesser degree, though," Xenalia replied. "Grievar brain structures have evolved quite differently than the Daimyo. I can barely feel it."

"But why the tingling in the Circle, then?" Cego couldn't help but ask.

Xenalia waved the little spectral close to Cego's face as she peered into each of his eyes. He could feel her warm breath—it smelled of some leafy green he couldn't place.

"The tingling you are feeling is likely related to the incident of last year and the resulting flux on your arm," she said. "Although the burn now seems to be completely dormant on the surface, it must still have some neurophysical connection, given that is the only reason your brain would be processing the feeling. Are you sure you would not be able to do an overnight wired study? We would be able to get far more data on the possibility of—"

"No," Cego said flatly. "I'm not going back in there."

"I understand your reluctance to enter the Sim," the cleric reasoned. "But wiring you for overnight processing of neural patterns would not be nearly as much of an immersive experience. It would pull on the existing outputs of your neural makeup, as opposed to the Sim, which injects an experience into your consciousness. And the resulting data would be especially useful in comparison to your prior brain wave patterns that we have on file. The experiment would certainly help ascertain some conclusions about what happened to you."

"No," Cego said again softly, trying to take a deep breath. "Xenalia, you know what the Sim did to me. The Cradle, I was plugged into it for nearly my entire life."

Cego could feel an ember of anger starting to rise in his chest. He sat up in the medward bed. "And now—now... you want to plug me back into something? To study me? Just like the other Daimyo did?" he yelled. "I was just their little experiment. Do you know what that feels like?"

Cego clutched his rib cage as a bolt of pain raced up it. He lay back in the bed, breathing hard.

Xenalia waved the spectral away with a flick of the wrist. She watched Cego for several silent moments, expressionless.

"Perhaps I have missed you," Xenalia said finally.

"...What?" Cego said, still trying to calm himself down.

"Pain," Xenalia replied. "Just now, seeing you become upset. Seeing you lose control. I felt like you were in pain. And I did not like that feeling, even though it was not my own. Almost as if I could feel the pain you were experiencing. So very strange."

Coming from Xenalia, that meant quite a lot.

"Perhaps you could visit again soon," she said. "Hopefully, not after getting your face *bashed* in."

"Okay, I'll try to," Cego said as he sat up from the bed and tested his footing on the cold medward floor. "Without getting my face bashed."

*   *   *

Cego managed to pull the second skin over his head and onto his body as he sprinted down the Lyceum's hallways.

Fighting Styles Around the World. The class had been a mandatory sign-up for Level Twos, and Cego had heard that the professor was quite eccentric. And now Cego was already five minutes late. He turned a corner, nearly colliding with two surprised students.

"Sorry, sorry," Cego yelled back as he narrowly dodged another Level Three boy he recognized.

He shot through the school's common ground, which was quiet during in-class session, and turned up a set of stairs. Cego's ribs started to pulse with pain again as he turned the corner of the second floor and closed in on his destination about twenty yards down the hallway.

"Wasn't that Doragūn?" Cego heard a passing student murmur to a classmate as he raced by them.

He stopped short right in front of classroom B22, a steel door with no discernible lock. A sign hanging on the door was abbreviated in a scrawling font: *FSAW.*

Ten minutes late.

Cego placed his face in front of the scanner and the door slid open.

A class full of students turned to stare up at him. In front of the class stood a lanky man with curly black hair draped over his shoulders. Cego fully expected a verbal lashing for his late arrival.

"Cego, correct?" the professor asked.

"Yes, Professor," Cego said between breaths. "Sorry to be late to your class... It's just that—"

"No need to explain yourself, Cego," the man responded. "I'm just glad you were able to make it at all. I'm Professor Drakken, as I'm sure you know already."

The teacher beckoned Cego down the stairs toward the center of the circular classroom. He reached out in greeting.

As Cego took the outstretched hand, Professor Drakken suddenly grabbed behind his elbow and dragged him forward, before sweeping Cego's leg out from under him. Cego landed on his back, dazed and feeling redness flush to his cheeks.

But Drakken looked down at him with a warm smile.

"And, as our friend Cego has just illustrated, it is of the utmost importance to know what to expect in every single Grievar culture."

Drakken motioned for him to stand up and take an empty seat up front. Out of the corner of his eye, Cego noticed Dozer in the back row with a wide grin on his face.

"For Corinthian Grievar, extending a hand for greeting, as we're accustomed to here in Ezo, is seen as a challenge to execute a takedown," Drakken said. "To not attempt such a technique on invitation would be quite insulting to a Corinthian."

Drakken fingered a small device attached to his leather vest, and a large colorful hologram sprang to life in the center of the room: a translucent globe that slowly spun sea-green oceans and crimson landmasses. Several small spectrals circled the hologram, like moons in orbit of the planet.

The professor took a long sip of water from a glass as he scanned the room.

A bead of sweat dripped off Cego's brow as he took a deep breath and settled into his chair. He'd been so focused on getting to class and meeting his new professor, he hadn't even looked around at the other students. He turned and saw Dozer again. His big friend was reclined in his chair, staring at the holographic image, and likely on his way to falling asleep. Knees, who sat next to Dozer, met Cego's eyes briefly and raised his brows in jest.

Cego's gaze fell across a few other familiar faces. Gryfin Thurgood, Mateus Winterfowl, Rhona Mitri, Kōri Shimo. The Bayhounds' captain, Shiar, sat beside his teammates with that arrogant smirk etched on his face.

And Rhodan Bertoth. The wide Myrkonian sat mid-row alongside two of his northern companions. The giant kid looked quite uncomfortable fully clothed, shifting back and forth in his new formfitting second skin.

Cego turned his head back toward the professor.

"Fighting Styles Around the World is indeed a class about just that: how Grievar from various cultures fight."

Drakken paced around the translucent globe as he spoke. "What their trademark techniques might be, their strengths and weaknesses, and ultimately, how we might learn to defeat them in the Circle.

"But," Drakken emphasized, "we are all one."

"We are all one," he said again, this time louder, watching his students to gauge their responses.

"Though our duty is to the Codes and to our nation, the men and women who stand across from us are Grievar-kin. Though they represent opposing nations and our end goal is to defeat them, we are all one."

Drakken pressed the device on his vest again, and one of the orbiting spectrals descended to illuminate a landform on the tip of the globe. "Myrkos," he said.

"The far northern reaches of the world, the icy tundras. Home to the proud Myrkonian Grievar, the Ice Tribes," Drakken stated. "And we're lucky to have our own northern warrior brood here with us, visiting this semester."

Rhodan Bertoth stood in his seat and slammed his hand against his chest.

Drakken focused the hovering spectrals on another landform, this time a large mass just north of the central Ezonian territories. "Kiroth. I can see even in your expressions now, the mere mention of our rival nation brings a sense of anger, even hatred." Drakken shook his head slowly. "But the Kirothian culture is complex and multifaceted, just as our own. We can learn from and respect our northern neighbors, despite facing them so often in the Circles."

The professor highlighted a series of islands to the south of Ezo this time. "The Besaydian islands. A loosely joined conglomerate of nation-states, each ruled by a maverick Daimyo, each with its own laws and customs, and each populated by a plethora of Grievar—native, immigrant, and those imported via the fight trade. Perhaps the most diverse of all the planet's nations."

Drakken nodded to a curly-haired girl sitting in the front row beside Cego. "One of our newest students, Brynn Mykili, was born of the Isles. She brings to us a variety of unique styles that she learned from the famous fighting pits, specifically footwork and movement in the variable terrains that are so common there."

The professor looked up at the class. "And of course, we need to consider our own nation, Ezo, home of the Citadel and our school, the Lyceum. A place where students both native and foreign are brought together for the sole purpose of excellence in combat, perfecting our skills for a greater cause. A purpose that has been written in the Codes and in our blood.

"I now turn the light to you," the professor said. He directed the spectrals to drift from the globe toward the seated students. "We'll need to learn where all your abilities are derived from."

Cego gulped as Drakken looked him directly in the eye.

"We won't always agree with the path of other nations, just as they might look down on ours," Drakken said. "But we are all one. We can learn from one another, just as you will face each other in the Circles through the semester. The same is true of your future opponents on foreign soil. They are your enemy, but they are also your blood. They are Grievar-kin."

*　　*　　*

Cego flopped onto his cot in the team dormitory.

He was weary. Not just from the toll his fight with Bertoth had taken but from the drain of a new semester at the Lyceum, organizing his mind around classes, subject matter, professors, and students. And this semester, without Sol's guidance for the entire team. The girl had acted as the knowledge base for all things Lyceum and otherwise.

Cego turned his head to the corner where Sol had bedded.

Usually, it would be the tidiest spot in the large room, her sheets neatly folded, all her clothes, fight gear, and belongings organized. Since she'd left, Dozer had decided Sol's corner was the biggest and relocated there. The difference was striking. Not only were the sheets unmade but Dozer's gear was strewn across the floor, and the remnants of his nightly snacks were starting to attract the rats.

Cego had seen a large black one scurry across the room just a moment before.

"Just once," Dozer shouted enthusiastically. "Just once, I wanna see you get my hand."

Dozer held his hands out in front of Joba, who swatted down at them lumberingly. Dozer easily pulled them away. The two had been playing the game for most of the midday break.

"See?" Dozer yelled. "I think my hands have gotten faster. Must've been all the speed-bag work I did last semester."

"That, or Joba's gotten slower," Knees remarked from a squatting position across the room, munching on a crisp fruit. "If that even be possible."

Dozer held his hands out. Joba swung and missed again, widely this time, but didn't appear frustrated. The usual smile was spread from ear to ear across his face.

"It's not fair," little Abel chimed in. "Joba too nice. He likes to see Dozer happy. He's missing on purpose."

Knees tossed his fruit core in the trash and walked to sit beside Cego.

"It's not hard to tell, y'know," the Venturian boy said to him in a low voice.

"Tell what?" said Cego, still lying on his back.

"You miss her," Knees said.

"What?" Cego's cheeks immediately flushed.

"You know...the longing looks at her old cot. And the deep sighs. Those deep sighs be a dead giveaway, brother."

Knees dramatically sighed to illustrate his point.

Cego was tongue-tied, not knowing how to respond to his friend's accusation.

Knees continued. "I know getting your face smashed by Bertoth rattled your skull. But I've seen you take worse. You've been acting strange since Sol split."

"No, it's not that. I don't—" Cego began.

"I know, I know," Knees interrupted. "You don't miss her. You just miss another good training partner."

It was like his friend could read his mind, which felt both comforting and scary, knowing what often went through Cego's head.

"To tell you the truth," Knees said, "I miss the prissy, purelight know-it-all too. Don't get me wrong, I like a bit of the chaotic here and there, but this—this be too much."

Knees looked to Dozer, who was now ducking his head under Joba's arms as the giant swung them back and forth. "Sol would've put Dozer in his place three, four times by now. Plus, I wouldn't have missed elective sign-ups this semester, because she'd have been up in my face with the schedule."

Cego's heart skipped a beat. Sign-ups.

On the first day of every new semester, Lyceum students signed up for their elective classes, some of which were highly sought after. Stratagems and Maneuvers taught by Professor Jos Dynari was one that almost always filled within the first few minutes. Even those students who missed the deadline by a mere hour were often placed in some of the more underwhelming electives, like Professor Sorba Myrandel's course, Methodologies for Increasing and Decreasing Heart Rate.

Cego had entirely missed the sign-up day.

Seeing his friend's wide eyes, Knees caught on. "You didn't. No, you couldn't have. You missed sign-ups today?"

"I was in the medward!" Cego protested as he snagged his

lightdeck from beneath his bed and powered it on. He quickly selected the schedule option to see what was available.

Nothing. There were absolutely no electives available anymore, not even Myrandel's course. Without enough course load, he'd need to take up a class over the semester break.

Knees looked over Cego's shoulder. "Uh-oh. Maybe you can talk to Administrator Albright to see if you could squeeze into some classes?"

Cego shivered at the thought of having to plead with Callen Albright, who had recently come on board the Lyceum's staff as head of administration. The man hated Cego's guts, probably because he reserved even more venom for Cego's mentor, Murray Pearson.

Cego sighed as he directed his lightdeck to view his current course load. Maybe he somehow already had enough credits. Fighting Styles Around the World. Elements of Combat Conditioning. Striking Level Three. Grappling Level Five. Core Enhancements.

Cego read the last class again, making sure he'd read right. Core Enhancements. There it was, listed on his schedule, three times per week blocked out for two hours.

"Wh-what...?" Cego stuttered. "I didn't sign up for this."

Knees glanced back over Cego's shoulder. "Core Enhancements? That be this year's most wanted class! How did you darkin' get into it, after skipping sign-ups altogether?"

"I didn't skip," Cego emphasized. "I was in the medward. But that doesn't matter. I didn't sign up for this; it must be some mistake."

Knees grabbed Cego's lightdeck and held it back from him. "Now, don't you be getting any ideas in that rattled skull of yours. If you be thinking that you'll go report this mistake to faculty, because it's the right thing to do, think again."

Again, there was Knees reading Cego's mind. The trend was starting to get annoying. "Well. What should I do, then?" Cego asked. "Just show up to class tomorrow?"

"That's exactly what you should be doing," Knees whispered. "Walk into class, sit in your seat, and listen to what Professor Zyleth has to say."

Professor Zyleth. The name had been whispered in the Lyceum's halls, by both students and faculty, the entire previous semester. The news that he was coming to teach at the Lyceum had been earth-shattering, to say the least. And quite controversial. After all, it was the first time that a Daimyo had ever taught at the school. Even the idea of a Daimyo stepping within the Lyceum's hallways was seen as unscrupulous to some of the Grievar faculty. And now, *one of them*. Teaching a class here. On how to make Grievar better.

"I guess so," Cego conceded. No matter what class he took, it would mean he could graduate to Level Three.

"Good," Knees said. "Now that's decided. Let's take over where Sol would have and put this dumb ox in his place."

Knees walked over to Abel, who was peacefully reading in his cot, despite the ruckus that Dozer and Joba were causing. "Hey, Abel…"

Knees whispered something in the little boy's ear.

Abel smiled and popped up. "Joba!"

The giant of a boy paused from letting Dozer kick him in the leg repeatedly to look at his tiny friend.

Abel said something in his native tongue to Joba, followed by, "Go for it!"

Joba turned toward Dozer and held his two hands out, waiting.

"Oh, so you want a turn at it now?" Dozer asked confidently. "You think you'll be as fast as me and I'll be stuck all day trying, huh? I don't think so."

Dozer held his hands up over Joba's, waiting for the perfect moment to move. Cego and Knees watched in anticipation.

Suddenly, Dozer brought his hands down, quite fast for the boy, Cego had to admit. Problem was, Joba didn't move his hands. He let Dozer smack down and then closed his giant fists, grabbing Dozer by the wrists.

"Hey!" Dozer yelled. "That's not how you're supposed to—"

Before the boy could continue, Joba dropped to his knee into kata guruma, draping Dozer across his shoulders.

Joba started to turn in a circle, swinging Dozer around with him. Joba's smile became wider as he spun faster.

"Don't let go!" Dozer yelled as his face began to turn green.

"Maybe you should've thought twice before eating third lunch just now," Knees goaded him as he swung past again.

"Let me go!" Dozer changed his tune as his cheeks puffed up in sick restraint. Joba complied this time and released Dozer, sending him flying across the room, right up to the entryway of the dorm. Dozer slid a few more feet before getting to his knees and retching a mess onto the floor.

"I'm not cleaning that up," Knees said.

"I hope no one thinks I am either, just because I'm new," said a voice from the entryway. A small girl with curly black hair and wide brown eyes stood in front of Dozer, looking down at him and his puddle of vomit.

Brynn Mykili. Cego recognized her from Drakken's class. The girl from the Isles.

Dozer looked up at her, clearly still dazed. "What're you doing here?"

"I've been assigned to your team. Hear you're down a member, with Solara Halberd leaving," Brynn replied. "I was wondering if there was a reason she might've packed up and left like that. Guess I've got my answer."

The petite girl deftly hopped over Dozer and walked to the empty cot. "This one looks just perfect," she said as she leapt onto it.

*   *   *

Cego was up early the next morning, before the sun had risen behind the grey Capital cloud cover. He looked out the single window of the dorm toward the luminous crescent moon suspended beside the Knight Tower.

He checked his lightpad once more to make sure his schedule hadn't suddenly changed. The class was still there: Core Enhancements, starting in less than an hour.

Most of the team still slept, as indicated by Dozer's loud snoring, but the new girl was already up and packing her gear.

"You have an early class too?" Cego whispered.

"Yes," Brynn replied. "Throws and Takedowns. There were two options for times, but I chose the early one. Still getting used to sleeping here, in beds and all."

Cego could see Brynn had stripped her bed and laid her sheets in a pile on the floor.

"What class have you got?" Brynn asked as the two walked out of the dorm together.

"Core Enhancements," Cego said.

"You got into that?" Brynn exclaimed. "I heard only Level Five and Six students were even eligible."

"I'm really not sure how I made it in, to tell you the truth," Cego replied. "I actually missed sign-ups because I was laid out in the ward."

"Yeah…" Brynn trailed off as the two ascended a staircase. "I watched your fight. You did pretty well, considering. That Bertoth boy looks like he eats Level Ones for breakfast."

"I felt that way," Cego said, rubbing his head. "But thanks anyways."

The two walked side by side silently for several moments down a long corridor.

"Well, this is me," Brynn said as she turned toward a classroom. "Good luck at the Daimyo's class today. Spirits be asked, he doesn't leech away your strength."

Cego looked at Brynn quizzically.

"Oh, just a superstition we have on the Isles," she said.

"Thanks, hope you get some good throws in today," Cego said as he continued on and up another flight of stairs.

Core Enhancements was set on the top floor of the Lyceum, reserved for upper-level students. Cego could hear the echo of his own footsteps as he continued to climb. The voices from below died down and he had the sinking feeling he was late to another class.

Cego finally reached an old wooden door, with several hanging plants outside it. No scanner. Just a brass knob that creaked as he turned it.

He entered a humid room with a high glass ceiling. There were plants everywhere. Vines crawling along the walls, trees sprouting from large pots, flowers of every color filling an assortment of containers.

Students sat awkwardly in mismatched chairs within the greenhouse. The space was obviously not meant to be a classroom. Off to one corner, a man knelt with his back to them. He silently snipped at a plant with a pair of shears, seemingly ignoring the waiting class.

Cego found a seat next to a golden-haired Level Five boy. Only one of the students seemed to even notice Cego, they were so distracted by the unusual environment and mysterious teacher. But a boy stared at Cego as he settled into his chair: Kōri Shimo. There was another Level Two in this class after all.

Cego thought back to last year and his strange experience with Shimo. The boy had pulled him from the onyx Circle in Professor Larkspur's classroom. Shimo had saved Cego from endlessly getting pummeled by the Guardian simulation. The boy had seemed so different from Cego, ruthless in the Circle, uncaring of whether he hurt or even killed another student. But now, after the matches of last year, after seeing that same darkness within himself, Cego wasn't sure that he was so different from Shimo after all.

The professor finally stood up and turned around, as if just realizing there was a class there for him to teach. Like most Daimyo, the man looked small compared to a Grievar. His skin was wrinkled, with veins running up and down his cheeks and along his forehead. A pair of spectacles sat across the bridge of his nose, magnifying jet-black eyes.

"Sorry about that," the Daimyo spoke in a soft but firm voice. "I often get caught up in my gardening and forget all else."

He walked to the center of the room and rolled out an old chalkboard on wheels. "I imagine my botany obsession might be akin to what Grievar feel in combat. A pull toward something greater."

He wrote the name of the class in big, flowing letters on the center of the board.

"My name is Zyleth," he said. "Just that. No need for this *Professor* nonsense. My area of expertise, in my world at least, is botany. Do any of you know what botany is?"

A Level Six girl with a shaved head and flux tattoos across her skull spoke up. "Working with plants. Growing them."

"Yes," Zyleth said as he peered over his spectacles. "Exactly. Growth. Taking a seed, a single embryo, and growing it into this."

He held his hand in front of a large vine that crawled up one wall, blossoming with sunset-orange flowers and, most notably, finger-length thorns.

"Why, do you ask, am I here? Teaching a very controversial class at the Lyceum?"

The class was silent.

"I certainly cannot teach you how to throw a punch." Zyleth awkwardly feigned throwing his fist forward, which elicited chuckles from the nervous students.

"But I can teach you about growth. How to select for desirable traits. This vine is called *Zymanthia hycathiea*, a rare species found only in the jungles of Carn. But in the wilds, this is not what zymanthia looks like. It does not have any of the thorns that you see here." Zyleth touched one of the thorns to his finger to illustrate, drawing a drop of his dark blue blood.

"Utilizing optogenetic radiation, I was able to modify the plant's core defense mechanism from one of camouflage to a more potent weapon. Plant this specific strain out in the wild, where it was found, and it would quickly overtake the entire forest. It is what we call an invasive species, due to its inherent enhancements.

"And that, my fighting students"—Zyleth wiped the blood from his hand—"is what this class is all about. Core enhancements. Except, instead of plants, we want to learn how we might enhance you Grievar."

Cego felt his stomach drop. He crossed his arms over his chest and shrank into his rickety chair. Some other students appeared to be on the edge of their seat, though.

"I have done my research on each of you already, no lightboard necessary," Zyleth said as he walked through the greenhouse between rows of students.

"Jal Perketu, Level Six," he said as he tapped a large brown-skinned boy on the shoulder. Jal already had a fairly thick beard for a seventeen-year-old, and his muscles were nearly bursting from the vibrant red second skin he wore.

"You have done incredibly well during your time here at the Lyceum, and I have no doubt you will make the current standards for Knighthood in the exit exams."

Jal nodded his head confidently.

"But." Zyleth stopped to pause in front of the boy. "I did see you lost a match in the frost container during first semester. To Mythandro, your compatriot here."

Zyleth gestured to another boy also wearing a red second skin, sitting beside Jal.

Jal started, "Well, yeah, but Mythandro had the advantage, given he's from the tundra and is used to footwork on the ice and snow. Plus breathing the cold air."

"Correct," Zyleth agreed. "Mythandro did have the advantage. And also correct, that is likely why he beat you that day. But do you think it will be different when you are a Grievar Knight, fighting for our nation? What will you tell your regiment commander when you fail against a foreign adversary who also possessed some advantage?"

Jal stayed silent.

"I have watched the footage of your fight," Zyleth continued. "And if you had maintained your pace throughout the bout, you would have won. Now, I know it is not realistic for you to have fully conditioned your lungs to the cold air. The time you can spend in the frost container is limited. But what if there was another way your lung capacity could find a way to grow? What if you could reach your full potential not only for this problem but for all your deficiencies?"

Jal seemed a bit taken aback by the suggestion. "I don't think I have so many deficiencies. But those I have, I'm sure I could shore them up in the training room."

"Right," Zyleth sighed, placing his hand on Jal's shoulder. "The training room. I understand the importance of proper hard work. But that will only take you so far. You have finite limitations, based on your physical and mental attributes. Just as my beloved zymanthia vine here used to have limitations. Until it was enhanced."

"I'm not taking no stims," a Level Five girl blurted from across the room. "It's not right. Not the natural way."

"Me neither," said Jal, shifting uncomfortably in his seat with Zyleth's hand still on his shoulder.

Zyleth remained utterly calm despite the dissent rising in the class. "No, no," the Daimyo replied. "I would not even think of it. I am well versed in the Codes. I would never have you forsake them."

"Then how?" Mythandro blurted out. "How do you expect us to get better than is possible?"

Cego felt like getting up from his chair and slowly backing out of the room.

"The same way I make these plants better." Zyleth seemed to

relish the path he was leading the students down. It was as if he were a fighter, five or six steps ahead, always with a counter ready.

"Light," Zyleth said flatly. "Spectral light."

He turned to the students. "Tell me, what is the effect of auralite in the Circle?"

A Level Five boy responded, eager to make a good impression. "Makes you want to please the crowd."

"Right, and rubellium?"

"Rising anger," another girl with fiery hair answered.

"And onyx? How about you?" Zyleth was looking directly at Cego. "Our gifted Level Two entrant to the course."

Cego felt his heart flutter. He knew firsthand what an onyx Circle could do to a mind. He remembered how he'd lost himself in the onyx last year, nearly killed another student when the blacklight had overtaken him.

"Onyx can be variable," Cego muttered. "For most, it evokes the past, for better or worse."

"Correct," Zyleth said as Cego released his breath.

"You all know the effects of the different Circles and their associated spectral wavelengths, given most of you have fought in Circles for your entire tenure at the Lyceum. What you do not know is that by focusing and intensifying spectral wavelengths, we can even further target and modify your physical and mental attributes. Permanently."

"You mean, you just shine some light on us and we can get better for good?" Jal asked, shaking his head in disbelief.

"It is not quite so simple, Jal," Zyleth said. "But that is what this course is all about. Core enhancements. You will be some of the first educated Grievar in the Lyceum to understand what it means to harness a new age of technology. This class will be about discovering exactly what your weaknesses are and then figuring out how we might remove them."

Cego shuddered at the professor's words.

"That sounds more than promising, Professor Zyleth," came a voice from the open door in the front of the room. Callen Albright, commander of the Grievar Scouts and now head administrator at the Lyceum.

"Ah, Sir Albright." Zyleth nodded. "So glad you could make our inaugural class."

"I wouldn't have it any other way," Callen said snidely. "And, as far as adherence to the Codes, I've run compliance checks, even with our resident scholar, Aon Farstead. He's on board."

Cego thought of Murray-Ku. What would his old coach have said about this? *Smells like deepshit*, he could imagine the grizzled Grievar muttering. Especially now that Callen Albright had stepped foot in the room.

But Cego couldn't believe Aon Farstead, the oldest Grievar in the Citadel, had agreed to this. He could not imagine the withered man nodding his head in approval to the words this Daimyo had just spoken.

"Shall we begin?" Albright asked Zyleth.

"Yes, let us begin," Zyleth said softly.

CHAPTER 3

A New Face

A Grievar burial is one without fanfare. A Grievar is not born to build legacy or history, to make name or impact. Only to fight and die in the Circle. And so death should be considered just as the wilting of a flower before the frost, noted and soon forgotten.

Passage Three, Fifth Precept of the Combat Codes

Solara Halberd ran her fingers through her hair, spreading the inky dye to each thick strand. She jammed a polished dagger into the rickety table in front of her, using the blade as a makeshift mirror.

Sol emptied the bottle of dye before holding the dagger at several angles around her head to make sure she hadn't missed any spots.

Good enough.

She looked the same as she had, just with black hair instead of red. Hopefully enough to separate her from the signature fiery mane of the Halberd family.

Sol stood in her small cabin: an undressed cot, desk, and chamber pot. No portholes there in the belly of the ship.

She wobbled and set herself steady as the ship rocked slightly. Sol certainly was no sailor. After three weeks on the *Erah Confligare*, she still had not found her footing, belowdecks or above.

The cabin was fine. In fact, it was an upgrade from the dormitory she was used to at the Lyceum. No need to share washbasins or chamber pots with her team. No need to hear the clockwork drone of Dozer snoring or the screams from the recent night terrors Cego had been having.

Sol snapped her mind away from the Lyceum, from her team and friends. They were now a thousand miles away, an ocean between them.

She left her cabin and went out to the craft's quarterdeck, where much of the Grunt crew lived yearlong. She made her way down a thin passage, taking care to avoid the creak of the damp-laden floor planks. She climbed the short stairs, raised the up-board, and was blinded by a fierce blue sky flecked with circling seabirds. The *Erah*'s white mainsail billowed as the eastern wind continued to carry the ship at pace, as it had over the past three weeks.

A Grunt seafarer mopping the deck looked up at Sol and nodded slightly. Most of the crew still didn't trust her. Sol wasn't a merchant, which was the primary sort of passenger on the *Erah*, most aboard to keep an eye on the goods they were transporting.

And Sol wasn't a man. It wasn't often the seafarers had females on board—let alone a Grievar.

Sol made her way to the iron railing bordering the deck and looked out to the choppy sea. She watched as an oily black curve broke the surface of the water, its back ribbed with small bumps and grooves.

When the *Erah* had first set sail from Ezo's Iron Harbor, Sol had flailed her arms and shouted at this same sight. She'd thought she'd seen her first basalm whale, but an amused seafarer had been quick to correct her.

Dyver. Submersible mech.

Sol watched as the Dyver overtook the ship in a few seconds and, within minutes, was nearly out of sight. Just another mech following the same trade route as the *Erah*.

"Had a cousin who crewed one of those," a husky voice sounded from beside Sol.

She turned to see the *Erah*'s captain, Diam. The Grunt was missing his front teeth and one of his ears, but he seemed to be the most approachable of the crew so far.

"Said they crossed the entire Cabrian Passage in a single day." Diam spat over the rail. "Imagine that. Heading from Iron Harbor at sunrise and squiggling your toes in the Isles' sands before nightfall."

"Are you curious what it might be like to captain one of those?" Sol asked, though she already knew the answer.

"Curious? Sure," Diam said. "Not curious enough though to cheat on my girl here."

Diam stroked the *Erah*'s railing. "Anyways, not always about getting places fast, Sayana."

Sol smiled at the Grunt captain. She'd taken the name Sayana for the journey, a distant cousin she'd heard Father mention a few times before.

"How much longer do you think ships like the *Erah* will be around?" Sol asked as she watched another Dyver streak beneath the water past them.

"Long as there's folks like you around." Diam squinted at her. "Real Code-abiding Grievar won't take no Dyver or Flyer anyplace. Plus, them gear and rations in *Erah*'s hold need to be Code-certified, which Diam here guarantees. No Daimyo mech-herder can say the same."

"Not many are so devout anymore," Sol said. "Most of the big teams travel by airship now."

"There'll always be some fighting folk who abide by Codes." Diam creased a broken smile. "Like you, lass."

Sol nodded, though she wasn't on the *Erah* out of adherence to the Codes. It was the way she'd always traveled as a girl. The old way. The way her father had traveled.

Sol furrowed her brow as she looked to the distance. An orange dusk was starting to creep into the blue overhead.

"My mam used to scrunch her head like that," Diam noted. "Buried her and she had the same look, still all creased up. Better you sit back and enjoy yourself a bit."

"No time to sit back while the rest spring forward toward action," Sol said automatically. She realized the words were her father's as soon as they left her mouth.

"That what this new hair coloring is? Springing toward action?" Diam asked as he eyed Sol's black braid. "Tell you the truth, old Diam here liked the fire-hair bit better. Who're you trying to be, Sayana?"

"Just myself—" Sol started as a seafarer from the crow's nest suddenly shouted.

"The Isles!" The man up high pointed a gnarled finger toward the dusky horizon.

Sol looked to see a lumbering shadow breaching the sea. Besayd.

She'd only ever dreamed of seeing this place, vague images buoyed by her father's travel tales. Markets where hawkers spoke a hundred different tongues, where carts brimmed with exotic foods and washed-up tech was sold beside glimmering treasures of old.

Diam slapped Sol on the shoulder and walked toward his command perch. The Grunt captain took several paces before turning back toward her.

"I seen that look before, Sayana," Diam said. "Many times. It's the look of those seeking something. Those planning on finding what's been lost to the Isles. I get it. Just make sure you don't find yourself lost too. I seen too many folks paying full for round trip, then leaving the *Erah* with empty cabins on the way back."

Diam wheeled around and climbed the stairs toward his perch.

"Pick up your line and don't dark up nothing, now!" the captain screamed at his crew. "Let's take our east wind to the end; we drop anchor at Emeraldi Harbor by sunfall!"

A strong wind picked up alongside the ship and took Sol's black braid with it.

*   *   *

The *Erah* found harbor on the largest of Besayd's islands, the Emerald.

Diam had told Sol that each isle was named for a prized gemstone, and the Emerald certainly fit its namesake: a dome of green-forested mountains that rose around a central valley. The sprawling harbor spanned out at the base of the valley, with an assortment of both high-tech crafts and old galleons crowding the dock space.

Sol craned her head up toward the lumbering green hills as the *Erah*'s crew found a spot at the docks. Even at this distance, she could make out one of the isle's unique features: the floating palaces that hovered above the slopes like sky lanterns.

Diam stood beside her at the rail and followed her gaze toward the giant homes suspended in midair.

"Few years ago, I personally made delivery to one of them," Diam muttered. "Man wouldn't trust the hawker middle, just wanted the goods straight from ship to stores. So, I carted up those hills, then climbed a set of floating stairs to the palace. Near had a heart attack by the time I made it to the lawn, which was big enough to fit a whole fish market."

"Was it the lord Daimyo's palace?" Sol asked.

"Nope. The one I saw was some bit-poor lord," Diam said as he spat down into the harbor. "Lord of the Emerald, Cantino, lives over the rise on the other side of the hills. Can't even see his palace unless you're coming in on Flyer."

"Thank you, Diam," Sol said as she heard the ship's gangplank crash to the docks. She reached out to grasp the Grunt's wrist.

The captain accepted the shake, firmly, meeting Sol's eye. "And you, lass, may you find what you're looking for. But keep your hands to your pockets and your eyes to the floor."

Diam's eyes flicked back to the floating palaces as he frowned. "Besayd may look pretty at a certain angle, but she's ugly deep below."

Sol nodded as she disembarked the *Erah*.

On the dock below, Sol was assaulted with a dizzying array of offers from surrounding hawkers, most speaking languages she did not understand. The goods on display ranged from frayed tech parts to prized pincer crabs caught on the rocks offshore, all shoved right up into Sol's face.

A pang of fear hit Sol in the stomach like a well-placed kick as she entered the fray of the large market that surrounded the harbor. She wasn't worried about her safety. She could handle herself, despite being all of one hundred forty pounds. Her fear came from not knowing. Uncertainty as to whether she'd be able to pull this off.

Sol took a deep breath and let the fear settle in her stomach. There, the nerves felt contained, even useful.

She listened to a merchant shuffle his feet as he tried to haggle the sale of a large sarpin. She smelled the burnt crisp of meat on a nearby grill mixed with the stink of rotting sewage pouring from the gutters onto the cobbles. She felt the path beneath her feet through the soles of her shoes.

Sol strode forward.

*   *   *

"Right here," Father said as he patted Sol's belly. "That's where the fear begins to form."

Sol stood alongside her father in the Grove, the top of her red braid only reaching up to his waistline. She looked up toward his towering figure as he guided her in their everyday practice.

"Then the fear will move up here," Father said in his baritone, patting her back, between the shoulder blades.

Artemis Halberd was built like a Grievar was made to be. A thick brow weathered with scar tissue from a career of head strikes. A jutting, chiseled jawline, designed to absorb impact, terminating toward two bulbous ears. A barrel chest and two muscle-gnarled arms, with such a span that they could reach his knees without him bending. Artemis Halberd was a golem of combat, strong like steel and yet sinuous like a whip.

"If the fear gets too high up, here in your chest," Artemis continued, "you won't be able to breathe, think, act."

Sol knew the fear her father spoke of. She'd never been a natural in the Circle. In her first bout, at the age of seven, the fear had overtaken her. It had caught in her chest, cut off her breathing, made her slow, an easy target for her waiting opponent.

"Keep your fear down here," her father said as he patted Sol's belly again. "Here, you can use your fear. Here, it is your friend. Here, it will keep your nerves electric, so that your senses can be heightened and your movements lightning quick."

Artemis demonstrated by breathing deeply himself, his stomach filling, before he pounced in and out on his toes, jabbing the air and then shooting in on a breathtakingly fast penetration step.

Most of those who watched Artemis Halberd fight were captivated by his dexterity despite his massive bulk. They marveled at the distance he could cover, a cross or a takedown coming from one side of the Circle to the other in an eyeblink.

Sol always watched her father's toes when he fought. The way his gnarled feet gripped the ground, as if they were another set of hands. Artemis would often crouch on all fours and bound around the garden grounds of their house, with little Sol trying to keep up, leaping over rosebushes and laughing so hard, it made it difficult to breathe.

"That's enough for today," Artemis sighed.

"But, Father! We'd barely just started working on the cross, jab, instep you showed." Solara pouted.

"I need to prepare on my own now, Sol," Artemis said gently. *"Shipping out tomorrow to the Isles for another grievance."*

Sol looked down at the dirt, digging her bare toes into it. She wanted to tell her father she missed him, that he was gone more often than he was there. But she knew it was useless. It was his duty to follow orders, to go in for every job that the Citadel called him up for. The Isles, Kiroth, Yorlen, Garrithston, a different place every few days now.

Artemis sensed Sol's disappointment. *"Sol, you know why I'm doing this."*

For you, Sol knew he'd say. She continued to look at the floor silently.

"For you," Artemis said as he patted her shoulder. *"For everything we have around us, for how far we've come."*

It was a lie and Sol knew it. She saw her father on SystemView, paraded down city streets with crowds of adoring fans showering him with praise. She saw the look on his face. He loved it. Artemis Halberd loved fighting in the Circles, he loved being Ezo's hero, the face of the Grievar Knight program.

Sol fiercely fought back the tears, biting her lip hard. She wouldn't give him that.

"Now, go get on with your studies." Artemis shooed Sol toward the house, and he turned and strode toward the estate's private training facility. He'd likely meet with one of the Citadel's coaches there to help him prepare for the upcoming bout.

Sol hesitated on the cobbled path. Sometimes, she'd sneak in after her father, crouch down by the window behind the overgrown hedges to watch his training sessions. She'd always been amazed at the team the Citadel put beside him: sparring partners, coaches, conditioning clerics, all devoted to making sure Artemis Halberd was ready for battle.

This time, Sol didn't care to watch. She didn't care if he was Ezo's hero or if he won the nation some prized resources.

All that mattered was Father was leaving again.

*   *   *

Sol clutched her bit-purse as she passed through the Emeraldi marketplace.

Crowded, loud, and filthy, at its heart, the market was not so different from those low-district pavilions Sol's father used to take her through back home.

She felt eyes following her, hawkers sitting atop crates puffing pipes and wrinkled old ladies peering out from their hoods. Sol's disguise felt thin, telegraphed like a sloppy cross. Could her newly darkened hair and foreign name really hide her identity? She pulled her cloak closer and continued along, eyes alert.

It wasn't difficult for Sol to locate the city's courtesan quarters. She passed several gaudy advertisements streaking sandstone buildings, massive works of graffiti that pointed tourists toward the section.

SEEKING PLEASURE BEYOND YOUR IMAGINATION? VISIT TIKAY-LA'S HOUSE ON AGATE ROAD.

Sol stared at the ad as she walked past. It depicted a feminine hand with a curved finger, beckoning onlookers forward.

She'd done her research and was aware of the myriad services a Courtesan House could offer wealthy visitors for a hefty bit-price. But Sol also knew courtesans heard things during their *practice*, anything from run-of-the-mill gossip to black market business dealings. The courtesans were the primary keepers and dealers of information on the Isles.

Sol needed information.

She followed the signs to the base of a sandstone bridge that connected two looming housing complexes. Long silver chains hung from the bridge's arch, each full of colorful gemstones that flashed in the fading sunlight.

Sol stepped from the shadow of the bridge and emerged into a different world. The raucousness of the market disappeared, replaced by the soft trickling of a fountain set in the center of a manicured square. Colorful jaybirds flitted to flower beds and roosted on the gutters of the surrounding stately houses.

Captain Diam's parting words floated through Sol's mind.

Besayd may look pretty at a certain angle, but she's ugly deep below.

Sol watched carefully as a hunched man, draped in fineries and accompanied by two burly mercs, shuffled to the front door of one of the houses. He knocked and waited a moment before gaining entry, while his henchmen stood guard outside.

Despite its tranquil façade, Sol felt exposed in the open square. Through several of the high windows she caught curious faces peering down at her.

She stepped into an alley, away from the prying eyes, and found herself in front of a wooden door with brass plates striped across it. A small logo was etched onto one of the plates: a feminine silhouette with a large eyeball in place of the head.

Sol took a deep breath and pounded the wood with the brass knocker.

The door creaked open and a sharp nose protruded from the crack. A sour-faced man eyed Sol up and down. "You here for apprenticeship? Too late."

Sol had been preparing to utilize the rudimentary Emeraldi tongue she'd practiced the past few months, but it seemed many on the island chose to speak Ezonian to her, as the language had been adopted for universal trade.

"I'm here to see the courtesan," Sol said.

The man scowled. "Lady Lilac already took a girl under her wing last month."

He began to shut the door.

Sol jammed her boot into the doorway, reaching into her pocket to produce two black bit-pieces. "Two onyx," she said, trying to sound nonchalant. "I'd just like to talk to Lilac."

The man's eyes gleamed as he grabbed the bits and sniffed them.

He looked Sol in the eyes as his long black tongue snaked from his mouth to lick the currency. "Three more onyx and she'll see you, whatever floats your fancy."

Sol fought back a shiver as she dropped three more onyx pieces into the man's hand. He opened the door with arms spread, "Welcome to Courtesan Lilac's."

The inside of the establishment was much like the exterior square: tranquil. A makeshift stream flowed around a rock formation in the entry room. Off in a corner, a musician strummed a lyre. The man's milky white eyes fluttered toward Sol's bootsteps. He was blind.

"Here to see Lilac, are you?" The blind musician smiled as he continued to strum seamlessly.

"Um...yes," Sol stuttered.

"Here shortly, she'll be." The man nodded toward a set of decorative cushions on the floor.

Sol felt a sudden calm wash over her as she took a seat in the pile of pillows. Perhaps it was the melodic strumming or the fragrant perfume that tinged the air.

She watched an ash-skinned man emerge from behind a waterfall of curtains, a girl on his arm. Veins coursed her skin like tears on marble. She wore a flowing crimson robe and an elaborate hair bun fashioned with glowing ties to hold it in place.

The Daimyo girl smiled warmly at Sol, who suddenly felt clumsy sitting on the cushions. She stood up awkwardly, shuffling her feet.

"Thank you, thank you." The grey man bowed his head to the girl. "Please see me again soon."

"We will see," the girl said soothingly. "Behave yourself, Lord Imiwara, and we will see."

The man left, leaving the Daimyo girl watching Sol curiously, her hands folded into her robe. Sol found herself fumbling for words.

"Are you...are you Courtesan Lilac?"

The girl held her lithe hand to her mouth and giggled, sounding like some exotic bird.

"I'm just an apprentice to Lady Lilac," she said softly. "Are you also to be an apprentice? To have a friend would be magnificent!"

"I don't think I'd make the cut," Sol said. "I'd just like to speak to her about someone I'm looking for."

"Lady Lilac knows many someones," the girl replied as she reached up to stroke Sol's braid. "And I disagree you wouldn't make the cut. Perhaps just a bit of time to fix you up."

Sol wasn't sure whether to take the girl's words as insult or compliment, so she just stood in silence and stared at the statuesque creature.

"I hear you seek information." A woman floated through the curtains, grey-haired and dressed in similar garb to the apprentice. Her steely eyes locked on to Sol's like a fighter prior to stepping into the Circle.

Sol could sense the lady reading her. Not discerning her weight or balance like a Grievar would but plucking at her very thoughts.

"Yes—" Sol started.

"Come with me." The lady floated back through the curtains, extending a curved, beckoning hand.

Sol followed her into a heavily cushioned room with a large circular bed at the center. Braziers at each corner burned perfume. Sol felt content and a bit fuzzy, as if she'd forgotten why she was there in the first place.

The lady draped herself across the bed like a cat and sighed. "I assume you've already paid off my doorman, but what you seek will require further payment, of course."

"I have more," Sol replied. "Are you Lady Lilac?"

The grey-haired Daimyo spread her arms wide. "In the flesh. Though it is not often I receive patrons who seek something outside the flesh. What may I call you, little bird?"

"Sayana."

Sol found herself drawn to the courtesan, walking to sit beside the lady on the bed. The perfume overwhelmed Sol's senses like a flowery, sweet sickness. She stared wide-eyed at the lady without any self-reproach, her only thought that she had no idea how old Lilac was; the courtesan could be either thirty or three hundred years of age.

"Sayana." Lilac purred the name. "You do not seem a Sayana to me. Is that who you really are?"

"No." Sol heard the word come out of her mouth, though part of her brain screamed in protest.

"I thought as much." Lilac batted her eyes. "Now, little bird, why don't you tell me your real name? After all, how can you expect me to help you find *someone* if we don't know who you really are?"

Again, Sol found her lips moving as if in some dream state. "My name is Solara Halberd."

Lady Lilac's eyes became wide, for a brief moment, before regaining their feline poise.

"Now, that's a name I've heard spoken quite often of late," Lilac said. "Halberd."

Like a slap to the head, her name snapped Sol back to reality, reminding her of the mission.

"What did you do to me?" Sol stood from the bed and backed up, shaky on her feet.

"I did nothing, little bird." Lilac grinned. "You came through my door and into my home, all on your own."

Sol felt familiar adrenaline flooding her veins. Whatever intoxicant she'd been exposed to, she knew her innate countermeasures would clear her system shortly. The pulse of combat began to lift the fog clouding her mind. Sol's hands balled into fists.

"You wouldn't hurt me, would you?" A pout tugged Lilac's bottom lip.

Sol shook her head. "No, but after whatever you did to me, I probably should."

"Just run-of-the mill airborne neuros," Lilac murmured as she stood from the bed and walked to a gilded mirror against one wall. "It helps set the mood with the patrons. Lets them forget all their worries and simply...be."

Lilac deftly plucked a brush from a small tin and began to apply rose-hued blush to her cheeks. The shoulder of her robe fell to one side.

"I know you were wondering." The courtesan stared at herself in the mirror appraisingly. "I'm one hundred ninety-two years old."

Now that the effects of the neurogen wore thin, Sol saw Lilac through different eyes. Though the courtesan's face still appeared a near-flawless porcelain, Sol could see cracks forming in the façade.

"I don't care about that," Sol said flatly. The Daimyo were known for enhancing, prolonging, fending off the inevitable. "But I do care about getting the information I came here for."

Lilac spun around, her eyes flashing. "Even if I decided not to *procure* your real name, did you really think I would not see through your disguise? Dear Solara, you didn't even properly dye the roots of your hair! I saw those fiery strands before you even stepped foot in this room."

Sol brushed her braid behind her shoulder and growled. "I'm not here to play games. You know who I am. So, you must know who I'm looking for."

"Of course," Lilac replied. "You seek the whereabouts of your father, the great Artemis Halberd."

It was strange hearing her father's name spoken out loud.

"During my own information gathering, I was able to determine that my father's body was purchased by one of the Besaydian lords," Sol said. "But that's as far as I could get. I was told speaking to a courtesan, I could get further. I want to know who bought my father's body."

"I hear many things in this room," Lilac said, turning back to the mirror to apply a finger of white cream to her face. "Daimyo nobles and politiks. Foreign diplomats, governors, and leaders of trade. Even an occasional lord of Besayd. Powerful men. Well, they all think themselves powerful. But in here, I wield the power."

Lilac turned back toward Sol and whispered, "One such lord... a regular, paid me a visit recently. Such a talkative man. He could barely close his mouth, even when I silenced him."

Sol found herself drawing closer to Lilac's whisper, though she made sure not to get too close, much as she'd avoid some strain of poisonous ivy.

"In his fits of blabber, my dear lord did release one tidbit that caught my ear, which I believe would be of the utmost interest to you." Lilac lifted her cupped hand outward, waiting.

Sol reached into her pocket and emptied her remaining onyx into Lilac's palm, enough to pay three months' rent in any Ezonian high district.

Lilac placed the currency on her table and smiled. "He said that the buyer of Artemis Halberd's body was the most well-known collector on the Isles. A man with a museum on his estate that rivals some of the greatest national museums, where thousands of archaeological specimens are kept and maintained. This man has a particular interest in Grievar historical artifacts."

"Who?" Sol couldn't help but betray her anxious curiosity.

"Lord Cantino himself," Lilac replied.

Sol felt like she'd taken a punch to the solar plexus.

Even before she'd come there, Sol had heard the name of the lord of the Emerald isle. Though Besayd did not have one single ruler, there was no debate that Lord Neferili Cantino wielded the greatest power.

Lilac read Sol's frown like a book and began to laugh, barely able to contain herself.

"Oh, sweet little bird! So naïve. You actually believed you would break into a lord's estate and steal your father's body, right under his nose?"

Sol steadied her breath.

Don't let the fear rise. Keep it down, where you can use it.

She steeled her gaze at the mocking courtesan. "I will do so. Neferili Cantino or the darkin' emperor of Kiroth, I don't care. I plan on getting my father's body back where it belongs. Not in some Daimyo private collection. I'm bringing him back to home soil. I'm giving him a proper Grievar burial. Wet earth and dry leaves."

Lilac let the contempt flee her face, as if she'd just removed a mask. "Ah, so. You are truly the daughter of Artemis Halberd. Courage runs in your blood, I see. Or perhaps stupidity. Either way, I have no doubt you are on a suicide mission, if you plan on trying to steal from Lord Cantino."

Sol didn't waver. "I don't care. We Grievar are always two steps from a plot of dirt anyways."

Lilac nodded. "I like you, Solara Halberd. Despite what you might think, you and I, we are not so different."

The courtesan raised her balled fists. "Of course, I don't fight like you, in the Circle. But I fight just the same, with the tools that have been given to me. Just like you, my bloodline has been bred into me. My path as a courtesan."

Lilac reached forward to grab Sol's hand. The lady's fingers were soft and sinuous.

"Go down to the Lake Kava dockyard, where the gondolas rise to the floating estates," the courtesan whispered. "There, look for a Grievar by the name of Beriali Timault. He pilots a gondola and happens to make regular trips up to Lord Cantino's estate. Look for him under the azure awning. Tell him his dear Lady Lilac has sent you."

Sol nodded. "Thank you."

She turned to leave, wanting to get out of this place while she still had her wits.

"Solara," Lilac called back to her.

Sol turned from beneath the curtains.

"In another life, perhaps I'd be where you are. Fighting in the Circles, in front of adoring, cheering spectators. And perhaps you might be here, seducing patrons in a Courtesan House."

"I don't think so," Sol replied.

Lilac's eyes twinkled. "You're not so far from this life as you think."

Sol didn't ask Lilac what she meant. She'd had enough verbal jousting. She turned and fled to the Emeraldi streets.

*   *   *

Sol found lodging at the Behemoth, a small brick-backed hostel in the slums that Diam had suggested. It was a Grunt establishment, the wood interior soaked through with stale ale and the floorboards infested with roaches. But the moment Sol lay back onto the stained cot, she fell into a dreamless sleep.

She woke the next morning sweating, the already-hot Besaydian sun burning against the window. Sol gathered her things and looked herself over in the makeshift dagger mirror, ensuring her hair had not suddenly reverted to red.

It seemed like only days since she'd lain on the grass in front of the Lyceum with her friends, staring up at the sky as they awaited the new semester. Sol had held back speaking about her father with the team, even Cego. The boy had delicately asked her about him, his eyes cast down at the floor, just once.

Dozer hadn't been so delicate.

Sol, you okay? Is this about your father getting flattened by that Kirothian Knight?

She grinned just thinking of her friends as she set out to the Emeraldi streets. She'd picked up a rough map of the city from the Grunt innkeeper, and it wasn't difficult to find the path toward Lake Kava.

Sol felt the hairs on her neck prickle and turned back to see a flicker of red cloth vanish behind the corner of a sandstone building. Perhaps a trick of the island light, or perhaps someone was following her. Sol had no doubt that Courtesan Lilac had likely sent someone to tail her, but she kept on track until she reached the edge of a steep sloping hill.

Though she'd already seen the hills when the *Erah* came to harbor, the rising slopes were starkly more beautiful from her vantage along the descending path. It was as if a giant had scooped the center out from a lush green mountain and filled it with sparkling waters. Lake Kava's docks bristled from the edge of the water as gondolas rose from each platform toward the mansions floating above.

As she descended toward the lake, Sol surveyed the colorful variety of dock awnings. She noticed a suntanned Grunt beneath a dark shade, prepping his gondola for departure. She walked out onto the dock and attempted to catch his eye. "Excuse me, are you Timault?"

The man looked at her quizzically, responding in his native tongue. *"Beth kissmet, mon voyagu."*

Sol knew a few words of Kirothian and had practiced some of the more prevalent Besaydian dialects, but she had no idea what language the man was speaking. She raised her hands apologetically. "Do you speak Ezonian?"

The man glared at her. *"Mon voyagu! Mon voyagu!"*

He did not appear to be happy with Sol.

A voice suddenly spoke from over Sol's shoulder. *"Facalis voyagu, tes von yuvel. Kissmet e yuvel. Mayas tissel von vivia?"*

The man nodded and went back to his work.

Sol turned toward the voice to see a figure cowled in a red cloak.

"I told him, he don't need worry about you taking his job," a girl said, lifting her hood. Her head was completely shaved. "These ferrymen, they fall in and out of favor of the lords, and he thought you been sent to replace him."

Sol's cheeks flushed.

"Don't worry, I told him you lost," the girl said. "Are you?"

Sol didn't answer the question. "Thank you for translating."

The girl extended her hand, grasping Sol's arm deeper than she was accustomed to, reaching all the way to the elbow.

"N'auri." The girl flashed a sharp-toothed smile.

"Sayana."

"You a fighting Grievar," N'auri said. "I can tell from your grasp. When I grasp a Grievar that don't fight, they squeeze hard, or try to pull. Prove a point, maybe. Fighting Grievar don't need show off. They already been training all day and need nothing else to prove."

Sol nodded.

"I hear you looking for Timault."

Sol eyed the girl carefully, unsure of whom she could trust here. She was aware that she stuck out like a sore thumb despite her disguise and was likely ripe for scammers, but Sol knew when she needed help.

"Yes, I was told he'd provide passage to where I need to get."

The girl pointed down toward the lakeside. "See, down there, the dock farthest out?"

Sol looked to where N'auri was pointing. A pack of kids were filing onto one of the larger gondolas. A barrel-chested man with a long mustache stood and yelled from the helm as another began to roughly shove the kids on board.

"That's Timault," N'auri said. "Not sure why you want to look for him, though. Man is no good. Finds slum parents, bit-poor to the bone, and buys up their kids to work the floating palaces. Servers, sweepers, polishers, hedgers. Some of the stronger ones he pawns to slave Circles. Weaker ones... even worse. What business do you have with him?"

Sol held her breath. Why would Lady Lilac send her to a slave trader? She didn't see any reason not to believe N'auri, but had the courtesan lied to her?

"I see your gears turning," N'auri said. "Who sent you to Timault? One of the courtesan, was it?"

"How did you know?"

N'auri frowned. "They got a deal, you see. Timault has the courtesan send him lost kids. Ones he might use. Courtesan are just like everybody else here on the Isles. Always something cooking below the surface, not what it appears."

Sol's shoulders sank. Her mission to take her father's body off these Isles seemed further away than ever, despite his lying not so far off in one of the palatial estates floating above.

"I'll help you," N'auri offered. "Anyway, I already know what you here for. What you looking for."

Sol held her breath. "How—"

"I already told you. Your grasp. Your stance. I know you a fighter. You looking for a proper Circle here on the Isles."

"Oh, well..." Sol breathed a sigh of relief.

"And that's what I'm here for too," N'auri said confidently. "I been waiting too long already to get myself on the path. We can help each other get there. Good training partner are hard to come by on the Isles. And seeing as you foreign and I'm native, we can trade technique."

Sol watched one of the gondolas launch, effortlessly gliding through the air over the glassy lake. She felt her plan slipping through her fingers.

"I can't," Sol said. "I mean, I'm not looking for a training partner. I'm looking for something else."

N'auri was undeterred. "Look, I understand. You don't trust me. I just told you everybody on these Isles is looking out for themselves. And you right. I am looking out for me. I need a good training partner to make it to Neferili Cantino's stable of Grievar. He doesn't take any slow—"

"Cantino?" Sol couldn't help but show interest. "I mean, I've heard of him before. One of the oldest Daimyo lords on the Isles, right?"

"Yeah, the Emerald lord must be three going on four hundred

years," N'auri said. "During those years, he built one of the strongest fight teams outside nation-funded ones. I been aiming to be on that team since I was a little *kika*. And I'm guessing, that's why you here too?"

Sol saw her opportunity, like a foot planted too far forward, ripe for an inside sweep.

"Yes," Sol said. "Either Cantino or some other Daimyo lord's team."

"Well, you know then that tryouts are one week from today," N'auri exclaimed. "All the lords will be there to watch. Cantino, Reginald, Sebeliun, Duvali. The richest and most powerful Daimyo will be looking to add to their teams. You win their favor, you get placed."

Sol felt excitement bubble in her stomach. Like fear, she worked to keep it down.

"I heard it is a great honor to earn a spot on Cantino's team." Sol mustered the lie.

"It is," N'auri replied. "And doesn't hurt that if you picked, you get access to his training center, best coaches on the Isles, food for a champ, not to mention a decent bed to sleep in his stables. Grievar dream, it is. My dream, at least."

Sol nodded. This was the path she needed to be on. She had no doubt that N'auri had been the one tailing her on the way to the docks, and the girl clearly wasn't telling the full truth, but Sol needed access to Cantino's compound before she could even consider how to retrieve her father's body. It would only be fitting she'd have to fight her way in there.

"You say you need a training partner, one week from the placement bouts," Sol said. She extended her hand once again. "I also need a training partner."

N'auri flashed her sharp white teeth and grasped Sol, again deep, down to the elbow.

CHAPTER 4

Dreams from the Surface

There is a way to suffocate an opponent without physical contact. At the start of a fight, each combatant thinks their skills superior; this creates an open space within the mind, an illumination that proposes any technique is possible. However, as the fight progresses, certain techniques are disabled, made untenable by an opponent's defensive abilities. If one can defuse all of an opponent's techniques, it will be as if they have been suffocated, snuffed out in the darkness with no viable option to move forward.

Passage Three, Fortieth Technique of the Combat Codes

Hey!"

Knees was shaking him, staring down from above.

"You be bugging out!" Knees yelled, continuing to shake him.

Cego sat up. He was in his cot in the dormitory. Sweat sheened his brow and soaked his body. He was breathing hard, his heart racing as if he'd just stepped from the Circle.

"You okay, Cego?" He heard Abel's little voice from the shadows at his side.

"Yes, I'm okay." His voice came out a parched whisper.

"Didn't seem like that a few seconds ago." Knees sighed as he turned and paced across the dorm.

"What happened?" Cego asked.

"You lit up!" Dozer's face suddenly popped up in front of his. "It was incredible!"

"What?" Cego rubbed his eyes. "What do you mean…I lit up?"

"Spirits be said, it was not incredible." Brynn Mykili was next to him now. "It was scary. You were screaming really loud."

The night terrors again. Cego had been having them since last year. But something about this one was different. He felt weary, as if he'd traveled some distance. His body ached in a strange way.

Knees walked back to his side. "They both be right; your screaming was pretty terrible as usual, especially because I've got to get up early for class tomorrow. But yeah, your arm. The Doragūn flux lit up again. I saw it floatin' up and down your arm, screaming bright light coming off the thing. And I'm pretty sure I smelled something burning."

Cego shifted his body and looked down at the cot. The canvas was blackened where his left arm had been resting, burned through down to the metal frame. He quickly shifted his body back over the charred spot.

"It's not doing anything now," he whispered.

Cego remembered the nightmare. There had been wind and snow, a cabin in the torchlight. A family and their screams. But it didn't feel like a dream. It felt like a memory.

He got out of his cot and checked the window, looking for the moon. Though the night sky was overcast, he could make out its luminescent form behind the clouds.

"What're you doing?" Dozer stood to look out the window alongside him. "What's out there?"

"Nothing," Cego replied. "Just seeing how far we are from morning.

Everyone should try to get some sleep. Class tomorrow and all. I'm sorry about this whole thing."

"Naw, that's all right." Dozer yawned as he threw his back onto his cot, nearly breaking the thing. "I wasn't sleeping anyways. Bored of that."

"That's 'cause you do all your sleeping during class, ya daft ox," Knees said as he also climbed back into bed.

"Can't help it if every semester teachers seem to get older," Dozer said. "And they talk slooower, like thiiisss..."

Brynn was still standing by Cego's cot. She put a warm hand on his shoulder. Cego could feel her big brown eyes on him. He glanced at her, not sure what to say. She nodded and padded off across the dormitory.

Cego lay down, breathing deeply. He tried to settle back in.

But sleep never came to him. He could still hear their screams.

*   *   *

Knees was always faster up the second ridge.

On the first slope, Cego could stay neck and neck with the Venturian, even pull ahead of him for a short burst, but he couldn't match his friend's pace for long. For every stride of Knees's lanky legs, Cego needed to take two.

Now Cego could see only his friend's heels as the boy disappeared over the crest of the hill. Cego leapt a gnarled root and cut a sharp angle as the forest trail quickly changed direction. He sprinted past rows of arrowhead pines, sparse along their trunks but providing a leafy canopy above. A morning mist mulled at the base of the arrowheads and crept onto the trail.

Conditioning class with Professor Tamil.

Once per week, they'd run Kalabasas Hill, which was set west of the Lyceum grounds in the Black Forest. The hill was made up of a series of interconnected trails, some threading deep into wooded canyons. The way down could be treacherous, but the climb back was the true test of conditioning for the students.

Though Cego wasn't the slowest in the class, he was far from the fastest. Knees usually finished the course near the lead of the pack. The Venturian and Gryfin Thurgood had been trading off second and third place. First place had been the sole possession of Damyn Zular, a girl who bounded down the trails like a gazelle.

The new Myrkonian recruits always shored up the bottom several spots. Their wide, stout bodies seemed completely unsuited for running.

"Thought we'd be havin' fights here, not running like winter hares!" Rhodan Bertoth had bellowed prior to the first sprint. By the end of the course, Rhodan looked like he'd seen a ghost, pale and far from his usual blustery self.

Cego heard rocks crunching on the trail behind him, someone coming up on his heels. Probably Kōri Shimo, who'd been gaining since the start of today's race and was usually neck and neck with Cego by the end of it. He glanced behind him; just the mist rolling across the dirt trail. Cego listened carefully but heard only his own rhythmic breathing and echoing footfalls.

He quick-stepped a series of stones to cross a brook. Again, he heard something on his heels, this time splashing, as if someone were stomping through the stream. But when he glanced behind him, it was just the babbling brook.

As he settled into a straightaway on the trail, Cego's thoughts drifted again to his missing friend. Sol would've been up at the head of this pack. Sol's conditioning always seemed to be optimized; she'd traded first place with Zular through first semester.

He jumped over a small boulder as sunlight pierced the pine boughs, momentarily blinding him in a flash of white. Cego was coming up on the final rise, a steep, rocky incline that would take him to the top. He prepared his mind as he would during the last minutes of a fight, attempting to maximize his efficiency.

Kōri Shimo suddenly appeared on his tail, silently surprising Cego and causing him to nearly topple over into the brook that ran beside them. Cego tried to maintain his balance but slid down in a spray of rock dust.

Shimo scrambled past and Cego took up pursuit.

Cego found his pace up the slope. The pines thinned and he could now make out several of the lead runners sprinting to their finish at the crest. As expected, Damyn was in the lead, although Knees wasn't far behind her.

His gaze focused, Cego started to pick up his pace, using his hands and feet to balance himself as he ascended the incline, just like he used to do as a boy on the island cliffs.

Cego felt a rush of energy pull him upward, as if a strong wind had found his back. But the pines did not sway. His feet felt light and his bones nearly hollow, as if he could leap to the air and fly the rest of the course.

All of a sudden, Cego had caught Shimo.

Kōri pushed the pace and the two rivals moved in parallel up the final ascent.

"You got this, brother!" Knees screamed from above. Cego turned to see his friend raising a fist in support. "Leave him in the dust!"

Cego felt momentum on his side. His conditioning was good. He had enough in the tank to finish with some breath to spare. He stayed right beside Shimo, smiling as he felt fresh energy course through his body.

Just as the two closed in on the top, Cego caught a glint from the corner of his eye, a flash of light in the brook that ran down the slope alongside the trail. He turned to see a reflection in the water, moving right beside him and Shimo.

A freckled boy smiled back at him.

Cego was abruptly spinning head over heels, tripped up by a rock. He met the hard earth in a tumble.

Shimo scrambled past him to reach the top first.

Cego lay in the dust, his head turned toward the running water.

No one was there anymore. Just the water and the mist snaking through the pines.

He'd recognized the face smiling back at him, though. There was no mistaking it.

It had been his brother's face. Sam's face.

*   *   *

Cego hiked the long stone passageway between the Lyceum's two wings, the Harmony and Valkyrie. Abel walked beside him, as they'd done all last year on the way to Professor Aon Farstead's Codes class. Sol had been the third of the team who had attended Codes, and Cego felt her missing presence as their footsteps echoed in the empty corridor.

Abel stopped for a moment to peer up at one of the old portraits that lined the torchlit walls. The Desovian boy had an unending curiosity. Things that others took for granted, Abel always questioned. He wanted to know.

"Gabard Greyspar," Abel whispered reverently. The portrait he was looking up at depicted a thick-shouldered Grievar with orange eyes and long grey hair running down his back. "In Desovi, we know all about the Greyspars, very famous," he said.

Cego got closer to the portrait and could see two boys in the background behind Gabard. They looked nearly identical.

"Those two grew up famous too," Abel pointed out. "They were known as Key and Lock. It was spoken, because they were twins, they knew each other so perfectly, their training sessions lasted entire days without either gaining advantage. Like mirrors."

Cego stared at the portrait in the flickering light. Although the twin boys looked the same on first glance, closer up he could make out differences between the two. One had a long scar running across his forehead and a piercing glint in his eye. The other twin's eyes were wide, as if he were caught by surprise.

Cego thought of Sam. There had been no mistaking his brother's face in the Kalabasas stream's reflection earlier in the day.

Wide-eyed, like the boy in this portrait. And curious, like Abel. Sam had always been exploring the nooks and crannies of the island.

And the scarred boy in the portrait reminded Cego of Silas, his older brother who'd always been so confident. Silas, now known around the world as the Grievar who'd vanquished Artemis Halberd. Cego had heard the announcers on SystemView, the whispers in the school's halls. They called him Silas the Slayer.

But to Cego, Silas was his cocky brother with the crooked smile. To Cego, Silas was the man who'd killed Sol's father.

"You okay?" Abel looked concerned.

"Yeah," Cego said without much confidence.

"I had many brothers and sisters back home," Abel stated. "I'm *Ka Sin*, which means fifth child from the top, out of eight. When we weren't put to work herding the goats, my oldest sister, *Ba Sen*, used to bring all of us to the fields when the poppies were in bloom, just on the edge of Desovian border. We wrestled under the sun for the entire day and then filled our bellies with delicious fruits."

"That sounds nice" was all Cego could say. He thought of the azure waters of the island, sitting on the black sand with Silas and Sam. Practicing ki-breath and listening to the breaking of the waves under the watchful eye of the old master. "You must miss them."

"I do," Abel said. "Very much, every time I close my eyes to sleep. But... they are *kythanta*." The little Desovian breathed deeply.

"*Kythanta?*"

"Yes." Abel paused. "It means... It's hard to describe in your language." The little boy stood for a moment, thinking. "It's like your arms." Abel held his two arms in the air. "They are separate, and they can do different things." He swung each arm in a different direction. "But even when they do different things, they are the same. Each knows what other is doing all the time."

Cego nodded.

"My brothers and sisters are far from me now," Abel said. "But no matter what, they are part of me. *Kythanta*, we are together."

"*Kythanta*," Cego whispered. He felt his arm tingle.

Footsteps echoed down the hallway, moving toward them. Cego half expected to see Sol emerge from the shadows, with some explanation that she wouldn't miss Aon Farstead's class no matter what.

"Beautiful, simply beautiful," a familiar voice said.

Zyleth, the Daimyo professor, walked toward them. He stopped beside the two surprised students to glance at the portrait on the wall.

"All this Grievar history, I simply love it," Zyleth said. "In our schools, we do not learn much about your kin. We learn of the great merchants, clerics, politiks, engineers, makers, even Bit-Minders. But Grievar are always just a footnote, the end of a chapter saying so and so fought in the Circle to finalize a negotiation."

Zyleth placed his hand on Cego's shoulder as he continued.

"But I had been missing out. Learning about the Grievar histories is simply fascinating. The different combat cultures, the fighting styles, I could spend all day reading the subject if I were not so busy."

Cego turned away from the man's cold fingers and made a move down the hall.

"Uh, we need to get going to Professor Aon's class," Cego stuttered.

"Yes, yes," Abel chimed in. "Don't want the great one to have us late."

"Of course," Zyleth agreed, nodding his head. "I greatly admire Professor Aon. In fact, I have just come from speaking to him."

"Oh," Cego said. "Are you friends?"

Zyleth laughed, a grating noise that Cego wished he could forget as soon as he heard it. "Friends! A Grievar and Daimyo. Let us just say there is a great deal I wish to learn from Aon Farstead. I wish you a good class."

They walked briskly down the hallway, away from Zyleth.

*   *   *

Cego and Abel climbed the long spiral staircase to the top of the Valkyrie. It was their second year of Codes class together, and they were the only Level Twos who had decided to opt in to the course.

Cego was looking forward to hearing the old Grievar's voice, oozing with wisdom from years of living and studying the Codes. Professor Aon had helped guide Cego through his first year at the Lyceum, providing a steady hand when things were anything but stable.

They reached the top of the stairs and walked through the open entrance into the professor's study.

Cego took the room in: the musty scent of paper and old book covers, the bronze light that filtered through the stained glass shield windows, the tall clock's methodical metronome. Aon's study was just as Cego remembered, a peaceful place where he could immerse himself in the histories of the world.

The class was seated. Only seven students had signed up for Codes this semester to study with Professor Aon. Cego and Abel found their seats beside Theodora Larkspur, a Level Four who was daughter to the Lyceum's professor of Circles. Like her mother, Adrienne, Theodora was tall, her shoulder blades rising above the chair backing.

The students sat quietly, listening to the clock's sharp clicks for nearly fifteen minutes. Cego began to worry that something was wrong.

They'd all heard the whispers last semester that Aon was sick, frailer than usual and confined to his bed after taking a bad fall. But in Cego's mind, Aon was a constant; he'd always been frail, but he continued on like the old clock with the steady hand.

"Heh, heh," a parched laugh broke from the shadows pooling around the doorway set between two towering bookshelves. A hunched form slowly made its way into the light. "Thought I'd not make it, did you? Heh, heh."

Professor Aon leaned heavily on his cane as he moved across the room toward his chair set at the front of the students' semicircle. Cego knew better than to try to help the professor. He'd been scolded quite pointedly for attempting to do so several times last year.

The professor slowly but steadily made his way, pausing at times to take deep breaths between spasmodic fits of coughing. Finally, Aon positioned his back to the seat and fell backward, expelling a pile of dust from the old cushion.

He coughed, a bronchial hack, and spat into a cup set on the side table before gazing up with blind, marbled eyes. He cocked his head, as if hearing something. "Yes, yes, I know," he said. "But I did make it, despite your best efforts!"

Cego felt a draft in the study as he watched Aon Farstead continue his conversation.

"Oh. I see, so you say, but why should I believe you?" Aon questioned no one. "Last time I trusted you, I ended up covered in a vat of gar oil. The rash was so bad, I spent two weeks in the infirmary."

The professor again broke out into a parched laugh, which gave way to a spasm of heavy coughing. The students looked back and forth at one another. Cego could see tears welling up in Abel's eyes.

"The cause and effect of such technologies on the Grievar's natural state need not only more study but a far larger pool of subjects before any rational determinations can be made," the professor stated, out of nowhere.

Despite Aon's disjointed statements, Cego watched Abel write everything down on the pad set in front of him.

"And so we come to the fourth passage, twelfth precept of the Codes: full nutritional intake may be ingested from the bounty of nature, plants that sprout and beasts that roam, but nothing shall be eaten that has undergone unnatural formation or modification."

It was the Larkspur girl who finally spoke up, standing from her seat to her considerable full height. "Excuse me, Professor Aon?"

The professor paused abruptly and cocked his head, as if realizing there was a small class of students in the room with him. He was silent for a moment, before a curved grin creased his thin lips.

"No! It was not the Desovians who gave rise to the widespread use of Cathilis shells for improved grip strength." Aon was gazing toward the tops of the bookshelves. "It was in the slave pits of Besayd where the practice originated."

Theodora sat back in her chair as Aon continued to babble. He went from deep discussions of history to random verses of Codes to seemingly mundane facts about his everyday life.

"Bathing! A waste of time!" His voice rose at one point. "Why would I waste time with such activities when the very fabric of my existence hangs in the balance?"

Students started to filter out of the room. Cego heard a blond Level Six boy muttering as he stood up and gathered his things. "Darkin' crazy as a bat in the sun. Wait until everyone hears about this…"

Soon it was only Cego, Abel, and Theodora left in the room. The three sat patiently, waiting for the clock to tick down to its designated end-of-class time. Abel continued to diligently take notes. Cego glanced over and saw the words scrawled on his friend's pad: *Six to seven bean pods per day keeps bowel movements regular.*

Finally, the clock sang out its chime.

"Discuss it with me next time, young Marta, and I'll be sure to have the experiment complete to help you." Aon didn't stop.

Theodora took a deep breath as she stood. "I feel bad leaving him like this. Should we do something?"

Abel walked to Aon's side and laid his hand on the professor's shoulder.

"May the fighting spirit visit you tonight and wake you from this dream, Professor Farstead," Abel whispered before rushing out, his sleeve over his face. Theodora followed, taking one last glance at Aon before she ducked out of the study.

Cego stood quietly as Aon continued his disjointed verse. He approached the man, feeling his stomach start to sink as he got closer, as if somehow the distance made Aon's infirmity less real. He knelt in front of Aon's seat, trying to block out the words and just watch the man's mouth moving, his blind eyes swirling. He tried to envision Aon as he remembered him, always with a wise answer to every question.

Suddenly, Cego realized the room was silent. Aon had stopped babbling. The old man sat silently; his head perked up as if listening to someone.

All at once, Aon's blind eyes focused and dropped down to where Cego was kneeling in front of the chair. Cego froze, his heart caught in his chest.

"Get out," Aon whispered, his voice a different, sober tenor. "Escape while you still can. Now is the time you must decide whether to walk in the shadows or the light."

Cego stood slowly and stepped back from Aon, keeping his eyes on him.

"Wh-what, Professor?" he stuttered. "Are you talking to me? I should get out?"

Aon seemed to stare at Cego for several moments more before his lips curled up. "Who wouldn't know the barrister of Mescalin? Heh, heh! The man is as wide as a full-grown ox and can eat as much as one too."

And just like that, Professor Farstead was back to babbling.

Cego kept his eyes on the professor for a moment more. "I know you're in there, Professor, and I'm not going to give up on you. You never gave up on me."

Cego turned and descended the staircase, Aon's raspy voice following him down.

CHAPTER 5

Price to Pay

Thoughts constantly barraging the mind are like thieves entering a home. First, a Grievar must learn to recognize the thieves upon entry, see them for their true nature. Second, a Grievar must accept the thieves within their home, the intruders have arrived and there is nothing to do. Finally, a Grievar must show the thieves that their home is empty, there is nothing to steal within.

Passage Two, One Hundredth Precept of the Combat Codes

The liquid burned Murray's stomach. He could feel it burrowing in like some acid worm seeking to destroy his innards.

"You're darkin' saying this stuff is supposed to help me?" Murray spat into a cup set alongside his cot. "Sure you're not trying to put me out of my misery?"

"Promise you, mighty one," a gentle voice replied. "Beelbub ichor will do the trick. But certainly isn't no stroll going down."

Murray looked up into a woman's grey eyes. "Leyna, you told me nothing but the truth this far, and I trust you. But darkin' hell, this shit is rancid."

Murray downed the rest of the vial of blue liquid and broke into a spasm of chest-racking coughs.

"Don't know if the old man will be able to handle another two weeks of this, from the looks of it." A lanky bald man stared down at Murray with pity.

"Well, he'll need to, love," Leyna replied matter-of-factly as she eyed Murray. "I've seen men with worse of a habit. Even cleavers, which gives the drink a run for its money, been weaned with beel-bub ichor."

"Right." The tall man rested a hand on Murray's shoulder. "I know you got this."

"Sure, he's got this, Anderson," Leyna said as she whipped her grey braid over her shoulder. She took Murray's vial and replaced it with a steaming bowl of mush. "It was not long ago when this one crawled in our door, needing to build back up, and he got right to task."

Murray thought back to his training in the Underground nearly two years ago. He'd fought for Cego under the lights of Lampai in a grueling battle against the Dragoon. Murray absentmindedly rubbed the lid of his artificial eye as he raised a spoonful of porridge to his mouth.

"This has become a bit of a habit, huh, old-timer?" Anderson asked as he helped himself to some of the Leyna's famous mush.

"Not voluntary," Murray sighed, working hard to down the food, which was usually delightful. "Never asked for your help this time, though."

"You show up to our doorstep in piss-poor shape, babbling about seeing ghosts of the past," Anderson said. "And what, we're supposed to send you back to the streets?"

"He was there, Anderson," Murray said. "Thought he was a ghost too at first, until he had a darkin' drink with me at Tlik's. Farmer's back and down here working for some Daimyo."

"Best if you try to forget it. Just work on recovering," Anderson said, clearly holding back what he wanted to say.

Murray had tried to forget Farmer. He'd stayed on the streets, spent every spare bit-piece on the drink. He'd tried to let the darkness take him, but the old man's words kept coming back to him. *The path still lies before you. The Codes are still within you.*

"You ready to tell us why you're back Deep in the first place?" Anderson interrupted Murray's thoughts. "I thought you were Upworld, teaching at the Lyceum with some cushy professorship."

"Yeah, I was." Murray paused as some of the beelbub ichor tried to make its way back up his throat. "I came Deep to find someone. I made a promise I'd meant to keep. But I got sidetracked."

"You can say that again." Leyna flashed her sharp smile. "Well, whatever you're here for, you know Anderson and I have your back. Us old-timers need to look out for one another."

"You've got my gratitude." Murray bowed his head. "Don't know how I'll ever repay the debt."

"Well, you can start by telling Thaloo's muscle to stop coming by here looking for you," Anderson said. "Since you showed up those years ago, his thugs been coming by. Leyna put her fist through some slagger's face not long ago."

"Thaloo's men came this way?" Murray's jaw clenched. "Why?"

"All of them have the same reason," Anderson said. "They're asking about that boy you brought Surface-side."

If Thaloo was involved, Murray knew something was rotten.

The slaver's den was where Murray had first discovered Cego. A gem in a pile of broken gravel. And he'd won the boy's freedom from contract with the notorious slaver. Though Thaloo was scum, he mostly honored his contracts; it was the only way to build trust in a place like the Underground.

The only reason Thaloo would be breaching contract would be if someone was pushing on him.

"Dark that, I gotta go," Murray said abruptly. He rose from the cot, and the beelbub ichor bubbled up again. He stumbled to the nearby pot and spewed into it.

"Where in the Deep do you think you're going in this condition?" Leyna scolded.

"I've got to take care of business," Murray said. "Still answers that've yet to be found and promises to keep."

Leyna sighed, knowing Murray was as stubborn as a cave bat in heat. "At least take Anderson with you."

"You know I would, Leyna," Murray said, looking at his silent friend. "But I need to do this one alone. Two ex-champions showing up at Thaloo's doorstep would draw too much attention."

Anderson nodded, as if he'd already known this. "Well, we'll be here if you need us."

*   *   *

Murray trudged down Markspar Row as the dawnshift rose in the Underground and the Grunt sweepers took to the streets to clean up last night's refuse. He gnawed on a stale loaf of bread, but the beelbub ichor rose in his stomach and warned him against any attempt at nourishment.

He tossed the crust to one of the mangy dogs tailing him.

Murray passed open-cavern bars with SystemView boards blaring, where harvesters gathered to drink before heading to a day's planting on the steppe. He loped by the honey-perfumed entrances of pleasure shrines set along the decrepit street.

Junkies and cleaver addicts, pickpockets and toughs peered out from shadowed corners of broken-down housing complexes. Murray could feel their small eyes following him hungrily, rats that determined the big man was no easy mark and returned to gnawing at themselves.

It wasn't long before that Murray had been among such rats, sprawled out on the filthy streets, only thirsting for his next drink, only working on forgetting.

Murray kicked at the stray dog nipping at his heels as he entered the row's hawker section. As if he'd wandered into some cacophonous jungle, his senses were overwhelmed with the competing caws of merchants selling their wares and the charred scents of sizzlers scorching vat-proteins.

Murray turned off the row onto a flimsy bridge with nails jutting from its planks. The wood bent beneath his weight as he crossed over a stream of sewage.

He stepped into a spectral-lit portico and caught a guard nearly asleep in his chair. The man's stomach bulged from beneath his leathers as he quickly sat upright at Murray's approach.

"What are you, daft, old-timer?" the merc asked, pointing up at the neon sign above his head. "Hours of operation are green to blackshift. No wagers or fight right now."

"I know you're closed," Murray said. "I'm not here to see the fights. I'm here to see your boss."

"That so?" The merc stood up from his chair and sized Murray up. "Thing is, boss told me he's got no meetings this dawnshift and to have him left alone."

The Grievar was younger than him by a margin and about two hundred fifty pounds. Strong enough, despite the stomach on him. Murray could tell the man favored his left leg. He likely had a good chin but looked like he'd get winded less than a minute into a scrap.

Murray knew he'd come out on top. Put this one down, gain entry, and find what he needed. But Murray also knew that there'd likely be more muscle down there.

"How about you go ask your boss if he'll see an old friend," Murray said as he produced an onyx piece and flipped it to the merc.

The man bit the piece. "Who should I say's asking?"

"Murray Pearson."

The merc's eyes widened slightly, though he did well to quickly rein in his surprise. Even decades since he'd been at the top of his game, Murray's name still rang loud in the Deep.

"Wait here," the man said as he descended the long stair. Murray waited, shifting his weight from side to side, doing his best to keep the beelbub ichor down while smelling the raw sewage flowing several feet below.

The merc emerged, nodded to Murray, and motioned for him to follow.

The last time Murray had been down these stairs, watched the lacklights fight for their lives in these pits, heard the jeers of drunks and Taskers, Murray had walked out with Cego at his hip.

This time, the den was quiet. Murray followed the guard to one of the back rooms and entered an ornate office.

Thaloo looked much the way Murray remembered him. Bulbous and jowled, his pockmarked face etched with a superior smile.

"On this yellowshift, the last thing I expected was to see you walk through the door, Murray Pearson," Thaloo said as he motioned for Murray to sit in one of the chairs across from the desk.

Murray reluctantly sat. "I never enjoy seeing you, Thaloo. But sometimes I need to, for whatever shit path I've been sent on."

"Not a gracious way to start, Pearson, if indeed you need something from me," the man said. "Wouldn't it pay to be more pleasant?"

After having dealt with the Citadel administration Upworld, with people like Callen Albright, Murray knew enough to forget his ego.

His fight was not the one in front of him.

"Sorry," Murray said. "It's been a tough couple months."

"So I've heard," Thaloo said, eyeing Murray up and down. "My eyes in the Deep told me you'd returned. I'd actually expected a visit much sooner, due to our shared history."

Murray held back a growl. Thaloo had forced him out of retirement to fight for Cego, made the kid's freedom from the slave Circles contingent on Murray beating the Dragoon at Lampai. He absentmindedly rubbed his bad eye.

Thaloo laughed, his cheeks undulating like gelatin. "Always stuck in the past, aren't you, Murray? Yes, the Dragoon took your eye in that fight, but you won, didn't you? The Mighty Murray Pearson, out of retirement after two decades, fighting in front of the entirety of Lampai. It was magnificent. Though the Dragoon was my fighter, I did have a pile of onyx running on you. Did you know that? Did you know I had faith in you, Pearson?"

Murray did not respond, and as usual, Thaloo paid homage to the sound of his own voice.

"And you got your boy, no?" Thaloo asked. "The golden-eyed one, I heard you took him Upworld, to the Lyceum. I heard that he passed the Trials, flawlessly, made it to the top of his class. You got everything you wanted, so why sour still; why not let yourself be happy for once?"

"I'm not here to reminisce, Thaloo," Murray said. "And I know you sent your thugs to Farmoss to bother my friends. So, let's cut the shit."

"If you say so, Pearson," Thaloo said as he stuffed a gummy wad of chew into his mouth. "And I've kept watch on your boy's progress because that information is valuable to some interested parties. Knowing such things is my path to survival down here. But why did you come Deep again, Murray Pearson? I certainly hope it wasn't to spend your time drunk and sleeping in your piss, as you've done for the past months."

"I made Cego a promise," Murray said. "Told him I'd find his younger brother, Sam. The kid grew up with Cego...in a darkin' bad place. He's been lost since, and I mean to find him."

"There are many bad places in this world," Thaloo said. "Care to be more specific?"

Murray watched the slaver's dull eyes flick back and forth. The man was probing him for information, though Murray had been the one seeking answers.

"I already know of the Cradle, if you're still worried about betraying your superiors Upworld." Thaloo smiled.

Murray shook his head. He should have suspected Thaloo

would somehow be embroiled in this darkness, in these Daimyo machinations.

"And what is it that you know of the Cradle?" Murray asked.

"A world as real as our own, created by the Bit-Minders to serve as a training environment for young Grievar from birth. To give the children weeks of practice in the span of minutes, decades of valuable training time before they even hit adolescence."

"You make it sound to be a good thing," Murray spat. "The Cradle is a darkin' abomination. Growing kids in vats, having them live their entire lives in a fake world created by the Bit-Minders."

"Fake?" Thaloo raised an eyebrow. "From what my sources have told me, the reality the Cradle creates is as real as anything here. Look at the junkies on the streets, their minds clouded by cleavers. Look at the patrons of the Courtesan Houses, the perfumes addling their senses. Look at the drunks stumbling from the bars, numbing their minds and trying to forget their pasts."

Thaloo's eyes bored into Murray, judging him.

"Are their worlds fake, Pearson?" Thaloo asked. "Is the Cradle not as real as these clouded perceptions of reality?"

"I'm not here to talk philosophy with you, Thaloo." Murray could feel the vile beelbub ichor bubbling in his stomach. "I want information on where I might find Sam."

Thaloo chewed voraciously. "You know that even someone like me, with my vast network of connections, has limitations. There are powers out there that would put my business interests at risk if I spoke the wrong words. All I've worked to build around me, gone. To anger them would be suicide."

"You must know something," Murray said. He didn't care about shame or what this man thought of him. "Anything...please. Tell me where I can find him."

Thaloo was silent, eyeing Murray carefully. "I don't dislike you, Pearson. In fact, as I've told you before, I see you as a kindred spirit."

Murray took a deep breath, readying himself for more of this man's blabber.

"And I know how you see me as weak," Thaloo said. "I did not grow up like other Grievar. I did not possess the physical skills that would enable me to fight, the preordained path for our kind. And I faced the world's wrath because of that. My parents, my siblings, other children, they all tormented me, made my life a living hell. They told me I was not made for this world. That I should end myself so that another mouth would not need feeding."

The spectral light flickered in the alcoves of Thaloo's office.

"But I found my place in this world, Pearson. Not easily like you, who found the path at your fingertips. I had to claw my way through the dirt, destroy those who would get in my way."

Thaloo stood, admiring one of his porcelain statues on the wall, wiping at it with a small cloth he'd produced from the folds of his robe.

"I see you in the dirt now, Pearson," Thaloo said. "I see you trying to claw your way back, and so I'll help you. But of course, a price must be paid."

Murray knew there was always a price with Thaloo. He produced his full purse and dropped it onto Thaloo's desk.

Thaloo eyed the open purse and began to laugh. "Pearson...this sum would pay upkeep of my den for less than a day. You think this worth it to risk my business, my life, my reputation?"

Murray shook his head. "We've been here before, Thaloo, and if you think I'll fight for you again, put on some show—"

"No, no," Thaloo said. "You returning to Lampai would be of no use to me. Much has changed since you fought your comeback there. The absolute best, men who would be otherwise at the top of their national forces, are coming Deep to fight. They're finding fighting for their nations might not be as stable, or honorable, as they thought. So, no, even the Mighty Murray Pearson coming back to Lampai would make no more than a whisper in these caverns now."

"What, then? Murray said. "All I can give you is my money or my fists; I've nothing else."

"You're right," Thaloo said. "That is all you have. And I do have use of your fists, as you say. Though not in the arena. Elsewhere."

"You'd have me become one of your mercs?" Murray raised his voice. "You're darkin' gone, trying to get me to stoop to that level."

"Need I remind you where you were not long ago?" Thaloo wiped the saliva from his mouth as he continued to chew. "Call it what you will, merc, Grievar for hire, fist-for-bit."

"No," Murray said flatly. "I'm not darkin' becoming some back-alley brawler for you, beating on folk that haven't paid their dues like the rest of your thugs down here."

"What I had in mind was something more specific, Pearson. Something more suited to someone of your skill set. And most of all, completely aligned with your own goals. Seems the spirits have some plan after all, matching both our needs in such a way."

"What are you talking about?" Murray said.

"Well," Thaloo drawled. "My ears have told me that the first group of Cradle kids that the Citadel ordered were said to have been a bad batch. They were to be wiped out because the Bit-Minder source code was corrupt."

"I know," Murray said.

"So, you have your sources too," Thaloo said. "But do you know what became of those children, those experiments like Cego's little brother?"

"Tell me." Murray slammed his hands on the desk.

"They aren't dead," Thaloo said. "Though the Citadel would have gladly terminated them, there are more opportunistic forces here in the Deep. The failed Cradle kids were still seen by some as an asset."

Murray sighed in relief. "Someone…bought them? From the Citadel?"

"Yes," Thaloo said. "Everything down here has a price."

"Who?"

"Well, now," Thaloo said. "If I were to tell you that, you wouldn't need me anymore, would you?"

"What do you ask of me? Spit it out," Murray snapped, barely able to contain himself.

"As I said, our goals are aligned. It so happens that the person who bought the Cradle brood has been problematic for me in the past. A thorn in my side, one could say."

Murray could read Thaloo; he knew what the slave Circle master wanted of him. "You need me to take care of your enemy."

"Yes," Thaloo said. "I'd have done it myself years ago, but this Daimyo has proven to be particularly hearty, defensible. And, while you raid his stash of tube brood, I figure it would make sense to kill two bats with one stone."

It was unthinkable for a Grievar Knight, even a retired one, to become an assassin. Fighting someone with honor, challenging them in the Circle under the eyes of the Codes, was the opposite of slinking into someone's home and killing them in the dark of night.

But that fog had lifted for Murray. He'd seen the Codes for what they were: a way to control his people, keep them in their place while the Daimyo profited and ruled. To Murray, the Codes were dead and so he'd do what he needed.

"Tell me who this Daimyo is," Murray whispered. "Tell me his name so that I might find him, free Sam, and free this man of his life."

Thaloo smiled. "It's good to be working with you again, Murray Pearson."

CHAPTER 6

Mothers and Fathers

There is the account of the famous Yagestari wrestler Lhadir, who was known to have the grappling prowess to put an adult gar bear on its back. When he fought against men, though, Lhadir never utilized his famed skills. His adversaries were so weary of his wrestling that they kept an awkward stance, making it easy for Lhadir to strike them down with punches.

Passage Four, Twenty-Fifth Precept of the Combat Codes

N'auri led Sol back up the ascent from Lake Kava. The two girls trekked through the Emerald's markets and found a dusty path that ran alongside the crowded harbor. The hawkers yelling on the docks were soon replaced with seabirds squawking from their perches atop the remains of sunken galleons.

"These shores are beautiful." Sol broke the silence as she gazed out at the crystalline waters.

N'auri nodded, looking out past the shore at some fishermen sitting on rocks. The Besaydian girl had gone silent.

Sol continued. "You've lived here on the Emerald your entire life?"

N'auri nodded again as the two broke from the shoreline onto a smaller path toward the isle's interior. The trail was barely decipherable from the tropical undergrowth that sprouted around them.

"I have, but not out here by the coast," N'auri finally replied. "Really, only fishers live out by the water. Though it's beautiful to look at, living on the water is a tough life. Storms come in often and destroy homes near shore. Beautiful seas, but deadly. Deceiving, like many things."

"I always dreamed of traveling here, as a child," Sol said.

"Why?" N'auri turned to her. "You from Ezo, no?"

Sol nodded.

"Then you lived in a stone-walled mansion, just like I heard stories of? Never having to spend a night hungry or hunt for food?"

Sol wanted to tell N'auri that not all Ezonians lived in mansions, that some were bit-poor and lived and starved in the streets, but she held her tongue. After all, Sol did grow up in a stone-walled mansion.

"Yes, I did live in a house before I was admitted to the Lyceum," Sol said. "My father used to tell me stories of the Isles. He told me of adventures in the wilds, exotic beasts, and unique people."

"Yes," N'auri said. "I love my home. But things here are not all so good like your dafé says. There are dangers in the wilds, storms that wreck lives. And many bad people, as you already seen."

The two continued in silence as the sun began to set behind them, casting long palm shadows across their path. Every hundred or so paces, Sol could see ramshackle homes through the thicket. She watched families settle in for the evening. Mothers hung fish out to dry on long lines strung between trees as packs of children peered out from the brush with curious eyes.

Just as dusk gave way to night, N'auri stopped abruptly, holding a hand up to her ear. Sol could only hear the pulsing drone of the insects surrounding them.

Two white eyes pierced the dark, along with a feral yell. Something pounced at them from the trunk of a nearby palm. In a blur of motion, N'auri grasped the figure as it leapt toward her, and rolled backward. Sol immediately recognized tomoe nage, the throw perfectly executed by her new Besaydian friend.

The figure flew into the nearby thicket. *"Owasaa!"*

A small boy sprang back out from the bush to stand in front of N'auri, hands on his hips, looking up at her with an expectant smile.

"Kinva tuvassa, Meao!" N'auri laughed as the boy moved in to embrace her.

The boy responded playfully, *"Matti Meao cerca naya, N'auri!"*

N'auri looked up at Sol. "This my youngest brother, Meao. Quite the trickster. Though he's still not fast enough to catch his elder sister off guard."

Sol smiled and reached out to grasp the little boy's hand. "Nice to meet you; my name is Sayana."

The boy, as if for the first time realizing Sol was there, stepped back a few paces while staring at her skeptically.

N'auri glared at the boy. *"Dinta shoon, Meao! Esha Ezo, shoon e yinvasa Meao enta see."*

The boy looked down at the ground, clearly reprimanded by his elder sister. He offered his hand out to Sol.

"I told him not to be rude to my new friend," N'auri explained. "And he could practice his Ezo-tongues."

Sol shook Meao's hand and smiled again.

"My name, Meao," the boy said sheepishly, putting his hand to his chest.

"Come on, now," N'auri shooed her brother. "Get in before Kinta eats your dinner."

The three turned from the path right into the thicket until they came to a clearing. A bright fire illuminated the palms and a few small shacks. Two boys, both bigger than Meao, were wrestling on the grass by the fire.

"*'Lo Yova, Kinta. Tuvaa mista yumafasi!*" N'auri yelled.

The two leapt to their feet and ran to hug N'auri before bolting toward the biggest of the shacks, with Meao sprinting after them. Sol and N'auri followed.

N'auri stopped at the entryway to the home and touched her finger to a small gemstone embedded in the doorframe. She kissed her hand and whispered several indecipherable words.

"This is a Kova stone." She turned back toward Sol. "Wherever family goes, they bring the Kova with them and set it in the entry to their home. Nothing else is needed to move homes, just this stone."

Sol didn't want to disrespect her new friend, so she moved to perform the same ritual. N'auri sensed the hesitation and chuckled. "No need for outsiders to do so, especially those who come from stone-walled mansions in Ezo."

They entered the home to a chaotic scene.

All three children seemed to be a blur of motion, frantically circling a large metal pot set at the center of the circular room. Three Emeraldi women worked on the outskirts, their long traditional garb fluttering as they moved frenetically. They pulled down vegetables from hanging baskets, set them on the cutting table, and chopped the roots with amazing speed before tossing them into the stewpot.

One man lounged off in a corner on a rope hammock, working at a bottle of swig. The man, his potbelly hanging from his garb, seemed oblivious to the chaos. His eyes were glued to an old SystemView box set in front of him. Exposed wires writhed from the rig, and the feed barely came in, but Sol could make out two Grievar exchanging blows in a Circle.

"*Kathedah! Maruu e etmemi, o Kathedah!*" the man bellowed at the feed. His eyes briefly left the box and landed directly on Sol, before floating to N'auri.

"*'Lo, Dafé, this is my new friend Sayana. She is from Ezo," N'auri said with precision, as if she'd rehearsed the line. "She is also trying out next week and will be my training partner leading up to the event."

"Oh, is she?" The man reverted to Ezonian, the words biting with sarcasm. "And I suppose that she also will win her way to a top lord's team? Against Grievar far better, from all over the world, and not to mention, but most importantly—men?"

Sol's cheeks reddened, but she saw N'auri barely flinched at the man's insult. "Dafé, I rather try and be a fighting Grievar than one sitting and watching others fight all day long."

The man's eyes narrowed. "I got me three growing boys to take that mantle, girl. All I ever wished for you was take your proper spot next to aunties, instead of chasing stupid fighting dreams."

He turned toward Sol. "Ezo girl, you see how she treats her dafé with such disrespect? Treat your parents like that, do you?"

"My parents are dead," Sol said. Immediately after the words left her mouth, she regretted it. She'd risk blowing her cover saying things like that.

"Ah, so," the big man said, bringing his fist up to his chest and bowing his head. "If they alive, though, you think they want you to chase shadows? Try to get what you never have?"

Sol started to respond, but N'auri cut her off. "Where she's from, in Ezo, they take pride in fighting daughters. They cheer them, throw flowers from the stands! They bury them a proper Grievar burial."

The man got up from his seat and looked fiercely at N'auri. "You know, girl. There was nothing I could do for her. She lies where she be. And you be there too if you keep this path."

Sol saw a wetness in N'auri's eyes as the girl turned away from her father.

"Eh, Ikareh!"

One of the Emeraldi ladies who'd been cooking stood in front of them with her arms crossed. She looked at Sol and smiled warmly.

"You a visitor in this home and we not treating you right. Instead of filling your head with our problems, we should be filling your belly."

The lady motioned them to the stewpot.

"*Karthoo*, Auntie Kess." N'auri took a deep breath and grinned. She took hold of Sol's hand and brought her to gather a bowl of the delicious-smelling broth.

Another of the ladies squeezed Sol's shoulder warmly. "Ever taste Emeraldi stew?"

Sol shook her head.

"Then you in for a treat. Fresh pincer crab caught just off the rocks, carmini clams, roasted besay root, and just a bit of taru spice for the heat!" The lady laughed from deep in her belly. "We Emeraldi women might not be fighting like you girls, but we bring the fight in other ways here."

The broth drew Sol. She hadn't eaten all day, and her stomach expressed the sentiment with a loud groan.

They brought their food outside, sitting on the large stones that surrounded the firepit, N'auri beside Sol and her two aunties chatting rapidly beside them. N'auri's father had decided to take his meal in front of the SystemView.

Big embers popped and crackled at their feet. Sol could smell the sea on the warm wind as she slurped her stew.

N'auri was quiet again, staring out into the darkness.

"You've lost someone too?" Sol asked.

"Yes," N'auri replied quietly. "My mafé. She was one of a few fighting Grievar women. Taught me everything I know."

Sol nodded.

"For years, she disguised herself like a man," N'auri continued. "Won her way onto Lord Cantino's team. Thousands of Grievar trying to make the spot. No help from anyone; her own parents even kicked her out."

Sol thought of her time at the Lyceum. She'd had to work hard to prove herself, especially because of her famous last name. But at least there, most of the teachers judged on merit and skill. She'd never had to hide who she was.

"She won hundreds of fights for Cantino, helped make him rich," N'auri said. "Even after they found out she was a woman, he kept her in the stable because they couldn't find a man to fight like she could."

Sol softly put her hand on N'auri's shoulder as the girl wiped tears from her face unapologetically.

"My mafé fell in the Circle. An honorable death," N'auri whispered. "I plan to do the same."

Sol desperately wanted to tell N'auri that her father, Artemis Halberd, one of the greatest Grievar to ever step in a Circle, was a lifeless corpse in Cantino's museum right now. Sol wanted to tell the girl this was why she was here too, that she would fight for her father.

But Sol said nothing. She couldn't risk her cover, despite the kinship she felt with her new friend. The two girls finished their stew as they stared out into the darkness.

"Enough for the sad stories of the past," N'auri said stoically. "Tomorrow, we look forward. Tomorrow, we train."

*　　*　　*

N'auri and Sol woke early. The two girls downed some of the leftover stew before stepping out into the dawn's rising light. N'auri's training Circle was out behind the house, set in the shade of several tall palms.

The Besaydian Circle was made of stone, not the spectral steel Sol was accustomed to. Just a formation of smooth grey and black rocks, with a pit of freshly raked sand at the center.

Even so, the second she stepped into the soft sand, a smile spread across her face. Sol couldn't help it. N'auri caught her smile and flashed her own sharp teeth. "Don't think I ever seen a girl so happy before."

"I didn't realize I missed it so much," Sol replied. "It's been too long."

Right about now, Sol's team would be stepping into their own Circles at the Lyceum. Gleaming Circles of auralite and rubellium steel, learning new techniques and strategies from the greatest fighting minds in the world. And Sol would miss it all.

But this was where she was meant to be.

N'auri squatted down and dug her hands into the sand before bringing her palms to her face, letting the granules fall through her fingers. A sign of respect.

"You done pit fighting before?" N'auri asked as she stood up.

"On the Isles, we fight on many different grounds."

"Pit fighting?" Sol asked. "You mean in the sand? I don't think I should have any problem."

"Why don't we see?" N'auri flashed her teeth as she raised her fists.

Sol met the girl's silver eyes, like those of a wolf. Noble and cunning at the same time. She took her own defensive stance. She'd see what the Besaydian girl had to offer, defend and probe until a proper counter opened up.

N'auri moved forward with a sudden ferocity, all her limbs in motion at once, looping punches coming from wide angles that drove Sol back onto her heels.

Create distance, circle, dodge, counter. Sol attempted to keep to her methodical fighting style. But N'auri stuck to her as she retreated, unrelenting in her offensive onslaught. The soft sand felt foreign beneath Sol's feet, slow, not like the canvas she was used to.

A fist grazed the side of Sol's head as she attempted to weave. An open palm strike caught the side of her ear. A knee burst through the center, which Sol barely got an elbow in front of.

Sol responded with a quick three-punch combination that N'auri jumped back from.

"Ah!" N'auri yelled, squatting in the sand, grinning. "You fast. I knew you be fast."

Sol knew the girl was faster than her, though, despite her technique appearing sloppy. N'auri moved like an animal, in frenetic bursts. Sol needed to bring the fight to the ground, where she could control the action without sustaining damage.

She waited for N'auri's next onslaught, the girl coming in even faster this time, with punches from all angles. Sol moved into one of the looping blows, taking the impact as it slung around the side of her head. But she'd closed the distance. Sol wrapped her arms around the girl's waist for a double-under clinch and drove in. She threw her leg behind N'auri's for the okuraishi harai trip.

To her surprise, N'auri unhooked her leg and threw herself backward. The Besaydian twisted her body as they moved through the air, landing on top of Sol and slamming her into the sand with an impact that took the breath from her lungs.

Sol had meant to take the fight to the ground but not like this. She quickly hip-escaped and wrapped her legs around N'auri's waist, grabbing ahold of the girl's head to prevent her from posturing to deliver strikes.

"Never seen kamata throw before?" N'auri asked between pants. She broke Sol's clinch and dropped a lightning-fast elbow.

Barely getting her hands up to deflect, Sol reached up to pull the girl down again. N'auri broke free, postured, and threw several quick punches, one rattling Sol's head against the ground. For her size, N'auri had surprising strength. Sol needed to act or she'd be overwhelmed.

Sol threw her hips into the girl's midsection, attempting to bump her over. N'auri planted a hand in the sand to balance herself and thwarted the sweep. Just as Sol expected. She grabbed the girl's posted hand and snaked her other arm over the top to latch on a shoulder lock—kimura.

N'auri immediately saw her mistake as Sol dropped to her back and started to wrench at the arm. "A trap! Ezonians have much trickery, as they told us." She laughed.

Again, Sol felt the girl's strength as she attempted to wrench her arm unsuccessfully. "You call it trickery. I call it technique," she replied.

Sol released the kimura and quickly switched her hips to throw her leg over N'auri's shoulder. Omoplata. She usually reserved the shoulder lock for larger opponents, but this girl had an unearthly strength to her.

N'auri squirmed frantically, like a snared animal, as she felt the pressure build on her shoulder. Sol had been there before. She'd spent countless hours attacking omoplata, setting her legs at just the right angle with one arm hanging over her opponent's back.

She started to flatten N'auri out by straightening her legs and inching her hips away. If she could push the girl's belly to the floor, it would be over.

Legs tight, pinch, push, inch the hips away. Over and over. Methodical, proper technique. This was Sol's game. She wouldn't fight like an animal.

N'auri seemed on the verge of giving up. Sol had felt it before. The last second before an opponent gave in to the threat of a broken shoulder, shattered kneecap, or constricted artery.

Training partners would sometimes fight through a submission and let the break happen out of stubborn pride. Then they'd work with a lost limb and most likely lose the match, wherever it went, not to mention spending a few days in the medward to heal.

Sol hoped N'auri wasn't that stubborn type. She didn't want to injure her new friend, especially as she doubted there was a medward anywhere in manageable distance. N'auri wouldn't be able to properly enter the Circles in one week's time if she was injured.

Sol hesitated, just briefly, but that was all N'auri needed. Feeling the pressure release on her shoulder, the Emeraldi girl rose to a knee and then to two feet. N'auri stood fully upright and hefted Sol's entire body off the ground.

Sol released the shoulder lock and dropped to the sand. She popped back to her feet, hands up.

"I felt you hesitate," N'auri said, her eyes flashing. The girl wasn't smiling anymore.

"I didn't want to injure you before next week," Sol replied.

"You injure me more by holding back, Ezonian," N'auri raised her voice. "You think Grievar in the pits will hold back when all is on the line?"

"No, of course not." Sol looked to the ground before meeting the girl's silvery eyes again. "But I am not them. And we are not in a contest. This is training. We need to help each other stay healthy, so when the time comes, we can commit our full energy to a bout."

"This is how they train where you from? Giving mercy? Giving away opportunity? How do they find the blood, go for the kill when the time comes, if they train this way? A wolf that doesn't bite the neck won't eat, is what my people say."

Sol shook her head. "I understand. It's something I've had trouble with, and I'm not sure. When the time comes, I hope my training will be enough to prepare me."

N'auri's gaze softened. She squatted on all fours again. "You speak truth, Ezonian. Perhaps we both have something to learn from each other. If you crack my shoulder, the fires of my dreams would be only ashes."

Sol watched as N'auri wiped sweat off her shaved head and touched a wet hand to the sand. Perhaps another ritual.

Suddenly, the girl leapt at her, flinging her hand out and spraying an arc of sand across Sol's face. N'auri hit Sol with a shoulder in the midsection and tossed her to the ground, landing on top.

Sol wiped the sand from her eyes to see that feral smile again, sharp teeth glinting down at her.

"And you must learn from me, Ezonian. From my people. Learn you must find the blood deep in your veins. The blood won't let you lower your guard. The blood won't let you ever give up."

N'auri stood and offered Sol a hand.

"Don't give up in those pits seven days from now," N'auri said solemnly. "If you do, you find yourself not just broken but buried."

CHAPTER 7

The Gift

A Grievar should spend some time every day feeling their own weight. Walking, sitting, or lying down, it is all too easy to forget the constant gravity that pulls a body to the earth. Becoming fully aware of the earthbound nature will let a Grievar realize their fullest capabilities.

Passage Five, Second Precept of the Combat Codes

Now, that's what I'm talking about!" Dozer yelled as he flexed his shoulders and turned to admire his exposed back in the long mirror. A freshly burned flux draped its tentacles down the length of Dozer's back, a sleek octopus inked in oily blacks and midnight blues.

Cego looked down at his right calf. He'd opted to have the Level Two flux burned onto his leg; though it was still dormant, he had a feeling the Doragūn pattern already possessing his arm wouldn't take kindly to having neighbors. He watched the octopus wrap its tentacles around his leg possessively.

"I mean, I wish it was a bit meaner looking," Dozer speculated. "But still, pretty darkin' nice. Sol doesn't know what she's missing."

He looked to his friend Knees, who'd gotten his shoulder fluxed with the same serrated cephalopod. The Venturian flashed him a quick smile before turning to Dozer.

"I'm just glad you didn't go ahead with the idea of getting it fluxed to your ass," Knees said, just loud enough so that surrounding students could hear. "Couldn't stand another reason for you to walk around the dorm, flexing."

"What?" Dozer yelled. "I never said—"

"I got mine arse fluxed when I was eight." Rhodan Bertoth stepped beside Dozer. "Ye must've not had the stones to do it!"

As they'd been doing all semester, Dozer and Rhodan squared off, sizing one another up.

"I hear where you're from, you bed with your sisters; that's why you all come out so ugly," Dozer retorted. Cego had heard his big friend practicing that line in the dorm for the past few days.

Rhodan let out a deep laugh, slapping Dozer on the shoulder. "Good on ye!" the boy spoke Ezonian with a thick accent. "In fact, it's our cousins we wed; my own pretty Lileth is waitin' fer me back north."

Dozer laughed but trailed off, suddenly unsure whether to believe Rhodan or not.

"Why did you not get a flux, Rhodan?" Abel piped up from beside the two boys, the little Desovian dwarfed by their collective mass.

"As ye can see, little brown one, I barely have the space." Rhodan happily ripped the second skin from his back, calling attention to the various designs floating across his body. Two great bears rearing up on his arms, a pair of mountain rams climbing his legs, a great toothed whale leaping through the ice across his back and splashing frosty water onto his neck and shoulders.

"And the way ye do it here, it's not what the Frost Mother allows us," Rhodan said with a furrowed brow. "Only an Ice Weaver can do such an honor to a Northman's body."

"Ice Weaver?" Cego asked.

"A shaman who can summon the blue spirits," Rhodan said reverently, holding his fist to his chest.

"You mean spectrals?" Knees said.

"Ye call 'em spectrals," Rhodan said. "But what ye do here isn't right. Summoning the spirits everywhere, all the time."

Rhodan pointed up at a cluster of yellowlight wisps floating past. The spectrals seemed ever-present in the Lyceum.

"This angers the gods," Rhodan whispered. "We only summon spirits for fighting or fluxing."

"That's why these southmen feel weak," proclaimed another Myrkonian boy named Zot. He grabbed Cego's arm and shook it, as if to illustrate how easily Cego's body flailed around.

"Let him go." Rhodan nodded to his fellow. "That one is not as weak as he looks."

Rhodan looked Cego in the eyes. "Before I got him with the skull bash, he nearly had me figured."

Cego shook his head. "That's not how it seemed at the time."

"How's the face?" Rhodan asked with a grin.

"I'll be fine," Cego replied. He didn't hold bad blood with the Myrkonian boy, who seemed honest enough. Rhodan was a different breed from the Bayhounds who roamed these halls. Cego glanced to Shiar, whose posse circled around him as usual.

"That's the stuff," one of them yelled as he admired the new wolf brand on his chest.

"Darkin' nasty!" another replied.

Shiar caught Cego looking his way and strode toward the Whelps.

"Admiring our work?" Shiar asked as his team of Bayhounds stalked behind him. "Lacklights from the Deep, imagining they could be a part of this. How sad."

"You be from the Deep too, same slave Circles we fought in," Knees responded.

Shiar cackled. "You remember that still, I suppose. Glad I was there too, so I could realize how helpless you really are."

"Helpless like when you were panting and retching up your greens all over the dirt?" Dozer interjected, stepping toward Shiar.

Shiar laughed again. "You're dumber than I remember, Dozer. You must be remembering your late friend, the one who was panting like a bitch before I put a heel to his head. What was the little shit's name, anyways? Weep?"

And just like that, Cego was inches from Shiar, as if he'd teleported. He didn't raise his hands, but he met the boy's eyes and did not waver. Cego saw something in those eyes, something he'd not seen before. Fear.

Cego remembered their last fight as if it were a vivid dream. He remembered rending Shiar's limbs, tearing his tendons apart, hammering his body with sharp blows and delighting when the boy's bones shattered.

Shiar remembered too. Cego could smell his fear now. He felt Shiar's heart beat a step faster, his breath catch in his chest.

Cego clenched his fists. He felt the energy welling up within, a vengeful force that wanted to break the boy again. His body coiled for action: feint high with a jab and blast through the middle with a cross to Shiar's throat. Shatter the windpipe, make it so the boy's taunting days were over.

"Oh, I see," Shiar said, practiced at masking fear. "This lacklight suddenly finds his balls and decides to show off for his team. Or maybe it's all show for these inbred northern fools?"

Rhodan took a step toward Shiar this time. "In the North, we have a type of shrew. Little mouse, very weak. But it screams, very loudly. It pretends it's a gar bear because it's scared of getting eaten up. Sometimes it gets away, fools the other creatures. But sometimes, the real bear finds it and stomps it into the ice."

Shiar yawned. "As much as I'd like to dance with all three of you, I plan on winning the first group challenge this semester. And that means I need to play nice out here. But in there, in the Circle, I plan on not playing nice. So, let's just say I'll see you soon."

Shiar strutted off, his crew of Bayhounds trailing behind.

"Spirits be said, is he always like that?" Brynn Mykili asked from beside them.

"Unfortunately, yes, he be like that since birth," Knees responded.

Cego looked down to see his strange flux suddenly alive again, slithering down his arm and starting to pulse with light. He quickly pulled his cloak across his body.

"Ye southmen, cold all the time." Rhodan laughed, slapping Cego on the shoulder. "See you in the Circle soon. Next time as a friend. Which means I'll fight harder than if you were my enemy, and ye better do the same."

Cego nodded as Rhodan and his brethren made their exit.

"We better get to work," said Knees. "Usually, Sol would be getting us prepped for the challenges."

"We don't need any of Sol's brainy strategy," Dozer huffed. "Let's just get in the Circle and fight."

"As much as I'd like to do that," Cego said, "Knees is right. We need to prepare. This year's challenges have more at stake than last. We need to maintain our cumulative score; otherwise, we're cut, no matter when during the semester. Professor Drakken said last year, half the Level Two teams were out before finals."

"Always so complicated," Dozer complained.

"For you, shitting on the pot is complicated." Knees punched Dozer in the shoulder.

"Well, there was that time after they served bean dip in the dining hall…" Dozer started.

"Please forget I mentioned that," Knees said as he walked from the room. "Let's get started with practice."

*   *   *

It seemed like Cego was always hurrying somewhere since the start of this semester. Professor Drakken, his instructor for

Fighting Styles Around the World, had scheduled Cego for a private meeting prior to class, and he was late again.

He arrived at Drakken's door and scanned the lightpad in front. The portal swished open and Cego was suddenly face-to-face with Shiar, again.

"What are you doing here?" Shiar scowled. He looked a little bit flustered, out of character for the boy.

"I've got a meeting with Professor Drakken; I'm in his class," Cego replied. "What are you doing here early?"

"I...had the same, just a meeting," Shiar muttered.

"What about?"

"None of your business," Shiar said, shoving past Cego.

Cego shook his head as he stepped into Drakken's classroom and Shiar hurried down the hall.

"Hey there, Cego," Drakken greeted him cheerfully. Cego looked around for the source of the voice but didn't see the professor.

"Up here!"

Cego looked above, toward the domed ceiling at the center of the lecture hall. There he saw Drakken hanging upside down, suspended by a series of ropes dangling from the ceiling beams.

"Professor?" Cego asked. "Do you need help?"

"No, no," Drakken said as he crunched his body upward, untied his feet, and deftly somersaulted to the ground.

"Timauldian ritual," Drakken explained as he brushed the matted hair from his eyes. "For a thousand years, their kin have suspended themselves upside down prior to fights, for an hour at least. They say it promotes circulation, blood flow, makes one quicker."

"I see..." said Cego. He'd certainly seen some strange training rituals, but this one might take the top spot.

Drakken sat cross-legged on the floor and motioned for Cego to do the same.

As Cego lowered himself to the ground, a memory flashed

across his mind: sitting across from the old master in the iron-wood Circle, the wise man reciting combat wisdom to the three brothers.

"Are you okay, Cego?" Drakken asked.

"Yes," Cego responded. "Just been in a bit of a rush lately."

"Are you sure?" Drakken pried. "Often, I watch you during class and you seem far off. Like you're preoccupied with something. Don't get me wrong—you're doing great so far—but I just want to make sure I can help you any way I can. That's why I asked you to come before class today."

Cego felt his stomach sink. Professor Drakken seemed nice enough. But he couldn't let go of his secrets. Could he?

"It's okay," Drakken continued. "I understand fully. I remember my schooling in Kiroth; I was coming in as a foreigner. A naïve, smiling Ezonian brood. It was tough coming from someplace different. Trying to fit in with the other students, observing their customs and rituals."

"Right," Cego responded. "It has been tough. Fitting in, that is."

"I would imagine so," said Drakken. "Even though it's technically an Ezonian province, the Underground is a fully different world. Completely different languages and customs, the slave Circles, not to mention the lack of a sun or sky. I can't even imagine your shock coming Upworld."

Cego thought back to first coming to the Surface with Murray-Ku. Riding the Lift from the darkness of the Deep and discovering that the sky wasn't always an unwavering blue like it had been on the island.

"Yes." Cego went along with it. "It was quite a bit. But it was all right."

"And then, after such a change, and finally after a year of starting to fit in..." Drakken trailed off. "Then the incident at the challenge matches last year."

Cego looked down at the floor.

Drakken put his hand on Cego's shoulder reassuringly. "From what I've heard, it was pretty intense."

Cego didn't respond.

"Sometimes, when something like that happens to us, our urge is to push it down. Forget about it. But that's not the right path," Drakken said. "The things we push down will fester. Eat away at our minds and bodies. Make us lesser Grievar."

"I'm not pushing it down," Cego said defensively. "It's just that I don't remember much from that day."

An excuse he'd used conveniently since then.

"I understand," Drakken said. "The mind does things under stress. It seeks to forget."

The professor stood and strode to the far wall of the classroom, beckoning Cego to follow. They stood in front of a shelf with a glass case on top of it. Cego peered within the case to see a crimson coin on a small pedestal, ruins engraved on its surface.

"Do you know what that is, Cego?" Drakken asked.

Cego waited for the answer.

"This is a reminder to me," the professor said. "Of a time when I was also under stress. In fact, a reminder of the most difficult time in my life. Right after I graduated combat school in Kiroth, at the empire's premiere academy. I'd been meaning to come back to Ezo and join the Knights, fight for my home nation. But I took a small detour first. I visited the Desovian highlands. Somewhere I'd always wanted to travel, since I was a little kid flipping through lightdecks of far-off places."

Drakken opened the display case and lifted the coin between two fingers, holding the glimmering treasure up to his face.

"I rode a roc across the Kirothian border. Followed the Beredeth River all the way to the Desovian highlands. It was beautiful, just like I'd remembered from the decks: waving high grass at the foot of the wise grey mountains, parting to give view of the vast Uropan Sea."

Cego found himself lulled by Drakken's words, as if he could see the man's memories.

"The small village I sought was set beneath the shadows of two large rubellium monoliths, jagged stones spiking from the earth to the sky. The Grievar who roamed the highlands were nomadic; they followed the herds of gentry goats feeding on the grasses. But one tribe had stayed put in that spot, between the giant elemental stones. They said the stones were the hands of the Earth Goddess reaching up to meet her sister, the sky.

"I stayed with the highlanders there for almost a year," he said. "One of the best years of my life. I learned their ways: how to milk and trim a goat in less than a minute, the warmth and danger of Desovian mead in front of a campfire, and even the embrace of a good woman on the coldest highland night."

Cego swallowed.

"I taught them what little I'd learned so far in the ways of combat," the professor said. "Of course, they had their own native styles, quite interesting, in fact. Entirely focused on clubbing at an opponent's ears, with round, looping blows. We'll cover it later this semester. But I was able to teach them some proper striking and grappling. Some of my favorite takedowns. They were fast learners, especially the children, like sponges. Before I knew it, I was known as *Kathardou Drakken* in the little village. Uncle Drakken."

Drakken turned away from Cego, still clutching the red coin in his hand.

"And then everything went bad," the professor whispered. "They came from the eastern passage. A rival Grievar tribe. Speaking another language, worshipping other gods. They might as well have been from a completely different world. They'd been told by the local Governance that they'd receive ample compensation, food, drink, slaves, for any new rubellium harvest. Especially the finest, purest ore, which was said to glow red like the sun setting on the Uropan.

"The villagers I lived with were peaceful. They knew how to

defend themselves, but they were not like this other tribe, who came in fast and swift, riding a herd of rocs. The invaders were not Code-abiding. They wielded weapons, spiked clubs, spears, axes. Their chieftain, set on the largest bird I've seen to this day, wielded a spectral rod."

Cego could hear Drakken's voice quiver.

"I tried to organize the villagers, get them in position to defend themselves. I'd studied the more warlike of the Desovian tribes, so I knew what they would be after. I tried to get the children, the old and weak, to safety, down to the river to escape on the few craft they had docked there. I tried . . . so hard."

Drakken turned back toward Cego, tears streaking from his eyes.

"But I couldn't do anything," Drakken whispered. "It was a slaughter. Every last man, woman, and child was killed on that day, before my eyes."

Cego held his breath.

"They left me alive, though," Drakken said. "They saw that I was not a native. They thought I might be with the Kirothian Empire, a Scout perhaps. So, I sat among the bodies, my friends, my love . . . as the invaders hacked at the monoliths of rubellium ore for hours. They filled their bags and loaded up their rocs with the metals. Then, after they'd had their fill, the chieftain rode to me. He looked down and handed me a big chunk of ore. A precious nugget, probably worth the whole village they'd just slaughtered in its weight. What he said to me I will never forget: *Bring this back to your people so that they can see the riches of the Desovian highlanders.*"

Drakken held up the gleaming crimson coin in front of Cego.

"After I returned to Ezo, I had this coin minted. I'd kept the ore with me; it had never left my side."

"Why?" Cego asked quietly. "Why would you want to remind yourself of such a terrible moment?"

"Because I don't want to forget them," Drakken responded. "Every time I look at this coin, it reminds me of those people I spent a full year with. Those people who changed my life for the better. I live always with the sadness in my heart. To this day, I wake sweating from night terrors. But this is how I remember them. This is how I honor them, so that they cannot be forgotten, so that their ways and memories will not be lost. I can live with that."

Cego nodded. He understood.

"Cego, that is why I'm worried that you are holding something in. Letting it fester, not letting it be remembered."

Cego looked up at Drakken. He trusted the man. But still, he couldn't bring himself to reveal his past. It was too much. But he did offer something.

"Ever since that day in the arena, when I lost control," Cego said, "I've felt something building inside me. It feels like...a darkness. Like something is taking over."

The professor listened patiently.

"I felt it with Shiar in the Circle," Cego said. "I wanted to end him. Kill him. And now, when I see him, after knowing what he's done to my friends, to me, I still want to make him stop talking. Permanently. I'm afraid I'll lose control again, not just with Shiar but anyone I face in the Circle."

Drakken nodded and stretched his hand toward Cego. He grasped the professor's hand and felt something smooth against his palm.

The rubellium coin.

"I—I can't," Cego stuttered. "I can't take this from you. It means too much."

"Hey!" a voice suddenly shattered their privacy. It was Dozer, bounding down the classroom stairs. "You coming to class early now?"

Drakken whispered to Cego, "Keep it. And remember, no matter what is going on outside us, we always have control of ourselves."

Cego put the coin in his pocket as Dozer slapped him on the shoulder.

CHAPTER 8

The Recruiter

A Grievar must be light like a floating flower seed but firmly planted like an ancient tree's roots. One must find the balance between flow and pressure, fluidity and firmness.
Seventeenth Precept of the Combat Codes

*S*ol looked out the window set on the far wall of the dining room. Ezo's Capital was often covered in fog or rain; today, though, the city was clear of both. Just cloud cover. Of course, no sun. Even so, what she'd give to be outside this room, training in the Grove, instead of here with these people.

The Halberds had visitors today and not the sort she liked. Sol loved the training partners her father would often bring by after practice. Those sorts of visitors would regale her with stories from the Circles. Stories of how their scars were won from far-off lands like the islands of Besayd or the deserts of Venturi.

No, today was not one for such visitors. Today's visitors were Daimyo. They seemed to come more often lately. Nobles, politiks, city governors, slavers, every occupation that made you bitrich. And the sort of Daimyo in particular that visited the home *of Artemis Halberd were those directly in touch with the Grievar trade: buying, selling, training, feeding, equipping, enhancing.*

Of course, Artemis Halberd had always fought for the azure flag. He'd been bred and trained on Ezonian soil, his fealty never wavering. That didn't prevent foreign suitors from coming by to try to sway him, or a wealthy noble from waving riches in front of his face to entice him to fight for their personal retinue.

Sol's stomach turned as she ingested pieces of the meal-table conversation. It was always the same. First, the Daimyo would make their attempts at compliments.

Sebeliun, the man's name was, waved his hand in the air as words slid from his mouth. "What a wonderful abode you have here. I particularly enjoy the quaint artwork you have adorned your walls with," he said, referring to the family portraits that lined the dining room.

The man continued, looking at Sol's father, who sat at the head of the table in his favorite unadorned steel chair. "And the gardens in front of your home, also quite beautiful. Especially for a Grievar, to have the ability to maintain flora in such an elegant way."

Despite their attempts at cordiality, the Daimyo never saw the Grievar as anything more than fighters, doing their bidding.

"It is important to maintain a balance with the natural world," Artemis Halberd replied in his deep voice. "I've tried to teach my daughter such things."

"Ah yes…" the Daimyo replied, not even looking at Sol.

After pleasantries, the visitors would bite into the meat of the conversation, like hounds.

"So, Sir Halberd," the particularly veiny one hissed. "We know that you've just completed quite a tour. Seven nations, seven fights, seven wins. As is expected for a Grievar of your caliber."

Artemis grunted a yeah. Her father never was one to talk about fights after they were finished.

The man continued. "With that grueling tour behind you, you surely could use some relaxation. A change of pace. Some time to spend with your family." The Daimyo's eyes flashed ever so quickly to Sol, as if for the first time revealing he knew she was sitting there.

Artemis ripped into the fowl set in front of him, seemingly oblivious to his suitor's efforts.

"Perhaps a year off on the Isles would suit your purposes," the Daimyo said. "We'd set you up at the most amenable of residences. A palace. One that would make your home here seem quaint. Your family would enjoy some of the Isles' greatest luxuries. Servants on staff around the clock to suit your every need. Grunt gardeners to save you and your daughter from such unenviable tasks."

Artemis continued to focus on his food.

"Perhaps your girl here could continue her fight practice." The Daimyo's cold black eyes swept over her again. "We have the best trainers, as you know. And educators as well, if you were so inclined to enroll her. She could learn new languages or even mathematics. If she has the mental capacity for such endeavors, that is."

Sol clenched her fists under the table.

"And your team here surely would not mind if you took a year off while you practiced with my own stable. Show them some of your famed techniques. Perhaps even step into the Circle for us on occasion."

Sol shut it out. She'd gained the unique ability to block their droning voices after much practice.

She looked to a faded portrait hanging across from her. In the picture, Sol stood next to her father, probably only five years old, a wide gap-toothed smile on her face, which was mostly covered in strawberry marmalade.

Sol remembered the day of that portrait clearly. Her father had taken a rare break from training and agreed to accompany her to the Capital's annual fair. Sol had gone every year before but never with her father. The fair held contests of strength, speed, and agility, and had a wide of array of animals to ride on and exotic foods from around the world.

Of course, her father had been swarmed with fans that day, like everywhere he went. But he'd lifted Sol up onto his shoulders above the crowds and paraded her around the fairgrounds. She remembered feeling so high above the crowds, safe up on those broad shoulders of Artemis Halberd.

Her father had even entered one of the contests of agility with Sol. He'd have easily won every other prize at the fair, of course, but agility was the one place that Sol had been able to keep up with him even at an early age.

The contest had required entrants to run an obstacle course, crawl through tunnels, leap over walls, go bar to bar across a muddy ravine. Sol had seemed weightless at that age and so she'd completed the course with little trouble. When it was Father's turn, Sol could remember him having difficulty squeezing through the little tunnels and bringing his considerable weight up over the high wall.

A small misstep crossing the ravine had left Artemis down in the mud. Sol had thought Father would be angry for falling, yet he'd emerged from the muck with a gleaming smile. He'd laughed as he grabbed Sol's foot and yanked her down along with him.

"You see?" the Daimyo's change of inflection brought Sol from her reverie. "Your daughter loves the idea of an escapade to the Isles. Just look at the smile on her face."

Sol hadn't realized she'd been smiling, thinking about that day at the fair. She quickly clenched her jaw and looked back down at her food.

*   *   *

The stadium was alive.

Sol had visited some of the largest arenas around the world traveling alongside her father, towering domes in the sky and glittering cages set on mountainsides, but still, her eyes grew wide as they approached Aquarius Arena.

Boats floated into the stadium down a tentacled mess of

waterways. Only small craft could squeeze through the narrow passages, most manned by hired Grunts paddling the long oar.

Sol sat in one such taxi beside N'auri, who was grinning ear to ear as they gently floated toward an entry arch.

"There's no other way in?" Sol asked, still dumbfounded that you couldn't just walk into the arena.

"Not unless you bit-rich enough to come by Flyer," N'auri responded. As if on cue, a black bullet streaked across the sky and then descended into the stadium's maw. "They do have landing pads up there for the lords."

The oarsman standing in front of them looked back. "Better enjoy the water; no fun flying."

"They say the old isle lords built the canals to scare foreign Grievar," N'auri explained. "They'd already be green in the face from the ocean voyage, so lords put them on another boat just before they stepped to the Circle."

Sol shook her head. Even in years past, before tech and enhancements, Daimyo had already been seeking to gain an edge.

Their taxi suddenly dropped, a quick coast down a slope in the canal. Sol's stomach dropped with it.

N'auri chuckled. "Not expecting that, Sayana?"

"No, well, I was just getting used to the slow pace—"

Sol was cut off as the boat descended again, this time down an even longer slide. She hadn't been able to tell from a distance, but she could now see the canals encircling the stadium sloped downward, with the arena's central chamber set below sea level.

"Originally, Aquarius was built out of a giant crater," N'auri explained as she watched Sol's curious eyes. "Some rock that struck the planet long time ago. They say Ancients fought in the crater."

Sol stared up as they floated beneath the stadium's undercarriage, a complex mesh of translucent tubes that funneled visitors throughout the dome like tiny insects.

N'auri continued speaking as the boat in front of them slowed to a creep. "When the sea filled the crater, the stadium was lost from histories. But then the Daimyo lords came to the Isles and did their magic. They used thousands of slaves to dig the canals. They conjured steel giants to draw out the water and set their shields to keep out the sea."

Shadows blanketed their craft as they entered a glowing tunnel. Sol peered over the side of the taxi to see swarms of spectrals flowing beneath them while a cacophony of chattering voices rushed overhead.

She could feel the power instilled within this stadium, the sea's suffocating pressure kept at bay only by the shields. Though Sol knew she should shun such Daimyo tech, she couldn't help but be amazed at the design, awed by these creatures who bent nature to their will and changed the world to fit their mold. She could imagine her father passing beneath this very stadium years before, his face dispassionate despite an upcoming bout.

The taxi slowed further, stuck in traffic. Some of the visitors ahead hopped off their boats onto a narrow stone walkway alongside the canal, choosing to move faster by foot.

"Let's go!" N'auri shouted as she flipped a bit to the oarsman and nimbly leapt off the craft.

Sol followed and the two girls melded into the tight pedestrian traffic on the walkway. They vaulted up a small stair directly into the brightness of one of the arena's main arteries. Sol stood still as the crowd flowed around her like a river. She could look clearly through the translucent floor beneath her feet. Green vines clung to the glass with spindly fingers and cascaded into the ocean waters below.

"Come on, what you waiting for?" N'auri hurried Sol along. The girl broke into a sprint, weaving through the crowds. Sol sighed as she gave chase; the Emeraldi was always full of energy, in constant movement without a moment for a deep breath.

They dodged dirt-covered Grunt laborers, heavily guarded Daimyo lords, and battle-worn Grievar from all corners of the world. Sol was amazed at the diversity. In Ezo's Capital, especially outside the Citadel, the Grievar population was uniform, most born and bred within the realm. But here in Besayd, it seemed every Grievar looked distinct; stout, bearded Myrkonians walked past tall, lithe Desovians.

N'auri turned a corner so quickly, Sol nearly lost her. She retraced her steps to see the girl already halfway up a stairwell. Sol followed N'auri's footsteps five levels up and finally out into a drab hallway far different from the sunlit floors below.

N'auri stood with her hands on her hips, waiting for Sol. "Maybe we should have worked your cardio a bit more."

Sol steadied her breath. "I'm fine; just wasn't prepared for a sprint all of a sudden."

N'auri smiled. "Always getting ready, Sayana. This how all Ezonians are, not knowing how to move in the moment?"

Sol shook her head as the two girls walked side by side down the hallway. "No, just me I guess."

They stopped at a dead end, as if the stadium architects had forgotten their purpose for the path. Exposed, leaky pipes dripped in several places from the ceiling, wetting the heads of some two dozen Grievar spread out in the hall. Some sat straight-backed against the wall, while others stretched out on the floor. Two local boys drilled techniques, trading a series of kicks and punches in rapid succession. One grey-haired man was crumpled in the corner, snoring loudly.

"We wait here for the recruiter," N'auri stated.

They found a place against a wall, Sol sitting cross-legged with her eyes closed to focus her breath. She worked to tune out the world around her, focus solely on her task ahead. The upcoming auditions would determine whether she could see her father again.

One more time was all she needed.

"You lost?"

Sol opened her eyes to see an ugly man with a long black mustache standing over her, his arms crossed. She recognized him as the gondola pilot that N'auri had warned her about when they'd first met. *Timault.*

"Daimyo viewing section starts three floors up, princess," the man said, before turning and spitting into one of the puddles beside them.

Sol stood, only coming up to the man's shoulder, as N'auri came to her side defensively.

"Why don't you bother someone else, Timault?" N'auri growled.

"Ah, if it ain't Tusava's girl!" Timault said. "How come your dafé hasn't slapped some sense into you yet?"

N'auri didn't flinch. "Better sight of me than eyes on a sad thing like you. Shouldn't you be off selling poor kids to the highest bidders?"

"I just do trades on the side. Fighting is what I'm here for. I even made second-round auditions last year," Timault bragged. "Got some good bit-work from the exposure too. But I'm more curious why you got some princess with you this time. This little girl got blue blood running in her? Think you'll be chosen as a pair, sway the lords?"

"She's no princess," N'auri said. "Sayana is Ezonian warrior blood. Citadel trained."

"Oh, right." Timault laughed. "If that's so, why's she here for tryouts in this shithole? Shouldn't she be at some polished school, sitting and learning how to throw punches from some old pissy clout?"

Sol stepped in front of N'auri. "I've dealt with his kind before."

She met the man's dark eyes. "You think you'll lift yourself up by trying to bring us down. Your type can't step into the Circle unadorned, with just skill and an opponent standing across from you. You need something more."

Timault stepped closer to Sol, smiling to reveal several missing teeth. She could smell the sour ale on his breath. He lifted his calloused hand and placed it against Sol's cheek. "We'll see if your bark matches your bite real soon, princess."

Before Sol could reply, the Grievar around them suddenly stood at attention. A tall man with obsidian skin and a shaved head strode into the center of the hall. The recruiter.

"Let's get this over with," he yelled, his Besaydian accent thick. "On the wall!"

N'auri and Sol followed the rest and stood against the wall.

"First-round auditions, we got space for only half of you," the man barked.

"Heard from local magistrate there would be spots for three dozen," a veteran Grievar grumbled.

"Heard wrong," the man responded. "Lord Cantino only got room in his stable for ten or so, maybe a few more if he's sufficiently impressed. Now, let's make this easy."

The recruiter paced back and forth, eyeing the Grievar up against the wall. He stopped in front of the grey-haired man with weathered skin. "You, go home, old boy."

The old man dropped to his knees. "Sir, I got nothing else. This be my last chance to make it, give real service to a lord. I been fighting slave markets for my entire life, living bit to bit. Please... one more chance; otherwise, might as well take to the waters and let the razor sharks find me."

"You've heard my say," the recruiter said unflinchingly. "Now, out before I get the guard on you. You don't want to end up in the lord's prison, believe me. That'd be far worse a fate than a fish-feeding."

Tears rolled from the old Grievar's eyes as he turned away to tread down the long hall. The recruiter continued down the line, stopping in front of two tall but thin brothers. "Get some meat on you first. You wouldn't stay standing for the audition, much less a stiff sea breeze."

He weeded out several more fighters until stopping in front of Timault, standing beside N'auri and Sol. "Back for more, Timault?"

Sol thought for a second that he'd tell the slaver to leave, but instead, the recruiter clasped hands with him and grinned. "Strength to you, brother. Let's take ales again over in the pleasure quarter real soon."

The man then towered over the girls against the wall. "You two. Too small and too...female. Out with you."

He turned and started to walk away.

"Wait!" N'auri yelled, a sudden desperation filling her normally confident voice.

"Oh, you going to plead now too?" The recruiter spun around. "Maybe say you like to stop by after hours to see my place?"

Sol could see N'auri's face frozen, caught speechless. Pleading certainly wouldn't work with this man, but there was another way to win approval. Sol had learned that the hard way many times before. She stepped forward again.

"If we aren't fit to audition for the lord, then none of these men are," Sol stated. "Especially strange that you are the one to keep us from fighting. You, with such a scarless face, smooth as a baby, looking like you've not seen a day of combat."

The recruiter spun around back toward Sol, his chest puffed out. This was about power. Everyone wanted to see who had it and who didn't.

He stood in front of her menacingly. "Pleading would have been a better idea, girl. Because I'm feeling merciful today, you two can still walk. Go home and cook your dafé a nice meal, now. Forget you were here. In fact, forget ever coming back here unless you sitting in the stands."

Sol knew the man's words before they came, and she'd already planned her counter.

"How about we forget about us and we talk about you instead?" Sol asked. The recruiter's job was to focus on other Grievar's skills, judge entrance to auditions. He took that little power seriously, as men tended to do. Their entire lives revolved around such things.

Sol meant to take that power away.

The man stayed quiet, but Sol could sense the anger rising in his chest as he held his breath. She noticed his clenched fists, his curled toes.

"In fact, I think the reason you even have this job, telling us we're not good enough, is because you aren't good enough yourself. Why aren't you trying out for this audition? Are you happy being some low-level arbiter for the lords? Like a scrap-picking dog at the dining table."

All the Grievar against the wall were silent, watching and waiting for the explosion.

"You're going somewhere you can't come back from, you little bitch," the recruiter growled as his jaw set, his pupils dilated. He wasn't there yet, though. Sol needed to push harder.

"Where am I going, scrap-picker? It's certainly not the same place you're heading after here, which is some arena back alley to grovel, to beg for a real fighter to pay you a bit or even a glance. How about we see how you fare against this girl in a little game of pick your shot? I'm sure you play it here on the Isles just as we do in Ezo, don't you?"

That was it. Sol could see the exact moment when the man's ego took over. He couldn't back down now.

"Let's do it," the man snarled as he stepped away from the wall and set his feet shoulder width apart. He held his long arms out in front of him.

Sol stepped across from the recruiter and planted her feet, the top of her head right beneath his outstretched fists. She lowered her arms to her sides, allowing herself to be fully exposed to any incoming strike. She could remember playing the game with her father nearly every morning in the Grove. Of course, Artemis Halberd would never use his full strength or speed against her.

"You first," Sol said calmly, though she could feel her heart pumping in her throat. She caught N'auri's stare from the corner of her eye.

She waited for the eruption of violence, as predictable as the tide coming in. Sol knew this man. He would try to take her head off, make a show of his strength in front of the viewers against the wall. She breathed out and met his eyes, waiting for the incoming attack.

The man's eyelid twitched just before he launched his strike. Sol saw the punch coming, but she couldn't raise her hands in defense or step aside to dodge the blow. Doing so would mean losing the game. All she could do was roll with the strike.

She turned her head just as the fist connected, letting it glance off her jaw, its power dissipating but still snapping her neck back. Learning to roll a punch was the difference between taking minor damage and getting knocked out cold.

"Is that the best you've got?" Sol stared back at the man in defiance as she wiped the blood from her mouth.

The man growled as Sol stretched her arms out just as he'd done. He came into range and let his arms down by his side.

Punches were the only strikes allowed in this contest, at least the way Sol had learned to play. She had no doubt she could put him down with a kick, but a single punch was a different story. Of course, he'd expect Sol to go for the face. He'd be ready to roll just as she'd done and even if she did connect flush, he wouldn't likely go down. And then, the man would get his turn to strike again.

Sol stared the man in the eyes and breathed steadily, watching the sweat start to trickle down his brow as he waited. She could see him clenching his jaw, readying himself for impact. Too bad she wouldn't get to hit him in the face.

Sol turned her hips and threw her full weight into a body punch, connecting with the man just below the right side of his rib cage. She felt her fist dig into his flesh.

At first the man didn't flinch; he looked down at Sol and smiled as if the punch hadn't bothered him a bit. But then, his eyes widened, his breath caught in his chest. The man dropped to his knees and curled up into a ball.

Liver shot always did the trick. Cego had shown Sol the art of that strike over countless training sessions.

She looked down at the man.

"We'll both be given entrance to the audition," she said. "Or we will leave, and we'll be sure to tell this little tale to every Grievar and Grunt on our way out."

The recruiter stood up slowly, not meeting Sol's eyes.

He nodded.

CHAPTER 9

A New Darkness

A Grievar should be mindful that their greatest attribute is often also their greatest weakness. A tall fighter will have range on an opponent when striking, but their long limbs will be easier to grasp and break on the ground. A stocky fighter, thickly muscled like a bull, will be suffocating when on top of an opponent, but when placed on his back, he will be like a turtle turned on its shell.

Passage Two, Seventy-Third Precept of the Combat Codes

T here is a central misunderstanding to the interpretation of the Codes," Professor Zyleth said. "Which is one of the primary reasons our little class here is so controversial."

Zyleth stood in front of the class, his inky eyes finding each student. "It is widely known that one of the Codes' main tenets is *no tools, no tech*. My friend, Professor Aon Farstead, taught you this lesson as Level Ones. But, as wise as Professor Farstead may be, he left out some integral facts."

Cego still wasn't used to seeing a Daimyo at the Lyceum, the little man seeming tiny in front of the class of upper-level Grievar, students nearly ready to test for Knighthood.

"No tools, no tech," Zyleth said again, loudly.

The professor placed his hand to the lid of a large metallic chest set on the floor. The chest swung open and Zyleth reached in, lifting out a steel rod with a bulbous head. He held the item in the air for all to see.

Cego recognized the weapon immediately. A spectral rod. He remembered seeing the Daimyo-paid guards wielding them, patrolling the Underground. Even some of the slave Circle owners had a few of the weapons, like the cruel weapon Tasker Ozark always had strapped to his side.

Replaced their Grievarhood with those darkin' metal sticks, Murray had always muttered.

"Now, what if I were to suddenly hand this spectral rod to you?" Zyleth asked, looking at Mithra Tentree, a Level Five girl who was eyeing the weapon cautiously. The professor offered the rod to her, but the girl shrank back.

"What? It's not even activated; it can't cause you any harm. Why not hold on to it?" Zyleth asked her.

"Because…because it's against the Codes," Mithra stuttered.

"Is it?" Zyleth asked. He pushed a small jeweled button on the handle to activate the weapon. A glowing crimson spectral sparked to life at its base. The light began to menacingly pulse up and down the steel's length as the weapon energized.

With the class's attention fully captured, Zyleth continued. "Is it against the Codes?" he asked again.

"If you were to simply—hold this weapon, without utilizing it, with no purpose but to hold it, you would not be breaking any Codes," he stated. "A less-cited verse, which is often conveniently left out of the rants of zealots, specifically states: *If a Grievar is in the presence of technologies, or has no other choice but to utilize a technological function, he may do so, as long as he does not have the intent to wield such technology with the goal of replacing his own function as a Grievar.*"

Zyleth powered down the spectral rod and placed it back in the chest. He reached in again and pulled out a small metal disc, the size of a spectacle lens. He deftly flipped the disc in the air, letting it spin and catch the light, before snatching it down.

"Anyone know what this is?" Zyleth asked.

None of the students answered.

Zyleth palmed the disc, hid it behind his hand, and flicked his wrist. A brilliant fan of electric light suddenly spread out around Zyleth's hand. He waved, flashing the light back and forth, the students' eyes following obediently, before chopping his hand down toward the desk in front of him. At first, nothing moved, until a heavy chunk of the steel slid from the desk and clanked to the ground, precisely severed by the little weapon.

"Spectral fan," Zyleth revealed. "Barely detectable but very lethal. Now, if I were to give this weapon to someone and they were to use it to…let's say, assault another student, in the Circle. Would that be against the Codes?"

"Yes," several of the students replied in unison, their eyes still wide at the power of such a small tool.

"Correct, obviously," Zyleth said. "Using technology to replace the natural-born weapons of a Grievar: your fists and feet, knees and elbows, shoulders and skulls. That, of course, is a clear violation of the Codes."

Zyleth dropped the disc back into the chest and closed the lid.

"Now, let me ask you," he said. "Is taking a stimulant against the Codes? Let us say the chemical of choice is neurovascular mitosin, which speeds up your recovery post-fight, gets you back in the Circle full force the next day. Is taking that against the Codes?"

The class did not respond. Though stims were rampant within the Knights' ranks, and even used by some students, they were not often spoken about openly.

"Labro." Zyleth pointed at a large Level Six boy, freakishly muscled, his veins nearly popping from his neck. "You took a dose of stims this morning."

Labro's face reddened. Coming from anyone else, this accusation could be grounds for expulsion from the Lyceum. "No, no, I didn't—" he began his denial.

"It is okay." Zyleth put his hand out to calm the large Grievar. "I won't tell High Commander Memnon. And even if I did, I don't think he'd bat an eye anymore."

Labro settled back into his seat uneasily.

"You did no wrong," Zyleth said. "You did not break the Codes by taking such an enhancement... What was it again?"

The professor flipped out his lightdeck and thumbed through it. "Ah yes, neurostatin mikropis, made specifically to increase your punching strength by lengthening your rotator cuff and shoulder ligaments."

Zyleth smiled, knowing that he was shocking the class in front of him, challenging their predisposed beliefs so aggressively.

"An enhancement allows a Grievar to reach their full potential," Zyleth stated. "Your kind has evolved over millennia for a specific purpose, to fight. The combat bloodline is stronger in some, pure-lights you call them, and more diluted within so-called lacklights. But all Grievar have the same purpose, this same goal of reaching combat perfection. Enhancement simply guides your body toward its natural purpose. So, is this an infraction? Is taking stims or enhancers against the Codes?"

The class hesitated this time. One Level Five shook his head slowly. "No, I guess not..."

A smile creased Labro's face, as if a weight had been lifted from his shoulders.

"Now." Zyleth held up a finger. "I'm certainly not saying everything is equivalent. Is it legal for a Grievar to don a mech suit, which drastically enhances strength and speed, and use that for fighting? No, of course not. That is a clear infraction. Grievar cannot use tech in this way; it is simply not permissible.

"But stims, neuros, and other methods of enhancing a Grievar's natural predispositions"—Zyleth's black eyes landed directly on

Cego and held for a moment—"there is nothing wrong with that. These are simply tools to lead you down your path."

Cego could only imagine Murray-Ku watching the lecture right now. He'd have already rushed Zyleth and picked him up by the throat for speaking such blasphemy.

"So, on that note of guidance," Zyleth said, "after-class studies are to contemplate a weakness you have in your fight game. What part of your skill set would you most like to strengthen? Think carefully, and we'll discuss tomorrow."

* * *

Cego squared off across the mats with Lunbar Degoas, a large Level Five boy with a mop of red hair and small eyes. Cego circled, looking for an opening to take a quick shot. A low single from the outside would be ideal, as clinching with a larger opponent wasn't usually a good decision.

Cego felt the urge to smile growing, though he didn't let it show. Grappling felt good. And some time apart from his team felt even better. The Whelps had been constantly packed together: in the dorm room, the dining hall, the training quarters, almost all his classes. Cego felt like he couldn't breathe lately, his second skin always tight across his back.

Grappling class was a good respite. Cego had placed into the Level Five skill set this semester. Only one other Level Two had placed into the class with him, a trend this year—Kōri Shimo. So far, Cego had handled himself ably despite being smaller than most of the older kids. Professor Tandore was a proficient teacher; the old Grievar made up for her clear lack of enthusiasm by demonstrating a variety of effective techniques.

On the mats, Cego felt like he could finally breathe, even now, with Lunbar smashing down on him. He'd taken an unsuccessful shot for a takedown and met a brick wall against Lunbar's quick sprawl, and now the Level Five boy was blanketing Cego with a smothering side control.

Cego framed up against Lunbar's neck and quickly escaped his hips from the heavy pressure, getting his legs out front in defense. The large boy smashed in again, trying to smother Cego's legs and crawl around them.

Cego writhed and twisted his hips to create space.

Kid, to get control of you, they need to blast through each line of your defenses. Your feet, your knees, your hands, then your hips. If they get your hips, you're darkin' done.

Cego could picture Murray-Ku shouting at him from the sidelines.

He looked to the clock on the far wall of the training room: still ten minutes left in the round. He could try to tire Degoas out; the larger, more heavily muscled Grievar would likely wind faster. But Lunbar was more often on top, grinding into Cego, using gravity to his advantage. Cego didn't want to find out if Lunbar could keep it up for the remainder of the round; his legs were already starting to burn defending the pressure-passing style.

He needed to take a risk.

Lunbar grabbed Cego's feet and lunged in again. This time, Cego launched his hips into the air while snagging a double-wrist grip on the boy's arm, pulling the limb in. Cego cinched the triangle choke with his legs, forming a figure four with his shin and the crook of the opposite knee, squeezing at his opponent's carotid arteries.

Lunbar's wide shoulders strained as he drove into Cego, trying to weaken the strangle. Cego framed his arms against the boy and shuffled backward on his shoulders, alleviating the incoming pressure. Cego couldn't finish the strangle straight on with an opponent this large, though; the proper angle was required to utilize the entirety of his leg strength.

But Degoas was wise to the maneuver; the boy suddenly jolted upward, no longer pressuring into Cego but instead lifting him into the air to release the leg triangle. Cego had been in this dilemma before. He could hold position and attempt to put Degoas out, or get spiked full force into the mats with his head leading the way.

Cego opted to not get slammed. Instead, he released his legs just as Degoas stood upright. Then Cego snuck beneath his opponent's standing base. He rolled upside down onto his shoulder, circled his shin behind Lunbar's knee, and thrust his hips forward to expose the boy's back.

Big Grievar, especially one on stims, you can break his arms and legs, but he'll keep coming. A good strangle, though, and he'll be napping like a baby, maybe even shit himself if you're lucky.

Murray had always had a way with words. Cego found himself resisting a smile again as he made a quick break toward Lunbar's back, separating from the boy's bulk before strapping his arms over a shoulder.

Degoas grasped Cego's forearm to protect his neck and struggled to his knees. Cego clung to him like a sloth, swinging his leg over a shoulder to trap Lunbar's defensive arm. He sliced his wrist across the boy's neck. The chin was still beneath the strangle, but it didn't matter. Cego had it on tight. He squeezed and ratcheted his elbow backward to compress the arteries.

Cego waited for a sign of submission, a tap from the boy.

As he squeezed harder, Cego's arm across the boy's neck suddenly felt warm and then itchy, as if a battalion of fire ants had crawled up the sleeve of his second skin. The restless warmth spread from Cego's arm through the rest of his body, swarming his chest, stomach, and legs, before moving outward.

Cego suddenly became acutely aware of the sweat-tinged air surrounding him. Somehow, he could sense the students training across the mats: a Myrkonian boy's heavy breathing, the beads of sweat dripping down a girl's brow, the impact from a swift double-leg takedown, the murmur under Professor Tandore's breath.

Cego could see the entire training room from afar. He focused on a boy with short dark hair and golden eyes. The boy was latched on to the neck of a larger opponent, squeezing. The large boy started to tap in submission, casually at first but then frantically as the golden-eyed boy kept the strangle on.

The golden-eyed boy was him. Cego knew that he was killing Lunbar Degoas, who was now unconscious and fast losing the precious oxygen supply to his brain. But Cego could do nothing to stop it. He watched himself as if he were a stranger, some demon that he had no control over.

Sometimes, we need to hurt ourselves to kill the demons. Sometimes, we need to feel the pain, every darkin' bit of it, raw as it comes, before we can pick ourselves up again.

Murray's voice cut through the darkness, thawing Cego's frozen body, letting him move toward the golden-eyed boy who was squeezing the life out of a helpless victim. Cego reached for himself, clawed forward with all his might.

"No!" Cego was screaming. He was lying on his back beside Degoas.

Professor Tandore was standing above him, wide-eyed and saying words that he could not understand. Degoas's body was convulsing beside him, the skin around the boy's neck smoldering, freshly burned from where Cego had held him with the strangle.

Cego looked down at his second skin. The material had burned away at his arm. His flesh beneath seemed to move along with the exposed dragon flux, fully awake now and writhing in the open air. Energy coursed along the serpentine body from his wrist to his shoulder. The flux didn't speak to Cego, a clear voice in his mind like the old master's voice, but Cego knew what the Doragūn said nonetheless.

I am hungry for blood, restless for violence.

Cego hid his naked arm and curled his body away from the watching eyes. He desperately wanted to check on Degoas, see if he was breathing. He wanted to tell the boy he was sorry for what he'd done, sorry that he couldn't control himself.

"I think I might be sick" was all Cego could muster as he looked up into Professor Tandore's probing eyes.

*   *   *

Cego shuddered against the cold glass of the second-floor training room. Shadows swayed beneath the heavy bag not far off. Cego had attempted to release his fear into that bag just moments ago, attacking it with more fury than he'd ever sent against a living opponent. He'd tried to sweat out the anger, reclaim his body somehow by wringing it of every ounce of hydration. But Cego could still feel it within him, the fear, the anger, the darkness that had risen up in the training room just hours ago. The unsettled energy sat in his stomach like a poison viper, curled and waiting to strike.

He would have killed Lunbar Degoas. If not for Professor Tandore ripping him off the stunned Level Five, Cego would have kept that strangle on until the boy's heart had stopped beating.

Dozer had taken Cego to the medward after the incident, though the place had been full of Grievar with far worse ailments than his queasy stomach. Dozer hadn't wanted to leave Cego's side when they'd been told they'd have to wait nearly an hour for a cleric.

"I don't need you here, Dozer," Cego had said impatiently. "You're making things worse."

Dozer had stared back at him with wide eyes before lumbering to the medward exit.

Cego hadn't waited longer; he didn't want to see Xenalia like this, even though he'd come to her in far worse a state physically. Cego retreated to this abandoned training room instead, where he came to hide away from others.

He stared down at his arm, the dragon flux dormant now, curled up at the base of his shoulder. But Cego could still sense it, growing stronger, sending dark tendrils through his body. The blacklight. At first, Cego hadn't been able to decipher the feeling he got when the blacklight rose up within him. That strange sensation as if he were watching himself from afar, out of his body and yet still able to control it.

It changes time, makes it slower, or faster, out of joint, Murray had said about the blacklight after Cego came out of the Trials last year.

But the old Grievar hadn't told Cego the blacklight would control him, make him murderous, uncaring of anything but finishing the person who stood across from him. That's where Cego was different from the others—he was born of the stuff. Even when he didn't stand in an onyx Circle, the blacklight was within him, somehow channeling itself through the Doragūn flux.

"You just gonna be staring out that window like a sad pup rest of the day?" a voice startled Cego.

Knees walked into the training room, his blue second skin soaked from class. He stopped at the hanging bag before spinning around to deliver a deft side kick to its midsection.

Cego stayed quiet while the Venturian continued to pepper the bag with jabs and kicks.

"I'm not like Abel, or Sol, you know," Knees finally said. "I'm not one to be talkin' you into the light with some lifting words. Not my custom. But when I hear my team captain's missing class, I figure I be checking for you here."

Cego wanted to thank his friend for caring enough that he'd skipped out on striking practice, but the words still wouldn't come. It was as if speaking would release whatever dark strain was inside Cego and infect his friends.

"I heard what happened in Tandore's earlier." Knees slammed an elbow into the bag. "Sounds like some bad shit. And doesn't seem like any good way to fix what's wrong with you."

Knees didn't sugarcoat anything. But he did speak the truth.

"So what can I do?" Cego finally whispered the words. It was all he wanted—to fix himself, get control again. "If I can't fix myself, what can I do?"

"No idea," Knees said. "And can't say I know what's even wrong with you. All I know is what's up here."

Knees tapped his skull as he walked toward Cego.

"For me, there's a lot of darked shit up here." Knees smirked. "Most nights, even days, I still be thinking back to my home in Venturi. Back to the digs my sister and me lived in. Back to my uncle... what he darkin' did to us every day."

Cego saw his friend's jaw tighten and he knew Knees was speaking the truth. The Venturian didn't ever seem to be fully here in the present. Part of the boy lived in his past, a dark childhood even by Cego's standards of having grown up in the Cradle.

"I always be feeling it," Knees said. "Everything the man did to us. Every time I had to hug my sis to sleep because she was crying too hard. Every time I should have stood up to him, even though I was small, weak then. I tell myself: I could have taken him by surprise, put him in the dirt. I still be feeling it all, sitting and festering and spreading through me."

Cego turned away from Knees, his eyes glistening.

"Whatever be in you," Knees said, putting a hand on Cego's shoulder. "We all be fighting back the darkness. Me, you, Abel, and Joba. Sol, wherever that girl be. Stupid as Dozer is, he's got some trouble in him too, that be for sure. We all need to be keeping it down, keeping it from controlling us. And then, we put one boot in front of the other."

Cego met Knees's eyes. He let a deep breath in, exhaled. He knew his friend was right. Cego thought of seeing the jagged scars running across Joba's back from the giant's time in the borderlands. He thought of feeling Sol's rage after her father had been killed, trying to talk to her when she was at her lowest.

"Sorry I missed class," Cego said.

"You be deserving a break," Knees said as he turned and moved toward the corridor. "We all do sometimes, I figure."

Cego got to his feet.

"That Brynn Mykili, though." Knees shook his head. "Not sure that Jadean be havin' any darkness to her. Cheery as a slaggin' sprite. Sort of sick, if you ask me."

Cego laughed as he followed his friend's lead.

CHAPTER 10

Offerings

Though one often returns to the past to learn from mistakes, they must remain feather-footed there. Treading too heavily in memories, dredging up either joy or regret, will only serve to impede the path of progression.

Thirtieth Precept of the Combat Codes

Murray enjoyed the blackshift.

When the massive arrays in the Underground's cavernous ceiling finally turned dark for the night, Murray found it easier to breathe.

Not that it was always quiet or peaceful during blackshift. Markspar Row still hummed with nighttime activities, businesses, and services that kicked into gear as the redlight faded. The mechs still churned against the eastern cavern wall, a never-ending search for deep elemental reserves.

Blacklight ain't no light, Murray's father had told him when he was young. The two used to sit on the stoop of their gutter-district home, staring out into the darkness of the gargantuan cavern, listening to swarms of bats overhead and hearing the distant echoes of nocturnal hawkers.

What is the blacklight, then, Da? Murray had asked Myrkoth Pearson. His father had been a middling purelight, still reliving his Knight's service long after he'd retired. Maybe that's why he'd slapped Murray around so often.

Like the onyx Circles, kid, Myrkoth had told him. *You can't see the blacklight, but it's there. It's grasping at your memories, what came before. Way up there during blackshift, there's onyx enough for all the Deep folk's nightmares.*

The distant blacklight tugged at Murray now, imparting a distinct nostalgia as he walked down the old gutter-district streets. That stoop he used to sit on with his father was gone, as was the single-story clay home he'd grown up in. In fact, the entire section had turned over years before, while Murray was Surface-side.

The Daimyo had bought up the area, grinding down the old homes to erect two- and three-story estates in their place. The old dirt path was now cobbled, the glowing lichen ripped from the low walls and replaced with spectral lamps. The soap-eaters had renamed the section Cavern Side.

It wasn't by chance Murray hadn't been back there since he'd buried his parents in the central boneyard after the Cimmerian Shade took them. There hadn't been any reason to come back.

Until now.

Murray craned his head for viewports posted on the estate awnings, saw none, and so kicked out a corrugated section of black fence in front of him. Another barrier to keep out folk like him.

Farther into Cavern Side lay the largest estates, homes owned by the Lords of Commerce, those who dictated the procurement of elements, along with the men who ran the chains of slave Circles and Courtesan Houses.

Murray flattened against the walls of one of the homes, staying out of the streetlight, as two voices broke the silence of blackshift.

"...And then she says to me, why didn't you throw down bits for the meal? Can you believe that?"

A low chortle came in response. "Can't believe you paid for it but didn't get any sweets. Shit deal on you."

Murray peered out from the shadows as two patrolmen crossed under the light. Though he hated slinking around in the shadows and had no doubt he could disable the two mercs, now was not the time. Now was not his fight. Plenty of that ahead.

Murray waited until the path was clear to move, quickly striding alongside the shadowed buildings and staying off the lit street.

He knew it when he a saw it: a four-floor Jadean-style estate, brass gutters atop black ironwood shingles with triangular crenellations marking each level. Wide shield windows peered out like glaring eyes from the central level. Maharu Manor.

Murray had played it out in his mind ever since he'd left Thaloo's, since he'd found out where Sam was being kept.

He hadn't told Anderson or Leyna about his plan. He knew they would try to stop him, convince him he was reckless, that he needed more time to wean himself from the drink, both of which were likely true.

Murray crossed the gardened grounds of the estate, strode up the front path, and knocked against the heavy door, opting to forgo use of the golden lion-head knocker. He lifted the hood off his head and stared into the viewport above, knowing someone was staring back at him, wondering who would show up at Lord Maharu's door at blackshift.

A robotic voice jumped from an audio implant fused to the door. "What business you got with the lord?"

"Lookin' for work," Murray answered.

"So, you think you'll get it showing up at blackshift?" the voice asked. "We don't need another pot cleaner."

Murray held back the urge to crumple the viewport above. "I heard the lord needs some new security."

"That so," the voice said incredulously. "And who're you to be asking?"

"Murray Pearson."

The audio box went silent. Murray could picture the lackey putting together how to turn this into a win for themselves, gain favor with their lord.

"Let me get back to you." The man went silent and Murray waited for several minutes.

He heard a click and the ornate door lifted, revealing a pristine room of dark ironwood planks sided with white tree-skin walls. Two broad-shouldered guards greeted him, likely ex-empire. They patted Murray down.

"Don't carry tech, not now, not never," Murray said.

"Murray Pearson, in the flesh," the younger guard whispered.

"Quiet." His partner elbowed him hard before nodding to Murray.

"Follow." The guard led Murray to the far side of the room, where he was herded into a cramped lift.

Gears groaned as the lift rose several levels. He breathed deeply as it settled to a stop and the door opened to two more guards who wordlessly waved Murray down a long ironwood hallway.

Murray listened to his heavy frame creak the pliable planks. Spectral torches illuminated more tree-skin walls and dark silhouettes behind the thin sheets. Some honey-sweet perfume tinged the air.

But Murray's attention was immediately drawn to the gleaming black form at the end of the hall, standing at attention in front of an entry portal.

From a distance, the mech appeared a suit of onyx armor that sucked in the light from the nearby torches. But as they approached, Murray could see the pilot posted within, the glow from the cockpit where the little Daimyo controlled the automaton. He noted this mech had no pulse cannon, like the Enforcers used Surface-side. A Sentinel.

They stepped toward the portal with golden sigils running up and down it, old glyphs concealing high-tech scanners inlaid to the frame.

"Arrived with Pearson, my lord," one of the guards said.

The entryway lifted and Murray breathed a sigh of relief to be past the Sentinel. He shuddered, acknowledging how small even he felt next to such a creature.

He stepped into the largest room of the estate, the entire floor he'd seen from outside with shield windows surrounding it.

Murray expected to see opulence typical of the Daimyo, lavish adornments or showy furniture. But, like the hall they'd entered from, this room was nearly unadorned apart from a utilitarian rack holding several long steel rods and a tall folding screen at the center.

"Welcome to my tearoom, Murray Pearson." A diminutive man walked toward him with two guards to either side. Three white-faced courtesans draped in flowing red robes came in tow.

"Thank you for seeing me, Lord Maharu," Murray responded, knowing this was where he had to play his part, resist the urge to fight.

"The pleasure is all mine," the Daimyo replied as he sat on the tatami. "I've followed your career closely, Knight Pearson. I was always a great fan of yours when you fought for the Citadel. In fact, I was there up in the boxes when you fought the Dragoon only a few years ago. I had a feeling you'd win, though most were betting against you."

"Those days are far behind me," Murray responded. "But they certainly have a fond place in my memory as well."

"Yes, yes," the Daimyo said, motioning for Murray to sit. "Can I offer you anything?"

Maharu nodded to one of the courtesans, who slipped behind the folding screen and returned carrying a tray of amber liquid and tiny sori glasses.

Murray recognized the high-end Hiberian liquor and shook his head. "I'm off the stuff."

"Ah, that is good to hear," Maharu responded. "I was most displeased when I'd heard you'd fallen on hard times. It is fitting that a champion like you would cleanse his body in such a way."

"Yes," Murray said impatiently, wanting to get past such formalities.

"Tell me, Knight Pearson." The Daimyo watched him with black, bottomless eyes. "Many have said you still follow the Codes. That you were unshakable and would never take on something as degrading as muscle work. And yet, here you are, telling me you'd like to be of service. What has changed?"

Murray had been waiting for the question. "My lord, you yourself said it. I've fallen on some tough times. I let the drink take me out of control. I spent everything, lost it all. I need a way to get back on my feet."

"Ah, so," the Daimyo said. "This makes sense. But why not return to the Citadel? After your Knighthood and Scout work, I'm sure they would be there to offer you a position."

"True, that they did," Murray responded. "But I'm done with them."

He left it at that, not wanting his feint to be too telegraphed. Sometimes, you had to let your opponent do the work for you.

"Yes, and my sources have told me as much, that you've had a falling-out with Commander Memnon. If you don't mind me asking, why was that?"

Murray sighed. "The Codes, as you said. I do still follow them. And the Citadel has broken their oath too many times over. Some of the things they were doing, trying to enhance their teams. It was too much."

Murray stared into the Daimyo's inky eyes, but Lord Maharu didn't flinch.

"I've heard of such things," the lord said. "As you can see around you, though I am Daimyo, I also am a strong believer in the Codes."

The little man stood and held his hands up to the tearoom.

"Most believe the Codes to be prescriptions for the Grievar way of life, but that is not the truth. They are a way of life for all, from the lowly Grunt to the highest lords. I have accepted that we Daimyo are meant to rule, but I've also come to accept that Grievar are meant to serve in their natural way. I don't make my security forces utilize weapons or tech, break their oaths. For that path would bring in lesser men, not the sort I'd want in my employ. Not men like you, who have standards, who follow the Codes."

Murray nodded. "That's why I came here, to be of service to you."

"It seems fated that you've come here, Knight Pearson." The Daimyo motioned for Murray to stand. "But truth be told, I'd most often not employ someone showing up at my door in the middle of blackshift, even if he is the Mighty Murray Pearson in the flesh."

"I wouldn't have been able to get into Cavern Side coming by dayshift," Murray said.

"No matter." Maharu waved his hand at the folder screen set in the middle of the room. "Fortunately for you, my head of security is on his way out. You'll need quite a bit of training and I'm sure he'll be glad to have you shadow him."

Murray watched as Farmer stepped from behind the folded screen. The old master looked as Murray remembered him from Tlik's bar, a withered body floating within a robe.

Farmer bowed low to Maharu and turned to meet Murray's eyes.

"Hello, Murray."

Murray could feel his plan slipping through his fingers. Why was Farmer here? It couldn't be coincidence that the man was working for the same lord that was holding the Cradle brood captive somewhere in this manor.

Maharu looked at Murray with a raised eyebrow, as if asking Murray why he'd be surprised the old master would be here, come back from the dead after so long to work as a lowly merc.

"It will be good to work together again, toward the joint cause of providing security for Lord Maharu," Murray said with a clenched jaw. The fight was not the one in front of him, yet.

"I am glad to show you how things are done here," Farmer replied.

Murray held his breath, barely believing that the plan would work, that this man would hire him.

"But." The Daimyo spat the word. "There's one more thing you must do to gain my employ."

Murray froze.

"Though your exploits are well known, you would understand that I'm wary of how your skills may have deteriorated since your time as a Knight," Maharu said. "So, you wouldn't mind me testing you, would you?"

"Of course not," Murray said.

Maharu nodded to one of the guards. "Yahalo."

A lanky Grievar stepped forward.

"Yes, my lord," Yahalo said, glancing nervously from Maharu to Murray.

Murray recognized him as the guard who had whispered his name in awe when he first entered the compound. Just a kid, probably barely out of empire training camp and hired Deep because he didn't make the cut as a Knight.

He'd hate to hurt the kid, but Murray knew he'd need to put on a show to make sure he was hired. He cracked his neck to both sides and tossed his cloak to the floor.

Yahalo advanced on Murray cautiously, throwing a few probing jabs as he got into range. Murray let the feints come, his hands down at his sides. One strike came in hard and Murray turned with it, not even bothering to counter.

The kid looked up at him with timid eyes and threw two more jabs and a cross. Murray let them connect, this time not even deflecting the strikes, letting one catch him square in the face.

Murray wiped the blood from his gums.

"Not bad, kid," he said as he dropped with startling quickness and shot his shoulder beneath Yahalo's legs. He tossed the merc over his head onto his back. Kata guruma.

Yahalo landed without time to recompose his guard and Murray was already on him, swinging his legs around the kid's head and extending his arm. Yahalo drove into Murray to prevent the arm break, but he fell right into the triangle trap. Murray squeezed his legs and the boy was out, snoring on the ironwood floor.

Maharu clapped rhythmically, looking down at his fallen guard. "I appreciate you not damaging my hires."

"Well," Murray said. "Wouldn't want to hurt those I'm going to be working alongside, right?"

"Yes, indeed," the Daimyo said. "Welcome to the team, Murray Pearson."

CHAPTER II

Fight for the Fallen

The inferior fighter is frustrated when recovering from injury or loss, unable to claim the strength they once possessed. A master understands that the path to recovery will reveal new techniques previously hidden by habit. A Grievar must always be ready to rebuild from nothing.

Sixtieth Precept of the Combat Codes

*T*hree weeks out from the Trials. Three weeks out from the Lyceum.

Sol had dreamed of training at the Lyceum since she could first speak, since her father had swept her away with stories of his own studies at the famed combat school. The Citadel held a place in Sol's mind reserved for lofty dreams: the domed central hall, the sister spirals, the rolling greens, and the glinting rows of shield windows.

But the Trials were no dream for Sol. The infamous entry test to the school had been the subject of her frequent nightmares. She'd wake, drenched in sweat and panting like she'd been in a real fight, fragments of horror stories she'd heard about the Trials flashing through her mind. Stories about kids never coming out the same.

Sol gritted her teeth and slammed an elbow into the practice dummy in front of her. She wasn't a little girl anymore. Nightmares were for little girls.

She threw two quick knees into the dummy's midsection, followed by a clinch. She swept the dummy to the ground with osoto gari, immediately transitioning to an arm bar on one of its rubbery limbs. She could hear the satisfying crack *of an elbow, the dummy's inner mechanism letting her know she'd found the target with her hips.*

Sol stood up, breathing heavily. She was almost thirteen and nearly ready for the Trials, with only one piece of her game missing. Strategy. That was what she needed Father for. He was to return from his tour today to help Sol prepare.

Sol looked up expectantly at the gated entrance to the Grove. Her father had swung that creaky gate open many times before, coming upon Sol practicing on this same dummy since she was a little girl. No hug or warm greeting when Father returned from his travels.

Artemis Halberd would simply say, in his deep baritone, Let's train.

To Sol, those words meant everything.

She set the dummy standing again and repeated the same sequence. Cutting elbow, clinch, two knees, osoto gari to arm bar.

Thunder rumbled overhead as raindrops started to fall from the sky.

Sol repeated the sequence again and again, feeling the dirt beneath her feet soften as the rain fell harder.

Father's words repeated in her head. Practice a technique once and you'll know what it looks like. Practice it a hundred times and you'll know what it feels like. Practice it one thousand times and you'll hit it on a lesser-skilled opponent. Practice it five thousand times and you'll hit it on an opponent of equal skill.

A lightning bolt lit the sky overhead. Sol's feet sank into the mud as she grasped the training dummy again, her fingers seeking a hold on the slippery leather surface. Two hard knees to the midsection. Osoto gari. Arm bar.

Her matted red hair fell across her face as she stood again. Sol heard the creaking sound of the gate opening. She swiveled her head, blinking the rain from her eyes as she looked across the Grove at the entry. Nobody there. The gate had become unhinged in the storm, swinging back and forth with the wind.

She set her jaw, hefted the dummy back up, and repeated the sequence. The storm grew fierce and Sol did too. Her father had always said never to fight with anger, but Sol felt the rage building inside her as she hammered the dummy with another elbow.

She forgot the sequence and began pounding the dummy with her fists. She felt the rain on her face and the wet leather of the dummy, nothing else. She didn't stop as her knuckles became raw, leaving bloody streaks across the equipment's white surface.

Sol didn't stop, because she didn't want to think. She didn't want to acknowledge the truth.

Father wasn't coming.

*   *   *

Sol stood beside N'auri in one of the large translucent travel tubes of Aquarius Arena. A stream of pedestrians passed behind the two wide-eyed Grievar girls as they pressed their faces up against the glass.

"Amazing, right, Sayana?" N'auri said as they peered down into the open arena from the fifteenth floor.

The two had come up to the highest viewing point they could reach; the next five floors were Daimyo only. They had several hours prior to their auditions, and Sol agreed that their time shouldn't be wasted waiting nervously.

"Yeah," Sol replied. "Like nothing I've ever seen. And when I was little, I visited many of the—"

She stopped sharply, realizing she was about to give away too much of her identity again.

"—I mean I've heard about many of the different types of arenas around the world," Sol recovered.

Aquarius Arena was a marvel. Under the glass roof of the main dome, there were five interior combat zones set along a track, each entirely distinct. Sol scanned the translucent enclosures, mentally preparing for the upcoming audition.

"That one is called the Isle," N'auri said, pointing to the zone closest to them. "Like a small version of the Emerald. And just like up on our real Peril Cliffs, a fall in there is bad too."

The Isle enclosure was filled with vegetation, birds and other fauna, as well as an angular cliff face that ran around it, descending into waters with sharp jutting rocks.

Another of the biomes housed a massive sandpit. "That's the zone you should aim for, the Pit," N'auri said. "Though you can use more practice, we did good sand work this week."

Two of the zones set on opposite ends of the circular track looked nearly identical, each with a grass field and a circle of palms within.

"What's the difference between those two?" Sol asked.

"They look the same," N'auri said, squinting her eyes at the two zones. "They call those the Constrictor and the Ancient. One of them is like it looks, a circle of palms, just like the Ancients fought in. No frills. But in the other, the Constrictor, those are no trees. Those are walls that squeeze in on you so it gets real tight. It becomes a close fight."

Sol's gaze drifted to the biome farthest from their vantage. The zone had an eerie darkness hanging against the confines of the glass walls, like a veil.

"And that there is the Nightmare," N'auri whispered, trepidation tingeing her voice. "The Grievar that defends the Nightmare is called the Wraith. Best fighter in Lord Cantino's stable, been with him a long time. So, when the fight horn goes off, make sure you go real fast. Follow the track to one of the close zones; else, you end up in the Nightmare. No one wants to be there."

Sol nodded. After seeing her competition, she was confident she could outrun the other Grievar to the zone of her choice. She'd been second fastest up Kalabasas Hill nearly every run last semester at the Lyceum.

The two girls continued to watch the crowd fill the stadium.

"Wonder if my dafé is out there," N'auri murmured.

"Do you think he'd come?" Sol asked. "He didn't seem to be too supportive earlier."

"Right," N'auri responded. "Man is an ass but he's got reasons. Dafé really just doesn't want me hurt."

"Better learn to dance with the viper than let it find you sleeping." Sol inadvertently let the words flow from her mouth.

"Huh?" N'auri said. "Don't think there are any viper in these parts."

"Right," Sol said. "It's just something my father used to say. Basically that training something that is dangerous is better than not training it at all. So, if your dafé helped you train, you'd be less likely to get hurt."

Although Artemis Halberd hadn't been there when Sol needed him, he'd been adamant that she follow her fighting path as a Grievar. The time her father had spent with Sol between trips had been devoted to helping her train.

"I don't know if my dafé could help me even if he wanted to," N'auri said. "I remember when I was a little *kika*, he used to be a proper Grievar. Even won a match sometimes. I was so proud. Then... then Mafé died, and everything went backward. Except Dafé's belly. That, he filled with drink."

Sol was silent. Even as she'd become closer with N'auri, she still hadn't let on about her real mission. She was afraid that the slightest slip could let it all spill from her grasp, like a telegraphed punch that opened you up to a quick counter. Still, Sol wished she could talk more about her father to N'auri.

"My father also died in the Circle, like your mafé," Sol said. "I didn't get to say goodbye to him. Last thing he said to me was *You've got some work to do on that jab, Sayana.*"

It felt good to tell someone that, to talk about those last moments she'd spent with her father.

N'auri's eyes flicked across the growing crowd, as if she'd be able to pick her father out from the masses.

"*This world is not built for you,*" N'auri said. "*You got to get after it hard for change to come.* That is the last thing my mafé said to me."

A curved smile crossed N'auri's face. Sol could imagine the same sharp-toothed smile on N'auri's mother, despite never having met the woman.

"We're down there not long from now," N'auri said. "I've been dreaming of this moment for my whole life, Sayana. Fighting in Aquarius Arena. Don't care for who. In front of the crowds, the lords, could be the darkin' governor of Ezo. Don't matter to me. I'm fighting for my family, for my blood. I'm fighting for Mafé."

Sol nodded, setting her jaw as she started to feel the adrenaline pump through her veins, picturing herself walking through one of the entryways into a combat zone.

"Who you fighting for, Sayana?" N'auri asked unexpectedly.

Sol froze.

"You fighting for your dafé in the ground?" N'auri questioned.

Sol was shaking her head before she even knew it. "No."

She wasn't fighting for Artemis Halberd. She was there for her father's body. That was her mission. He needed a proper Grievar burial back home. Wet earth and dry leaves. It wasn't right he was encased in some Daimyo museum. But Sol wasn't there for him. She wasn't fighting for her father.

Just as Sol was about to reply, a tremor ran through the glass in front of them, a great vibration that shook the entire arena for several seconds. The pedestrians froze in the hallway, and the crowds out beyond the glass seemed to go static. A lightboard planted on the far wall dropped to the floor and shattered as a cloud of dust spewed from the ceiling above.

And then, just as it seemed the world would end, the shaking stopped.

"Sea tremor," N'auri whispered, and she put a hand to her forehead. "Only get one of those every few years. A sign."

Sol had never felt the world shake like that. Ezo had its flooding rains and its greatstorms that caused considerable damage to infrastructure, but never had the earth heaved beneath her feet.

Sol breathed deeply, planting her boots on the floor, ensuring there was still stable footing beneath her.

CHAPTER 12

Back to the Circle

A Grievar shall not gather in a group for any joint purpose. The path of servitude is a road that must be taken alone. Though we might work together to teach and learn martial technique, every individual must still be separate and identifiable from the mass. A mob formed, devoid of individual purpose, will only serve to detract from the greater good.

Passage One, Thirty-Fifth Precept of the Combat Codes

We got to still get our necks in it!" Dozer protested.

"We'd be down two," Knees responded, pacing across the dorm room. "Which is a lot, considering we're also missing Sol this time around. No offense, Brynn, but you be no Solara Halberd."

"None taken," Brynn responded in her cheerful fashion. "But what if we could still pull it off? I mean, what's the risk?"

"Now would be when Sol would lecture us on the exact risk of it all, probably until the sun started to rise," Knees said. "But the basics be we got Joba here with a broken knee, and clerics won't be able to patch him up full in two days. And we'd be set to face the

Myrkonians in the first round of challenges. We all saw what Bertoth did to Cego. We could skip this challenge and take a small hit to the rankings, but then we'd be missing our chance to climb. Or we fight and potentially get beat bad, in which case we be digging ourselves out of a hole for the rest of the semester."

Cego nodded, only half listening to the team's discussion. He saw the way Dozer and Knees were looking at him. Like they expected him to step up, act the team leader. Formulate a plan. Tell everyone it was going to work out, that they could win this first round of upcoming challenges against the Northmen.

But Cego didn't feel like saying those things. He felt like a liability. He still didn't know when he was going to lose control again, when the darkness would suddenly take over. It had only been a week since the incident in Tandore's class. How could he lead his team when he didn't even know if he could lead himself?

Cego looked out the window toward Ezo's Capital. The Tendrum District's white skyscrapers pierced the clouds and loomed over the lower dregs like some noble bird perched above the swamplands.

Cego hadn't walked the dregs since Murray-Ku had left. The old Grievar used to take him along the broken roads, past the dilapidated homes of Grunts and lacklights, beneath the giant abandoned bridges where the neuro-junkies camped out, to the steps in front of the old domed Courthouse where lines of poor folk waited for their turn at PublicJustice.

He wondered where Murray was right now. Hopefully, the old Grievar had found what he was looking for, but the team could certainly use his advice back here at the Lyceum. *Cego* could use his advice. Murray always seemed to know how to fight against the odds.

"Cego." Knees was standing next to him, waving his hand across his eyes. "Man, you here with us?"

"Yes," Cego said, turning away from the window and his thoughts. "Just thinking."

Knees put a hand on Cego's shoulder. "We need you here."

Cego felt like he needed Dozer to land a heavy slap to his face to get him out of the strange stupor. He shook his head. "What have you got so far?"

"All we can come up with is you, me, and Dozer match up with the Myrkonian trio in the first round," Knees said. "We need at least two of us to make it through, so that second round we'll have Abel and Brynn fresh for whichever team we're up against."

Abel chimed in. "I am ready. There is a chance Joba might be too. He says he wants it."

The giant boy nodded, keeping the smile on his face even while wincing as he tried to take a step toward the group on his hobbled leg. Abel had said that Joba injured himself training takedowns with some of the Northmen out in the practice yard. Joba had been doing fine until Rhodan Bertoth hit him with a blast double-leg takedown and lifted all three hundred pounds of him clear off the ground.

"I know you guys don't think I'm much of a fighter, but spirits be said, I'm going to prove you wrong," Brynn added as she stepped forward.

"So," Knees said, looking at Cego again expectantly. "What do you have to say?"

Cego reached into his pocket and clutched the coin that Professor Drakken had given him. He had to put his own problems behind him, take control again. He couldn't leave his team behind.

"I think you've put together a solid plan, Knees," Cego said, breaking his silence as he put his hand on his friend's shoulder. "Sol would approve."

"You want Rhodan?" Knees asked. "Wasn't sure if you be wanting to square off with another one of the Northmen instead."

"No," Cego said. "I want Rhodan. I'll be ready this time."

"All right, then," Knees said, looking at Cego with newfound confidence.

"Let's do this!" Dozer slapped Cego on the back enthusiastically, hard enough to send him nearly sprawling to the ground.

Cego steadied himself and took a hard look at the team in front of him. A mismatched bunch, that was for sure. Lacklights and foreigners, lumbering giants and agile sprites. And himself, whatever he was. But a worthy group of friends; his teammates had sacrificed themselves to help him over the past two years. Cego would give anything for them; he'd go through the Deep's darkest passages and back to keep them safe.

Cego nodded determinedly. "Let's do this."

*   *   *

Stepping out onto the challenge grounds again was like a swift kick to the gut, reminding Cego of everything that had happened there.

There was an electricity in the air for the Lyceum's first combat contest of the semester, Level Two teams at the center of attention. The first challenge was a time when precedent was set, where new students could establish themselves as forces to be reckoned with or the old class could reassert their proper place in the rankings.

Cego looked out toward the stands of eager spectators housed within the tall gymnasium. As usual, both students and faculty were in attendance: watching to appraise the Level Twos, gauge upcoming opponents, or simply sit back and enjoy the violence that Grievar were born for.

Cego rotated his arms in small circles as he jogged alongside his teammates, following a track along the perimeter of the grounds. Several of the other Level Twos also warmed up on the track, though most students were front and center, testing out their techniques within the dormant Circles set on the canvas.

"There's Rhodan," Knees said, jogging beside Cego as he pointed out the hefty Myrkonian shooting penetration steps, back and forth like a caged bull.

"We see Rhodan all the time," Cego noted as he made extra care to loosen up his right arm.

"Right, but most of the time, you're not about to square up with him in the Circle," Knees responded.

"Are you trying to mess with Cego's head or something?" Brynn chimed in, running beside the two boys. "At least where I'm from, it's best to focus on your own fight game, not the guy across from you."

"Hey, you've been on this team for what, a month?" Knees said defensively. "Me and Cego came up together. Fighting in the slave Circles. Taking the Trials. I know him. Second time around against a beast like Rhodan, he needs some better strategy."

Unfortunately, the only strategy Cego had been focusing on was keeping control of himself. He absentmindedly reached for his pocket to palm the coin that Professor Drakken had given him, but the gift was back in the dorm with the rest of Cego's possessions.

Dozer pulled up beside the three Whelps. "I thought we were warming up," the big boy huffed. "Not trying to wear ourselves out for fight time."

Knees chuckled at Dozer, who was already breathing heavy. "I just hope your opponent has a worse gas tank than you. I mean, he looks big, but you never know."

"I got this," Dozer said between breaths. "Just need to stop... running so much."

The big Grievar pulled off the track as Cego, Knees, and Brynn continued at their brisk pace.

"How about you, Knees?" Brynn asked. "You got a strategy for your opponent?"

"Yeah," Knees was quick to respond. "Watched a bit of him on local SystemView last night. Before he got to the Lyceum, he actually had a bunch of fights up in the Northlands. No Knighthood or anything like that out there. They be putting their boys in the Circles early, even before proper schooling."

"What did you see?" Cego asked, now feeling stupid for not having checked out any of Rhodan Bertoth's past footage.

"He's a southpaw, for one," Knees said. "Got a good shot, like most of these Myrkonians. But I think I can wear out his legs with some nice low kicks, then bring it up high later in the round when he's fiending for a breath."

Cego nodded, though he wasn't fully listening anymore. He was focusing on his breathing, willing the world around him to calm. He expelled the air from his abdomen and slowly brought it back in, letting it climb his spine and disperse across his limbs.

He'd practiced ki-breath on the island every day of his life, sitting on the black sand beach alongside his brothers, Sam and Silas.

The breath is stronger than the mind. The breath does not wander; it does not live in the past or future. It is there with you now, only as it draws inward and then out again. If you want control of yourself, you must control your breath.

Even now, with the knowledge that the old master was some figment of his imagination, some wiring of electric impulses between synapses, Cego trusted the man's words. In a way that he could trust no one else. Farmer was forever a part of him, integrated into Cego's hard wiring, and whether that guided him on the right path or wrong didn't matter. It was the path he was on.

Cego breathed again deeply as he continued to pace the perimeter of the grounds.

His little brother, Sam, never had the patience for ki-breath. The boy had been like one of the sand runners pecking at the shore, never stopping, always frantically seeking a new sunken mollusk to dredge up.

But Silas had breathed as if he were the wind or the tide. A permanent fixture, a force of nature that didn't need to contemplate past or future.

It felt good to acknowledge them. Cego had tried to force his brothers from his mind since last year. He hadn't been able to fathom their existence along with the groundswell of changes within his brain and body.

But now, jogging the challenge grounds, the place where everything had changed, Cego felt his brothers within him.

He saw Sam's freckled face, heard the little boy's singsong voice on the ocean wind. He saw Silas's stern, disapproving eyes. That curved smile on his thin lips. And his fist flashing toward Cego, always one step faster.

Cego's brothers were alive. Not just in his mind, like the old master or the island. His brothers were out there in this world, somewhere. Cego had seen Silas with his own eyes on SystemView. His brother had stood over the body of Artemis Halberd, fresh to the kill, flashing that same smile Cego had been so familiar with.

And if Silas was alive and fighting, then Sam was out there too. *Somewhere.*

"Hey, you planning on taking a nap before the fights or what?" Knees woke Cego from his reverie.

His friend was standing in front of him. Cego realized he'd stopped his jog. He was standing at the center of the challenge grounds, staring out into the crowd.

"No," Cego said. "Just remembering."

"I got you." Knees put his hand on Cego's shoulder, squeezing it hard. "But I hope you're remembering how Rhodan nearly put his fist through your head a while back, because we're on."

"What?" Cego asked.

Knees pointed to the wide lightboard planted at the center of the rafters. Dozer's face was on display, trying to look tough in the promotional image. Then Knees's and Abel's and Brynn's visages flashed across the screen. Cego was last. His image stared back at him, captured last year; his golden eyes had been hungry then to prove himself to the faculty, to the other students, to Murray.

Now Cego didn't care about proving himself to anyone. He just wanted control of himself again. He needed to know he was the master of his path, his destiny.

Cego breathed deep as he stepped toward the awaiting Circles.

*   *   *

This is a normal reaction to auralite.

Cego repeated that to himself as bluelight spectrals rose in the air around the metallic Circle he stood in. Auralite, and the bluelight spectrals that the alloy attracted, made the crowd seem louder than it was. The element influenced fighters to follow the mob mentality. Cego had never had a problem with bluelight before, but now he kept second-guessing himself, afraid he'd lose control again.

Rhodan Bertoth stood across from him. Despite the Lyceum's insistence that students wear their second skins during their challenges, Bertoth had ripped the blue material from his back as soon as he reached the Circle.

"Darkin' thing's itchy," the Myrkonian boy said as he flexed his considerable muscle mass.

Cego couldn't help but smile. He liked Bertoth, despite knowing the boy was about to try to take his head off.

"Don't hold back this time," Bertoth growled intensely as they squared off, waiting for the sounding bell to chime. "I want to see the real Doragūn in action."

Cego nodded, glancing up as their biometrics flashed across the large lightboard above. Bertoth was a beast. The Northman's physical stats were well above average in nearly every category, particularly size and strength. The bell rang out, cutting through the din of the crowd and bringing Cego's gaze back down across the Circle.

Bertoth came at Cego with the same berserker fury that he'd channeled in their first fight, a direct sprint across the Circle to throw an anvil-sized fist at Cego's skull.

Cego managed to weave his head but was still caught off-balance by the brunt of Bertoth's body weight following the fist. Cego steadied himself with an outstretched hand and turned to meet the Myrkonian again.

Bertoth gave Cego no breathing room to set a pace. Two clubbing overhand rights, which Cego ducked, followed by a knee blasting up the middle. Cego lowered his hands defensively as he felt his ribs shudder beneath the knee's impact.

With Cego's hands down, Rhodan smiled and launched his head forward like a battering ram. It was the same skull strike that had put Cego out earlier in the year, so he bent his entire body backward to avoid it this time. Rhodan capitalized on the opening with a front kick that sent Cego tumbling to the ground.

Cego was almost relieved to feel the canvas against his back, somewhere he might be able to control this beast of a boy.

The relief didn't last as Bertoth drove his hips into Cego's feet to set up a torrent of ground-and-pound, his massive fists rearing up and crashing down like an avalanche. Cego covered his face, squirmed his hips, kicked up hard to stay the onslaught.

Cego landed one of his upkicks, a hard heel to Rhodan's chin that would have stopped most in their tracks. But the boy didn't seem to notice; his forward motion continued as he rained down blows, one rattling Cego's head against the canvas. Warm blood seeped into Cego's eye and blurred his vision.

Perhaps Cego should not have been so worried about keeping himself under control when he was up against this beast, Deepbent on breaking him in two. He needed to focus on controlling Bertoth somehow.

Cego caught Rhodan with another square upkick, this time to the chest. He used the opportunity to spring to his feet, circling around and away. He held his hand up to his face, tracing the deep gash above his eye.

Rhodan had slowed just a bit, a barely discernible sluggishness to the Myrkonian's footwork, his incoming punches not quite as hard to track. Still, any one of those anvils that landed flush would be the end.

Cego breathed. He countered one of Rhodan's punches with two quick jabs, the second sliding over the boy's shoulder and finding his chin.

Rhodan stopped. He nodded at Cego before slapping his jaw several times, far harder than Cego had punched it.

"My little sis hits harder than that!" he yelled, his hands up toward the crowd as he waded in again.

Cego sighed as he wiped the blood from his eye. Why couldn't he just match up with someone his own size for once?

Rhodan came with a quick cross, followed by a thundering body shot. Cego moved into jab range again, throwing several in a row, catching Rhodan beneath the eye but still not fazing him. Cego fired a low leg kick that felt like it met a steel beam.

Bertoth grinned and swiped out an open-palmed slap, catching Cego on the side of the head and knocking him back to the canvas. Cego's ears shrieked like a horde of cave bats. He rolled over his shoulder and back to his feet, wobbling as the crowd's cheering seemed to increase a decibel, urging him to wade in for more punishment.

Fighting this Northman felt like fighting a force of nature. Whatever Cego did, Bertoth kept coming forward, with a seemingly unstoppable momentum.

Cego's mind drifted as he floated in and out of Bertoth's range, weaving, covering up, countering. Surviving.

*   *   *

Silas stood in front of Cego.

The two brothers squared off within the ironwood Circle, where blood and sweat soaked through the tatami from thousands of rounds of training. The Circle where Cego had cried and laughed alongside his brothers. The Circle where he'd spent the majority of his life.

"Try again," Silas said.

Cego tried harder than the last time, attempting to blast through his older brother's defenses with a series of punches and kicks.

Cego's movements seemed perfectly timed, and yet Silas was always faster, a step ahead and ready to parry or evade. And just when Cego was off-balance, Silas countered with a lightning-quick strike, not made to put Cego out but to teach him a lesson.

This time it was a round kick to the neck that left Cego stumbling.

"Try again," Silas repeated.

"I've been trying!" Cego yelled. He hated when Silas made him react in anger.

"Yes, you have been trying, but not successfully," Silas said calmly, infuriatingly.

Cego came in again at Silas, this time with power behind his shots. He rammed a series of jabs forward, followed by a cross and then a spinning elbow. Nothing touched Silas. He taught Cego his lesson again with a stinging kick to the thigh.

His brother seemed to be on another plane of combat. A force of nature that was out of Cego's control.

"What should I do?" Cego asked, almost ready to give up, even though he knew Silas wouldn't let him.

"Try again" was all Silas repeated, that curved smile now crossing his face. His brother was enjoying this. Enjoying Cego's failure, over and over.

Cego looked out beyond the ironwood Circle they trained in, to the black sand beach set beneath the sand dunes. There, the old master sat cross-legged. He'd been seated the entire day on the shore, unmoving, practicing his ki-breath since the sun rose with the low tide. Now dusk dragged the waters back in, wetting the old master's grey robes. Cego knew Farmer would let the water flow around him, envelop him. He'd become a part of the waters, his robes swirling in the currents like seagrass.

Cego looked back to his brother. "Okay," he replied as he returned Silas's smile.

He would be like the old master and let the water flow around him.

Cego threw another series of attacks at Silas. No different from the last several bouts. Double jab, cross, round kick. In and out. Hard cross, body shot. Cego didn't throw his attacks harder or faster than last time. As expected, Silas parried. But when Silas launched his own counter, Cego was ready. He sidestepped to avoid the front kick and responded with a hook that grazed Silas.

Silas stopped and nodded approvingly. Though Cego had barely touched his brother, he'd unbalanced him. Something he'd never done before.

Let the tide come in.

*   *   *

Bertoth was the tide. The mountain that could not be moved. The raging river that could not be dammed.

Cego could not divert Bertoth's path, but he might flow around him.

Every punch the Myrkonian threw, Cego accepted, countering with several shots of his own but not expecting them to derail the big Grievar. Cego's counters were part of the natural course of the fight. Bertoth responded in kind but Cego kept pace, always throwing two counters for each incoming strike.

Soon, it was Bertoth who stepped back with pause.

He smiled. "This is what I was waiting for. This is the Doragūn I've heard of."

Rhodan roared, invigorated, charging forward again with a manic grin on his face. The Myrkonian became a whirlwind of violence. Cego joined him, dancing with the fury, allowing Bertoth's offense to fully emerge.

Cego was still standing after the storm was weathered. Now it was his turn. He launched a volley, peppering Bertoth with a rapid series of jabs and leg kicks. He cut the Myrkonian across the brow with a hard cross, bleeding him just as he'd bled Cego earlier in the bout. He railed a spinning side kick into the Northman's gut and followed with another kick up high, cracking Bertoth in the jaw to send him stumbling.

Cego felt alive. The crowd's eyes were on his Circle. The blue-light let him hear them murmuring from the stands, wondering if he'd lose control again.

Listening to his body, Cego scanned himself for any signs of the incoming dark energy.

He was still there. He was in control. This was his fight.

Bertoth was visibly winded now, sweat beading his brow. Yet the Northman still came forward. He didn't know how to stop. Cego ducked a looping shot and responded with a series of body punches, each thudding into the Myrkonian's midsection, sapping what remained of his stamina. Cego was getting faster, as if he were feeding on Bertoth's vigor.

Cego threw another buckling leg kick and then a switch kick to the other side that slammed into the boy's midsection.

Bertoth shot in for a desperate takedown, but Cego easily sprawled his legs back. He pushed Rhodan's head to the ground, whirled away, and came back with a knee to the face. Bertoth's nose exploded as he fell to the canvas. Cego could swear he heard the ground shudder.

The Northman started to crawl back to his feet. Cego hoped Bertoth wouldn't stand again, but of course, he did. The Myrkonian staggered toward Cego, swinging like a wild animal with the strength he had left.

Don't hold back, Bertoth had told him.

Cego wouldn't hold back. He launched two quick jabs, bring-ing Bertoth's hands high, and then stepped into a spinning back kick, putting his entire body weight into the movement, landing his heel against the big Grievar's liver.

Bertoth paused for a moment, looking at Cego as if he didn't quite believe what had happened, before doubling over. The Myrkonian dropped to the ground and curled into a fetal ball.

The spectrals dispersed to the air and the buzz of auralite dis-sipated just as rapidly from Cego's mind.

Still, though, he heard the chant from the crowd loud and clear, ringing across the grounds.

"Doragūn! Doragūn!"

*   *   *

Cego barely recalled talking to his team between challenge rounds. The adrenaline and lingering high from defeating Rhodan Bertoth still fogged his mind.

Knees had won and Dozer had lost in their first-round matchups.

"Didn't know Myrkonians knew leg locks," Dozer had repeated after his fight, visibly upset that he'd been submitted by his opponent.

"Toe hold off the inside cross," Knees had chided his friend. "You should've seen that coming a mile off."

Most importantly, the Whelps had made it through the first round. Abel and Brynn stood ready for the second round of challenges, and Cego was already back in the Circle, as if he'd never left. The rubellium alloy and the redlight glowing around him were designed to heighten heart rate and amplify fear, resentment, and anger. In rubellium, more than ever, Cego needed to make sure he didn't lose control.

Especially considering his opponent this round. Shiar.

Cego couldn't think of anyone he hated more than the boy who stepped into the Circle across from him, staring back with those haughty eyes.

Shiar was a lacklight who posed as a purelight. He was a vicious boy who thrived on the pain of others. One who tormented and killed for pure pleasure.

Cego felt the hairs on his neck stand up at the mere sight of Shiar. How much he would love to smash his hand through the boy's face, get ahold of him and tear his ligaments apart, shatter his bones.

But Cego knew he couldn't let the rage take hold like it did last year. Standing in this same spot across from Shiar, he'd lost himself to the blacklight within him. That would not happen again. He was there for his team, for his friends. Not for his own vengeance.

Cego steadied his breath and observed his opponent. Shiar looked like he'd put on about thirty pounds of muscle since last year. His shoulders were broader and his legs thicker. Of course, the boy was a growing Grievar, but Shiar's growth was unnatural. He'd likely been popping stims, probably with the help of Professor Zyleth and the upper levels.

Crimson spectrals lifted from their dormant position on the Circle, casting their light on the combatants. Cego could feel the rage sitting in the pit of his stomach, rising with the wisps as the fight bell sounded.

Shiar advanced as Cego stood stationary, waiting for the boy to come to him. The two had danced to this rhythm before.

Just before Shiar came within striking distance, Cego sensed something out of place. Shiar's eyes shifted back and forth. The boy was hesitant.

Was it fear? Did Shiar remember the punishment Cego had dealt him last year?

The two boys circled each other, probing with the occasional range-finding jab.

Cego launched the first strike: a quick side kick that Shiar evaded.

Shiar returned with his own kick combination, low and then high. Quite fast but far too telegraphed.

Cego replied with a jab-cross, pushing Shiar back on his heels, and followed with a hard leg kick that found its mark.

"Keep on that one," Knees yelled from the sidelines. "Punish him!"

Shiar winced. His eyes darted toward the stands.

Cego capitalized on the opening with a quick right hand and uppercut that sent the boy reeling backward.

Shiar regained his composure with two quick jabs before clinching up, grasping behind Cego's head to pull him in. Cego flowed with the movement. He dropped to his knee and circled his arm beneath Shiar's legs for the kata guruma throw. Shiar sensed the imbalance and shifted his weight backward, but Cego seamlessly transitioned into a single-leg takedown, grabbing the boy's thigh and driving forward to deposit him on his back.

"Be keeping him floored," Cego heard Knees's voice from the sidelines. "No escaping from the Lyceum's best grappler!"

Cego closed the distance quickly, knowing he had the clear advantage on the ground. He drove in with his head, pushing Shiar's chest flat, while wrapping his arms around the boy's back in a tight grasp. Shiar desperately attempted to writhe away, unsuccessful despite his newfound strength advantage.

"No," Shiar whispered under his breath. "I can't do it here."

Cego nearly stopped his offensive, not sure what to make of Shiar's strange words. Likely some mind game the boy had devised to gain an edge.

Shiar shoved Cego back with his steely forearms and swung his hips away, before scrambling back to his feet. He clearly wanted to keep this fight standing.

Cego nodded. He'd give Shiar what he wanted.

Cego dropped low as if to shoot for a takedown but instead launched a fist into Shiar's gut. He followed with a powerful uppercut that found the boy's chin.

Shiar dropped to a knee and wiped the blood from his face.

Cego let him stand. He could feel the rising urge to punish Shiar for everything he'd done. He wanted to hurt him.

Shiar grinned, blood filling the gaps between his teeth. Cego had seen that smile before. He'd seen it when Shiar had killed his friend Weep, as the boy had hammered his boot into the little boy's skull.

Shiar took an unorthodox stance, one hand forward and the other cocked beside his head, as if he were feigning a punch.

"Shiar be up to something," Knees yelled. "Watch for the counter!"

Cego stepped forward and threw a cross that Shiar wove his head around, but found his target with his next strike: a thudding body shot that smashed into Shiar's rib cage.

Shiar's eyes glinted as he endured the punch with a grunt. He'd let it come through. Shiar was setting up a counter, though a seemingly sloppy one: His right hand arced toward Cego.

Cego ducked the punch with ease, but as it passed over him, a flash of blue caught the corner of his eye.

He didn't have time to consider the strange light before Shiar was on him again with a straight cross.

This time, Cego saw it clearly. Shiar's fist lit up like an azure flame.

Cego instinctively sucked his stomach in and jumped back. Shiar's strike had clearly fallen short.

But then why was Shiar grinning like that?

Cego looked down at his stomach. His second skin had burned away, revealing a roaring bloody gash beneath. Cego stumbled backward as he stared at the gaping wound. Searing pain raced through his abdomen like a shock wave.

Shiar cackled gleefully as he stalked forward. The boy's fist sparked to life with blue fury again as he threw a winging haymaker. A fan of electric light spread from his fingers, sizzling as it sliced toward Cego's head.

A spectral fan. Cego instantly recognized the weapon he'd seen earlier this semester in Professor Zyleth's classroom. Daimyo tech in Shiar's hands.

How could Shiar be so bold, so blatantly breaking the Codes? He was concealing the weapon, only the size of a coin, in the sleeve of his second skin, but still—couldn't anyone else in the crowd see the fan as it flared to life?

Cego looked to the sidelines, desperately searching for help as he backed away from Shiar.

"Keep on him, don't let up," Knees yelled, unable to see the blood now soaking Cego's dark pants.

Lightboards flashed across the challenge grounds and glowing spectrals floated through the air. From a distance, the flash of light in Shiar's hand must have appeared as nothing more than a strange reflection, some optical illusion.

But the weapon was no illusion. Cego reached down to feel the gash on his stomach. It was deep; the fan had cut through his flesh like a scythe through a blade of grass.

Shiar stalked him like a predator, his weapon humming and ready to release its lethal charge within the span of a punch. That's why the boy wanted to keep the fight standing. On the ground, Cego could grasp Shiar's hands to restrain him and Shiar couldn't activate the weapon so easily with a flick of the wrist.

Cego needed to take the fight back to the ground, fast. He already felt faint; he'd bleed out if the contest lasted much longer.

He threw an outside leg kick and jumped back as Shiar loaded his weapon hand up, advancing slowly, a wide grin spread across his face. Cego started to shoot for Shiar's forward leg, but the boy merely waved his hand to stop him in his tracks. Cego couldn't clinch up. He couldn't get past the weapon's lethal arc.

If he couldn't come in from the front or side, he needed to attack from beneath. He'd seen Sol practicing the technique before she'd left. A springing forward roll toward an opponent to entangle their legs and topple them like a tree.

Cego had barely practiced the technique, just a few times in the training room with Sol, but he needed to take the risk. The alternative was getting sliced in two by Shiar.

He faked a backstep and then dove forward full speed. Shiar lashed out with the crackling fan, but Cego was already beneath him, wrapping his legs at the knee.

Cego pushed his hips forward and felt Shiar's balance begin to give way. But Cego's legs were covered in slick ichor, his stomach wound still spewing blood. Shiar ripped free from the entrapment and launched back to the offensive.

Cego watched helplessly from the ground as an overhand right sliced down at him. Shiar snarled as his weapon blazed blue. All

Cego could do was hold his arm up in defense and wait for his body to be cut in half.

Suddenly, Cego felt an immense heat rise in his arm, a volcanic torrent of energy racing up from within. The fan's electric current met Cego's raised arm.

Everything exploded.

A tremendous white pulse of light obscured Cego's vision and roared in his eardrums like a mech engine.

The world twisted around Cego in a tornado of brightness and pain. He reached forward, grasping at the unyielding light.

Flashes of electricity formed into faces. The old master's wrinkled face watching the waters. Silas, wrapped in shadows, trudging through the snow. Freckle-faced Sam, huddled and shivering in the dark. Murray-Ku, torn down and hunched over a bottle. Sol, with the wind and blue skies at her back.

The faces spun manically, crying and laughing and screaming at Cego. The ground rose up beneath him, his body rooted to the cold canvas. He opened his eyes to see the challenge-ground rafters above, still spinning in silence until they stabilized into a static frame.

Cego's ears popped and the world became intact again, filled with screams and the piercing wail of a siren and the stifling smell of burning flesh.

He reached to his stomach and felt the gash still there, weeping warm blood onto his hand.

His head lolled to the side. There, across the Circle, lay Shiar.

He was on fire.

CHAPTER 13

Another Traveler

The knee is both one of the weakest and most integral structures within a Grievar's body. Thus, a Grievar should be practiced in attacks directed at the knee in order to severely disable an opponent. From standing, the oblique kick is an effective technique for keeping an opponent at bay while also causing damage to the knee. From the ground, the heel hook is a versatile attack to tear vital ligaments within the knee joint. A Grievar should be well practiced in both these techniques.

Passage Four, Twenty-Third Technique
of the Combat Codes

This world they've built, it is not for us.

He trudged through the storm again, unyielding snow blasting back at him. Winds raged and howled, cutting his vision with icy white sheets.

Every step forward was a hardship, every breath of frost a battle. But he savored it. It was real.

He knew the ache coursing through his muscles was real, the frost biting his skin was real. He was real, finally. He'd been released from his cocoon of darkness. After waiting so long, he could walk this world. He could follow his path.

Soon, this storm will come to them.

He knew what would happen next before it even came. Over the hillside, the torchlight flickering through the storm. The cabin in the distance. The voices of life and laughter echoing from within, and then the urge, coming on strong. The door flung open to the frigid night air, the cries of terror. The blood and silence and the wind howling across the chimney.

He licked blue blood from his hands, savored the taste of fear and death.

And then he was outside again, back in the storm. He screamed into the night, a primal howl vibrating his throat.

He called to his pack dispersed across this world. They were out there in the night, ready for him to come and take his place. They needed him. They'd been sheep for too long. With him, they would become wolves once more.

Snow covered him as he screamed into the wind again. They had taken everything from his kind: honor, wisdom, and knowledge. And freedom, most of all.

He felt the familiar electric anger coursing through his veins. The blacklight. The rage boiled within and then pulsed from his skin. The snow that had fallen on him evaporated like a phantom in the night air.

He walked forward through the snow, steam rising from the earth in his wake.

Soon, we will find our path home.

*   *   *

Silas didn't travel with the fanfare.

The flag-laden caravan trumpeted as it entered each Kirothian district. The Knights paraded in front of the townsfolk, like pieces of gentry goat freshly butchered and set for auction.

He'd not be a part of it. So, Silas followed alongside the Knight battalion, parallel to the road in the higher-elevation forest, mounted on his roc as it trotted amid the barren trees. The bird's three-pronged talons left their fresh mark on the snow.

"*Sathedah.*" Silas barely whispered, but his roc stopped in its tracks, as if mech-wired. The wide-eyed bird swayed back and forth as it caught its breath. Steam trailed up from two palm-sized nostrils on the top of its beak. It had been a long journey, at least a hundred miles in the last day. But he'd kept up with the caravan running on the strength of mechs: Enforcers and rumbling tanks and old, rusted transports.

But his roc was tired now. Silas would let it rest for the night, just as those mechs below would charge their onyx and rubellium cores. The bird ran and then rested to recover. No tools, no tech needed to make it better. No need to improve what was perfect already.

As Silas dismounted, the cold wind lifted his cloak and attempted to cut into his black leather second skin. He rustled his roc's neck feathers to calm it.

"Karo," he whispered. Silas had named the bird on a whim when they first rode together, the beast barely strong enough then to support his weight.

Silas pulled kindling from his rucksack and set to work starting a fire as night fell on the Kirothian wild. He knew his roc was not the largest or fiercest of beasts that prowled the northern forests. Gar bears the size of tanks with claws like daggers. Or tuskers that were known to charge and gore men twice their size.

He tethered Karo to a nearby elm and sat to munch some dry bread as the red dusk gave way to the eerie blue of night.

Karo's head perked up. The roc could always hear the faintest of footfalls long before Silas. Even Silas could hear the runner coming from a mile away, though. A clumsy, flat-footed scout, sent from the Kirothian caravan camped down the hill. The boy was out of breath by the time he reached Silas.

"Sir…Silas," the boy sputtered, his breath visible in the cold night air.

Silas did not speak; he stared at the boy, scanning the scout's freckled face.

"We set up camp down in the ravine," the boy explained, as if Silas couldn't clearly spot the light streaming from below.

The boy continued. "Marshal Vlador wanted to see if you're prepared for Zytoc Province. He said your presence would be greatly valued."

Silas gave a slight nod. He'd do what was required of him. The fanfare, speeches, posturing, they left a bad taste in his mouth. But he needed the Kirothians, just as they needed him.

Silas was their hero. He'd dispatched the famed Ezonian Knight Artemis Halberd with ease.

They wanted to parade him around the land with their battalion. Tarthyk, Kakenstan, Lathen, and now Zytoc Province. Each city the same as the next: Vlador speaking lofty words to a crowd gathered at the city center, his Knights surrounding him wearing their full Kirothian reds. Most of the crowd too bit-less to even afford their next meal.

Vlador would raise his fist to the air triumphantly as he'd recall Artemis Halberd's fall, again and again, as if he himself had brought the famed Knight down. And then he would beckon Silas from the shadows to show him off like a prize roc.

Silas noticed the boy staring in silence, looking down at his hand with wide eyes.

Silas pulled his black sleeve up to the elbow to let the boy see the full flux tattoo.

A silver wolf with gleaming red eyes reared its head and gnashed its teeth at the edge of Silas's wrist. The flux was hungry for violence.

The boy stepped back, eyes still wide. "Is it…?"

"Shirōkami," Silas said. "The white wolf."

It was almost as if the boy wished to reach out and touch the beast, but he stopped himself, remembering his orders.

"Will you be there?" the boy asked.

Silas examined him for several more moments in silence. "Where are you from, boy?"

"I've just come from the camp down below—"

"No, where are you originally from?" Silas whispered. "Your home."

"Gaslyk," the boy responded timidly. "A little village in the western reaches, not far from the Desovian border."

"Do you miss your home, your family?"

"Uh…" the boy stammered, likely thinking Silas was trying to trick him. "I'm very grateful for the opportunities the marshal has provided me."

"You think you show weakness by missing your home, boy?" Silas questioned.

"No, no." The boy's breath caught. "It's just that down there with the battalion, no one ever talks about their homes."

"Do not follow like a sheep," Silas said. "Tell me the truth."

The boy met Silas's burning eyes. "Yes, I do miss my home. Every morning I wake and every night at camp."

Silas nodded before he suddenly cocked his head to the side, listening. The boy stared at him in silence for near a minute.

Finally, Silas relaxed. "What's your name, boy?"

"Varik."

"Tell Vlador I'll be at Zytoc."

And with that, the boy was off sprinting back through the forest, whether to avoid the beasts of the night or another minute with him, Silas wasn't sure.

CHAPTER 14

Free to Fight

A musician in training may believe there to be only seven notes on their lyre, and an apprentice painter might see only twelve central colors. But the masters see beyond that; they can decipher the myriad of mixtures to produce harmonious melodies and glorious artworks. Each Grievar has only four limbs and a head, and yet using these appendages in combination, an infinite number of techniques are at a master's disposal.

Passage One, One Hundred Fifteenth
Precept of the Combat Codes

G ood luck," Sol said to N'auri, clasping the girl's wrist firmly and looking her in the eye. "Your mafé would be proud of you."

The two girls stood in one of the bulbous joints of the track that ran around Aquarius Arena. Grievar contestants waited in the wide room, stretching and warming up to prepare for the coming auditions.

Sol felt like a rat trapped in a maze. The instructions they'd been given were to simply run as fast as they could to their combat zone of choice. The first to make it to an entrance would be the first to fight in that zone, where a Grievar from the lord's personal retinue would be waiting.

"Where I'm from, we don't wish for luck," N'auri responded. *"Kinvasa bevadia."*

Sol had heard the utterance from some of the other native islanders preparing to fight.

"Find yourself fighting," N'auri translated.

Sol nodded. *"Kinvasa bevadia."*

Sol squatted and reviewed her strategy. She'd decided to take N'auri's advice and break for the Pit. Sol had considered the Nightmare zone briefly as a way to distinguish herself; she'd practiced blindfolded fighting with her father, though she wouldn't consider herself an expert by any means. But the darkness that hung over the Nightmare looked formidable; it looked *heavy*.

The Grievar in the room jumped to their marks as the announcer began his countdown. Each stood on a designated spot around the circular room, ready to sprint in one of two directions around the track.

"Ten, nine, eight, seven..."

Sol looked over to N'auri out of the corner of her eye, facing the opposite way. The Emeraldi was still scanning the crowd outside. Having her dafé there must be more important to her than she'd let on.

"Six, five, four, three..."

The Grievar standing next to her, one of the twins she recognized from the administration room, looked back at her with fierce eyes and grinned. Sol nodded back.

"Two, one... go!"

Sol sprang forward as two portals opened on either end of the room. She was set on reaching the Pit first. She didn't even make it to the track's entry, though, before she sprawled across the floor. The twin beside her sprinted ahead and out the portal. He'd tripped her.

Sol returned to her feet and followed the boy onto the track. In her periphery she saw several of the other Grievar entangled in combat, trying to stymie each other from getting the head start. Nowhere in the rules had she heard that the contestants could start their fights before they'd even reached a zone.

Fair isn't worth roc dung in combat. What's fair is determined by the winner, whether they fought by the rules or not.

The stern teachings of Artemis Halberd were certainly there with her in Aquarius Arena.

Sol sprinted toward the first zone, either the Ancient or the Constrictor; she couldn't tell. The entry portal was sealed shut, which meant that a Grievar had already claimed the zone. She continued past, focusing on each step, not the massive blur of the crowd that surrounded the track or the shouts she heard farther ahead.

She'd just set a solid pace when she came upon an unexpected sight in the tunnel: another Grievar lying face-first on the floor.

"If it isn't our little princess," a voice came from just ahead.

Timault stood with his arms crossed, blocking Sol's way. She stopped and eyed the mustached slaver with caution.

"Just a bit of a nap for that one." Timault nodded to the twin on the floor, twitching. "He'll be up shortly but not before he's lost chances at the lord's favor."

Sol thought about trying to make a quick break past the man— she was certainly faster—but it was too much risk if he got a hand on her. The difference between an opponent squared up front or at a blind angle was significant.

"Why don't we both continue on our own path and get to the zone we want?" Sol reasoned. "I'll even give you a head start."

She felt confident she could take Timault on, but sustaining any injuries in the process would hurt her chances of winning against one of the experienced fighters within the combat zones.

"You think the lord is just looking at what we do in the zones?"

Timault sniffed and spat a gob of viscous liquid on the floor. "He wants real fighters in his stable. Men who do whatever it takes to win. That's me. Ain't you, princess. Nice little performance you gave earlier, but I'm not some desk-spawn Grievar you can drop like my friend. So, why don't you hang tight here until Papa Timault's all done, then you can take whatever's left over."

Sol could see the man wasn't going away easy. She stepped forward. "Now's your chance to turn around and reconsider what you're doing here."

Timault's eyes narrowed as he took an answering step. "What's a pretty thing like you doing here, anyways? Could still swear you got Daimyo blood running through you, princess. There's many a Courtesan House on the Isles where you'd fit in better, find yourself a nice bit-wage."

Sol growled and lifted her hands to a fighting stance.

"All right, princess," Timault said as he spat again. "If that's the way you want to dance, we can do it the hard way. Just don't say I didn't warn you."

Timault closed the distance, walking Sol down with his hands by his sides. She'd fought bigger Grievar before, put her speed against greater strength. Sol needed to stay outside the pocket, counter, throw the man off-balance, and then pick her shots.

He continued to pace forward with his hands down, letting Sol back up and circle. She threw range-finding jabs, but Timault bobbed his head and smiled as he kept coming.

Just as Sol was lulled into the slow pace, Timault burst forward with unexpected speed and grabbed her with a bear hug. Sol exploded her hips backward and framed in front of the man's face, focusing on breaking his grip before he ended up on top of her. Out of instinct, she countershot for his leg, connecting and lifting the man's foot.

Stupid. Timault was too strong. He pushed his leg down, bringing Sol's head toward the ground, and dropped a hard elbow directly to the back of her skull.

The world melted. The translucence of the tube, the blur of the crowd outside, the ringing of the announcer on the megaphone, all became a gelatinous blur.

Sol knew she was on the floor; she could feel the smooth surface beneath her cheek. She heard Timault's voice from above.

"Told you you're not meant for this, princess." The man chuckled.

A warm gob of spit splattered on her face, followed by a boot pressing hard to her neck.

Maybe Timault was right. Maybe they were all right. She'd gotten this far, fought her way through the Trials, performed well in the Lyceum. She'd gotten by with meticulous work, planning, strategizing, optimizing her performance for every opponent she'd stood across the Circle from.

But when it came down to it, when she was face-to-face with this man with his boot on her throat, slowly squeezing the life out of her, what did she have? She was a little girl, the daughter of Artemis Halberd, always sheltered beneath his massive shadow.

Now her father was gone and Sol was nothing.

*   *   *

Jab. Jab. Jab.

Jab. Jab. Jab.

Sol's red hair matted her face, covered her eyes, yet she kept punching the wooden practice board. Over the past several days, her knuckles had bled, scarred over, bled again, blistered, and calloused from repeated strikes to the wooden plank, which was now permanently crusted crimson.

Jab. Jab. Jab.

Her father's final words echoed in her mind; she couldn't rid herself of them. It's all he'd said to her before he left.

You've got some work to do on that jab.

Nothing she'd ever done had pleased him. He'd always asked for better. No matter how hard she worked, Sol couldn't live up to

Artemis Halberd's lofty expectations. Even from the day she was born a girl, the Grievar champion had looked down at her with forlorn eyes, as if she'd failed him already.

Jab. Jab. Jab.

Sol felt the hot flush of anger rushing through her as she threw the punch repeatedly. She'd believed that she could release the emotion, as she usually did, with some time at the practice board. She'd sweat it out, feel the rage seep through her pores and escape in her heavy breath.

This time, the anger wasn't leaving. So, Sol kept punching.

A week had passed since she'd found out about her father's death, Artemis Halberd's great failure in front of the world, falling in a heavily contested bout on foreign soil.

Jab. Jab. Jab.

Why hadn't he said something else to her that day before he left? Something she could take with her? Some inspiration for the tests that lay ahead for Sol's second year at the Lyceum?

You've got some work to do on that jab.

And now he was gone, without anything to say to his daughter, again.

Jab. Jab. Jab.

Sol punched harder and faster, ripping open her calloused knuckles again. The blood spattering the wood dripped to the floor of the empty practice room.

Her fist wasn't even hers anymore. She watched it move in front of her eyes as if it were thrown from another body. She heard the dull thud as it hit the practice board but didn't feel the impact through her numbed-out nerves.

You've got some work to do on that jab.

She kept punching, not even breathing anymore. Tears streaked her eyes and fell to mingle with the puddle of blood and sweat beneath her.

"Ahh!" Sol screamed at her father for leaving, for dying. She

screamed at the Kirothian Grievar for killing him, the one they called the Slayer. She screamed most of all at herself, for failing, over and over, for not being the brood that Artemis Halberd had wanted.

"Sol." She heard her name, though she kept punching.

"Sol!"

"Father?"

She must be delusional, hearing him there in this empty practice room.

"I'm working on my jab," she said through clenched teeth as her fist slammed over and over into the board.

"Sol!"

A hand was on her shoulder. She grabbed it, instinctively dropping to her knees and threading her arm, tossing someone over her shoulder onto the hard floor. Seoi nage.

"Ouch!"

Sol looked down through sweat and tears. Cego. Her friend was lying on the ground, holding his head, looking up at her with his worried eyes.

Sol panted, finally letting her arms rest at her sides. She looked at Cego, not knowing what to say, not even bothering to wipe the tears from her face.

He got up slowly.

"Sol," Cego said. "We've been worried about you. The whole team."

"I'm sorry" was all Sol could muster.

"Don't be sorry," he said. "You've every right to be feeling sad. The way you found out, on SystemView like that. With everyone, the whole world watching. It's not supposed to be like that."

Sol let her legs fall out from beneath her, sitting on her knees across from her friend, feeling the exhaustion of several sleepless nights finally touch her. "That's not what bothers me," she said. "That's not why... not why I've been here."

Cego waited patiently, sitting across from her. Shadows rippled through the practice room.

"I'm angry." Sol felt ashamed saying it. "I feel like I can't get rid of it. Usually, I can do something about it. I can change what I don't like. This time, I feel like I don't have any control over it."

Cego nodded. He'd always been a good listener.

"I can sense it in my stomach, just sitting there," Sol said. "It's like a weight. A heaviness. And I don't know what to do."

"I understand," Cego said.

A heavy cloud passed outside, darkening the room.

"I feel it too," he said. "The weight of my past. Everything I've ever believed is a lie."

Sol looked up at her friend, sensing the gravity of his words.

"I can't say it all, not right now," Cego said. "But I want you to know. Of everyone, I want you to know. But I'm still figuring it out myself. I want to get it right in my head."

"Figuring what out?" Sol asked quietly. "What's happened?"

"I used to believe I was from some place," Cego said. "I used to believe I had a family. I used to believe I was...someone."

"Someone?" Sol touched Cego's hand, squeezing it. "What do you mean? You are someone. You're here, talking to me."

"I know," Cego said. "But I'm not. I'm different."

Cego's hand was ice-cold. She kept her hand encased around his, as if she could impart some warmth to him.

"I'm different too," Sol said. She wanted to tell him everything. Her guarded secrets. But Sol's breath held and caught her words like a defensive hand dropping to guard a body shot.

She held Cego's hand and the two sat silently across from each other.

"I'm not telling you this so you feel bad for me, though." Cego broke the silence. "I'm telling you because I think I know a way out. Out of the darkness. A way to lift the weight pushing you down."

Sol looked at Cego expectantly.

"Don't run from it," Cego said. *"I've done that. I think I've been doing that my entire life. Running away from my past, trying to escape. And I know now that path only leads deeper into the darkness."*

"So, what then?" Sol asked. *"If we can't get away from it, what can we do?"*

"Embrace it," Cego said. *"Welcome the weight of your past. Don't run from it. Stand in front of it and let it flow through you. Let it make you stronger."*

Sol let go of Cego's hand, looking him in the eye. Something was different about this strange boy she'd grown close to over the past year.

"You're free," Cego said. *"When you no longer fight it, when you're no longer held down by your past, by the burden of every moment that's come before, you are weightless. You can fly. You're free to follow your own path. Not the prescribed path that someone told you, or the path that someone's created you for. This is your path, Sol. Stop running."*

Sol breathed as if she hadn't breathed since the day she heard news of her father.

"Stop running," Sol whispered.

*   *   *

Timault's boot crushed down on Sol's neck, but she didn't care. She could die now, let this man destroy her. Yet she'd rather not die. She'd rather continue on. This was her path.

Sol grabbed Timault's boot, far too heavy to push off, rolled onto her shoulder, and curled her legs around his planted leg to snare it. She used the leverage of her crossed legs to pull her head from beneath his boot and swept the man to the ground by twisting her hips.

Sol immediately dropped back to snag the blocky corner of Timault's boot in the crook of her elbow. She ripped, torquing his heel with her entire body. She felt the ligaments in his knee snap, a series of audible *pops*.

Timault screamed but Sol wasn't done. She kept her legs entwined and turned her hips back to their starting position. And then she repeated the process, ripping at his knee another time with greater force, feeling for any intact connections, listening as any remaining tendons snapped, hearing him scream again.

Sol disentangled her legs and stood over Timault. He tried to stumble to his feet, but Sol helped him find his place back on the ground with a hard front kick to the face, crumpling his nose and bouncing his head against the floor.

Timault lay still with his eyes open as Sol looked down at him, sitting on his chest.

She wanted to spit in his face as he'd done to her. Timault was a bad man. N'auri had told her of the things he'd done. But the crowd was watching. The lords were watching. Perhaps Father was watching, somewhere.

"You've been right all along," Sol whispered as she moved in closer, looking into the man's fearful eyes. "I do have Daimyo blood. My real mother, she was a courtesan. I never knew her. And my father. My father was Artemis Halberd."

Timault's eyes widened. His mouth started to open, but Sol slammed her fist into his face again, several times, further bludgeoning his smashed nose until he was calm again.

"I can't let anyone know that secret, though," Sol said. She slid her arm around his neck with her head braced against his opposite shoulder. She began to squeeze.

Timault started to writhe, instinctively thrashing his hands to push Sol off him, but she kept her body close and her strangle tight. Sol held the position, focusing on her own breathing, looking up calmly at the crowd beyond the glass, many with their eyes bearing down on her even though she wasn't even within a combat zone. Timault had been a favorite to get the lord's attention.

When she was satisfied, Sol stood, letting Timault's head loll to the side listlessly with a string of spittle hanging from his mouth.

The twin lying beside them had woken from unconsciousness and run ahead during the scuffle. Sol didn't care.

She walked down the hallway at a measured pace. It didn't matter what zone she ended up in. She'd handle whoever stood in front of her, in whatever environment.

She was done running.

CHAPTER 15

Blind Again

The omoplata is an often underutilized offense from the ground. Most Grievar opt for the leg triangle as a choice strangle from bottom position; however, against a larger and stronger opponent, the triangle's effectiveness can be negated. Against such powerful foes, the omoplata will serve to keep weight off the attacker while systematically applying breaking pressure to the shoulder.

Passage Six, Nineteenth Technique of the Combat Codes

Cego thought he must be blind again.

"I am with you. I am your friend," a voice said to him.

Cego's eyes were open, but he only saw white, like a snowstorm blanketing him.

Once, Cego had pretended to be blind. When he'd first arrived to this world, freshly born from the Cradle and tossed to the Underground's slave Circles, he'd kept his eyes welded shut for a month to fool his captors.

Now he really was blind.

"Cego, can you hear me?" the familiar voice said.

"Yes," he answered.

A cold hand touched his forehead. Lithe fingers lifted his eyelids. Cego tried to move, protect himself, but he couldn't. His arms and legs didn't work.

"To clear your vision," the voice said again as Cego felt some liquid flood his eyes, stinging like acid.

He tried to thrash his limbs and turn his head, but he couldn't. Nothing worked. A murky shape took form in the whiteness, swimming up from the depths and breaking the surface.

Cego knew the form, the face. Xenalia.

"I'm with you. I am your friend," she said, hovering over him. The cleric looked quite worried.

"I'm not blind," Cego said as if to convince himself.

"No, you are not," Xenalia replied. The medward ceiling took shape around her face, a familiar sight in what seemed a very unfamiliar world. "The *serashi* drops I just applied to your eyes sufficiently cleared the retinal blurring caused by the blast."

"But I think I'm paralyzed," Cego said. "I can't move."

"You are not paralyzed," Xenalia answered. She frowned.

"Then why can't I move anything?" Cego asked.

"You are restrained," Xenalia replied. She lifted a small lightpad over Cego's face. It displayed a live feed, showing the medward room they were in from above. Cego saw himself, lying on the bench with little Xenalia beside him. Steel clasps encircled his feet, legs, arms, and neck. He was locked down.

"What the… Why?" Cego asked.

Xenalia held a finger to her lips, whispering, "You are in holding."

The cleric waved her hand over the lightpad to display the exit to the medward. Two large broad-shouldered forms stood guard there, armored with steel plate and black visors across their blocky heads. Cego had seen their kind before. Mech suits. Daimyo Enforcers.

He looked up to Xenalia with wide eyes. "What's happening?"

"They are restraining you until you are to be moved," the cleric replied. "You have been charged with a crime."

"What? What crime!" Cego tried to keep his voice down, though he had the urge to shout.

Xenalia applied a salve to Cego's stomach. His abdomen seared with pain as the memory surfaced of Shiar slashing the spectral weapon across his gut.

"He...Shiar, he had a spectral fan," Cego whispered. "He attacked me with Daimyo tech in the Circle."

"I know," Xenalia said. "I have observed over fifteen hours of footage from various angles of your fight. I ran the data, accounting for margin of error due to spectral flashes and illumination from the lightboards on the challenge grounds. The boy you fought, Shiar. He was employing Daimyo tech, utilizing an illicit weapon."

"So, why am I the one that's shackled to a bed?" Cego raised his voice this time, struggling against the restraints.

"They will not listen to me," Xenalia whispered. "I have told them what I know already. But they do not believe me; they will not accept the evidence."

Xenalia reached back to the lightpad and turned the display to Cego.

An official notice scrolled across the screen:

CEGO, UNKNOWN BLOODLINE, AGE FOURTEEN

BORN, UNDERGROUND OF EZO

ARRIVED AT LYCEUM, 3044 P.A., FIRST MONTH, FIFTH DAY, 15:02

CHARGED ON 3045 P.A., SIXTH MONTH, FIRST DAY, 11:34

POSSESSION OF DAIMYO WEAPONRY, EXPLOSIVE CLASS, BREACH OF THE COMBAT CODES SECTION 1, ARTICLE 1.

UTILIZATION OF DAIMYO WEAPONRY, EXPLOSIVE CLASS, BREACH OF THE COMBAT CODES SECTION 1, ARTICLE 2.

Cego read the two lines over and over, his eyes growing wide.

He was being charged for using Daimyo tech in the Circle. But Shiar was the one who attacked him with a spectral fan.

"I didn't use any weapon," Cego stuttered. "It was him; Shiar should be the one getting charged!"

Xenalia looked down before meeting Cego's eyes. "Unfortunately, that is not possible."

The cleric pointed back to the lightpad. Cego read the last charge on the screen:

MURDER WITH INTENT, GRIEVAR VIOLENCE OUTSIDE OF A CIRCLE, BREACH OF GOVERNANCE LAW, MARK 31.

Cego understood immediately. "He's..."

"Yes," Xenalia answered. "Shiar is dead. Explosive wounds."

Cego hated Shiar, but this was not what he wanted. This was not the way for a Grievar to die.

"They all, everyone at the Lyceum..." Cego trailed off, having to catch his breath. "They think that I killed him? That I planned this all?"

"I do not know what the faculty and students of the Lyceum believe," replied Xenalia. "What I do know is what the Daimyo Governance believes, which is why they are charging you. They believe you illicitly used Daimyo tech to kill a fellow student in the Circle. They will charge you for this crime and others in the halls of PublicJustice by end of week."

Perhaps Cego was still dreaming.

Xenalia placed her cold little hand over his shackled wrist. "I know the truth, Cego. I know what happened in there. I will help you."

Cego felt himself growing faint, the white edges returning to his vision, the snowstorm starting up again.

"Shiar somehow came into possession of a spectral fan." Xenalia's voice brought Cego back momentarily. "He employed the weapon during his match with you. Your body reacted to the Daimyo tech, to the incoming lethal attack, with an intense catalytic reaction. Much like the release of antibodies to combat a virus, your body released energy instead. Explosive, radioactive energy that resulted in Shiar's death. Somehow, you were not affected by the heat of the blast. But you did suffer from temporary blindness due to the high-spectrum light that the blast emitted. Nearly a quarter of the spectators in the stadium also suffered from some vision impairment."

He tried to process the cleric's rapid words. He'd somehow defended himself against the spectral weapon attack.

Xenalia continued. "The change your body is undergoing, what we spoke of days ago, caused this reaction. I'm not yet certain of the specific mechanisms employed, but it has all the hallmarks of the Grievar catalytic reaction, which is usually internal, a way for your body to heal incurred damage. Somehow, your body has adapted, evolved to make this internal defensive mechanism... external."

Xenalia's voice became fainter. Cego felt himself falling away from her, falling away from the medward despite the shackles on his body. The white edges encroached further upon his vision.

"The primary question I am still attempting to solve is where a spectral fan might have come from. Especially on Lyceum grounds, where no weapons of any sort are permissible, it is highly irregular, nearly impossible, that Shiar would have been able to obtain such technology."

Cego grunted, trying to expel the truth he immediately knew. "Zyleth."

He heard Xenalia repeat the name softly, *Professor Zyleth*, as the white of the storm fully enveloped him.

*   *   *

Cego wearily woke to the light of a spectral, one of the wisps crossing directly in front of his nose, dispelling the dense fog over his mind like a salt sniff.

He was sitting in a cold steel chair within a small room, surrounded by blank white walls and a spotless glass window set in front of him. Another room lay on the opposite side of the window, identical to his, except *that* room had an exit.

Shackles no longer constrained Cego; his neck, arms, and legs were free. He clenched and unclenched his fists, circled his arms. He could move again. He started to stand but his legs gave way like pudding beneath him, unaccustomed to carrying his body's weight.

Cego pushed himself up, using the chair for aid, his legs shaking.

"You'll be able to stand shortly," a voice came through a speaker set in the room. Cego looked up and saw an unexpected sight.

The high commander of the Citadel, Memnon, sat in the little room on the other side of the glass.

Cego hadn't seen the man since the Myrkonian march at the semester's start. Memnon's hair looked whiter, his face wearier and more wrinkled.

"Boy, are you doing all right?" the high commander asked.

Cego didn't respond. He was tired of responding to people who wanted something from him, interrogators asking him questions that he had no answers to. He stared back at Memnon with defiant golden eyes.

"I understand," Memnon said. "I understand you must be confused right now. Angry, even. Everything has moved so fast since your fight."

Cego stayed silent and so Memnon kept talking.

"But you need to understand. There is protocol to follow." Memnon eased his bulk into a chair. "Governance needs to have full control of this case. Even I can't do anything to help you, boy. The only reason I'm here speaking to you now is because I owe Murray Pearson a favor. If he knew what was happening, he'd be here by your side. Probably trying to smash through this glass in front of us."

Cego thought of Murray-Ku and felt an upwelling of despair. If Murray were there, he *would* break through that glass. He wouldn't care about protocol or Governance or anything but coming to help Cego. But Murray wasn't there. He was gone. Just like Cego's friends were gone. Sol, off somewhere on the other side of the world, and the rest of his team probably back at the Lyceum.

Cego was alone.

He'd been there before, though. Without anyone else, fending for his own survival.

Memnon reached into his pocket and produced a flat slice of hard bread. He pushed it through a small slot in the wall onto the floor of Cego's room.

Cego's stomach growled. They'd hooked him to a feeding tube in the medward, but now his body ached for real sustenance.

He hesitated, looking up at Memnon with feral eyes.

"Take it; you'll need energy for what's to come."

Cego's hunger won. He snatched the piece of bread and stuffed it into his mouth.

"That's the thing with Murray Pearson, though," Memnon said. "He's rash. But he's not often right. The fact of the matter is you've been charged with serious crimes. Possession of Daimyo tech. Murder of another student."

Cego started to protest, yell what he knew to be the truth. But he knew it wouldn't help. He stayed silent, gritting his teeth.

"Now, if you'd just come clean…" Memnon sighed, as if he'd had this conversation before. "Tell us exactly where you came into possession of the weapon, who put you up to this. I can relay that to the Judge, and *it* would certainly be willing to lighten your sentence."

Cego kept his mouth shut.

"Not to say that even with a lighter sentence you'd survive Public-Justice," Memnon said softly, regret tingeing his voice. "You must know how it works."

Cego did know how it worked, but only because Murray had

been a PublicDefender and used to rant about the entire process, especially when he was under the drink.

Entire System's shit, kid. PublicJustice is a disgrace.

"I'm innocent," Cego said, as he'd done so many times over the past week. "I didn't have any weapon. Shiar did."

Memnon shook his head and sighed again. "That little cleric friend of yours in the medward, she said as much to me. In fact, she darkin' followed me all the way up to the door of my quarters, nonstop talking. Had to shut the thing in her face to quiet her."

Cego couldn't help but crack a smile, thinking of little Xenalia hunting Memnon down.

"Whether you're innocent or not, you've been accused. Means you need to sit arguments, plead your case to the Judge. If you tell us who helped you, you'll take on a lesser opponent in your Trial by Combat."

Cego remembered Murray telling him about those who were found guilty, especially those charged by the full prosecutorial might of the Daimyo Governance.

You'll darkin' be fightin' to your grave, no matter who you are.

"I told you," Cego said again. "I'm innocent. There's been a mistake."

"Listen, boy." Memnon stood up impatiently, his weariness suddenly replaced with anger. He closed in on the glass, looking down at Cego. "I saw the footage. I saw what happened there. Now is your only chance to tell me the truth, make a deal for a lesser opponent. And this'll be the only deal I or Governance will be giving you. Most don't get this chance. This is only happening because I owe Pearson a favor."

Cego didn't care anymore. He'd take on the entire Citadel Knighthood if it meant fighting for his innocence. He didn't care if they buried him in the process.

Wherever Murray was, Cego knew that's what he would do. And Cego knew exactly, at that moment, what Murray Pearson would say as well.

"You can take your darkin' deal and shove it up the Deep side," Cego growled. "I'm innocent."

*   *   *

Cego had only seen the old Courthouse from the outside, its tall white dome streaked with burn marks from fire, its crumbling stone stairs lined with poor folk and junkies, low breeds waiting for their turn at PublicJustice, moaning, spitting, crying, clawing at one another while the dealers waited in the shadows to reclaim their prey after processing.

The interior of the Courthouse was not what Cego had expected. The halls were deathly quiet, without any of the chaos from outside, as if upon entry, the poor masses were immediately pacified. The masses were still there; Cego saw them huddled and waiting in line to gain entry to one of the many processing booths. What kept them subdued was a force stronger than a junkie's neuro habit or the rage that some Grunt sweeper felt for abruptly getting evicted from his home of thirty years.

Fear. Fear kept these men and women quiet. Daimyo Enforcers stood at attention along the wide halls of the Courthouse, armored in the full might of their mech suits. The Enforcers stood nine feet tall, muscled with auralite-reinforced steel and armed with built-in spectral cannons that could incinerate even the mightiest Grievar in seconds. The mechs stood silently, unwavering, but promising instant death to any low breed who brought chaos within the halls of PublicJustice.

One such mech dragged Cego behind it. His hands were shackled once more, chained to the massive arm of the suit. Cego had caught a glimpse of the Daimyo pilot within the mech, a little blue-veined man peering out through the circular window set at the center of the suit.

The mech jerked his hand forward and Cego stumbled, smashed to the floor and pulled along like some toy on a leash.

"Keep moving, two hundred twelve," the pilot spoke through a speaker. The man had called Cego only by that number, 212, since he'd pulled him out of the interrogation room.

Cego's legs still felt weak; his body still sought to regain its balance. For a moment, he considered letting this thing pull him like some piece of trash across the smooth Courthouse floors.

But Cego was not going to let that happen, just like he was not going to proclaim his guilt.

Cego grabbed the chain and pulled himself off the ground, straining to keep in step under the mech's shadow. They marched through the Courthouse's main atrium. He stared up at the tall domed ceiling curving toward the skylights above as spectrals fluttered through the air and descended to observe the masses moving in all different directions below.

"Cego!" a familiar voice cut through the quiet of the hall.

Dozer. The big boy was pushing up against the fencing that separated the security check from the main atrium. Beside Dozer, Knees, Abel, Joba, and Brynn stared back at Cego. His team, the Whelps, all right there in the halls of PublicJustice. How had they gotten here? There's no way the Lyceum administration would have given them the pass.

"Cego!" Dozer yelled again. "We know you're innocent! We got your back, brother!"

Cego wanted to call out to Dozer, tell him how much it meant to have someone to stand by him. But he didn't want to call any attention to his friend; he saw one of the mechs stationed along the wall take a menacing step toward the chain security fence.

Cego found Knees's eyes as he was dragged past. The Venturian looked tired, deep circles ringing his eyes. Somehow, Cego knew Knees was behind the team's visit to the Courthouse; that boy had a way with breaking the rules.

Cego felt grateful to have such loyal friends, so much so that he could feel the strength returning to his body, as if a flood of energy suddenly rushed through his nervous system.

"Where are we going?" Cego had almost forgotten he was being dragged along by an Enforcer.

Surprisingly, the pilot responded. "The Hall of the Grievar."

The mech pulled Cego out of the atrium, beneath a massive stone archway with the symbol of a fist emblazoned atop it. The Hall of the Grievar. This was where Murray-Ku had spent his time as a PublicDefender, fighting for those who could not fight for themselves, those who could not afford representation.

They marched past scores of courtrooms, some in progress with sealed portals and others open and waiting for the next case to be heard.

"I'm darkin' innocent!" a bedraggled white-haired man yelled as he was dragged out of one of the courtrooms. "I've not fought for ten years! Give me another chance!"

The guard pulling the prisoner's chain guffawed, a gap-toothed smile spreading across his face. "You'll get a chance, old man. Out in the Killing Fields."

Cego listened to the prisoner's screams echo down the hallway.

"Where are they taking him?" Cego asked.

"Quiet, two hundred twelve," the pilot snapped. "You'll find out soon enough."

As they marched in silence, Cego noticed engraved words repeating and running the length of the hall: *The light of justice shall shine on the innocent, giving them the strength to prevail. The guilty shall find no quarter, only death in the darkness.*

The mech finally stopped in front of one of the steel portals, turning and pressing its hydraulic arm against the surface to unseal it. It dragged Cego into the courtroom.

"Two hundred twelve arriving," the Enforcer announced. "Here to stand trial."

CHAPTER 16

Blood and Power

The greatest of Grievar lose their heads in the Circle. Not to say that they give in to fits of rage, or that they are literally decapitated, but that they do not look out from their own eyes at an opponent. They do not carry the weight of their head: pride and fear, past and future. The truest incarnation of combat is a headless one, a body moving in complete autonomy from mental tethering.

Passage One, Eighty-Sixth Precept of the Combat Codes

Sol heard nothing but her own breath, though she knew another Grievar was somewhere in the darkness beside her. The Wraith was waiting for her to make the first move.

N'auri's words echoed in Sol's mind. "Avoid the Nightmare, whatever you do."

But Sol's unsanctioned bout against Timault in the halls of Aquarius Arena had held her back. She'd been the last to find a Circle. And so, she'd stepped into the darkness of the Nightmare knowing she was up against the Wraith, the most feared of Lord Cantino's stable of hired mercenaries.

"I know what you're up to," Sol spoke, her own voice surprising her through the silence. "I've played this game before."

Sol thought back to the blindfolded exercises her father had trained her with, limiting her to other senses in anticipation of the next strike. But then, she'd been able to hear her father's heavy steps, perhaps because Artemis Halberd had been playing nice. This was the Wraith and he certainly was not playing nice.

She took a quiet step forward.

Even in the darkness, you can sense shape, form, feeling, Artemis Halberd's voice echoed in her head. She breathed out, tried to steady her nerves, tried to make some shape of the glistening darkness in front of her.

"You're waiting for me to move, to come into your range, so that you can strike first," Sol said, not sure if she spoke to keep her own nerves at bay or to test if any response might come from the Wraith.

Nothing. Silence. And then suddenly, a white blur whipped through the darkness, slamming into Sol's face and sending her reeling to the hard ground.

A form was standing over her, the room spinning.

"I was waiting," the Wraith whispered. "But I decided I'd wait no longer."

Sol expected the finishing blow to fall, but all she felt was the cold floor on her back. Her vision adjusted to see a pale form with glowing yellow eyes peering down at her.

Sol stood and backed away, her hands up again.

The Wraith didn't move, he just watched.

"What are you waiting for?" Sol asked, feeling a mix of anger and shame rise up in her. The man was playing with his food.

"How do we learn if we don't observe?" he said. "Don't you wish to learn?"

Sol nearly dropped her hands, so strange was this question coming from a man who meant to take her head off.

"*This is no class.*" Sol gritted her teeth and took a step toward the Wraith.

The Wraith shook his head, frowning. "*Combat, whether two children play-fighting in the grass or two Knights battling for the sake of their nations, must always be for the purpose of learning.*"

Sol took another step toward the man, who remained utterly still. "*These trials are meant to determine who gets on to Cantino's team. And I need to be one of those fighters.*"

"*Another mistake,*" the Wraith said. "*You should not need anything. If you need, you've already lost.*"

"*Stop this.*" Sol raised her voice. "*I'm not your student. I'm not here to learn your lessons. Just fight me and be done with it.*"

The Wraith stared at her in the darkness. "*You may still learn—*"

Sol took the opportunity to launch a long side kick at the man, but his hands were up and wrapped around her leg in an instant. Sol somehow found herself back on the floor and this time the Wraith didn't wait, he didn't observe.

But as the first kick found her ribs, Sol couldn't help but think the Wraith was still attempting to teach her a lesson.

*   *   *

"Can't believe you stood toe-to-toe with the Wraith for that long," N'auri exclaimed. "In the Nightmare!"

Sol shook the cobwebs from her head. *Toe-to-toe* was an overstatement. In the darkness, he'd been too fast, too slick. She hadn't stood a chance.

Sol gingerly drew her hand across her brow, touching the now-cauterized gash from the strike that had put her out. She'd sustained quite a bit of damage before that blow: broken ribs and nose, a torn knee ligament, and a nearly shattered hip. Somehow, she'd kept standing back up, kept moving toward the Wraith until he'd finally put her out.

Miraculously, Sol felt nearly whole again, just two days after the match. Lord Cantino's clerics had worked diligently to repair Sol while she'd been evacuated by Flyer to his personal medward.

N'auri had not taken quite as much damage in her close-quarters bout within the Constrictor, a dislocated shoulder and broken hand. The Emeraldi girl had been cleared from the medward and visited Sol with stories of life from within the lord's famed stables.

"By the way," N'auri said, "I seen Wraith around the stables a few times now. He's not all bad. Quiet, sure, but he even showed me one of those kick combos he used to put you down."

"Great," Sol chuckled. "Not only does he easily finish me, he then spreads the way he's done it."

N'auri laughed, baring her sharp white teeth. The girl looked happier each time Sol had seen her since they'd arrived at Lord Cantino's compound. And Sol could understand why. N'auri's life had been devoted to gaining entrance to this house and she'd done so, in spectacular fashion. N'auri had soundly defeated her opponent during the audition, tossing him on his head with a sacrifice throw.

Sol still wasn't quite sure how she'd received the lord's favor after getting dismantled by the Wraith. She had a feeling it was related to her encounter with Timault on the track. That fight had played through Sol's head repeatedly throughout her medward stay. Had the man deserved the fate Sol had handed him?

As if reading her mind, N'auri grasped Sol's shoulder. "Sayana, I see you worrying when your face scrunches up like that. Let it go. Timault deserved it. Believe me, I knew that man and he did many bad things. If you didn't put him in the dirt, he would've killed you, maybe even gotten someone else."

Sol nodded. Timault had gotten in the way.

Sol slid from the medward cot and attempted to stand. She gingerly placed weight on her hip and then walked beside N'auri around the room. At least two dozen cots lined the medward, each equipped with its own tech suite and manned by a personal cleric. The facility was nearly as expansive as the one at the Lyceum, despite being owned by a single Daimyo.

"I want to see the grounds today," Sol said suddenly. She'd felt like she was missing out, recovering in the medward while the rest of Cantino's new crew had been free to explore the compound. "Show me around."

"You sure you discharged?" N'auri asked. "Don't think the lord would be happy if one of his new Grievar didn't heal up proper before she went exploring around his manor."

Sol had always followed the rules. She'd prided herself at the Lyceum for precisely taking instruction. After her audition experience, though, something had shifted within her, like the sea tremor that had shaken the stadium.

"That's all right." Sol smiled. "A little fresh air could do me good."

N'auri led Sol along by the crook of her elbow as they made for the medward exit.

*   *   *

Lord Cantino's manor oozed opulence. Every inch of the grounds was perfectly manicured by a horde of Grunt servicers who were shipped to the manor every morning and then descended back to their dregs by evening.

It was midday when Sol and N'auri stepped out from the medward onto the high path, and so the servicers were in full force in the gardens, clipping hedges, polishing giant granite statues and fountain heads, washing the manor's massive bay windows.

"Wow" was all Sol could say.

"I know, right?" N'auri responded. "I'd always imagined this was how the lords lived; just didn't think it was actually true."

Sol had not been raised in the spartan manner of many Grievar. Although her father had abided by the Codes, the influence of Daimyo culture had been clear at the Halberd house. They'd been provided luxuries by Governance that would make most Grievar blush in shame. But Cantino's compound made Sol's home look like a shack.

The two continued along the balconied path that circled the gardens. From this vantage, peering over the high hedges, Sol could see the world: palaces hovering above the sloping hillside like birds in a headwind, and farther down the city, a staccato of grey stone rooftops and brown market awnings, spilling onto rose-hued shores with minuscule boats docked in the gridded harbor, and finally the sheets of verdant water bleeding to the horizon.

The girls walked down a pair of marbled stairs into the gardens. They stopped to watch as a palanquin passed in front of them. Four stout laborers carried the gilded box on their shoulders. Within sat a woman veiled with an elaborately patterned silk. A courtesan.

"One of the old Grievar told me a few ladies come through here every month," N'auri whispered to Sol. "Spend a few days in the lord's manor to do their job and then leave, just like that."

Sol met the woman's dark eyes as she passed.

She imagined her own blood mother getting carried around on one of these silly things, draped in fineries and jewels worth the value of a village. Her mother wouldn't have come into the light of day to see Sol's father, though. The little Sol knew about the affair was that it was a highly guarded secret. Most courtesans only attended to their own kind: Daimyo lords and politiks who paid enormous sums to carry on their bloodline with the most pure-blooded women.

And so, the question still burned in Sol's imagination: Why had a courtesan attended on her father? Though Artemis Halberd had been one of the most famed Grievar on the planet, he was still just that, a Grievar. What had brought them together...to make her? It was one of the many questions Sol would never be able to ask her father.

The girls continued to explore the winding paths of House Cantino, getting lost in the maze of hedges. They walked along the fenced perimeter of the lord's aviary, which housed at least a dozen magnificent rocs of varying colors. Sol thought of Dozer back at the Lyceum; the big kid would have been slack-jawed to see the flock of giant flightless birds in front of her. She felt a twinge of guilt, being so far away from her home and her team of Whelps.

The two continued past trimmed topiaries and exotic flower beds, before they crossed over a miniature wooden bridge and sat beside the tranquil koi pond beneath it.

"When Mafé was living here, I could never come visit," N'auri said as she tossed a smooth stone into the pond, watching the colorful fish dart away.

"Why not?" Sol asked.

"Grievar are stuck here," N'auri said, looking down at their reflections in the water. "We're not allowed to see family, friends, anyone from a past life. When I was little, I wanted more than anything to come see her. I imagined what it would be like, living in a castle in the clouds. Getting all the best training, learning from teachers only the lords could afford. More than that, I just missed her."

N'auri's words conjured Sol's own memories, desperately wanting her father to come home from some far-off fight, and then the sharp pang of loneliness that hit her when he didn't return.

"How often did your mafé come home?" Sol asked as she lobbed a white stone into the pond and watched the ripples expand outward.

N'auri shook her head. "She didn't. Hard to gain the lord's favor. But it's even harder to get out. The lord doesn't take kindly to his Grievar turncoating, giving over team secrets to some rival."

Sol's entire plan was focused on earning her way into Cantino's house. She hadn't yet thought about getting out, let alone making an escape from a fortresslike manor while transporting a large and very famous Grievar corpse.

A sleek Flyer streaked through the sky above them, shaking the serene garden with a seismic thunderclap, before descending into the center of the compound.

"Patrol keeps a sharp eye on anyone going in and out of here," N'auri whispered as the two looked up in awe.

"Your mafé, how long was it that you didn't see her, before she... she died?" Sol asked.

"Oh, I saw her," N'auri responded, flashing her sharp smile. "I saw her many times during those years she was in the lord's service."

"How?" Sol asked expectantly, her heart skipping a beat. Perhaps she was so lucky that her friend had discovered a secret exit from the grounds.

"Of course, in the arena," N'auri said. "I watched all her matches. Though it cost me every bit I earned, and though I sat in the dankest section with a bunch of Grunt bootleggers, I saw Mafé fight."

N'auri's eyes sparkled like the Emerald Sea. "And she fought. Hasn't been a Grievar since, man or woman, that fought like Maliora Pali."

A loud chime sounded across the compound. Sol had heard the noise in the medward but had no idea what it signified.

"I'll enjoy their foods, though," N'auri whispered as she stared down at her reflection in the pond. "I'll drink their fresh water and build myself strong with their meats. I'll sleep in their soft sheets and get rest and wake up stronger and better each day. And I'll be ready when time comes."

The bell sounded again.

"That's dinner," N'auri explained as she grabbed Sol's hand. The two headed back toward the manor.

*   *   *

Sol managed some restraint with the feast set in front of her, though not much. After being fed intravenously in the medward for the past few days, she was hungry for real sustenance.

She palmed a freshly baked sweet roll and chomped its crunchy exterior, letting the buttery dough sit on her tongue before gulping it down.

Beside her, N'auri was not nearly as restrained. The Besaydian girl was a whirlwind of hunger, grabbing breads, fruits, and meats from the decorative table at a frenetic pace. Her feeding was like her fighting, chaotic: She ripped into a ram shank, wielding the large bone like a club, before suckling at one of the juicy pink papayas grasped in her other hand.

Sol couldn't help but smile at her friend. She'd seen N'auri laid bare moments before in the gardens. And yet, there she was in full force at the dinner table, making even the veteran Grievar sitting across from her chuckle.

"You know you freshlings going to be running the floating stairs later this eve?" A man with a shaved head spoke from across the table. "Hope you'll be able to keep that all down."

N'auri looked up momentarily from her food lust. "Sure I will," she spoke through a stuffed mouth before continuing to clean her plate.

"Don't you remember doing the same, Gull?" a thick-shouldered Grievar woman said from beside him. "Coming into this house dirt-poor off the streets and suddenly having everything you could ever ask for?"

The Grievar named Gull nodded. "Yup. Though I think I must've paid for it a few weeks at least. Spent more time on the pot than training. Just trying to give these kids a heads-up. That's what we veterans are here for, right, Nayassa?"

"Right, just saying we were all sitting in those seats once," Nayassa replied.

Sol glanced farther down the long table at the man who had been silent for the entire meal, barely touching his food. She'd only seen the Wraith before in the darkness of the sphere, but he looked no less imposing in the daylight. The man's skin was pale with long, jagged scars crisscrossing his face.

Nayassa noticed Sol's gaze. "Oh, don't mind Wraith," the lady said. "He's just pissed that he's got to help out now with fresh recruits. Normally, all he does is train."

Nine Grievar sat in the ornate dining room, five veterans and four new recruits. Sol recognized one of the twins from the auditions sitting beside N'auri. The bulky man sitting farther down the table was unfamiliar.

"Over at Lord Kothos's, we had *chalik* meat every night," the man said in a nasally voice. "Don't see that here."

"Better not let the lord hear you taking dislike to what he's given you, turncoat," Gull said. "Just because you think you were someone in another house doesn't mean you're anyone here yet. We all prove ourselves in House Cantino."

"I'm no turncoat," the big Grievar replied. "Your Lord Cantino brought me on board because his team was getting old and couldn't handle the pressure. And he paid well. I'm simply going where the bits are."

Wraith suddenly stood up directly across from the man and stared at him with full-moon eyes. "Jon Mayv," he said in a monotone. "You performed well for Lord Kothos. Only one loss in his service over a span of six years. Do you remember who you lost to?"

"I'm better than I used to be," the man said. "I was a freshling back then. Plus, you got the drop on me; I wasn't used to fighting in no close quarters then—"

"Oh, I do remember that one," Gull interjected. "Wraith put you down in all of twenty seconds without breaking a sweat."

Jon's face flushed red as he stood to his full height, nearly seven and a half feet. He slammed his hands down on the table, shaking the entire thing and sending silverware crashing to the floor. "Why don't you try and do that again, right here!"

The Wraith stood and calmly folded the dining cloth from his lap, setting it neatly on the table.

"Told you this would be a good meal," N'auri said to Sol, her mouth still stuffed with food as she watched the two men square off.

A voice from afar suddenly turned the heads of all in the room. "Now, now, my friends! We are all one team here at House Cantino.

Our past is irrelevant when we are working together to accomplish a goal."

Lord Neferili Cantino strode into the room from the far entrance between two massive marble pillars. The Daimyo looked diminutive beside the two thickly armored Grievar who flanked him.

"Sit, sit," Lord Cantino said, not raising his voice, and yet the veterans in the room were quick to take their chairs. Sol and N'auri slid back to their seats and kept their eyes on the man they'd heard so much about.

Sol examined Lord Cantino as he took the seat at the head of the table. He looked like many of the nobles Sol had encountered visiting her home every year to entice her father. Pale, paper-thin skin, with translucent blue veins that tangled on his face and snaked down his neck.

Something was different about Lord Cantino's eyes, though. Most Daimyo had dark eyes. Sol could only describe Cantino's eyes as pitch-black: two holes in his skull that leeched color and light.

The lord sat straight-backed in his jewel-studded chair as he scanned the table of Grievar, the two armored guards standing at attention to either side of him.

"Conflict is necessary," Cantino broke the silence. "That is why we are all here, correct? Conflict. You Grievar fight in the Circles, each of you born from the embers of war with the blood of combat running in your veins. You can feel it, no?"

Cantino sipped from the crystal goblet of wine set in front of him. "Now, I have heard your kind talk, whispers in the armories or fits of anger in the city streets. I have heard the Grunt servicers in the gardens. You think I cannot hear? They say Daimyo are lazy. They say we rest easy in this world while the rest toil. They say we partake in the spoils of labor and war."

He took another long sip of his wine, swirling the vintage around his mouth before swallowing.

"But I am also a creature of conflict, like you," he said. "Business, trade, diplomacy, technology: These are my fists and feet, my elbows and knees. You would not quite understand how it works, but I can wield these tools with the precision that you can throw your sharpest punch."

Cantino waved his hand and Grunt servicers emerged from the pillared entryways lining the hall with crystal glasses in hand, placing the drinks beside each Grievar.

"Not all Daimyo are the same, though," Cantino continued. "There are many lazy ones, those nobles and lords who have luxuriated too long and let their minds waste away. These men are useless, with no purpose in the world, no ambition to grasp for, no self to constantly better. And there are also Grievar who have lost their way. Those who have forgotten why they are here, to fight, to serve the greater purpose of the Codes and enable the cogs of trade and diplomacy to turn. There are those who have become weak."

Cantino's black eyes found Sol and she felt as if she were staring down a bottomless well.

The Daimyo lord stood and slowly walked to Sol's side. He placed a frail hand on her shoulder, and she felt a shiver run through her.

"Sayana," he spoke her false name as if he had a bad taste in his mouth. "Perhaps you wonder why you have made it onto my elite stable of Grievar?"

"I will prove myself—" Sol began.

"The Wraith puts everyone down," Cantino interjected. "You are not weak because the Wraith defeated you in the sphere. In fact, what I observed is how many times you stood up again. I watched how much punishment you were willing to withstand to try to gain entrance onto my team. Though your skill is lacking, you can learn these things. But some things cannot be learned..."

Cantino continued on past Sol around the table and she breathed a sigh of relief. "You have been chosen carefully. I take pride in the Grievar I keep in my stable. You stand for me. And so, I expect you to conduct yourselves properly, to show no weakness."

Cantino walked to Jon Mayv's side, placing his hand on the big Grievar's shoulder. The two men's heads were nearly of equal height despite Jon sitting in his chair.

"Now, Jon, I understand you are quite a proud man," Cantino said. "That is why I sought you, paid a heavy bit-price to make the trade for you from House Kothos. It is not your size or strength that attracted me when I watched your footage. It was your pride, the way you held yourself."

Cantino nodded to one of his armored guards, who obediently trotted to his side. He held out his hand and the guard unholstered his spectral rod and placed it in the lord's grasp.

Sol felt her heart jump. She could see a sudden panicked look on the big Grievar's face as the lord hovered over him.

"You do need to understand," Cantino said. "Pride is a good thing. It keeps us sharp, strong, ambitious. But pride must not interfere with duty. And your duty is with me now, Jon. You are here to serve House Cantino with every fiber of your body. To not do so... is weakness."

Cantino flipped a switch on the handle of the rod and it started to hum as a spectral spark twirled around the bulb-shaped head of the weapon. The spark picked up speed and the buzz of the weapon filled the marbled room.

"I understand, I understand," Jon stammered, sweat beading his forehead. "Won't happen again, Lord Cantino."

"Yes, I believe you, and thank you for that," Cantino said. "But we are all creatures of habit. You know this, right? And we must learn our ways by habit. We must burn these habits into our minds, into our bodies."

"I know, I'll—"

Jon's groveling was cut short, transformed into a bloodcurdling scream as Cantino lowered the fully powered spectral rod onto the Grievar's shoulder.

Jon's body moved as if it were possessed, like his bones were trying to escape from his skin. His huge arms flailed and smashed down repeatedly against the table in front of him, shattering the dishware into shards. His head rocked back while his eyes rolled into his skull, before slamming forward into the dense wooden table, nearly cracking it.

Sol stood along with N'auri and the twin, the three new Grievar jumping upright as if they'd woken from a terrible nightmare. The veterans across from them stayed seated without surprise, watching the spectacle. The Wraith picked at his food.

Sol smelled a terrible burning, as if the Grunt cooks in the kitchen next door had sizzled a loin of ram for too long. It was Jon's shoulder sizzling beneath the rod. As the lord lifted the weapon, a thick patch of Jon's skin clung to it, and beneath it, the white of bone gleamed from within the charred cavity.

Lord Cantino casually handed the rod back to his guard and returned to his seat. Jon Mayv remained facedown on the table.

"With that bit of unpleasantness out of the way," Cantino said, "let us raise our glasses to our new Grievar and to our preparation for the first challenges of the year at Aquarius Arena."

Cantino held his glass in the air, motioning for those at the table to do the same. The Wraith, Gull, and Nayassa lifted their drinks high with their heads low in salute. N'auri and Sol met each other's eyes.

The girls slowly reached for their glasses.

"To House Cantino!" the veterans barked. "To House Cantino!"

CHAPTER 17

The Trial

Justice shall not be considered by a Grievar. A Grievar fights and dies to serve the greater purpose of society but does not consider why. Examination of the complexities of justice will only render a Grievar ineffective on their true path toward combat mastery.

Passage Three, Thirty-Third Precept of the Combat Codes

Though the courtroom was certainly unique, unlike any room Cego had ever stood in, one thing captured his attention immediately. Not the small crowd sitting within a glass box behind him, nor the three additional armed Enforcers stationed at all sides of the room. Those sights did not turn Cego's head.

It was the translucent tube, spanning from floor to ceiling and set at the center of the courtroom, that drew his gaze. Within the tube floated a creature that Cego had only heard spoken of in hushed whispers, in the manner that Abel spoke of his old gods.

A Bit-Minder.

Cego had thought Daimyo were strange-looking creatures, but the Bit-Minder made those blue-veined people seem ordinary.

Male or female, Cego couldn't distinguish. The thing was the size of a small child but with arms and legs barely formed, as if the growth of such limbs were unimportant to its existence. The Bit-Minder's head took up most of its body mass, a bulbous, wrinkled organ with a squished face and two tiny black eyes, staring out from the tube directly at Cego.

Cego felt a shiver run through his body as the Enforcer pushed him into a seat directly in front of the Bit-Minder, locking his manacles to the chair. He had no idea what to do; in the Circle it was obvious, no matter the opponent that stood in front of him. But here in this foreign courtroom, with this even stranger creature observing him, Cego was lost.

"Do not be lost, Grievar-child," the Bit-Minder somehow said without moving its mouth, a voice that sounded soft yet seemed everywhere at the same time.

"Everything that has led you to this point, your entire path before this moment here in my courtroom, has already passed. You look at the stream of time behind you to gain perspective, but you can never swim it again. And everything that will happen in the future, the evidence we will hear, the upcoming arguments of the defense and prosecution, the verdict that I bestow on you, your success or defeat in Trial by Combat; those moments are set in time as well. You cannot do anything to change the future, what I know will come to pass."

The Bit-Minder paused for a moment, staring at Cego again as if it could see through him. Spectrals wafted down the tube and began to spiral around the creature.

"So, Grievar-child, set your mind at rest. For you, like all your kind, are feeble in this way. This is a blessing. You should not preoccupy yourself with such things as the past and future, for there are minds far greater than yours to occupy those realms."

Cego realized he'd forgotten to breathe. He sucked in air.

"Now let us begin." The little creature waved a vestigial arm awkwardly and the spectrals dispersed, some floating past Cego as if obeying orders.

Cego managed to pull his eyes from the Bit-Minder for a moment to glance around him.

Set above and behind him was a glass box with several seats inside. Cego didn't recognize most of the spectators until he saw Commander Memnon sitting up there, looking large next to several diminutive Daimyo. Beside Memnon was another face that Cego did not welcome. Callen Albright, head of the Scouts.

"To those present," the Bit-Minder addressed those in the box, "know that I care not whether the truth is spoken today in my courtroom. Truth, coming from the minds and mouths of lesser breeds, is a subjective reality, inherently flawed and based on limited cognitive processing. I will process words, expressions, actions, even what is not said, and come to my judgment with the utmost certainty. Today we hear the arguments of guilt and innocence of the Accused, two hundred twelve."

Cego tried to meet Commander Memnon's eyes, but the big Grievar stared straight ahead.

"Let us call forth those who will conduct the arguments." The Bit-Minder waved his tiny hand and the spectrals flocked together over the entryway to the room. "First, our Prosecutor."

The entry portal slid open and a Daimyo stepped through, wearing a grey robe and a strange bulbous cap. He walked to the front of the Bit-Minder's tube and addressed the creature as the spectrals trailed him.

"Prosecutor Makail Wenceforth, representing the Governance of Ezo, on this day, eight of the sixth month, in the year three thousand forty-six post-Armistice, seeking the guilt of the Accused, two hundred twelve."

The man bent his head toward the Bit-Minder. "I thank you, Minder of Justice, for passing judgment on this day, in your infinite wisdom."

The Prosecutor walked stiffly to one side of the room, standing behind a small wooden pedestal. His dark eyes landed on Cego sitting in the middle of it all.

The Bit-Minder spoke again. "And now we welcome our Defender. The Accused is not of age to provide his own defense during arguments, and so he will be provided a PublicDefender set forth accordingly by the Governance of Ezo."

The spectrals again flocked to the portal to welcome the Defender.

Cego's eyes widened when he saw the man who entered the courtroom. A Daimyo, just like the Prosecutor, walked forward assuredly.

"Defender Tamail Zyleth, representing the Accused, on this day, eight of the sixth month, in the year three thousand forty-six post-Armistice."

Professor Zyleth.

Zyleth bent his head to the Bit-Minder. "I thank you, Minder of Justice, for passing judgment on this day, in your infinite wisdom."

He walked to stand behind a pedestal on the opposite side of the room. "It should be entered into the System, Minder of Justice, that I have a prior relationship with the Accused, two hundred twelve. He is a student within the class I teach at the Lyceum."

Zyleth met Cego's eyes, unblinking, without emotion.

Cego's mind raced. Zyleth must have provided Shiar with the spectral fan, the weapon the boy had attacked him with. The professor was the one who had caused all of this. And now Zyleth was the one who was supposed to defend him and prove his innocence.

The Bit-Minder interrupted Cego's racing thoughts. "We congregate, on this day, eight of the sixth month, in the year three thousand forty-six post-Armistice, to determine the guilt or innocence of the Accused, two hundred twelve, who is charged with possession of Daimyo-designated technology, intent to utilize Daimyo-designated technology as a weapon, and premeditated murder utilizing Daimyo-designated technology. We will proceed with arguments immediately. First, our Prosecutor, Wenceforth, will provide his case to the System."

The little grey Daimyo stepped to the foot of his pedestal as the spectrals swarmed him.

"Seven days ago, at the Lyceum, during the first of the semester's challenges, our Accused utilized unauthorized technology to slay a fellow student," Wenceforth said dramatically, waving his hands in the air.

"I intend to provide irrefutable evidence to the System that the Accused not only stole the unlawful weaponry in question but also then premeditated its use for murder within the Circle. We are a nation of Codes. The heart of this matter strikes not only the very soul of Ezo's legal system but our civilization's long-standing armistice between nations: Grievar must never utilize weaponry for combat. They are authorized to use only the tools that nature has given them for the sacred purpose of standing in the Circle, representing those souls who cannot fight. They fight so the rest shall not have to."

Wenceforth slammed his hands down on the pedestal. "Due to the gravity of the crime and the clear proof we have at the ready, the prosecution requests only the most suitable opponent in the Accused's upcoming Trial by Combat. We request the Goliath."

The Bit-Minder stared out with blank, beady eyes. "The prosecution's Trial by Combat request is heard. As you should already know, Prosecutor Wenceforth, whether your request is granted will be determined by the evidence presented. Now let us hear from Defender Zyleth."

Cego barely heard the Prosecutor. He was helpless, shackled there to the courtroom chair. He couldn't even voice his own defense, and now this man, Zyleth, was set to speak for him.

Professor Zyleth met Cego's eyes as he spoke pointedly.

"The Accused was a good student," the professor said. "He is a good student, and he will continue to be one. I know this because I've had many students, both Daimyo and Grievar. His desire to learn, to attain new knowledge, outshines the thirst of even some of the greatest minds in Ezo's Capital."

Why was Zyleth complimenting him?

"Which is not to say that makes him innocent of the charges we've heard," Zyleth said. "No, someone who thirsts for knowledge in such a way certainly would be able to commit crimes, and perhaps they might even be more likely to explore that which is forbidden, unlawful, or out of reach."

Here it is. Now Zyleth had started to turn the blade, sink it into Cego's chance of proving his innocence.

"But did the Accused commit these crimes?" Zyleth asked, raising his voice. "I am in a unique position to evaluate, because the first charge stipulates the weapon in question was stolen from my own classroom. From my own unique collection. And I know, for a fact, with hard feed evidence, that it was not the Accused who stole the spectral fan. It was Shiar, the boy who was killed in the explosion at the Lyceum."

Cego's heart raced. Zyleth *was defending him.* The professor was telling the truth.

"I submit my first piece of evidence." Zyleth reached into his robe and placed a small sliver of metal on the pedestal in front of him.

The Bit-Minder's eyes seemed to dilate and suddenly a holographic image emerged, suspended in the liquid of the tube.

It was a holo-feed of Zyleth's classroom. Cego recognized the professor's strange plants growing wildly around the room. A shadow crept into the feed's view. The shadow turned toward the light to reveal Shiar's sharp face. Cego would recognize the boy's nasty smirk anywhere.

The feed tracked Shiar as he crept to the far end of the room, where Zyleth's weapons chest rested against the wall. Shiar moved his hand toward the lock and the chest opened. He reached into the chest, rifling around, before withdrawing and running from the room.

The holo-feed dissipated from the tube.

"As you can see, clear as auralite, the Accused was not the one who stole the weapon from my classroom," Zyleth said. "It was the now-deceased boy Shiar. The real question is, who put him up to it? Who provided a student with biometric access to my classroom and, somehow, a key to my private weapons chest? Now, I realize that's not the central question of the arguments, but it is related and certainly should be further investigated."

What was Zyleth playing at? Cego had previously thought it was the professor himself who had provided Shiar with the weapon.

"Prosecutor Wenceforth, do you wish to enter any comment into the System regarding the submitted evidence?" the Bit-Minder asked.

"Yes." Wenceforth seemed prepared for his counter. "The question the defense posed, as he stated himself, is unrelated to the charge in question. It doesn't matter who accessed his classroom, his weapons chest, or how they did it. All that matters is whether the Accused came into unlawful possession of the spectral fan. Yes, the feed does show Shiar entering the classroom and accessing the chest, but there is no clear view of him taking the weapon itself. For all we are aware of, the boy could have just looked in the chest out of curiosity. This may have even provided the Accused an opportunity to enter the room afterward and access the chest, which was already ajar."

Zyleth produced an audible snort at the Prosecutor's suggestion.

"Silence," the Bit-Minder forcefully reprimanded Zyleth. "Prosecutor, do you have any evidence to submit at this juncture?"

"I do," Wenceforth said, eyeballing Zyleth.

The grey-faced man placed his own sliver of metal on his pedestal, triggering another holo-feed within the tube.

It displayed an overhead view of the challenge grounds, the students in their Circles with the crowd looming around them. The feed swept in from above, zooming in on the action.

Cego saw himself, leaping in and out, squaring off with Shiar. He saw the wild expression in Shiar's eyes and the smirk on his face as he lashed out with looping blows.

Cego remembered this part of the fight. It was when he'd first realized Shiar had some sort of weapon. But the feed didn't catch the blue spark in Shiar's hand as Cego had remembered it. Missing from this view was the wide slash of light that had trailed the boy's punches, threatening to dismember Cego.

Cego watched himself clutch at his stomach after he'd been slashed. The feed zoomed in and paused just as Cego attempted a counterpunch.

"There!" Wenceforth yelled excitedly, pointing at the holo. "Notice the Accused's hand as he attacks. The illumination that surrounds it—blue and white. Though of course we cannot see the weapon itself, given the metal of the spectral fan would be nearly invisible when activated, there is no other reason why this ring of light would be surrounding the Accused's hand, other than him having possession of the murder weapon."

Cego stared at the image, questioning what he saw with his own eyes. There *was* a faint halo of light surrounding his hand.

The feed restarted, and Cego eerily watched the events from above that had replayed in his mind so often, how he desperately tried to avoid the weapon, evading punches with techniques he'd never use in unarmed combat. He was only fighting to survive.

He watched himself trying to take Shiar to the ground, unsuccessfully attempting the iminari roll. And then Cego saw the moment when he raised his arm in defense against Shiar's slash from above. A fiery explosion burst from where the two combatants met, enveloping their bodies just before the feed went white.

"Now, the question of what caused the explosion has an easy

answer," Wenceforth said. "For that, I'd like to call my first witness."

"Permission granted," the Bit-Minder responded.

"I call Maker Machiron Symutron, weapons engineer first class of ArkTech Labs."

The Bit-Minder's beady eyes bulged as a new holograph appeared in the tube: a dirt-covered witness wearing a glowing pair of goggles that made his eyes seem especially large.

"Greetings, Maker Symutron," Wenceforth said. "I appreciate your time, especially given I know you are currently across the world introducing some proprietary tech to emerging nations. I'll get right to it."

The maker nodded as the holo-feed wavered briefly.

"Maker, in your vast expertise on all modern weapons, do you also have sufficient knowledge of the spectral fan?"

"Well, considering I personally developed three of the last four fan models, I'd say yes, I do," the maker deadpanned.

"As I thought," the Prosecutor said. "And, with that significant expertise in building, testing, and utilizing the spectral fan, could you please comment on the weapon's purpose?"

"Of course," the maker said. "The spectral fan is a close-quarters defensive weapon. Deactivated, it appears as an easily concealable, small metal disc. When activated via a small pressure trigger, the disc releases seven auralite filaments from its core. These filaments rapidly channel spectral energy via the metallurgic principle, which I don't have near enough time to explain right now. But the generated result is a spectral blade in the shape of a fan."

The holo-feed of Maker Symutron cut out again for a split second before reappearing. The Bit-Minder furrowed its brow.

"Using a spectral fan, a politik, lord, or even a maker such as myself can maintain anonymity without the bulk of a mech suit, while still remaining safe from any assailant. Just one week ago,

Vice-Governor Kaverstraw was walking through a low district with his family when he was attacked by a Grievar thug twice his size. He was able to successfully deploy his concealed spectral fan and cleave the beast in two with not so much as a hand flick."

Wenceforth smiled at that note. "You said *concealed*. How concealable? Would such a weapon be easily hidden from plain sight in the Circle, within the palm of a hand or sleeve of a second skin?"

The maker nodded. "Yes, though the weapon would likely be put to clumsy use in the hands of some Grievar."

"And when activated, what would the outward appearance of the weapon be to onlookers, when swung in the heat of combat?"

"It would appear a flash of light," the maker responded. "A halo, barely visible, but apparent to an astute observer."

"Thank you for this expert testimony," Wenceforth said. "One more question for you, Maker Symutron. What would happen if a spectral fan were improperly used?"

"What specifically do you mean by *improperly used*, Prosecutor?" the maker questioned.

"What would happen if the spectral fan wielder were to not release the trigger on the charge?"

The maker shook his head. "Spectral charge is generated and increased with continued pressure on the trigger. If the user held the trigger down after the weapon was already at full power, the safety would activate to prevent an overcharge of the weapon."

"And if the safety were removed or tampered with prior to use?" Wenceforth asked.

"That would be an immensely ignorant action, forgoing any knowledge of weaponry. But, in such a case, if overcharged, the spectral fan would explode."

Wenceforth nodded. "Thank you, Maker Symutron, that is all the prosecution will need from you."

"Defender Zyleth, would you like to question the witness while present?" the Bit-Minder said.

"No," Zyleth said flatly, prompting the holo-feed of the maker to dissipate.

Cego could barely follow the rapid words of the Daimyo in the courtroom, but he could tell things weren't going well for him.

"Would you like to call any other witnesses, Defender Zyleth?" the Bit-Minder asked.

"Yes, I would," Zyleth responded. "I call Xenalia Disthik, cleric second class."

Cego's heart skipped a beat as his friend appeared in holographic form within the tube, her black hair tied back in a bun. Xenalia's eyes met Cego's briefly but quickly returned to Zyleth.

"Thank you for your valuable time, Cleric Disthik," Zyleth stated formally. "I have called you today as a witness not only for your broad medical expertise but also because you are highly familiar with the Accused's physical and mental profile."

Xenalia nodded as Zyleth flung his first question out like a jab. "How long have you known the Accused, and how familiar are you with him from a medical perspective?"

"I have known the Accused for one year, seven months, and fifteen days," Xenalia responded in her succinct fashion. "During this time period, I have attended on the Accused forty-three times, which is far more than I see the average student within this time span. I do have quite an expansive medical and psychological profile built on the Accused."

Xenalia showed no warmth in her words when she spoke of Cego. Not that she ever showed much emotion, but Cego had become accustomed to considering Xenalia his friend. Now, though, she referred to him like he was a stranger.

"Good, good," Zyleth said. "You spoke about psychological profiling. I do know for a fact that the Lyceum, under orders of Governance, compiles risk profiles on each student. Can you elaborate on this and provide the specific data you have on the Accused?"

Xenalia hesitated a moment, her eyes flashing to Cego, before responding. "Yes, we compile psychographic profiles on every student that enters the Lyceum, using a wide array of data points including bloodline, peer interaction, and combat history. The primary goal of these profiles is to determine the probability of the student graduating and entering the Knighthood, so that we can determine the appropriate level of resources to devote to the student. The secondary purpose of the profile is to determine the risk level for the student: how likely they are to engage in unlawful activities, specifically those not in compliance with the Codes."

Cego stared at Xenalia. Had she simply been analyzing him the entire time? Did Xenalia care how he turned out or was she just tuned in to whether he was worth the Lyceum's resources or at risk to break the Codes?

"The Accused's profile is a data torrent of disparities," Xenalia continued. "In regard to our evaluation of success potential, his likelihood to become a Grievar Knight and succeed in the Circle after graduation, the Accused has the highest score we've ever seen."

Even Zyleth seemed to be taken by surprise at the statement.

"Ever?" the Defender asked. "You mean to say he has a greater success profile than even Artemis Halberd had?"

"Yes," Xenalia responded. "By a wide margin."

"And tell me of his risk profile," Zyleth prompted.

Xenalia again met Cego's eyes, briefly but pointedly. She was one of the only people who knew about his secret, his unorthodox upbringing and how he'd been losing control of himself during combat.

Cego was a risk and he knew it.

"He has little to no risk of straying from the Codes," Xenalia said. "From all the data I evaluated, he only displayed behaviors in accordance with the laws and procedures of Governance."

Cego breathed out.

"Let the System show that our expert witness has stated the

Accused was a superior student at the Lyceum, perhaps the best ever, a potential massive asset to the Knight team and our nation," Zyleth summarized. "In addition, our witness has stated that the Accused did not have any heightened risk potential of breaking the Codes, including the risk of utilizing unauthorized Daimyo tech or weaponry, as he's been charged with.

"Now." Zyleth continued his questioning. "Tell me about Cego's state after the incident in question, when he was brought to you in the ward."

"The Accused came to me unconscious, in critical condition." Xenalia's pitch-black eyes fluttered. "He suffered from contusions to the face, torso, and legs, including three broken ribs. I speculate those injuries were incurred during the first of his challenge fights, though. His primary injury was a ten-inch-long, four-inch-deep laceration across his abdomen, which ruptured his stomach lining and punctured the large intestine."

"Cleric Disthik," Zyleth led. "Would you say the stomach wound on the Accused would be consistent with that which a spectral weapon would inflict, even more specifically, a concealed spectral fan?"

"Yes," Xenalia responded. "Although I cannot say with complete certainty that it was a spectral fan that inflicted the damage, I would venture to say that this weapon or one similar to it would be the only tech able to cause such a wound in such a short period of time."

"Indeed," Zyleth responded, nodding his head enthusiastically. "Thank you for your help, Cleric Disthik."

"Would you like to question the witness, Prosecutor?" the Bit-Minder's voice echoed.

"I would." Wenceforth stood at the pedestal, peering up at the holo-feed of Xenalia. "I'll be brief here, Cleric."

Xenalia nodded.

"Would it not be entirely possible that the mentioned abdominal wound on the Accused was self-inflicted? Especially when an unauthorized wielder, a Grievar, were utilizing such a weapon, would the likelihood be high that they injure themselves rather than any intended target?"

"I cannot rule out that possibility," Xenalia responded.

Wenceforth flashed a gum-filled smirk. "Cleric, I'd like to ask a final question, perhaps to satisfy my own curiosity after reviewing the case file."

Zyleth interjected. "Why should we waste our witness's valuable time attempting to satisfy the Prosecutor's own curiosity?"

"Prosecutor Wenceforth," the Bit-Minder interceded. "Does your line of questioning provide any additional evidence to the System in relation to the charges?"

"Yes," Wenceforth responded. "It does; I misspoke. I am curious, naturally, as a Prosecutor who likes to seek the truth. But the witness's response should also provide further data for the System's ruling."

"Then proceed," the Bit-Minder commanded.

"Cleric," the Prosecutor said. "You of course are aware of the medical profile of the Accused and his physical state after the incident in question. You stated his most grievous wound was the stomach laceration, and yet he was at the center of a major explosion, one that temporarily blinded hundreds and killed another student. Why or how did the Accused avoid any bodily injury from the explosion?"

Somehow, Cego knew the line of questioning with Xenalia would lead to this point. He knew the cleric's theory: The energy reaction had come from his own body as a defensive mechanism against the weapon.

Xenalia met Cego's eyes once more before looking back at the Prosecutor. "As a medward officer, as a cleric of Ezo, I pride myself in knowledge. My life is knowledge, attempting to figure out why things happen, in particular within the bodies of Grievar. But I can say with absolute certainty I have no idea how the Accused did not sustain any burns or concussive wounds from the explosion."

Wenceforth frowned and stared at Xenalia for several long moments. Finally, he relented. "Thank you for your time, Cleric."

Xenalia's face disappeared from the holo-feed.

Though she'd never set foot in the courtroom, Cego missed Xenalia's presence the second she disappeared.

He was alone again.

CHAPTER 18

Becoming the Enemy

Every defensive movement should be paired with an offensive one. When raising a hand to block a body kick, that same hand should be ready to catch the leg. When escaping from beneath an opponent's mount, one should be seeking an arm or leg to attack immediately. A purely defensive or offensive fighter will fall prey to their own imbalances.

Passage Three, Thirty-Fourth Technique
of the Combat Codes

Though Murray had always held a special place of hatred in his heart for mercs, he had a surprisingly easy time becoming one.

Lord Maharu respected the Grievar path in many ways that the Citadel had not. It was strange that a Daimyo who Murray thought must be so far from the Codes would be one to abide by them, at least for his subjects. Maharu did not force his Grievar to use any tech, and he provided them suitable spartan living accommodations. He let his Grievar train their skills every day, not only sit passive guard duty to ensure his estate was safe.

Most of all, Maharu didn't force his mercs to use stims.

"Grievar were made for combat," the lord had said to Murray. "You are well-oiled fighting machines; why change what nature intended?"

Murray paced the ironwood planks of the estate's first level. He'd gotten better at preventing the floor from creaking beneath his considerable weight, though the wood still let out an occasional squeal of protest. What haunted Murray was beneath these floors.

He knew that Maharu had purchased the failed Cradle experiments from the Citadel. He knew the Daimyo lord he was serving was letting little kids grow in tubes beneath the floor that Murray patrolled.

He stopped to breathe, nodding to another merc posted at the estate's front entrance, one he'd sparred with earlier in the day.

After being stationed at Maharu's estate for a month, Murray still had nothing to show for it. No information on the kids down below. No confirmation that Sam was among the experiments. No plan to rescue them.

Murray hadn't even had the opportunity to go down to the basement. His current post was providing security for the upper floors, most often wherever the lord was stationed.

Murray listened to all sorts of irrelevant conversations through the days. Maharu ran one of the largest elemental mining companies in the Underground, so he had a constant influx of incoming trade leaders, makers, dignitaries, and national representatives to deal with. Many of the high-profile Daimyo brought entire teams with them for protection, so Maharu often kept Murray close by his side.

In fact, Maharu was quite proud of retaining the service of the Mighty Murray Pearson. He'd be forced to stand at attention while the Daimyo ate and drank, talked politics and philosophy. Every so often the soap-eaters would interrupt their conversation and ask

Murray to regale them with some story from the Circles, a choice fight that they'd heard stories of. Murray knew he had a part to play there, so he did his best to dredge up those memories.

But he heard nothing about the Cradle. Not a single world from Maharu or his staff about the supposed kids stored below. Murray had racked his mind endlessly, lying awake at night—could Thaloo have been lying? Could the insidious slave owner have tricked him? It was unlikely, given the fat man was still waiting for Murray to deliver on his end of the bargain.

Murray knew one man there who had the answers he needed, though: Farmer.

He'd seen the old man on occasion, in passing; Farmer was Maharu's head of security and spent most of his time in a top-floor office, watching the feeds, analyzing the histories of incoming guests as potential threats. Farmer commanded the merc team with an efficiency that Murray remembered well from his time leading the Citadel's Knights.

As far as Murray could tell, Farmer was fully devoted to the lord. After coming out of the Cradle, the old man had found his path again, a suitable use of his highly sought-after skill set. And in the end, could Murray blame him? Was serving Lord Maharu so different from working for the Citadel, as Murray had done as a Scout for the past decade?

On either path, they were pawns.

But Murray wasn't there to set himself on a new path. He was here to dig up the old, make good on a promise he'd sworn to Cego. And to do that, Murray needed to see the kids below for himself. After a month of establishing himself as a competent bootlicker, he needed to move forward.

Tonight, he'd been stationed on the first floor, which was somewhat unusual, though Murray suspected it was because Maharu had no significant guests to the estate this evening, not even the standard courtesan coming by his bed quarters.

Murray made sure to make the usual rounds on the perimeter before taking the route to the basement lift, knowing the many viewports above were tracking him.

The entrance to the basement lift always had a guard posted in front. Through the entire night, the unsleeping Sentinel took watch in front of the lift's entry, and at dayshift, a guard switched places with the mech.

As he rounded the corner to the lift's hallway, Murray was relieved to see a familiar face posted in front of the door.

"You always on this shift?" Murray attempted to make casual conversation with the young guard that he'd strangled unconscious a month before.

"Yes." Yahalo barely made eye contact with Murray.

"How long have you been doing muscle work for the lord?" Murray asked.

Yahalo finally met Murray's eyes before answering. "A few months before you arrived. Finished training camp in Karbrok and tried for Knight's team...but I got cut."

Murray nodded. "I heard they make some hard cuts in Kiroth. Though I've met some of the fighters that didn't make it, and they still gave me hell. Darkin' pressure of those bastards still giving me nightmares."

The compliment worked; a grin cracked Yahalo's face. "My older brother. He's head wrestling coach with the empire's southern force. Taught me most of what I know."

"Incredible," Murray said. "I'd still like to learn from a wrestler of that caliber."

"Yes," Yahalo said. "Lord lets us have a break every year, and I head back Surface-side to see him and my family. We wrestle in the dirt like when we were kids, and he still always gets the edge on me."

Murray feigned interest. "What sort of techniques does he favor?"

Yahalo crouched into a wrestling stance with his hand forward. "First he loves to blind me, puts his hand right in front of my face to mask the shot."

Murray chuckled and mirrored the stance. "As would be expected."

"Then he slaps on a clinch and drives forward." Murray let Yahalo grab his head.

"When I react and push back, he snaps me down into a front headlock, every time," Yahalo said with pride, showing Murray the technique.

"That's good stuff," Murray said. "If I was still teaching at the Lyceum, I'd be showing that to my students."

"Right..." Yahalo trailed off. "What happened there, anyhow? Why'd you leave a cushy job with the Citadel?"

Murray sighed. "Complicated. Didn't see eye to eye with the commander. You know how it is."

"Yeah, I do," Yahalo said as he settled down.

Murray saw his opportunity, like a body punch ready to be thrown on hands held too high. He felt bad doing it to the kid, but he needed answers.

"Hey, kid," Murray said. "Mind if you do me a favor?"

Yahalo stopped smiling. "Maybe. What is it?"

"Hrm...well, this is a bit embarrassing," Murray said. "But I got a lady in town. Plan on seeing her on my day off. But thing is I need to bring her something nice. You know how ladies are. I know Maharu lets us pick up rations, but wondering if you might grab a bottle of some sweet wine up from the kitchen for me. I know you got in tight with the sizzler up there."

Yahalo contemplated the ask. "Maharu doesn't like us to leave our posts, especially this one..."

"Well, not to brag, but you do have Murray Pearson to watch it for you."

Yahalo eyed Murray carefully before acquiescing. "All right, I'll be quick!"

As soon as Yahalo turned the corner, Murray started for the lift.

"Where are you going?" Farmer's soft voice made Murray stop in his tracks.

How in the dark did the old man creep up on me like that?

"Where do you think I'm going?" Murray tried to regain his composure. "Down there."

"I don't think that's such a good idea," Farmer replied.

"You used to know me," Murray growled. "And I'll tell you, I haven't changed much over these years. Have you ever known me as one to only follow good ideas?"

"No, I haven't," Farmer said as he took a step toward Murray. "But I've also known you to not be entirely suicidal. You go down that lift right now, you'll be dead before it rises back to this floor."

"Well, maybe some things do darkin' change," Murray said. "I don't care too much about ending up dead nowadays, that's for sure."

"Back at the bar, do you remember what I told you?" Farmer asked. "Your path isn't over yet. Don't throw it away, Murray."

"I don't consider rescuing the kids trapped down below as throwing anything away." Murray kept his voice low. He watched Farmer quickly glance at the viewport posted above.

"That's only storage down there," Farmer whispered.

"So, the lord has a Sentinel watching over protein packs and washcloths all night. That so?" Murray said.

"That's so." Farmer met Murray's eyes and held the stare. Though the man's eyes had dulled and his face had sunken in, Murray saw a glimmer of something there. Maybe it was some last vestige of hope, some naïve seed planted within Murray that good people stayed good. That this man he'd looked up to his whole life, one who'd taught him so much about living, could see the truth beyond this game of pawns and lords that they played at each day.

"How can you do this?" Murray's voice shook. "How do you wake up every morning, get yourself dressed, put down your mush, and do this?"

"We do what we must to survive, Murray," Farmer said.

"So, that's what it's all about?" Murray said. "Survival? Even if that means others getting put beneath the ground?"

"There's always someone getting put beneath," Farmer said. "That can't stop us from waking up each morning and moving forward. There must be a balance."

The hope Murray had seen again in Farmer dissipated, like a candle snuffed out. This was the man who had lived in the darkness of the Cradle for a decade. The man who had been a tool of the Bit-Minders, feeding on their blacklight like a leech.

"I'm not about to see these kids down this lift get put under," Murray growled as he clenched his fists. "Even if it means making your survival a little less likely."

Murray hadn't fought Farmer since he'd graduated from the Lyceum, since he was a fresh-eyed Knight. It hadn't gone well for Murray back then. Farmer had been lightning fast, sinuous like a whip, and a master tactician. But that man was gone. And this man was standing between Murray and Sam.

As Murray was about to make his move, he saw Yahalo scramble back down the hall, a gleaming bottle of sweet wine in hand.

"Thank you for scouting the front gate for me, Yahalo," Murray spoke before the kid dug himself in too deep.

Yahalo slid to a halt and stood at attention, the wine bottle behind his back. He averted his eyes from Farmer. "I, um…Of course. I'm sorry it took so long. Captain—"

"Not a worry, Yahalo," Murray interrupted again. "Captain Farmer and I were just discussing what great work you've been doing. Do you have anything to report?"

Yahalo glanced at Murray with wide eyes, clearly trying to read his intention.

"No, no, nothing to report," the kid stammered.

"Good, then," Murray said.

Farmer met Murray's eyes once more before silently turning

away. Murray stared at his old coach as he walked away, waiting until the man was fully out of sight until he turned back to Yahalo. Sweat was beading the kid's head as he stood in place, likely unsure what to do next.

"Don't worry." Murray reached out and took the wine bottle from Yahalo's trembling hands. "I'll make sure Farmer knows it was my idea if it comes up."

"All right…" Yahalo murmured.

"And I owe you," Murray continued. "You covered for me and so I'll cover for you, soon. Perhaps you can take a shift and find some lucky girl to bring some sweet wine to."

*   *   *

The redshift cast crimson bars on the ironwood in front of Murray's tatami. He eyed the flask of Hiberian sweetlye. The drink sat about three feet in front of him on a teal wood tray. A beautiful, rounded glass of amber liquid, fizzling with seduction.

A toast to your service, Knight Pearson.

The note was scrawled in beautiful calligraphy and propped against the glass. Murray had seen Lord Maharu writing thousands of such notes within his office over the past month, the little man moving his ink brush with the grace of martial study.

Murray could picture the lord swiping this note aside after scribing it before handing it to his servicer. The Grunt had delivered it along with the rare Hiberian liquor to Murray's quarters this morning.

He had to admit Maharu was a master of his craft. A month of close observation watching the lord occupy his natural habitat had shown Murray the sort of man he was.

The path to mastery required repeated practice, success against a resistant opponent. Lord Maharu had such skill in his ability to control. He'd wave away hawkers trying to cheat him, let them think they were about to win a contract at discount, when his real goal was to sweep the tatami out from under them, take their entire trade with a swift stroke. He'd make his servicers think they were free to go as they pleased, that they were following their true path even though they were doing his bidding.

Despite the façade Maharu upheld, his apparent observance of the Codes, Murray knew the man was dangerous. He'd seen many killers and Maharu was one of them, perhaps one of the most skilled. The Daimyo lord had shown nearly no bad feints.

All except one: the bottle of Hiberian amber sitting in front of Murray now. He knew of Murray's weakness and was throwing a shot at it.

But Murray had been in too many Circles to let up on his defense. He'd been caught with his hands down before, and he didn't plan on getting knocked on his ass this time.

He stood, palmed the curved glass of liquor, and tossed it into the piss pot set beside the tatami.

"Darkin' kid," he growled as he produced the vial of beelbub ichor from his vest pocket, downing it with clenched teeth. "Made me give the good stuff up for this."

Murray would make the first move. He slung on his vest and stepped through the lichen-silk curtain beyond his room into the living quarters of Maharu's service folk. The security forces, sweepers, sizzlers, and window washers lived apart from the Daimyo branch of the compound.

Some of the Grunts called the area Little Markspar, after the famous bustling trade street of the Underground. Stolen goods from every closet of the estate were bustled into the service quarters—canned greens from the pantry, dried fish jerky from the rations closet, rice paste and potted plants, all traded and bargained for among Little Markspar's inhabitants.

Murray had befriended a neighbor, a Grunt named Gib quartered right beside him who happened to be the best wire-tech in Cavern Side.

Murray put his boot softly against Gib's door.

"Yup, I'm awake, all right." The man opened up and smiled through his missing teeth.

"Thank you, friend." Murray genuinely liked Gib. He worked hard and appeared happy in the lord's service. "You got it?"

"Right here, right here." The Grunt nodded, reaching into his pocket to produce a fist-sized orb. "Like we talked about, right?"

"Like we talked about." Murray nodded back, placing a sizable stack of onyx in the Grunt's hand. He took the azure ball and pocketed it.

Murray walked briskly out of Little Markspar, past the washroom and training quarters, beyond the laundry and the steel-rimmed well. He found his way across the main entry court and down the hall to the basement lift.

Yahalo was gone from his post, as planned. Murray felt bad for tricking the kid, but some fights required misdirection.

Murray lifted the gate and stepped into the lift as quietly as possible.

As the gears creaked and his stomach dropped, Murray gripped the orb with a sweaty palm. He could feel the energy budding within the device.

Use the Codes like a blanket, not a board.

Old Aon Farstead had said those words to Murray not long ago, when he'd been seeking answers about Cego's past. Murray had needed to lie, play mind games, even talk with a Bit-Minder to get those answers, to discover the terrible truth of the Cradle. He'd had to break the Codes to get those answers about the kid, and he was about to break them again now to find Cego's brother. But did it really matter when the man who'd taught Murray the Codes in the first place was a part of all of this? Did the Codes matter when Farmer was as much a monster as the Daimyo lord he served?

Murray breathed deeply as the lift jolted to a stop. The door slid up and he bowled the orb beneath it. The glimmering device seemed to roll in slow motion, grating along the stone floor, until it came to a stop against the steel basement entry.

Murray held his breath. Nothing happened. Had the darkin' Grunt sold him a defective device?

Just as he was about to press the lift lever back up, the orb erupted in a brilliant flash of white. Murray looked up to the viewports stationed above, hopefully scrambled for the time he'd need, as he raised a hand to the brightness and walked into the hall. He'd have mere minutes to get in, get Sam, and get out fast.

The buzzing brightness began to dim just as Murray reached the gate and shoved it open. He stopped in his tracks, lowering his hand from his eyes as he stared into the wide storage room.

"How stupid you must think I am, Knight Pearson."

Lord Maharu waited, stone-faced in his blue- and gold-trimmed nightrobe. His towering black Sentinel was posted next to him.

Them, Murray had half expected.

But beside them stood Farmer.

"I told you to forget all of this, Murray," the old man said. "Now you have gone down a path that you cannot return from."

CHAPTER 19

Judgment

A Grievar's facial expression should remain the same through victory or defeat; to smile broadly or frown in displeasure is to stray from the path.

One Hundred Fiftieth Precept of the Combat Codes

*C*ego inhaled deeply, breathing the cool mist as it rose from the tide before him.

The sun had just peeked over the horizon, but Cego could already feel the gathering heat of midday. The warm air blanketed the cool seawater and vaporized to ghosts swirling on the sunrise.

The low tide always brought with it scuttling sea creatures: armies of big-clawed crabs marching toward their homes in the sand dunes and barnacled giant clams gasping for air as they burrowed beneath the muck. Millet birds chattered happily as they hopped in the black sand surf, picking at easy prey.

Where was Sam?

Usually, Cego's curious little brother would be giving chase, trying to scoop up the creatures as they fled the sound of his smacking wet footsteps in the surf.

Cego stayed seated but turned to look for his brother down the shoreline, toward the rocky tide pools, and then back toward the compound, where Sam would often peer through the beach grass like some feline waiting to pounce.

There was no sign of Sam, strangely, not even the sound of the little boy's raucous laughter after he'd played some ill-chosen joke on Silas. Silas would give Sam a swift smack across the face when he caught up to him, but playfully—he'd always had a soft spot for the youngest brother.

Thinking of his older brother, Cego peered out toward the horizon, looking for Silas's dark form crashing through the whitecaps, often bringing with him a catch of netted sarpin, ready to toss into Farmer's stewpot. The waves rose and fell, but Silas was not swimming out there.

Cego breathed deeply again, trying to focus his ki-breath and stay solely in the present moment, hear the surf, feel the warmth of the rising sun, sense the steady beat of his heart. But Cego couldn't focus. A strange thought kept invading his mind, like an unwanted intruder.

Where is everyone?

As if reading his thoughts, the old master suddenly stood in front of Cego, the man's grey robe dancing in the morning breeze.

"Where is everyone?" Farmer parroted Cego's thought.

"You're here," Cego replied. "But I don't know where Sam and Silas have gone off to."

The old master seemed rooted to the ground, like one of the ironwood trees that grew on the island's interior. Cego couldn't shake the thought that Farmer had always stood there, in that very spot in the surf in front of him.

"I've always been here," the old master echoed Cego's thoughts again. "Where is everyone?"

"I thought maybe Sam was hiding up in the grass, near the compound, but I couldn't see him," Cego replied. "And Silas, maybe he's out swimming and just hasn't returned yet."

The old master stood still as a gust of wind lifted black sand from the shore and peppered his face.

He repeated the same question. "Where is everyone?"

Cego suddenly felt very alone. Though Farmer stood with him, the man seemed like another natural formation on the island: the sharp cliff face or the ironwood forest or the Path that illuminated the water when the sun set.

"They're gone?" Cego asked timidly. "They won't come back?"

The old master did not reply, but the ocean breeze kicked up, sending another gust of sand into Cego's face, blurring his vision.

Cego needed to know where his brothers had gone. He spoke into the rising wind. "Where are they?"

The wind grew more aggressive, sending a stream of stinging black into Cego's eyes while howling in his ears. He could barely see Farmer anymore, only the man's glowing eyes through the maelstrom. A red streak of lightning flashed in the distance.

"Where is everyone?" Cego screamed this time while trying to hold firm to the ground beneath him, digging his hands into the sand.

Suddenly, the wind stopped. The black sand buffeting Cego froze midair and plummeted back to the beach.

Farmer stood, still firmly rooted, unmoving, and covered in sand. Then he slowly lifted a robed arm toward the sky. It was an otherworldly movement, as if Cego had just seen a tree extend its branch or a mountain bow its granite head.

Cego looked up toward the old master's raised arm, and the world around him changed. The rising sun sped through the sky overhead and then sank back below the cliffs. Night blanketed the world and stars pricked the sky as the glowing moon raced on its own path toward the sea. The sun rose and fell again, and the world blinked from light to dark.

Cego saw time dance around him.

He breathed, deeply, following the inhale and exhale from start to finish as days and months raced by him.

He put a hand to his face, expecting to feel something different, perhaps new scars or wrinkles like those on the old master's brow, but all Cego felt was his own smooth face.

Farmer lowered his arm and the world slowed again.

Cego watched a red crab emerge from the tide and scuttle across the beach. He heard the cry of a seabird circling overhead. He felt the grains of black sand sifting through his fingers.

"It's time," the old master whispered.

"What?" Cego asked, again feeling alone. "If everyone is gone, what can I do? How can I do this myself?"

"It's time," the man said again.

*   *   *

The prosecution and defense traded off barbed examinations of witness after witness over several days: a mentalist specializing in criminal behavior, the metallurgist who had constructed the Circle that Cego and Shiar fought in, a forensic examiner who called forth grisly images of Shiar's charred corpse. Even Zyleth himself was interrogated by the Prosecutor about his proximity to the case.

Though Cego had no idea who was prevailing so far, he knew a well-matched fight when he saw one. Zyleth proved to be an experienced Defender, ably holding his own against Ezo's appointed Prosecutor, Wenceforth.

Just when Cego thought he wouldn't be able to sit through another argument of what constituted possession of unauthorized weaponry, the Bit-Minder's voice cut through the heated back-and-forth.

"We will now recess shortly," the creature said. "Though I require no rest or breaks, breeds such as your own do have necessities to take care of. Go and do so, and return in fifteen minutes."

The spectators above filtered out of the box. Wenceforth

exited the courtroom expediently and Cego was left manacled to his chair. Zyleth stayed put, taking a seat next to Cego, crossing his legs in a relaxed fashion as he stared up without pause at the Bit-Minder, who returned his gaze. It was the first time during this trial Zyleth had not left Cego alone through recess.

"Ugly-looking thing, is it not?" Zyleth said to Cego.

Cego wasn't sure how to respond; the Bit-Minder was looking right at them. He whispered, "Um...can't it...can't it hear you?"

"Yes, most definitely," Zyleth said. "In fact, this Bit-Minder can likely hear and see everyone who just left the courtroom, as well as hundreds of other people around Ezo that it is currently observing."

"How?" Cego asked.

"Not many know with complete certainty how they work, but it is speculated one way the Bit-Minders retrieve their data is through observation spectrals."

Cego warily watched the luminescent wisps circling the tube, the same spectrals he saw everywhere: in the halls of the Lyceum, through the city streets, even in the dorm room where he slept. He shivered.

"Do not worry," Zyleth said. "Yes, they are likely observing much of your waking life, but they do not care what you do or say. Not, at least, in the same sense you would care. For example..."

Zyleth stood up, walked up to the tube, and tapped the glass several times. "Hello there, Sir Bit-Minder. Did you hear me earlier? I had mentioned that you were ugly. But I had not fully expressed myself. You truly look the epitome of horridness, like some sort of unborn discarded fetal sac. In fact, though I am not quite sure how your kind reproduces, the perfect punishment for any criminal passing through your courtroom would be a visual re-creation of the very act that created you in the first place."

The Bit-Minder watched Zyleth without expression, just two black eyes staring out of the tube.

The professor tapped the glass a few more times before turning back to Cego. "See? It hears, but it is not all here. It is... everywhere."

Cego truly understood now why Murray-Ku had lowered his voice to a hushed whisper when he'd talked about the Bit-Minders.

I'd rather be five feet under, clawing my way up, than stuck in a room with one of those darkin' things again...

The thought of Murray brought Cego back to his current predicament: He was manacled to a chair, being charged with murder and without anyone to help him. Except, strangely, the man he'd thought had framed him in the first place. Zyleth.

"Why are you helping me?" Cego couldn't contain himself.

"It is my job," Zyleth responded flatly. "PublicDefenders are tasked with providing as persuasive an argument as possible in defense of the Accused, whether they believe them to be guilty or innocent."

"So, it's a complete coincidence that you, my professor at the Lyceum, somehow ended up as my PublicDefender?"

"You are not all brawn, like many of your kind," Zyleth said. "Correct, I do have ulterior motives in representing you, and I did put in a request with Governance that I take on this case."

"You want to figure out who put Shiar up to stealing your spectral fan," Cego guessed. "You want to know who orchestrated all of this."

"Again, you are sharp," Zyleth said. "Which is why I like you. Another reason I do not want you to end up in a grave for a crime you did not commit."

"You think I'm innocent?" Cego asked.

Zyleth eyeballed him. "Yes, I do believe you are innocent. And so far, I think we have a good position with the System. There is too much uncertainty, not enough direct evidence that ties you to getting ahold of the weapon. And hopefully, if we finish arguments strong, you will end up in Trial by Combat against some weak Lyceum dropout hired by PublicJustice. Take the win and you will be back in class by end of week."

Cego's future suddenly did not seem so dark.

"Though I also believe there is something you are hiding," Zyleth added. "Some secret that is connected to this unorthodox attack on you in the Circle. You do realize hiding anything from your PublicDefender can only hurt your chances at exculpation. Is there anything you would like to tell me now, Cego?"

Cego gulped. He did believe Zyleth wanted to help him. But he still didn't trust him with his secrets as far as a stone's throw.

"No, there isn't anything else," Cego said.

"That is what I thought you would say." Zyleth stood up, moving back toward the tube and staring at the Bit-Minder. "Do not forget, though, whatever your secret is, whatever you are hiding, this thing in the tube knows it already."

Cego swallowed hard, looking at the lifeless thing.

The Bit-Minder abruptly spoke, staring back at Cego with sudden clarity as if it had just come to life. "Court will now commence. In this session, we will finalize the determination of guilt or innocence of the Accused, two hundred twelve. All in attendance, return to your positions immediately."

*   *   *

Not much longer, Cego told himself as the proceedings continued. Even if it meant fighting for his life in Trial by Combat, Cego merely wanted to move his body, escape from these confining shackles.

He glanced behind him and saw Commander Memnon had returned to his seat and was peering through the glass intensely.

"If we do not have any more witnesses, we will proceed to the closing portion of arguments," the Bit-Minder droned.

"I'd like to submit a final piece of material evidence to the System," Prosecutor Wenceforth announced.

"Proceed."

The Prosecutor reached into his pocket and pressed something shining and small to the pedestal. The item magnified in the holo-feed. There was no mistaking the coin that Professor Drakken had given Cego, glinting crimson under the courtroom lights.

Professor Drakken had handed the rubellium coin to Cego after telling the tragic story from his past. Cego had kept the gift close by since, only leaving it behind in his dorm when he left for the challenges.

"There are two people in this courtroom who certainly recognize this coin," Wenceforth started. "The first is the Accused himself, given the coin was found in his personal effects."

Cego shifted in his seat uncomfortably. What did the gift he'd received from Drakken have to do with this trial? Was the coin another unauthorized technology in his possession they planned on charging him for?

"The second person here familiar with this coin is our very own Defender Zyleth," Wenceforth revealed. "This rubellium coin is in fact a crypto-key that unseals the weapons chest in Defender Zyleth's classroom."

The words cut Cego like another slash to the gut.

"We are unsure of how the Accused came into possession of the key that let him access the murder weapon, but we do have testimony that it was missing for a period of time prior to and after the crimes."

Cego felt the room start to spin. The image of Shiar walking out of Professor Drakken's classroom that strange morning flashed across his mind. He saw Professor Drakken placing the red coin in his hand firmly, telling Cego to keep it close.

"Why would the Accused have the key to the weapons chest in his possession, if not to steal a weapon? Here we have irrefutable evidence that ties all three charges against the Accused together: possession, intent, and murder."

Had Drakken made up the entire story of the Desovian tribe's slaughter just to get Cego to take the key? Had he also been the one to hand off the key to Shiar? Cego stared blankly at the spinning holograph until it disappeared.

"Does the defense have any rebuttal to this evidence?" the Bit-Minder questioned.

Zyleth shook his head wearily.

"If that is the last of the evidence submitted to the System, we will proceed with closing arguments to determine the guilt or innocence of the Accused, two hundred twelve," the Bit-Minder drove forward.

Both Defender and Prosecutor stood at their pedestals like Grievar squaring off in the Circle.

Wenceforth stayed silent and so Zyleth punched first.

"I came here to fulfill my professional duty: proving to the best of my ability the innocence of the Accused. But I must confess, I had other motives."

What is Zyleth doing?

"Personal motives," Zyleth sighed. "I wanted to discover how someone stole my property and used it for murder. I wanted to discover who had orchestrated this entire scheme, for no matter what you believe to be the truth, no student could have accomplished this level of deception and guile working on their own.

"I came here to have questions answered regarding the Accused, the victim, the weapon, and the events surrounding the murder," Zyleth said. "But, sadly, at this trial's end, I have almost no answers to satisfy my questions.

"But!" Zyleth threw the word like a jab. "I did have one question answered. The most important question, in fact. The only one that matters. An answer to the central charge in this trial: Did the Accused utilize unauthorized weaponry to murder Shiar in the challenge Circle? I now know without a doubt that the answer is no.

"We have clear evidence to the contrary," Zyleth stated. "We have the feed of Shiar breaking into my classroom to steal the weapon. We have Cleric Xenalia's medical testimony, an examination of the gash on the Accused's body, which was clearly cleaved by Shiar utilizing the spectral weapon. We have the venerable maker's testimony of how a spectral fan could be overcharged, which is instrumental in demonstrating how Shiar set off such an explosion and killed himself in the process. And finally, we have character testimony, from myself and Cleric Xenalia: The Accused has no clear motive for the crime, no risk profile to break the Codes, and no secret, vengeful, evil side to him as the Prosecutor has attempted to convince the System of."

Cego shivered as he heard Zyleth defending him passionately. Lying for him. The professor knew Cego had a secret, and though he didn't know what it was, he still was risking his own reputation to provide the defense.

"The System should see this all clearly. I have no need to further elaborate." Zyleth emphatically pounded his hand on the pedestal. "Our argument is sealed."

"Prosecutor Wenceforth, you will proceed with your closing argument," the Bit-Minder intoned.

Cego turned to see who remained in the courtroom. The spectator box was filled now. Memnon, Dakar Pugilio, Callen Albright, nearly the entirety of the Citadel's command gazed down on him with judging eyes. Several Daimyo Cego didn't recognize also stared out from the box, all wearing the pressed grey uniforms of Governance officials.

"Minder of Justice, System, and all else who watch today," Wenceforth began. "I repeat what I said at the start of this trial. This goes beyond a theft. This goes beyond a murder. What is at stake today in deciding on the guilt of the Accused is our very way of life."

Cego saw Zyleth hold back another of his snorts.

"Some may think me dramatic," Wenceforth continued. "But I

contend if we do not successfully and aggressively prosecute those interlopers who break the most sacred of Codes, then the tide will start to turn. In Ezo alone over the last decade, Grievar-on-Grievar crime utilizing illicit technology has increased twofold. Grievar crime against innocent Daimyo-kin, our lords and politiks, makers, clerics, and courtesans has increased threefold. *Threefold.*"

Wenceforth slammed his fist down on the pedestal. "I will not stand idly while our society is uprooted by brutes and buffoons. Wherever a Grievar stands in our strata, Knight or administrator, diplomat, mercenary, slave, or student, they must know their place. And that place is fighting. Doing their job to continue supporting our shared history of assured peace between nations and conglomerates. Following their preordained path to fight so that the rest shall not have to. And adhering to all Codes that facilitate this path."

Wenceforth's eyes landed on Cego, filled with righteous rage. "The Accused's crimes are clear. The evidence is clear. He broke the most sacred Code, took hold of one of *our* weapons and used it to strike down another student. If we do not prosecute him to the full strength of our laws, if we do not ensure he is executed during his Trial by Combat, the Accused will surely act heinously again. Next time, he won't strike out at another student. Next time, his rage will push him further; he will turn our weapons on us. Next time, Daimyo blood will flow.

"Our argument is sealed." Silence filled the courtroom as Wenceforth sat back down in satisfaction.

The Bit-Minder closed its eyes. Cego hadn't even been aware that was possible until now; the creature had stared wide-eyed out into space for the entirety of the trial. The thing appeared to be in a strange dormant state.

Cego felt Zyleth's hand on his shoulder, giving it a squeeze. The professor looked down at Cego, manacled to the chair.

"I know you are innocent," he said softly. "Whatever the sentence, I'll make sure your...family knows the outcome."

Cego looked up at Zyleth, confused. His family? Did the professor somehow know about Sam and Silas? Did Zyleth know about the old master?

Suddenly, the Bit-Minder's eyes flared back to life, staring directly at Cego, burrowing into him.

Cego wanted to break the manacles, leap from his chair, flee this place. He wanted to find Murray in whatever dark hole he'd dug himself into and stay lost in the Deep. Cego closed his eyes, unable to bear the Bit-Minder's gaze any longer. He was back on the island, sitting on the black sand beach, when he heard the thing's voice cut him.

"On the charge of possession of Daimyo-designated technology, the Accused, two hundred twelve, is found guilty."

Cego winced, keeping his eyes squeezed shut.

"On the charge of intent to utilize Daimyo-designated technology as a weapon, the Accused, two hundred twelve, is found guilty."

Cego felt the stinging wound on his stomach as if it were reopened, gashed and weeping again.

"On the charge of premeditated murder utilizing Daimyo-designated technology, the Accused, two hundred twelve, is found guilty."

The words the Bit-Minder spoke lost their meaning. Cego heard them, but they were just a collection of sounds, garbled and not making any sense.

"The sentence for the Accused, two hundred twelve, will be Trial by Combat," the Bit-Minder spoke. "The severity of retribution will be set at maximum. As requested by the Prosecutor, the Goliath will be utilized to ensure the Accused does not walk free and put the population at future risk. At this juncture, I ask the defense whether the Accused will undergo Trial by Combat himself or would rather be represented in the Circle by one of Ezo's PublicDefenders."

Zyleth looked down at Cego, pity welling up in his dark eyes.

"Cego...do you want a PublicDefender to fight in your stead?"

Cego could nearly hear Murray muttering.

PublicDefenders are a bunch of darkin' weaklings modernday. Even fighting for the innocent against some two-bit merc, they're likely to botch the job.

"No," Cego said. "I'll defend myself."

Zyleth looked at him again in despair. "Are you sure you do not want to reconsider? I feel I need to inform you about the Goliath. He is the Grievar you would face in Trial by Combat. No one... not even convicted Knights have gotten past him over the past decade. All of them were struck down in moments. At least with a PublicDefender, you would stand a chance. And, if your Defender loses, the Governance would utilize mech cannon fire for your execution. A quick death, at least. Not like with the Goliath. I have seen him...He is not a normal Grievar. It is always a grisly—"

Cego cut Zyleth off. "No, I'll defend myself."

Zyleth nodded reluctantly. "I understand."

The professor turned back to the Bit-Minder.

"The Accused, two hundred twelve, wishes to defend himself in Trial by Combat."

The Bit-Minder's eyes flashed, processing the information.

"Tomorrow at the sixth hour, the Accused, two hundred twelve, will defend himself against the Governance-appointed Grievar, the Goliath, in Trial by Combat. The event will take place in the Capital's Central Square for public viewing. If the Accused prevails, he will win his freedom. If he loses, his corpse will be incinerated immediately following death. His memory will be forgotten and scattered alongside the ashes of all other Code breakers."

CHAPTER 20

The Execution

Every offensive movement should have the aim of disabling or dispatching an adversary. Techniques that rely on an opponent's pain compliance should not be pursued. Though these methods may be successful on lesser Grievar, they will be a wasteful expenditure on veteran fighters with resilient minds.

Passage Two, Third Technique of the Combat Codes

I t was one of the Capital's rare days of sun. The blue sky cast a cloudless blanket overhead.

High Commander Memnon shifted uncomfortably in his seat as he watched the gathering crowd in Central Square below. Parents dragged yelling children behind them to find suitable viewing spots as street vendors loudly peddled their wares off wooden carts. Central Square's surrounding eateries had transported their grills outdoors to feed the sudden wave of patrons.

Memnon hadn't seen an execution in Central Square for some time. Technically, the crowd had gathered to view a Trial by Combat, but Governance had successfully charged the Accused with the full weight of the law. They would release the Goliath on Cego. The spectators had come fully expecting an execution.

"It's a travesty, I'm tellin' you." Dakar Pugilio sat beside Memnon, taking another long swig from his metal flask. The commander of PublicJustice had been drunk during yesterday's arguments in the courtroom and he was drunk again now, sitting at the far reaches of the square's amphitheater-style seating.

"Jus' a boy, this Cego is," Dakar slurred. "And I for one am not convinced he should be getting put in the ground today."

"The laws of our nation are clear," Commander Callen Albright responded, sitting on the opposite side of Memnon. "The Accused had his day in court and the System found him guilty. Now he faces retribution in his Trial by Combat. If he is to prevail, he will walk free, as the Codes dictate clearly."

Dakar knocked his flask back again and snorted. "We both know the boy won't prevail, Albright. The Goliath is gonna crush him like a freshly laid hatchling."

"If destiny preordains his survival, then he will—"

"Dark your destiny!" Dakar yelled at Albright, spraying his foul-smelling drink in Memnon's face. "You've seen the Goliath just like I have. Do you know how many of my PublicDefenders that beast has put in the dirt just this past year? Do you know?"

Callen chuckled, amused at the line of questioning. "No, Pugilio, I have no idea how many of your inept Grievar the Goliath has killed this year. Why don't you enlighten me?"

"Twelve!" Dakar yelled. "Twelve of my men, mangled, ripped apart, not even fit for proper burial. I'm the one to tell the news to their wives, their mas and pas, their darkin' little ones..."

Callen sneered. "If your Defenders were properly trained, if they had some actual discipline, then they'd score some wins for those they represented. The problem with PublicJustice isn't the Goliath, Pugilio; it's that disgraceful team of yours and their leadership."

Dakar stood up to his full height, red-faced and towering over Callen. "You sniveling coward! You think because you got some shit promotion recently, you're gonna walk over—"

"Please, Dakar, sit down," Memnon sighed, standing between his two commanders as he did so often.

Dakar fell into his seat and pressed the flask back to his lips. "You both know well as I that freak that the Governance puts out there... Goliath. It's not even a fair chance to the Accused. Whatever the Daimyo have done to it over the years, it's Grievar no longer. It's a monster."

"It gets the job done," Callen said. "It serves its purpose to supply justice to those that deserve it. And this boy, Cego. I know justice has been seeking him for some time now, since Murray first dragged him up from the Deep."

Memnon's shoulders sagged upon hearing Murray's name. He knew his old champion would be standing in Central Square right now in Cego's stead, facing the Goliath fearlessly. Even the Mighty Murray Pearson would fall to this beast, though. The only reason the Governance didn't use the Goliath as a Knight to represent international disputes was because it was volatile. Uncontrollable. There'd been too many incidents gone wrong, friendlies and training partners found on the wrong side of its rage.

"Murray'd be here, standing in the way of this injustice," Dakar mumbled, mirroring Memnon's thoughts.

"Murray isn't here, though," Memnon growled, frustration rising within him. "Murray abandoned his post, his people, and his nation. He left us without saying a word. And he left the boy, who will die if he must."

Murray had disappeared after Memnon had offered him a commander's position. The shit-stubborn Grievar had laughed in Memnon's face, after everything the two had gone through together.

"Murray is probably the reason all of this is happening," Callen said as he sat back in his seat with his hands behind his head. "With his constant need to disobey orders, walk his own path, no wonder his so-called protégé, Cego, turned to crime."

Memnon knew something was out of place. He knew of Cego's hidden past. He knew of the boy's upbringing in the Cradle, the first of many in the Governance program to create a superior Knight force. The Daimyo were cooking something up, as usual. But there wasn't anything Memnon could do. Somehow, the boy had gotten himself in deep. And now he'd need to fend for himself. There weren't always heroes out there to save people. Some had to respond to the call of duty—serve a greater cause.

Suddenly, a wave of silence washed over the crowd beneath the Citadel's commanders.

"It comes," whispered Callen Albright as he lifted a magnifying monocle to his eye to get a better view.

Memnon looked toward the north side of Central Square to see a hulking form approach. Two fully armed mech Enforcers guided the Goliath, each grasping a long steel rod attached to the thing's arms to keep it at a distance.

Even the high commander held his breath, looking at the Goliath. It was the largest Grievar Memnon had ever seen, if it could even be called a Grievar anymore.

As the Goliath entered the Circle at the foot of the square's amphitheater steps, it screamed, an unearthly bellow, displaying rows of sharpened teeth. Its veined muscles pulsed as it thrashed against the Enforcers' restraints, forcing the mechs to dig their steel boots into the dirt.

"Simply incredible," Callen whispered under his breath. "If only we could get the beast into the Knights' ranks. We'd fill Halberd's spot and more."

Memnon shook his head wearily as he stared down at the scene alongside the slack-jawed crowd.

The Goliath's head was massive and malformed, centered on

two rage-filled eyes hugging a wide, bulbous nose. Its ears hung like leathery pus sacs, each pierced with numerous bone ornaments.

Memnon had once looked into those eyes with familiarity. The Goliath had once been a man. A Knight whom Memnon had served alongside with honor. Bernathon Grimbly.

The team had just returned from a successful campaign on the Adar ridge, winning a series of matches against the Kirothians. Bernathon had always been homesick when the Knights were sent abroad, speaking constantly of his wife and three sons waiting for him in the homeland. The man had returned to find his entire family murdered. And then he'd disappeared.

Memnon had asked about Grimbly's whereabouts, but Governance had been tight-lipped. Years later, the Daimyo had delivered the Goliath to PublicJustice, made a show of the creature's freakish strength to Command. It was only the man's eyes that hadn't changed, the one way Memnon had recognized the beast as once a man at all.

"Cego." Commander Pugilio pierced Memnon's reverie with the boy's name.

The crowd's silence turned into an eruption of raucous jeers. Memnon looked to the south entrance to see the boy dragged behind an Enforcer. Cego was hooded, blind to the world, and looking so small, he appeared like any of the other children standing in the crowd, many who were now tossing rotten fruit at the Accused.

Memnon felt the cold steel of Dakar's flask against his arm. He met his commander's eyes and took the offering, throwing back a swig of the powerful liquid.

What had he done?

*   *   *

Cego blinked as the hood was ripped from his head and the brightness of the world exploded into view.

Something skidded across Cego's shoulder and splattered onto his face. He stared out wide-eyed at the crowd surrounding him, unnamed faces screaming, jeering, and hurling fruit as Cego knelt on the ground, still manacled to his Enforcer.

The reverb of a megaphone blasted atop the din of the crowd. "We gather here, in Central Square, joyous for another day of justice in the Capital of your nation of Ezo!"

The crowd hooted and clapped. Cego tried to cover his face as another fruit careened toward him, its hard shell slamming into his skull.

Why were they doing this to him?

He looked out into the crowd. He watched a man hoisting his little daughter up on his shoulders, the girl smiling and laughing. He spotted an old lady hunched up against the barricade, staring at him silently with judgmental eyes. He saw a massive Grievar boy pushing his way through the crowd like a steamroller.

Joba.

Joba used his bulk to clear a path right up to the steel blockade, the ever-present smile dressing his face even as he waded through the chaos.

"Cego!" Dozer followed behind Joba, shoving aside spectators as he bellowed. "We're here, brother!"

And then they were all there. Dozer, Knees, Joba, Abel, and Brynn. His friends were there for him again. Cego even saw Kōri Shimo, awkwardly standing beside the Whelps, staring back at him without expression.

Cego started to shout back to his friends, but the Enforcer shoved him to the ground, belly first, mashing his face to the concrete of the square.

"Silence, two hundred twelve," the mech's voice droned in Cego's ear. "I will remove your manacles shortly; stay still until you are told to do otherwise."

Cego watched his friends from his flattened position. Abel frowned deeply and Brynn appeared on the verge of tears. Knees watched him with wide eyes, but Cego realized the Venturian was not focused on him. Knees stared at something beyond him.

Cego turned his head to follow Knees's gaze.

What he saw, towering across the Circle, seemed a nightmare, some horror that woke children from their sleep.

It was no Grievar, not even close. The thing met Cego's eyes with its own, two unforgiving orbs set atop a deformed skull. It bared its teeth, gleaming rows of daggers meant for the mouth of some wild beast, not for a man with arms and legs.

This was the Goliath. This was the creature Zyleth had warned Cego of. Staring at the Goliath as it roared and struggled to break its restraints, Cego could only think one thing: Perhaps the professor had been right to recommend Cego take the cannon fire for a quick execution.

He looked back at his friends still jostling with the raucous crowd to keep their spot alongside the barricade. He wanted to appear brave, confident in front of them. He wanted to act a leader. But Cego was not confident. He was terrified, a scared boy who didn't know why this was all happening to him.

The Enforcer removed Cego's manacles and violently jerked him back to his knees, forcing him to look at the Goliath. The beast was raking its feet in the dirt like a bull as it reared against its restraints. It gnashed its teeth and hurled its bony fists in the air as the two Enforcers at its side prepared to release it.

"You all know why we are here on this glorious day!" the announcer called into the loudspeaker. "We've got a Code breaker in our midst. We've got a cold-blooded murderer that once walked among us."

The crowd erupted into jeers again, even louder this time, a throbbing chorus that struck Cego in the chest like a front kick. Another barrage of fruits showered him, some bouncing off the Enforcer's steel armor.

"But we have our justice," the announcer continued. "We have our Governance-appointed justice, who will serve to destroy this criminal. The outlaw will be eradicated, buried in the dirt and no longer a threat to our nation. To do this noble task, we have our Goliath!"

The crowd screamed in approval, mothers and fathers and little children raising their hands in the air, cheering on the snarling beast in the Circle.

"Let justice be served!" the announcer sang the words, hanging on each like some violent melody.

Cego stumbled to his feet, his arms limp after being manacled for so long. He helplessly watched as the Enforcers released the Goliath, unclasping the steel rings that circled its bulging biceps.

Cego met the Goliath's eyes. Perhaps once there was a man within this gargantuan body, but Cego could see nothing but a wild beast springing toward him on all four limbs, leading with its open maw.

The crowd chanted, "*Goliath, Goliath, Goliath!*"

The bright sun glinted in Cego's eyes. He could feel the concrete beneath his bare feet. The odors of sweat and urine and charred street foods filled his nostrils.

Through it all Cego heard a voice, crystal clear and ringing out to him.

"Cego, I'm here."

The Goliath was locked in place across from Cego, its face frozen in a vicious snarl as it reached forward with a claw, the knuckles shaven and sharpened down to the bone.

"Cego, I'm here, over here."

Cego followed the voice to the crowd, where expressions of bloodlust and fear were captured in a sea of frozen faces.

"Cego, I'm here," the voice repeated.

Cego's gaze caught movement in the frozen world in front of him, some disruption of continuity within the shadows of the crowd. One of the shadows seemed to be sliding forward, apart from its comrades, across the ground and unburdened by a body above it.

The shadow slid toward Cego, stopping just at his feet before it broke the plane of the pavement and stretched up toward the sky, like some feline just waking. The shadow shimmered and grew in depth, suddenly filling itself with color and tone, morphing into a familiar human form.

A face took shape on the body, smoothing out and freckling and protruding into a sharp nose. Finally, two eyes blinked to life, colored like beach grass.

Sam.

There was no mistaking Cego's little brother.

Sam was shirtless and sun-kissed, just as Cego remembered him.

"Hullo, Cego," Sam said casually.

"How can you be here?"

"I've always been here, Cego," Sam replied. "I starved with you on the streets of the Underground. I walked the halls of the Lyceum and stood with you in the Circle. I sat beside you at your trial in the old Courthouse. And I'm here with you now."

"How?" Cego asked. "You can't be here. You aren't real."

"We're brothers," Sam said as he reached out toward Cego and rested a hand on his chest. "We're connected, you and I and Silas. We brothers share many things, not just memories of the island or the techniques Farmer taught us. We brothers share much more than that. We share blood and light and time."

Cego shook his head. "I don't understand."

"I felt it when you were released into this world, Cego," Sam said. "I cried with you when you were left for dead in the slave Circles, and I felt so much pride when you made it into the Lyceum. We are connected; we always will be."

Somehow, Cego knew it. He'd always known it. Sam and Silas were a part of him as much as the heart nestled in his chest.

"Sam, I've missed you," Cego said, wanting to reach out and

embrace the boy standing in front of him. He held back. "Are you doing all right?"

"Yes, I'm doing all right," Sam said.

"And Silas?" Cego asked. "I saw him on SystemView. I've felt him too."

"Silas is where he needs to be," Sam said confidently. "Don't worry about either of us. Focus on what's in front of you."

Cego turned toward the Goliath, completely frozen but still terrifying.

"How can I possibly win against that monster?" Cego asked in despair. "I've got nothing on it. Size, speed, strength. Those people out there. They're here to watch me die, Sam."

"You do have something that the Goliath does not, brother," Sam's eyes twinkled. "Something far more valuable."

"What?"

"Time," Sam said. "Time is how we grew strong on the island. How many sunrises and starry nights did we spend there, training, preparing?"

Suddenly, Cego could hear the crowd again, low murmurs emerging on sloth-like lips, forms and shapes and light around him awakening from deep hibernation.

"Brother," Sam whispered. "You think you only spent thirteen years on the island. But it was longer. Far longer. Time is something you have in abundance that no man or Goliath has."

Sam's freckled face started to fade in front of Cego, his body blurring and dripping back into the shadows on the concrete.

"Sam," Cego yelled. "Where are you going?"

But Sam did not respond. His brother had already dissipated to shadow and shrunk back into the crowd.

The Goliath's giant arms and legs shook and strained toward Cego like some machine finally given enough charge to complete its brutal task. The clamor of the crowd rose again, and the light dispelled the shadows.

The Goliath's gnarled feet exploded off the ground.

The beast arrowed toward Cego like a maelstrom of violence, thrashing fists carrying the force to blast through a stone wall. And then Cego was within the whirlwind, the mad rage of the Goliath swirling around him.

Even inside the chaos, Cego saw patterns. He watched a massive fist careen over his head and a lashing elbow following it. He noticed a weighted forward leg propelling the beast, grasping at Cego, trying to squeeze the life from him. He saw a long cross hurtling toward him, coupled with a sudden, jerking head butt.

Cego evaded. He ducked and weaved, dove in and out, sidestepped. He knew the stakes: Letting the Goliath connect with even a glancing blow would shatter him.

One of the Goliath's jagged fists, knuckles of carved bone, swiped Cego across the shoulder. Blood spattered the concrete, eliciting the crowd's roar of approval.

Cego didn't feel the raw open wound painting his chest crimson. The crowd was no more than a distant murmur.

He felt an electric rush course through his body, some untapped well dispelling the ache from his unhealed injuries, shedding the torpor from his days unmoving in captivity and breaking the hesitation of his unsure mind. The blacklight.

The energy surged up his arm; he felt the Doragūn flux come alive again, streaking across his skin as if his veins were on fire. But this time, Cego controlled the blacklight. It was not the uncaged chaos that would take his mind. The blacklight would not force him to watch his own body as an outsider. Instead, Cego channeled it within: He knew he'd been born from the blacklight, a lifetime of perfecting movement and technique in the Cradle.

The Goliath paused its onslaught for a single, disparate gulf between raging waves. Its monstrous chest heaved as it stared at Cego, questioning how its prey could prove so difficult to catch.

The gulf expired and the Goliath crashed back at Cego with another barrage of furious attacks.

Cego continued to evade masterfully; he couldn't let in another knuckled slash or he'd bleed out before the Goliath had a chance to bash his brains in. He needed to counterattack between the beats of violence. He needed to bring this beast to its knees.

He slammed his hardest side kick into the Goliath's kneecap. Cego's own leg buckled. Whatever this thing was made of was not simple bone and muscle. How could he bring down something so massive, so fortified?

To bring a mountain down, remove one stone at a time.

The old master's martial wisdom was still within Cego, a tool he could easily draw from his belt.

Cego shot a quick penetration step beneath the Goliath's towering legs, emerging at the thing's backside. The beast began to turn, but Cego timed a well-placed kick behind the knee, finding soft tissue and ligament. Still, the Goliath did not flinch.

Cego flowed atop the Goliath's violent patterns, constantly maneuvering himself to the back and side of the creature, again and again slamming the heel of his foot into the soft tissue behind its shell of a kneecap.

Cego chopped at the giant repeatedly, not even bothering to feign strikes elsewhere. All his energy focused on disrupting a single, load-bearing joint in the Goliath's frame.

He evaded another massive cross, shuffling to the side and rotating his full body weight into a spinning kick, his heel directly connecting with the Goliath's knee. This time, something buckled. And just like that, the gargantuan leg above the knee gave way, shuddering and collapsing.

The Goliath roared, the guttural sound of a starved animal being deprived of its meal.

It tried to return to its feet, putting weight on its shredded knee, only to fall back to the ground. Undeterred, it bellowed and launched itself toward Cego in a sprawl, throwing a hammer fist that cracked the concrete where it landed.

Cego took advantage of the opportunity, springing forward and slamming his fist at full power into the Goliath's skull. His hand shattered. Cego felt his fingers break as if he'd tried to punch through a steel wall.

But Cego couldn't stop; this beast certainly would not. He launched a flying knee to the Goliath's lowered chin. The beast's head jerked upward and back, and suddenly the thing stopped coming forward. It unexpectedly shrank away.

Had he somehow wounded the Goliath?

He needed to finish it, fast. Cego leapt forward, throwing a side kick aimed at the soft tissue beneath the beast's rib cage. He'd used the same kick to finish Rhodan Bertoth.

But the Goliath was not Rhodan Bertoth. It was not any normal combatant. Something within the beast twitched, and it moved faster than Cego thought possible for something so large. It whipped an arm out and wrapped a massive hand around Cego's incoming foot.

"Heh, heh," the beast chuckled, a deep and terrifying noise. The Goliath slung him into the air by the foot like a frail plaything.

Cego saw the blue sky, the glint of the sun, and then the crowd, appearing upside down, before the concrete rushed to meet him with terrible speed.

He felt his shoulder explode, as if he'd fallen from the top of one of the Tendrum District's tall towers. The shock wave of impact unraveled his body.

The Goliath picked Cego back up, dangling him upside down and peering at him like a broken toy. The crowd roared, delirious for the final blow as the Goliath cocked its spiked fist, ready to pulverize another victim in the name of justice.

"Goliath! Goliath! Goliath!"

Cego squeezed his eyes shut, waiting for impact. He heard the

Goliath chuckle again, clearly taking in the adoration of the blood-thirsty crowd, the one thing that seemed to feed the beast.

But the blow didn't come.

The chants for the Goliath were suddenly broken by jeers. The crowd was distracted. Cego opened his eyes, still dangling upside down, to see a familiar form steadily climbing over the far-side barrier.

Joba.

Cego's friend was not smiling for once. A determined look had invaded Joba's gentle face as he strode forward, uncaring that two Enforcers had just turned from their work across the square at the sight of an unauthorized entry to the combat zone.

"No...please. Turn around, Joba." Cego struggled futilely against the Goliath's strength. The beast appeared confused, stunned for a moment, unsure why the crowd had stopped chanting its name. But still, it tightened its grasp on Cego's ankle and raised its other hand for the killing blow.

"Urgh!"

Cego suddenly saw two thick arms wrapped around the Goliath's neck, setting in a strangle. A fat head peeked out from behind the Goliath's shoulder. Joba had taken the Goliath's back and was squeezing the beast's neck with all his might.

The Goliath dropped Cego to the ground in annoyance and grasped back around its shoulder. It ripped big Joba's arm free like a child's before rearing forward violently. Joba sprawled to the concrete.

Cego watched from the ground as Joba stood again. His friend steadily walked back in front of Cego, staring down the Goliath, protecting him.

A raucous chorus of jeers erupted from the crowd and the Goliath continued to look confused. Two opponents in the Circle. This wasn't supposed to happen.

And then Cego heard a noise he'd never forget. Like the sound of the undertow after you'd been pulled beneath the sea by a large wave.

Cego met Joba's eyes and his big friend smiled again for a moment before he looked down at his midsection to see a giant hole in the place of his stomach, burned all the way through. On the other side of him, an Enforcer's smoking spectral cannon hissed blue.

The crowd roared in approval as Joba fell face-first to the pavement. The Goliath joined in with a primal scream as it crawled on all fours toward Cego.

Cego stared at Joba's torn body on the floor. He heard a wail through the crowd, cutting above the screams of rancor. A shriek of sadness. *Abel.*

Somehow, Abel's cry brought strength to Cego's legs. He propped himself to his knees and then back to his feet. Cego stood to meet the incoming beast, his arm hanging limply at his side.

The Goliath launched itself at Cego and he dodged, replying with a quick combination, pulling his initial punches but ending with a power shot, a cutting elbow that landed flush on the creature's orbital, finally finding some soft tissue to rupture.

The Goliath roared and leapt toward Cego again, grasping at him with its razor-boned hands. Cego evaded and targeted the same soft spot, the eye socket, this time with a straight kick that landed flush.

The Goliath held back for a beat, breathing heavily and watching Cego warily through its remaining good eye.

Cego met the beast's stare as he felt the blacklight energy surge through him again. The Doragūn flux exploded in brilliant colors down his arm before compacting into a pulsing core at his fist. Cego launched himself forward, far faster than he knew he could move, and slammed his hand into the Goliath's eye socket with his entire body weight behind it. His balled fist was the perfect projectile, puncturing the Goliath's lens, traveling through the vitreous resistance, severing the optical wiring and continuing even farther, until Cego's arm disappeared into the skull to the elbow. He torqued his hand to find the soft, sinewy path past the hard musculature, finally burying it in a thick bundle of nerves.

Cego ripped his arm free, slick with ichor and brain matter.

The Goliath's massive head rocked back and then plummeted to the pavement with a *thud*, an empty socket still staring lifelessly toward the blue sky above.

The crowd was silent.

*   *   *

High Commander Memnon had nearly polished off Dakar Pugilio's flask, clenching the metal case in his hand as he watched the crowd go silent.

"Lord Patron's blessed shit," Dakar slurred from beside Memnon, staring down at the spectacle in Central Square. Cego knelt on the concrete, covered head to toe in the Goliath's blood. The boy looked tiny next to the massive corpse beside him.

Even the hawkers around the periphery of the square had gone quiet, holding their squawks along with the spectators, as if they all expected the Goliath to breathe again, stand and fight as some undead creature of combat.

"He cheated," Commander Callen whispered, standing on his feet and still peering through his monocle. "He had to have cheated again somehow. He's using Daimyo tech."

Memnon tried to stand but nearly toppled over as the effects of Dakar's drink unbalanced him. Despite his inebriation, he knew what would happen next. Memnon knew these people in the crowd, those who had come to view PublicJustice in action. These folk came seeking retribution for all those wrongs against them. They came to rectify their own wretched lives, filled with regrets and loss, all channeled into rage against the Accused. And now that retribution had been taken from them.

Memnon watched as the first stone flew, skidding to the concrete beside Cego; launched from the hand of an angry father or some rebellious adolescent, it didn't matter. He knew more would follow.

Without thinking, Memnon began to stumble down the stands toward Central Square below. His heavy boots crashed onto the amphitheater steps, trying to find footing within the packed crowd that was now shouting with fury.

Memnon saw the mech Enforcers standing at attention against the barricades, patiently waiting for the first in the mob to attempt to break through. Though Governance had attempted to execute Cego, they would not let PublicJustice appear weak in front of a mob of low breeds.

More projectiles flew from the crowd, rocks, discarded food, and globs of mud. Memnon watched a glass bottle strike Cego in the neck. The boy didn't flinch, just stared straight ahead as if he were in some sort of trance.

Memnon reached ground level and the thickest of Central Square's mob. He used his considerable bulk to push through the surge of people, many now chanting their demand in unison: *"Justice! Justice! Justice!"*

Memnon watched as a potbellied Grievar with wild eyes swung his fists at anything that came near him, smashing the head of a small lady trying to escape the mob with her child under wing. The high commander moved in, grabbed the man's arm, and tossed him to the ground, pinning him with a knee and staring him in the eye.

"Stop." Memnon said the word before smashing his fist into the man's face.

He kept moving, shoving aside a stalled food cart and leaping over two men wrestling on the ground. Chaos had broken loose. The mob didn't care who or what they destroyed; they just wanted to destroy something.

Memnon finally saw the barricade and the surge pushing against it like a herd of wildebeest.

He watched as a man attempted to leap over the barrier only

to get caught full force in the chest by an Enforcer's steel arm, hurling his broken body back into the crowd. A junkie with blue hair screamed as he tried to crawl over the other side, meeting an Enforcer's loaded spectral cannon. The unleashed blast melted the man's chest like ice on a Besaydian hot stone.

Memnon arrived at the barricade, grasping another unruly man by the hair and smashing his face into the steel.

"High Commander Memnon of the Citadel; I'm here to protect the boy," he called out to the nearest Enforcer.

The Enforcer nodded its visored helm and Memnon hurtled over the barricade, feeling the familiar pain streak up his back. It didn't slow him. He marched toward the Goliath's giant body spread out at the center of the Circle.

Cego sat in the same spot, covered in blood, staring out into nothingness. Another rock struck the boy on the shoulder hard, but he didn't flinch.

"Cego!" Memnon yelled as he grabbed the boy by the shoulders to pull him to his feet. Cego's legs were like pudding, collapsing beneath him and sending him back to his knees.

The boy didn't look up at Memnon or even register that the high commander stood over him. Another projectile sailed through the air, a metal bolt that thudded into Cego's chest, knocking him backward. Cego sat back up, his eyes still blank.

Memnon threw his body onto the boy's, wrapping his bulky arms around Cego.

The high commander of the Citadel felt the mob's wrath, the hail of projectiles falling on his back. Something sharp punched through his skin, hanging at his rib cage, but Memnon did not care.

This was his fault.

Memnon had known something was amiss at the trial. He'd known the Goliath was invoked to execute Cego. Why had he let it go so far? For what? Duty to his nation? The greater good? Memnon wasn't even sure what that meant anymore.

All Memnon knew was that he wanted to protect this boy. Cego had won his Trial by Combat.

"I've got you," Memnon whispered as he squeezed his arms around the boy tighter.

The high commander shivered suddenly as he felt something run through his body. Not the pain from the barrage of rocks raining onto his exposed back but something else, as if a fault had cracked inside him and released a long-buried artifact.

Sacrifice. Not in the symbolic way that he'd carried the Knights' team for so long, strategizing from afar and commanding his men to fight in Circles around the world. Not his sacrifice to the nation of Ezo, giving everything up. He'd taken no wife, bred no children, had no life outside of his position as high commander of the Citadel. No, this was not some far-fetched devotion for Memnon. This was the sacrifice of right here, right now: wrapping his arms around this boy to ensure his safety.

A large jagged rock smashed into his back, but he barely noticed. He felt the heat from a spectral cannon scorch above him, incinerating another mob member trying to scale the barricade.

Nothing mattered to Memnon but protecting this boy. Cego had won his freedom. He deserved to live.

Memnon heard a shrieking noise overhead. The scream became the whirring of an engine, and Memnon gazed up to the sky to see an obsidian Flyer descending on Central Square as one of the Enforcers waved it down.

"We've got him from here." An Enforcer put its steel hand on Memnon's shoulder. The high commander didn't want to let Cego go.

"We've got him," the Enforcer said with menace this time as Memnon felt the heat of a spectral cannon charging. He unclasped the boy from his bear hug, and the Enforcer lifted Cego like a house cat into its steel arms. The mech marched toward the waiting Flyer.

Memnon stood and watched, the mob still raging at his back, as the Enforcer carried Cego's limp body up the dropped entry plank, which then withdrew and sealed.

The Flyer ascended to the air, fire exploding beneath it to char the concrete black, before racing away into the cloudless sky.

Memnon wasn't sure how long he stood there watching the Flyer get smaller on the horizon. The crowd behind him had dispersed as several more Enforcers arrived at the scene.

It was quiet again. The Goliath's body was left carelessly on the concrete along with numerous members of the mob. And the big boy, Cego's friend from the Lyceum. His shredded body was laid out, his open eyes facing the sky.

"Memnon!" The high commander turned to see a familiar red face. Pugilio.

"You all right?" Dakar asked in his brusque way.

Memnon looked down at himself. Just flesh wounds. Nothing more than he'd endure after a good practice. "Yes, I'm fine."

"That was some charge, man!" Pugilio slapped him on the back, too drunk or uncaring of the welts spread across Memnon's shoulders. "Haven't seen you move like that in a while. Maybe even since we served together."

"Yes," Memnon said, keeping his eye trained on the Flyer. "The boy is safe, though."

"Right…" Dakar trailed off. "But I fear he's heading someplace worse than the hands of the mob now."

"What do you mean?" Memnon said, turning to Pugilio.

"You didn't see?" Pugilio said. "That Flyer. Wasn't any standard transport mech. I know it because I've been on one before. That was inmate transport. Where do you think it's going now?"

Pugilio pointed toward the Flyer, nearly gone on the horizon already.

"That thing's not heading back toward the Citadel," Dakar said. "That boy's off to Arklight Prison."

CHAPTER 21

The Show and the Squire

Loyalty is adherence to a path, a preordained way of life. A Grievar shall have loyalty to their fighting nature.
Passage One, Fifty-Second Precept of the Combat Codes

Silas couldn't see the path ahead in the storm and yet he trudged forward through the deep snow. The wind howled in his ears and burned his lungs, punishing him for every breath, every step forward.

He looked to the sky for the moon, but there was nothing, only frost blasting across the darkness, sheets of icy pain whirling down.

Silas continued forward, somehow pushing through the pain. He could feel his skin burning as the frost cut it, a thousand electric knives lighting up every nerve ending. He welcomed the challenge like an old friend.

He mechanically trudged through the snow with no sense of time or distance.

Finally, something appeared through the black. Torchlight flickering in windows. A small cottage in the distance, off down a long ridge. A fire burning, smoke drifting through a cobbled chimney.

And then he was at the doorstep, as if the wind had carried him. A forgotten scent filled his nose, something savory cooking within.

Silas paused, hearing voices, laughter. He felt a desperate urge to leave, to return to the tundra that he'd trodden. He wanted to retreat to the darkness, but he couldn't. The voices called to him; the light beckoned him.

This world they've built, it is not for us.

Silas was inside then, the heavy oak door shattered on the floor, wide-eyed creatures staring back at him. Little ones screaming, crying. Big ones yelling, swinging at him with fists and sticks and blades.

The torch flames set along the cottage walls danced to the intruding wind, and so did he. Silas felt the blacklight rise up within him, waiting to be released. His body found purpose; he was flying. He felt the crunch of his knuckles against a soft skull, the explosion of his foot against a kneecap, the sharp torque of an exposed neck.

Soon, this storm will come to them.

Screams were replaced with moans as the wind found its way to the fireplace, dousing it with frost and flicking out the torchlight.

And then there was only the darkness and the night wind passing over the chimney.

Silas's mouth curved up into a crooked smile.

Soon, we will find our path home.

*   *   *

Silas ran his hand through Karo's feathers, eyeing the pelts strung between buildings across the thoroughfare. The hides of every imaginable beast were draped on the streets of Zytoc Province, like flags flapping in the wind. They trotted beneath a line of assorted bear pelts, some already tanned to the skin and others still sporting fur and fresh blood.

"Good you're feathered, my friend," Silas whispered to his roc, though he knew the large bird was a delicacy in some parts around there.

The people of Zytoc Province specialized in making leather goods. They tanned and dressed pelts for an assortment of needs, though mostly to produce jerkins fit for Grievar combat training. The villagers took pride in constructing leathers thick enough to absorb impact, yet flexible to allow for agility in the Circle.

Most often, Zytoc's streets were near empty while the townsfolk worked within the tanneries. Today, though, the leather makers were out in abundance, cheering on their beloved Grievar Knights.

Silas rode his roc at the rear of the Knights' caravan, following in the shadow of an old, grinding transport mech. He ruffled Karo's feathers again to calm the bird.

Up front, the Knights rode atop a flotilla on wheels, garish machinery made solely to parade these men down city avenues. Marshal Vlador stood up front with his weathered face contorted into a smile. Ulrich towered behind Vlador, at least two heads taller than all the other Knights. The giant raised his fists in the air as if he'd just won a match. Beside Ulrich was Devana, the marshal that Silas could at least tolerate. He watched from the shadows as the Grievar woman's wild hair caught the wind and flowed behind her.

As they traveled toward Zytoc's central square, women threw flower wreaths from rooftops and open windows, while men on the street pounded their chests and hooted. Dirt-covered kids darted through the crowd to catch a glimpse of their favorite fighters.

Silas could see those set behind the crowds, though. He glimpsed townsfolk with grimaces on their faces, those who didn't cheer for the caravan. These were the ones who could barely buy milk to feed their infants and yet were forced to replenish the empire's bit-tax with what little they had.

The caravan pulled to a stop in the square, the mechs forming a perimeter around the Knights' flotilla. Vlador stepped forward.

"Dear folk of Zytoc," his amplified voice boomed through the square and down the city's narrow alleys. "Today, we stand before you in honor and victory. Today, we stand before you, having given our blood for you. Today, we kneel before you, Grievar Knights of the Kirothian Empire, at your service."

All the Knights bent to a knee and bowed their heads to the crowd. Vlador had a flair for the dramatic, such was the performance the caravan gave at each of these towns.

Silas stopped listening as Vlador droned on, speaking of the sacrifices his men gave, the training they put in every day so that they could be victorious within the Circle. The marshal spoke of how the support of towns like Zytoc helped the empire continue to win for the people.

Silas knew it wasn't true. Only a small percentage of the bit-tax went to Grievar programs. The Daimyo took most of the bits of these poor folk for their own opulence: to put bounties on their tables, buy slaves, and build their own personal empires.

It was all a performance, just like Vlador's little speech. And everyone was a loser: Knight, servicer, grower, leather maker, or crafter. All except for those at the top of the food chain. The Daimyo.

Silas was jostled from his reverie at the mention of his own name.

"Ahem, again," Vlador said. "The man who single-handedly brought honor back to the empire. He defeated Ezo's champion, Artemis Halberd, putting him in the dirt while barely breaking a sweat. Silas the Slayer himself!"

Vlador swiveled his head, not knowing if Silas was even in their presence.

Silas dismounted his roc and stepped out from the shadows behind the tank. The crowd parted as he strode to the pavilion, their collective breath held as the man in black leapt atop the stage like a cat.

Silas stood unmoving as he always did while the crowd cheered him. *For what?* Destroying an unworthy opponent? The champion, Artemis Halberd, had been broken already. Silas didn't deserve these mindless cheers.

The applause finally died down as if the crowd expected Silas to say something. He did not speak.

"You have a silent hero, my good folk," Vlador yelled. "He lets his technique in the Circle speak for itself!"

The crowd roared again. Vlador seemed to feed on it, soaking in the adoration for Silas.

"And now, let's have a demonstration of that storied technique, shall we?" Vlador asked, prompting even more approval.

A neophyte Knight, Leor Karrin, stepped forward onto the stage. He tightened the bands on his red leather jerkin. Silas had sparred with Karrin at each town they passed through to demonstrate their fighting competence. It was a dance of sorts; Karrin was to throw a variety of punches, kicks, and clinches his way. Silas would parry each, prior to going on the offensive. He'd put Karrin down with a throw, mount the downed Knight, and finish the whole charade with a feigned strangle.

The crowd went silent as Silas stepped forward, his black cloak whipping in the wind.

Silas didn't even put his arms up in a fighting posture as Karrin came at him. He simply used head movement to avoid the Grievar's punches.

The crowd gasped at Silas's dexterity, the way he moved seamlessly to dodge Karrin's blows. Silas played his part. He danced like a marionette, bobbing, weaving, fading in and out until it was his turn to go on the offensive.

As Silas attacked, the world slowed around him. He noticed the sky's blue tint fade to grey as wispy clouds formed overhead. He heard the barking of a dog in the distance. He felt the eyes of the onlookers bearing into him.

And he noticed a child, freckled and shirtless, standing barely four feet tall amid the chaos of the crowd. But the boy's piercing eyes shone out from the dirt and dust, and his voice was clear, despite the clamor.

"Silas, we're still here."

Was it him, speaking to Silas again? Telling him the truths of this world?

No, this was different. The boy's voice was unmistakable. Silas knew that voice as well as he knew his own.

He called out to the boy, "Where? Where are you?"

"We're still here," the boy repeated.

Silas screamed the boy's name. He knew this child's favorite path down to the black sand beach, the way he twisted his nose at the smell of the saltwater pools, how he forgot to move his hips when trying to escape from side control.

Silas was frantic, screaming the boy's name over and over. He could hear himself, like a wolf howling for its pack. He felt the hair on his neck prickle up. He heard his own panting breath and he saw the mist leave his mouth into the cold air.

Silas looked to the sky. A lone snowflake fell toward him from the clouds above. More snowflakes followed, crystalline clusters falling on the stage.

Silas looked toward the ground. There, covered in red snow, was Karrin, his lifeless eyes looking up at Silas from the strangest of angles. Silas turned back to the silent crowd, unaware of their stunned faces.

All Silas noticed was that the boy in the crowd was gone. Sam was gone.

*   *   *

The boy sat at the corner of the tent, staring at the grass. Though he'd been serving the Daimyo for the past month, he hadn't been able to shake the old beliefs, the fear his kin had instilled into him.

Despite the fear, the boy couldn't help but glance up at the confrontation.

"He is a liability." Spittle flew from the Kirothian viceroy's mouth.

"Yes, but he's our liability, at least," Marshal Vlador responded. "Otherwise he could be, let's say, an Ezonian liability."

Grunts had erected the makeshift assembly hall when they'd first arrived at camp outside Zytoc Province. More than half of the empire's combat council sat around the circular table within the large tent, three Daimyo viceroys representing Kiroth's largest cities and three Grievar marshals representing the Knights.

"He's doing what you civs want him to do, right?" Marshal Ulrich asked as he ripped into a boar shank. "He's fighting."

"He is here to fight enemy combatants," the viceroy named Mansher responded as his black eyes briefly cast over the boy. "Killing our own is not part of the deal. Do you know how much the yearly bit-cost of training a Knight is? And have you seen how the man speaks to himself? He's clearly mad. A liability."

The viceroy of Karbrok stood formally to make his statement, peering over a pair of glowing spectacles. "The people of Karbrok do not condone actions that stray from the Codes; however, we are a united front behind strengthening our forces, with the dual purposes of displaying the empire's might in the face of foreigners encroaching on our land, as well as providing exemplary leadership within our Knights' program."

Marshal Devana snorted. The boy liked the Grievar woman, who stood in her thick furs, whipping her long hair over her shoulder. She'd always been unable to contain herself in these meetings, near the Daimyo with their formal graces.

"Whatever the dogs of Karbrok or Tolensk or any of your stinkin' nobility-infested cities want, it's just piss to the wind." Devana stalked the circumference of the table, glaring at each of the Daimyo as she passed.

She sniffed the air. "Smells like we have three bluebloods in this tent. And three Grievar-kin to round out the council."

Devana didn't even notice the boy's presence. He was a Grievar after all, and though not yet a Knight like the rest of the three adults, he felt his pride momentarily injured.

"Last I remembered, three in the black means we break the pact," Devana said. "You know my vote already. He should be free to fight where he likes; nothing holds him here."

Another of the viceroys stood, a small lady with a smirk on her pale blue lips. "As Marshal Devana so eloquently stated, she is correct that three dissenting votes to release Silas from our Knights' battalion will unseal the pact."

"Lady Millisand, I assure you that Devana understands as well as I how important the asset is right now for the empire," Vlador interjected, sensing conflict.

"Thank you for your assurance, Marshal Vlador," Millisand purred as she walked toward Devana, barely coming to the Grievar woman's shoulder and yet staring up at her with confidence. "But I do not believe your compatriot does fully understand."

The boy watched as the Daimyo woman stared directly into Devana's eyes, before moving on to stand beside her fellow viceroy.

"Mansher, I understand your anxiety that the asset is becoming uncontrollable." Millisand placed her gloved hand on the man's shoulder and looked to the council.

"My estate recently purchased a rare azure lioness, which was similarly uncontrollable after we separated her from her pride. She gave in to fits of rage and even dismembered a few of my choice servicers. At first, I tried to control the beast with a closed fist, caging and branding her when she acted out. But she continued to follow her retaliatory nature. So, I decided to learn more about the lioness, watch her and discover what she truly wanted. I soon found her quite taken with a particular sort of prey: newborn hind. We gave her fresh hind every meal, and suddenly the lioness was tame. Now she sleeps at my bedside like a kitten."

The boy shivered, thinking about this soulless Daimyo woman

and her bloodthirsty beast. He was once again relieved that no one was paying any notice to him in the corner of the tent.

"So, you're sayin' we should feed Silas more deer meat to keep him happy?" Ulrich belched from across the table.

"No, Ulrich," Vlador answered. "Lady Millisand is saying we need to know more about the asset to keep him under control."

"Again with *the asset!*" Devana yelled, her face flushed red. "Can't call your kin by their real name, Vlador? Just because you're starting to talk like these bluebloods doesn't mean you're one of them."

Millisand ignored Devana's outburst and continued. "We simply need a way to properly observe the asset on a regular basis. A way to collect information so that we know what he truly wants."

"Perhaps we could amend the current situation by giving Silas some help," the viceroy of Karbrok interjected.

Vlador eyed the man. "What are you suggesting?"

"Most of our top Knights do have squires, do they not?" the spectacled Daimyo asked. "If we were to put the right squire in place, one with a more intimate knowledge of our goals, they would be able to...communicate with us when necessary."

"A spy!" Devana shouted. "You want to have a darkin' spy in Silas's tent, slinking around and then coming home to your ears, just because you don't have the balls to control him on your own."

"Again"—the viceroy of Karbrok coughed—"as I stated, it is not uncommon for our Knights to have squires, and Silas has not been assigned one yet. Not a spy, simply a man to keep an eye on him."

"I agree with this proposal," Millisand said as she returned to her seat. "Mansher, would this strategy soothe your wired nerves about our asset?"

"It would indeed, Millisand," Mansher said. "Marshal Vlador, I trust you can find the right man to serve as a squire?"

Vlador nodded. "I have someone in mind already."

The marshal suddenly turned toward the corner the boy sat in.

"Varik here has been a fine servant, tending to us on our travels. But he's no Grunt. He's Grievar stock, and is meant for more than service work."

All eyes in the room were suddenly cast at the boy, those pupilless gazes of the Daimyo viceroys burrowing into him. The boy withered back into the corner. He thought of his wrinkled grandmatron, who had told him as a child that meeting the eyes of the Daimyo would mean losing his strength, his vigor, his soul.

The viceroy of Karbrok stood as he examined the boy like a piece of meat. "It is settled, then. We continue to employ Silas the Slayer as a Knight of the empire. And we install our trustworthy squire, Varik, to…help him. Vote if you hold true to this."

Three Daimyo held their open palms to the air along with Marshal Ulrich, who still held a shank in his clenched fist.

The boy watched Vlador meet Devana's eyes as the man slowly raised his palm. The Grievar woman returned his gaze with disgust and stood up.

"I once knew an honorable man." Devana spat on the ground. "But now he's gone."

"It is done," said the viceroy of Karbrok. "The boy will accompany the Slayer, serve him, and not let him out of his sight unless it is to report to us."

Varik thought back to just before this meeting in the tent, when he'd watched from the crowd as Silas beat the other Knight bloody. He recalled the empty stare in the Slayer's eyes as he'd torn apart one of his own teammates.

Varik shivered again.

CHAPTER 22

Broken Specimens

A Grievar does not let external circumstance influence technique or strategy. Whether fighting in the light of the masses or in the shadows of a training study, a Grievar moves with equal purpose and efficacy. One who caters to environment with a changed mind will falter.

Passage Two, One Hundred Twelfth
Precept of the Combat Codes

Sol flipped her black braid to the side and took a deep breath as she appraised herself in the mirror.

A serpentine form flowed up her left shoulder and slithered out at her collarbone. It must have been her imagination, but the little whelp flux that she'd received as a Level One seemed to watch her lately with judgmental eyes.

Have you forgotten your team back at the Lyceum? Here you are, sitting in the lap of luxury in some Daimyo lord's house, while the Whelps struggle... What if they need you? What if he needs you?

Sol averted her eyes from the whelp flux and looked to the newest addition across her opposite shoulder. A crimson roc with its hooked beak curved around her shoulder blade raised its feathered head proudly, staring back at her, reminding her that she was now a fighter in Lord Cantino's famed stable.

I'm here for a reason.

Sol sighed as she pulled a tunic on and exited the room. She knocked on N'auri's door across the hall. The two had just a few moments free from training each week, and Sol had made it clear she wanted to visit Lord Cantino's famed museum filled with artifacts of Grievar history. Sol did not mention that the artifact she was most interested in was *her father's corpse.*

At one point, she considered divulging her entire plan to N'auri. If anyone could understand, it would be her Emeraldi friend. But Sol had dismissed the idea after considering that N'auri would have to risk everything to help her: her dreams, her promises to her mafé. Sol couldn't let her take those risks. She'd have to do this alone.

Sol knocked on the door, eyeing the glittering Kova stone that N'auri had latched to the wooden frame on her first night there. *Wherever I go, wherever my home is, this will be on the door,* N'auri had said.

N'auri opened up, dressed in the same bedraggled combat skin that she'd been wearing the night before.

"'Lo, Sayana," N'auri said.

"Didn't you want to wash up before our visit to the museum?" Sol asked. She'd made use of the ample washroom, bathing and scrubbing off the grime from a day of hard training, but it didn't seem like her friend enjoyed sitting in a hot bath as much as she did.

"No," N'auri flatly stated. "I aim to smell like a Grievar. I'm not using all these soaps and oils they give us."

The girl bent forward and sniffed at Sol playfully. "You're the one that stinks."

Sol pushed her away and chuckled as they walked down the hall.

"Plus, I really only like washing in the sea," N'auri explained. "Used to make the trip once per week back home."

Sol nodded in understanding. She could see how the veteran Grievar here had settled into their new lives, become accustomed to the luxuries that House Cantino had provided them. Meats that weren't vat-grown, purified water, fresh clothing every day. Things that Sol wouldn't have thought twice to be without normally, and yet now she considered them upon waking in the morning.

The two girls descended the stable's main stairwell from the living quarters to the ground floor, where the training facilities were housed. Despite having attended the greatest combat school in the world, the Lyceum, Sol was still quite impressed at Lord Cantino's facility. He had everything he needed to train an elite regiment of Grievar.

The girls nodded at Wraith, who nearly never left the training room. He was methodically working a heavy bag like a slab of meat, striking it with the same switch-kick combination over and over. The same combination that had knocked Sol senseless over a month before. Of course, the strange man didn't acknowledge their presence as they passed by.

The Besaydian sun was high and hot as usual as they exited the stables and crossed through the gardens to the west end of the grounds, where the lord's famed museum was located. Though several of the Isles' Daimyo lords had notable museums that visitors came far and wide to see, Cantino's was considered the gem of the lot.

The girls made their way to the west end of the gardens and broke onto a smaller path until they reached a raised dome covered with manicured grass. Two armed guards stood at attention at the head of the museum and stood to block their way.

"No entrance," one of them said mechanically through his visored helmet, which had a large dent atop it.

"We're in the lord's stable," N'auri responded. "Don't you recognize us?"

The large guard took an aggressive step toward N'auri, but Sol quickly intervened.

"My friend didn't mean anything by it, just that we were told by Lord Cantino that we would have access to the grounds during our time off from training."

"Not today," the guard answered. "Today's maintenance day for the museum. Closed for access."

"I don't think so, dent head," N'auri growled. "My friend here been in my ear since we arrived about going to this museum, and I don't plan to disappoint her."

Had Sol really been that transparent about her plans? She didn't have time to consider it as the guard began to reach for the rod holstered at his waist. N'auri darted forward, ready for the move, grasping the guard's wrist so that he couldn't draw the weapon. In response, the guard raised his other gauntleted hand to strike the girl down.

"Hold!" a commanding voice broke from behind them.

Lord Cantino, dressed in his full regalia, galloped toward them from across the gardens, mounted on a large bloodred roc. The magnificent bird halted and lowered its plumed head to the ground.

"I do not aim to see my newest recruits wasted on fighting my own guards," Cantino said as he dismounted.

The guard lowered his hand and dropped to a knee. "Yes, my lord."

"Now, if what I hear is correct, you would like to visit the museum?" Cantino asked, looking at Sol with his inky black eyes. He was just about the same height as her.

Sol nodded. "Yes, I'd been hoping to see it."

"Well, I do not think there is any better person on the entire isle to give you a proper tour," Cantino said as the guards moved aside. "I will take you."

They passed under the museum entryway made of two curved

white spikes meeting at their tips. The two guards started to follow, but Cantino turned back to stop them with a raised hand. "You think I cannot trust those from my own stable? Do something useful and take Firenze back to the roost."

Cantino handed the roc's bridle to the guard before leading Sol and N'auri down a series of polished, mismatched stairs, almost as if they were designed to trip visitors.

"I see you have already recognized this first exhibit," Cantino said. "These stairs are all bones from one creature. The ribs and teeth of the mega-seraphin. Once, the seraphin was said to patrol the waters that surrounded the Isles, a leviathan so large it could swallow fishing galleons in its maw and smash shantytowns with its tail. To this day, Grunt fishers swear they have sighted the beast offshore. Though it is more likely they are seeing one of my transport mechs coming in."

They descended from the sun-streaked day into a dimly lit world beneath the gardens, not illuminated with the brightness of spectral light but with oil torches evenly spaced on the stone walls. The stairway fed into a cavernous entry hall. Hanging from the ceiling was the skeleton of another behemoth, this one fully formed with four limbs and a skull filled with razor-sharp teeth.

"My oldest specimen," Cantino said proudly as they stopped to look up at the skeleton. "The giant tartarus, an early relative of modern wolves but, of course, quite a bit larger. They did hunt in packs like their modern cousins. Can you imagine that? A dozen of these beasts chasing a mammoth down, their teeth rending flesh like candle wax."

"What happened to it?" Sol asked, trying to sound interested. "How did a beast this powerful die out?" After all, she was supposedly there because she wanted to see the collection, not just one body in particular.

Cantino seemed to be delighted that someone was taking interest. "Good question, Sayana. Even the strongest of beasts succumb to nature's selection. All the behemoths of ancient times are gone today because they could not adapt to a new world. They could not change their feeding and hunting habits to accommodate to new pressures."

"Didn't you kill them all?" N'auri said bluntly. "Your kind. The Daimyo are the reason the behemoths are gone. Your tech destroyed their homes; your mechs hunted them to the end."

Cantino turned his black eyes on N'auri, the torchlight from the great hall flickering in their depths.

"Yes, you are correct," he replied. "My kind became one of the greatest pressures on the behemoths. And they could not adapt to our needs. They were not able to find their place in this world alongside us."

The three continued walking from the great hall into a series of smaller dome-shaped rooms, each with a variety of bestial skeletons displayed in cases and suspended from the ceilings. Cantino stood in front of an avian skeleton about the size of a Grievar.

"A roc!" Sol said, wishing to continue showing interest in the lord's collection.

"Yes," he said. "An ancient roc. This bird ran the steep mountainsides of these very Isles before the great seaquakes separated them. Then all the Isles were part of one landform called Gatalan. This roc ran alongside the behemoths of Gatalan: the tartarus wolf and the mammoth and the Golian bear. And yet this roc survived while those behemoths perished. Do you know why?"

"Adaptation?" Sol guessed.

"Yes," Cantino whispered. "This roc adapted to the world we built. It served as a worthy mount for us to ride long distances, a beast to carry burdensome loads or pull wagons full of grains. This roc in front of you shared the exact same blood as my mount tethered in the gardens above. This roc survived because it did not fight back against us like those behemoths, those giants who believed themselves kings of the world. They were stupid, and so they perished."

Cantino led them on toward the next room. Sol observed N'auri for a moment; her friend was scanning the room, looking around, but not at the exhibits. N'auri seemed to be more interested in watching the comings and goings of Grunt servicers mopping the floors and wiping every smudge off the display cases.

"And here." Cantino held his hands out to welcome the girls to another room. "Here is the pride of my museum. I would say begrudgingly it is dwarfed only by the Ezonian national museum's own exhibit. My Grievar collection."

Sol unintentionally held her breath as they entered the long hall, which was set up eerily similarly to the previous bestial exhibits. Skeletons of men and women, Grievar, were meticulously labeled and displayed in glass cases alongside the walls.

Cantino stood beside one of the first skeletons, an ancient-looking specimen that seemed to be missing several key bones: a hip, shoulder blade, femur, and one full arm.

"This is Aron," he said proudly. "My teams unearthed him in Western Myrkos, and now researchers around the world use him as a defining benchmark of Grievar evolution. Though they con-stantly argue about whether he should even be classified a Grievar at all."

N'auri appeared to show more interest in this exhibit, finally chiming in. "He's missing some limbs, so not sure if he'd be any good in the Circle."

Cantino laughed, a high-pitched sound like a cave bat made to find its way in the darkness. He pointed toward Aron's skull. "See the brow ridge? It is not quite as defined as a modern Grievar's, jut-ting out for protection against head strikes. Like yours."

Cantino brushed his hand against Sol's brow, pushing aside her hair and making her shudder. "And his hip, the left side that is remaining; look closely and you can see it does not have the same grooves that a modern Grievar would, the ambiothic track where ligaments are bundled to promote greater flexibility."

Cantino made another move toward Sol to demonstrate on her body again, but she was able to awkwardly sidestep toward the exhibit case and evade him. "But why was he different from us?" she asked.

"This is why Aron is so interesting," Cantino said. "He was alive during a unique window in time, a time when the Codes had only recently been established. Perhaps it had only been ten generations at this point that early Grievar had bred exclusively for the purpose of selecting for combat prowess."

"So, he...Aron might have bred with a Grunt or Daimyo?" Sol asked, thinking of her own creation.

"No," Cantino answered, his black eyes flicking back and forth between the two girls. "Each bloodline was still being established during this time period. There was no Grievar or Grunt or Daimyo as we know them today. Just as Grievar were racing toward the goal of a species evolved to fight in the Circles, the other bloodlines were also driving in their unique directions. The Grunts breeding toward their specific roles to provide labor and servitude. And my own kind, the Daimyo, slowly weeding out those many unnecessary traits, selecting only for those that benefited a ruling species: intelligence, ambition, cunning."

This was not the story Sol had been taught like so many other Grievar from an early age. "But what about the Codes?" she asked. "The story of the Endless Wars...my kind rising from the darkness to stop the bloodshed, to prevent the annihilation. Fighting so that the rest shall not have to."

Cantino laughed again. "So naïve! So childlike!" he exclaimed. "You never cease to amaze me, and yet...this is why I love your kind. This is why I've created this!" He held his arms out in mock embrace of the exhibit.

"The stories you have been told are not entirely incorrect, but, like most stories the lesser breeds learn, they are simplified," Cantino said. "The Grievar did come from the darkness to fight for us.

It is true. They came to prevent total annihilation, to stop the End-less Wars."

Cantino continued speaking as they slowly followed him down the long exhibit hall, passing less dated and more anatomically modern Grievar skeletons.

"But, of course, your kind did not just appear like in the sto-ries. Like everything important, it took time. Thousands of years of breeding, selecting for the correct traits. *That was the dark-ness the Grievar emerged from.* Over millennia, you emerged from the blackest night, one where all men were the same, without any merit or purpose or specialization. This is why ancient men fought, constantly warring over land and resources and power and every other tribal notion: It was because they were all the same."

Cantino pointed out a Grunt servicer quietly polishing the glass across from them. "Does that Grunt care that he is in servitude? Working through his life without any other ambitions? His only goal is to clean my floors, wash my glass. No, he certainly does not mind at all. He has been bred for this. To him, he is fulfilling his destiny by wiping away those smudge marks.

"And these specimens throughout history." Cantino waved his arm toward the Grievar skeletons lining the hall. "And you. Fulfill-ing your destiny by fighting. Does it not feel that way when you are in the Circle?"

Sol could not deny this feeling. When she was fighting, she felt free. Free of the cares of the world, not living in the past or the future. Simply flowing through the present moment, one tech-nique at a time. And yet half of Sol's blood was not Grievar. Half of her was Daimyo. What did this mean for her path, for her destiny?

The group entered the far part of the hall, reserved for the mod-ern era of Grievar specimens. Sol's breath caught in her chest as she prepared to see her father again after so long.

Here, the specimens were not just skeletons; they were pre-served bodies. Sol recognized the nameplates beneath some of the cases, famous fighters from only a few generations past. N'auri peered in, closely examining one of them.

"Nafari Mikoto." She whispered the name under her breath, dropping to one knee as she looked up at the man's embalmed face. Sol could see her friend was restraining herself, shudders running through her body.

"I suppose you know Mikoto's story well, being from the Isles yourself," Cantino said casually. "Often considered the greatest fighter to come out of Besayd. One of the greatest of his era. He is worshipped on an almost godlike status among the natives. I am sure N'auri here had the traditional altar for him within her home."

"We did," N'auri said. "Every night, my dafé made us all kneel in front of it, say our prayers to Mikoto."

"Yes," Cantino continued. "Although many do not know the full history. That Mikoto attended the Lyceum. He was trained by the best at the Citadel for years before coming back to the Isles and reaching his potential. The natives usually forget that part of the history. Their mythology tells that he trained in the wilds, braving the strongest undertows and wrestling the caimans in the swamplands. Mikoto built his famed kicking strength in the forests, knocking down so many trees that the locals hired him to clear groves for their new homes. Does this sound familiar, N'auri?"

N'auri nodded slowly. She stood to her full height across from Cantino. Sol saw the glint in her friend's eye. The same glint she had before she threw a punch. But if N'auri so much as laid a hand on Lord Cantino, both she and Sol would be corpses before sunset, like the Grievar staring back at them from within the cases.

Through clenched teeth, N'auri hissed, "If we are to talk about covering up history, talk about forgetting reality, let's talk about Maliora Pali. My mafé. Where is she standing with these great fighters, these men forever trapped in your collection?"

Lord Cantino didn't look surprised in the least at the mention of N'auri's mother. His black eyes moved back and forth. Cantino was in his element there, conversing, using his mind and words to determine the outcome of a situation.

"I had been expecting you to bring this up at some point, N'auri," he said. "I am glad we can finally discuss your mother."

N'auri took a step back. "You knew...you knew I'm Maliora Pali's kin?"

Again, that laugh. The high-pitched chortle escaped from Cantino's mouth and echoed through the exhibit hall, as if it were mocking all the noble Grievar souls housed here.

"What, you do not think I make sure my recruits are thoroughly researched prior to joining my stable?" Cantino asked. "Again, I cannot overstate how much I love your kind. So simple, so naïve. The fact that your mother was Maliora Pali *was the reason* you were brought on."

N'auri was silent.

"Yes, you had a decent performance at Aquarius. But I have seen better. But the fact that you are Maliora's daughter. And even better, that you are here to avenge her death, to become even greater than her so that your family name can finally be remembered. That is ambition. That is a path that I can support."

N'auri shook her head, attempting to hold back the violence surging through her veins.

"Ah...I see now. You blame me," Cantino whispered. "You blame he who brought Maliora Pali up from being a nobody, a peasant off the streets. You blame he who gave her the training and the facilities to progress within for years. The man who enabled her to become one of the best of her time. The man who let her fulfill her destiny by fighting in front of thousands of fans and countrymen. You blame me for giving all of that to her, correct?"

N'auri stayed silent.

"She died an honorable death," Cantino said. "In the Circle. One that any Grievar would seek. And yet you wanted more, loyal child. You wanted her name to be spoken on the streets, to be revered, perhaps even worshipped as our friend Mikoto is, at altars in homes across the Isles."

"No!" N'auri yelled. "I don't care about that. I just want her to be remembered. I want her memory to be honored, just like any Grievar in the Circle, giving their life for the fight, giving their life for... *you*."

"Is she not remembered?" Cantino asked. "I certainly remember Maliora. She was fiery, just as you are. Stubborn to her core. Fast as a reef shark. And a wonderful woman to bed. So strong and supple those nights she lay with me."

N'auri's eyes widened. She trembled with rage, saliva glistening on her lips as her fists clenched. Just when Sol thought it would be the end, when N'auri would strike out at Lord Cantino, the Emeraldi girl spun on her heel and walked away. Her boots echoed down the long hall.

Sol was left alone beside Lord Cantino, her heart pounding, sweat beading her forehead. They stood in silence for several moments at the foot of the dead-eyed island hero. The lord turned his black eyes to her.

"Do you remember how we started this tour with the roc specimen?" he asked Sol.

"Yes," she replied.

"So many similarities," he whispered. "The reason the roc did not go extinct like its behemoth brethren was because it did not fight back against us. It adapted to the Daimyo way. And the Grievar— why are Grievar still here? Why have you not gone extinct?"

Sol looked down at the ground; she couldn't bear meeting the man's nightmarish gaze.

"Grievar are here for the same reason as the roc," Cantino answered himself. "They do not fight back. They have adapted to the way of the world. To *our* way."

Sol nodded silently, not knowing what to say.

"Perhaps we should head back now; we have been beneath for quite a while and I do not want to keep you from your training."

Sol wanted to scream. She wanted to tell Cantino she needed to keep moving farther down the hall, toward the end of the exhibit, where the shadows seemed to pool. She needed to see *him*, her father, Artemis Halberd.

But Sol could only mouth a quiet yes.

The two walked from the hall, past the Grievar corpses and ancient skeletons and behemoths, all staring out with their dead eyes, questioning what they did to deserve this fate, ending up in this man's collection.

They reached the long bone stairwell back to the surface, where the dusk light now streamed in.

Cantino broke the silence. "Do you know what else the Grievar and roc share?"

Sol didn't respond, knowing this man would answer his own questions.

"They need to be broken," Cantino said. "Like my roc, Firenze, waiting for me in the gardens above, who was proud before he was loyal and obedient. N'auri needs to be broken, just like her mother was."

CHAPTER 23

The Arena Without Breath

When the wild tusker encounters an adversary, it does not attempt a charge at the onset of confrontation. The tusker first seeks to negate all of its adversary's attacks. The beast dives in and out, testing and thrusting before retreating. It proudly accepts small gashes on its face and flank with the realization that each failed attack is a blow to its adversary's confidence. After its opponent's attempts have been exhausted, the tusker charges in against a weary body and broken mind. A Grievar should take note of such a beast.

Passage Four, Thirty-Fifth Precept of the Combat Codes

Silas watched the rain.

It thrummed on his roof, pooled on the cobbles, created rivulets and streams that flowed to the city's gutters.

Silas listened to the methodical drumming, the way each droplet careened from the sky to find an individual place in the dirt. It was peaceful for Silas to acknowledge these forces of nature beyond his control. The frigid snowstorms of Myrkos, the heavy rains that came in the spring to the Kirothian highlands.

He pushed his face to the window like a young child as a vein of lightning streaked the sky. The steel frame of his room shook with the thunder that followed.

The Daimyo couldn't control the rain. They found shelter in their palaces, bound their shutters, immersed themselves in their simulations, but the rain still fell atop Daimyo roofs. It still accumulated in their gutters, flooded their city streets. And sometimes, if the rain continued to fall for a long time, things started to break. Shelters fell, pipes burst, wells overflowed.

Silas enjoyed when this happened, when the world the Daimyo had built began to collapse.

He shook his head as he surveyed his quarters: the roof above his head, the tables and shelves surrounding him, the humming icebox filled with vat-cooked meats. They'd insisted he stay nearby this time, his quarters set in downtown Tolensk.

Silas suddenly spoke, though he was entirely alone in the room. "Oh, should I? Right now?"

Silas nodded, before stepping outside the door into the rain. He looked up to the sky from the middle of the street, letting the droplets find his face and the inside of his mouth, soaking his black cloak and filling his boots.

He closed his eyes and let the passing storm fill his senses; its electricity tinged the air around him. Silas listened. Perhaps he'd have more instructions. He'd always guided Silas when he needed it.

The sky lit up again, blue-white electric flashes that reflected in Silas's glowing eyes and illuminated the curved smile on his face.

No instructions. Just be here.

Silas laughed out loud with the crack of thunder; his diaphragm trembled as the ground shook beneath him. He wasn't sure how long he stood there or how long the storm lasted, but he didn't care.

And then Silas opened his eyes and it was over. The rolling

thunderheads had passed, and the sun had peeked from the clouds. A boy was standing in front of him, soaking wet with brown hair matted over his eyes.

Sam.

"Sir! Sir Silas," the boy stuttered, wiping the water from his brow. "Reporting for duty."

The boy shifted his boots in the mud. He wore the crimson reds of Kiroth, a metal wolf sigil pinned to his cloak. He looked up at Silas timidly.

He wasn't Sam. Messy brown hair, a short nose, and long eyelashes topped with water droplets. Silas recognized the boy. He'd been the runner from outside Zytoc Province, notifying Silas of the battalion's movement when he'd camped in the high forest.

"Duty?" Silas asked, his mind still caught somewhere between the storm and this place, where the city street in front of him was busy again with townsfolk, merchants hawking their wares, smiths resuming their pounding, outdoor grills flaring up.

"Yes, Sir Silas," the boy replied. "Squire duty. My name is Varik. Varik Thandros. I've been assigned the post to serve as your squire."

"I need no squire," Silas replied, turning on his heel and heading back toward his door.

"Wait!" The boy followed. "They said, Marshal Vlador said I needed to—"

"Marshal Vlador has already asked too much of me." Silas whirled back toward the boy. "The fact that his Knights need squires is proof enough that his mind is addled, the Codes lost to him."

Silas continued to the door, wrenching it open and slamming it behind him.

"Wait!" He could hear the boy from behind the steel plate. "I've nowhere else to go! If I can't squire for you, they'll think I've failed. They'll…" The boy trailed off.

Silas was silent behind the door, watching the water droplets streak his window. The boy's face appeared in the glass, trying to peer in.

"Please! Sir Silas, I would be honored to learn from you. I promise I'll be helpful, only do what you ask of me."

The boy continued for some time, knocking on the door and pleading. He was persistent, Silas gave him that, like his brother Cego; when that boy latched his teeth on to something, he tended to not let go until his teeth broke.

Finally, a prolonged silence. Silas slumped down against a wall, thinking the boy had given up, when suddenly he heard a peculiar sound: soft melodic notes plucked and strummed on a lute.

Silas could visualize the boy's little fingers cascading over the tusker-hair strings, and then he heard Varik's voice carry through the steel of the door.

> *A little stream, o'er there,*
> *Brothers three skipped stones.*
> *The first went far, the second near,*
> *The third fell in and disappeared.*
> *A little home, o'er there,*
> *Brothers two returned.*
> *No fish in hand, or water pail,*
> *So their father's rage was turned.*
> *A river rushed, o'er there,*
> *Brothers went in to the waist.*
> *They found their third in too deep,*
> *Wearing a secret grin.*
> *An ocean vast, o'er there,*
> *Three brothers swam away.*
> *Left their home to breathe again*
> *The air above the blue waters.*

Silas closed his eyes, listening to the boy's tune. He saw cerulean skies and emerald waters, black sands and towering cliff faces. In the darkness he saw another world, a place where he'd once belonged.

And when the musician outside his door fell silent again, Silas heard another voice speak to him.

"Yes." Silas nodded. The instructions had come.

*　　*　　*

When Silas opened his door the next morning, the boy was still there, sleeping with his back up against the wall, his lute propped by his side.

He slammed the door shut behind him and the boy's eyes sprang open.

"Sir Silas! Good morning to you. I hope you had a restful sleep in preparation for today's fight."

It was almost as if he'd forgotten Silas had not answered his calls from outside. His eyes still shone bright. Silas thought again of Cego's stubbornness, how his younger brother would always readily return to his feet even after Silas had beaten him bloody.

Silas didn't respond to Varik as he untethered his roc from the shed beside his quarters. He met Karo's hard avian eyes and put his hand to her feathered head gently before guiding the bird outside.

"Amazing that you ride the roc still, just like the Grievar of old in the stories!" Varik exclaimed. "My uncle once told me about a Kirothian Knight named Penthalas Tovalyn who rode the largest roc in the entire land, standing nearly ten feet tall. The story said he fought it before taming it! Is that how you got your roc?"

Silas continued to ignore the boy as he opened a pouch of dried jerky and held it to Karo's beak as she devoured it. When she'd finished breakfast, Silas tossed a few pieces of meat in his own mouth and set the ropes to mount the bird.

"Wait, let me help you." The boy clumsily attempted to help Silas mount the roc, kneeling in the dirt and offering a boost. Silas lithely sprang onto the bird's back.

"Of course, you don't need help there," Varik said as Silas pushed his boot against Karo's side to spur her into a trot down the cobbled street.

Varik began to sprint alongside the roc to keep up, gasping for breath but still managing to talk. "I'm not sure I can...keep up this pace all the way to the...arena...sir...but..."

Silas spurred Karo harder and she took off into a gallop down the street, leaving the boy behind in the dust.

"I'll see you at the stadium!" Varik shouted.

Silas shook his head as a smile crept onto his face.

*   *   *

The wind whipped Silas's cloak behind his roc as they galloped down the wide dirt thoroughfare. The Grievar Road ran from town to town along Kiroth's western front, all the way south to the Ezonian border and north to the foot of the frostlands. The road skirted the major cities, dodged the bustle of trade and mech traffic. Only those traveling on foot or by beast took the Grievar Road.

Silas watched Tolensk as he passed it by. The city was not large, but it held a key position alongside Kiroth's western border with Desovi.

The city was shaped like an arrowhead, with the bulk of the Grunt and Grievar populations living in the wide neck and the Daimyo nobles set at the tip where the hills began to rise. Tolensk's stadium was set outside the city walls in the mountains, where the air was thinner, and the empire believed they had an advantage over aggressors.

Silas had been stationed in Tolensk at least a half dozen occasions over the past year, each time matching up against a Desovian Knight, the best the westerners had to offer. Of course, he'd dispatched them all easily.

Marshal Vlador had made sure to illustrate the importance of these matches to Silas when he'd first been stationed here.

The Desovians have been pushing into the western front. Our Knights were occupied with defending Ezonian incursions to the south, while we ourselves were starting to move north toward Myrkos. They took the taiga and then the blackwood forests sitting border-side. Then they won the auralite mines even farther into our territories. By then, we knew they were making a real drive for the western front, something they'd been eyeing for the past five decades.

Silas had mostly ignored the marshal's political talk. He didn't care. It was all froth bubbling on the water, sure to get swept away by the next big wave. The empire's motives, each nation squabbling over land and resources. Each using Grievar for their own purposes: to enrich the Daimyo nobles and to grow their slave hordes.

Silas worked with them, though. He'd been told to.

This world they've built, it is not for us.

He urged Karo forward as they broke off the Grievar Road onto a steep stony grade that climbed the mountain to the back side of the stadium. Silas preferred not to travel on the main artery, which was clogged with mechs vomiting their fumes alongside the noble palanquins, gilded craft carried on the backs of slaves, like show-cocks spreading their plumage.

His roc deftly made her way up the treacherous slope, her long talons grasping and propelling over jagged rocks, leaving a cloud of kicked-up gravel dust behind.

Silas enjoyed this climb, surveying the lands in the distance. He could make out the grey curve of the Tusi River snaking its way to the blackwood forests and then back out to parallel the Grievar Road.

The air grew thinner as they continued to ascend, the chill discernible even through his thick cloak and black leather. He watched a mother golden hawk arc through the sky, her yellow eyes peering down at him before moving on to seek some exposed prey.

Two stronghorn rams clashed their heads on an adjacent rocky outcropping, the impact echoing across the stony hillside. Juveniles attempting to prove their worth to the flock. The rams parted, expertly finding the proper footing on the treacherous terrain. The two combatants met eyes, snorted, and kicked up dust as they prepared for the next clash.

Silas sighed as he watched the rams. Their combat was pure. When they looked each other in the eye, they saw an equal opponent. Yes, one was stronger, the other had an injured hind leg, but it didn't matter. In their minds, they were equals. No matter their differences, they were joined in combat.

Silas could remember possessing that same feeling. Fighting not for lands or riches or even pride. But locking horns simply for the purity of the act, because that was what he was created for. With no end goal, only with the flight of action, the buzz of excitement and adrenaline pumping through his veins, making him feel alive.

No longer. Now he did not fight for purity, for himself. He fought for them. Those who didn't know combat. Those who only saw the outcome.

Silas watched as the stronghorns charged again. One ram cut a superior angle at the last moment, slamming into the other's undefended side, causing it to lose its footing and tumble off the precipice. The ram shrieked as it fell, its hillside grace gone as it was battered on the sharp stones, finally thudding to rest, unmoving.

A good death. One that any Grievar would want, hope for.

Silas saw Grievar-kin dying in their old age, felled by time, unable to dance in the winds of combat. They followed the Daimyo path instead, attempting to enhance their bodies unnaturally, living for hundreds of years as if they were the gods. During their pitiful tenure, they grew their lands, their wealth, their spawn.

For what purpose? Why did any of it matter without the purity of combat? Without the ability to look into an opponent's eyes and know you were equal, there for the same purpose?

To live, to fight, to die.

Silas turned back to his ascent. Karo had climbed surely; they were now nearly at the back side of the stadium, which loomed like a stone giant, its highest colonnades dipping into the clouds.

Nonrespar Arena. The Arena Without Breath.

Silas pulled onto level ground, his roc trotting on the thin mountain grass beside the giant boulders that made the base of the stadium. Silas dismounted, ruffling Karo's head feathers as she bent low.

"You climbed well, my friend." Silas led her forward with harness in hand.

He looked up to the sky, a sheer wall of stone in front of him. Crows circled above, watching and waiting, prepared to dive for the discarded food of patrons or the greatest prize of all: the fresh meat of some downed fighter.

Silas found the back entrance set up for Grunt sizzlers manning the kitchens or cleaners sweeping the stadium halls. Most Knights would parade into Nonrespar's grand entrance, welcoming the cheers of their adoring fans.

A Grunt looked up disinterestedly from a smoke break beneath a tattered awning, making eye contact with Silas and then shifting his attention to the roc.

"Nice bird you got," the Grunt said. "Fighting bird?"

"No," Silas said. "Just for riding. Though she won't hesitate to rip your arm off if she doesn't like you."

The Grunt nodded, seeming somewhat satisfied with the answer as he took a long puff of his burner while eyeing the roc.

"I'll tie her out here," Silas said as he looped Karo's rein around a wooden post. "She doesn't like the indoors."

"Need someone to watch?" the Grunt asked, clearly angling for a payoff.

"No, she can watch herself," Silas said. "But I'll give you another of these if you make sure she's fed."

Silas flipped the Grunt a shiny bit.

"What she eat?"

"Anything alive or recently killed," Silas said. "She prefers larger mammals, but if you have rodents down below, she'll enjoy those too."

"Yup." The Grunt nodded again. "All them rats like the lower levels, same as down where we stay."

"You live in the arena?" Silas asked. Though he knew Grunts were treated poorly, for some reason he'd assumed they traveled in to work from Tolensk's dregs.

"Yup. Hundred of us about," the Grunt said. "Boss says makes it quicker for us to get here, plus sometimes stadium needs night work."

Silas had never been below Nonrespar, though he'd explored the undercarriages of some other stadiums during his travels. Even for Grunts, the living conditions would be horrific. Most of the sewage from the latrines above traveled through pipes and let loose to the ground of the lower levels.

Silas threw another onyx bit to the Grunt. "Make sure my roc gets fed; I'll be out to get her shortly."

The Grunt pocketed the bit with an enthusiastic expression. Silas let down the hood of his cloak and turned to enter the stadium.

"Where you go now?" the Grunt asked.

Silas turned back. "Same as you, I'm going to work."

* * *

Silas stayed in the shadows as he awaited his entrance to the arena. He was the main event tonight, and so they would blast his name across the stadium's speakers. There was no chance he'd miss his time in the light.

He'd found his quiet corner while other Grievar fought in the preliminary bouts, minor disputes of the day: Daimyo lords squabbling over land, hawker merchants trying to finalize some business deals, even slavers testing some of their purchases in the big show.

Silas sat cross-legged on a crate in the storage room filled with servicer cleaning tools. Slivers of light cut through the slots in the wood-framed wall. He could hear the roar of the crowd as a fighter was dispatched, the wooden boxes beside him trembling.

"And now, for our next preliminary bout, we have Lord Klad-stok's Prime Knight, the swiftest kick in the westlands, Madrigal Harris," the announcer proclaimed.

"And representing Lord Balis, we have the notorious merc, brought here all the way from the Isles of Besayd, Nat Kinkade!"

Silas felt anger rising in his stomach. Though he was used to it by now, he was disgusted at the mere thought of Grievar serving at the leisure of a Daimyo lord, doing their every bidding, fighting for their petty disputes, living in their stables like some beast.

Silas understood that even he was a cog in the machine, a pawn, but the fact that some Grievar sought out such a life on their own volition, for bits and fame—it was revolting.

The crowd roared as the two Grievar clashed. Silas closed his eyes in the darkness. He saw the endless emerald waters of the island, the Path sparkling like a gemstone necklace to the horizon.

Silas practiced his ki-breath, quieted his mind as he'd done so many times on the island with his brothers. The world around him began to dim. It was here, in the darkness, broken from time, that he could hear him best. Silas had spoken to him since he'd arrived into this world. He'd told Silas where to go, revealed to him the truths of the past and the future. But Silas could not hear his voice now; he couldn't force the words to the surface.

Silas felt the hard crate beneath him, the sound of the crowd shaking the walls, the announcer's robotic voice echoing in the hallway, the hushed breathing from beside him in the storeroom.

Silas's eyes flared open. Breathing, though faint, was coming from behind a stack of crates. Perhaps some stowaway slave or Grunt worker taking a nap.

Silas stood up silently and moved toward the stack. Just when he was in range, he launched a front kick to blast through the crates as if they were kindling, exploding them in a shower of wooden planks and dust.

"Ahh!" a familiar voice yelled from the shadows. "It's me, it's me!"

The dust cleared to revealed Varik, his would-be squire, shielding his eyes and curled up in the corner of the storeroom, now covered with wood splinters.

"Were you spying on me?" Silas asked threateningly.

"No, no!" the boy responded. "I'm here, I just got here, I'm supposed to help you—"

"I told you I don't need help. I don't need a squire," Silas said.

"I know, but Vlador told me I needed to help you or else. And I came in here and you seemed so comfortable. I thought maybe you were resting before your match, so I thought I'd just wait here until you woke up so I could do what I needed."

"What is it you think you need to do that will help me?" Silas asked, genuinely curious what Vlador thought this boy's supposed purpose was, outside of spying on him.

"I've been trained in massage, to make sure you're fully loose without a muscle off-kilter prior to your fight," the boy replied.

Silas nodded. Grievar massage was an ancient art, one of body empathy that some of the greatest Knights had been masters of. Learning to destroy a body systematically also provided great insight into how to repair it.

Of course, Silas needed no such thing.

"I also have your rations, pre- and post-fight," Varik said. He loosened the drawstring on a sack he held over his shoulder. Within it were a variety of dried fruit, jerkies, and hydrating liquids.

"Is that all?" Silas asked.

"Uh...I guess," Varik replied, though he looked down as he said it.

"Fear," Silas said. He could smell it. "There it is. What else have you?"

Varik hesitated before he produced another case from behind him, hidden in the shadows of the crates. The box was steel-plated. "They also said I should try to offer this to you."

Silas didn't even need to open the case to know what was within. Stims. Neurogens. Standard modern Grievar enhancements, used both prior to a fight to boost a variety of attributes and after to promote faster recovery.

Silas had watched the majority of the Kirothian team take an assortment of stims during training. It was commonplace now, despite the Codes explicitly forbidding their use.

"And why are you hesitant to give me this case?" Silas asked.

"Because . . . well, I know about you," Varik replied. "I know you don't take stims. I heard the story from Cartage, where you killed a Grievar in the Circle, and then afterward, you . . . ripped his arm off. To show the crowd where the stims were in effect. Where the blood had clogged up."

Silas smirked. Stories traveled fast and legends were created even faster.

"Yes, and Vlador and the empire have pushed me to take enhancements numerous times; why is it he thinks this time is any different?"

"He just said offer it, let him know they're there for him if he needs a boost," Varik said.

"Do you take these?" Silas asked, stepping closer to the boy and taking the steel box from him. He opened the lid to reveal a black foam interior cushioning several containers: liquids, pills, an orb that glowed softly.

"No, I don't, I swear I haven't," Varik responded, looking down at the floor again.

"Why do you lie?" Silas asked as he lifted the small orb to his face and peered at the white light pulsing from its center.

"I'm not!" Varik reacted quickly, looking up at Silas, meeting his glowing eyes. "Just once. I tried a small dose of the neuros once."

Silas nodded as he grasped his hand around the orb.

He continued to interrogate the boy. "Tell me, supposed squire, that one time. Why did you take this enhancement?"

Varik paused with his breath held before the story emerged. "It was last year. They were holding the annual rainy season fight festival in my village, Gaslyk. My two older brothers have always been a bit ahead of me; they said there were some big Scouts coming in to the festival, direct from Karbrok."

Silas knew all about the scouting efforts Vlador had initiated over the past decade. The empire swept every small village across the land, looking for talent. They separated children from their families to pull them into early training programs.

"Only once before had the big-time Scouts come by our village, and that time, the winner of the festival had been recruited. He actually became a Knight of the empire! Now he's famous where I'm from. So, a few months out, my brothers and I trained on the constant for the festival. We were ready."

Silas watched the boy carefully as he spoke. He was a product of their system, but he was not yet fully tainted. His eyes still had some light to them.

"Day before the festival, all our matches were set. I walked in on my brothers before training. They were taking something, I saw it. A vial of liquid, black like tar. I don't think they would've offered it to me if I hadn't caught them, probably just wanted to keep it to themselves. But because I was there, they told me to take a swig. They told me it would give me the edge the next day."

"And did it?" Silas asked. "Did you have the edge?"

Varik looked at the ground again. "No, I lost in the first round. Some kid got me with a strangle."

"And your brothers?"

"Yes." Anger flashed in Varik's eyes. "My older brother, Harbak. He won the tournament, finished all his opponents. Right now, he's training as a first-year in Karbrok. He's going to be a Knight."

"Perhaps," Silas whispered. "Or perhaps he'll dry up like a rotten fruit and get tossed to the streets like so many others."

Varik looked up at Silas curiously. "What do you mean?"

Silas held up a vial of viscous black liquid from the case, right in front of Varik's eyes. "The edge," he said again. "All of this is made to give Grievar the edge. Enhance their stamina, strength, agility, awareness, reaction, and recovery time. Everything that a Grievar is made to have, thousands of years of combat blood running through our veins, and this little salve is supposed to make all of that better."

Silas squeezed the vial in his hand, shattering it, letting the black liquid drip through his fingers onto the floor. Probably the monthly bit-worth of any small village like Varik's slipping through to the stone cracks below.

"Do you know who makes this?" Silas asked, venom creeping into his voice.

Varik shook his head.

"Them," Silas growled. "The Daimyo. Their makers in labs study us, figure out how to make us better. They figure out how to change us for their purposes so that their perfect world can continue on. So that we can settle their disputes, win over their lands. Only our blood is spilled."

Silas took the next piece of equipment from the steel case, a translucent container full of pills. He dropped it on the floor and stamped his boot atop it, grinding the pills into dust.

"Do you think the Daimyo have your best interests in mind?" Silas asked. "When they peddle these neuros, stims, cleavers, do you think they reveal how these enhancements will destroy the users? Do you think they tell a Grievar they will be addicted long after they are finished fighting in the Circle, after they are no longer useful to the Daimyo? Do they speak of how a Grievar will shrivel up soon after they decide he's not worth the bits any longer?"

Varik shook his head again.

"We are nothing to them," Silas spat. "We are tools to be used. They throw us parades, laud our victories, make us out to be champions. But we are nothing. We are slaves, just the same as the Grunts, constructing their monoliths and mechs. We Grievar are just another way for them to keep building their version of this world."

"But we're made to fight," Varik said. "If these enhancements make us fight better, isn't that good for us?"

"We are made to fight," Silas responded. "That is true. We are born to fight, to determine the most skillful, the strongest, the fastest. But we were not born to fight for them. We were born to fight for ourselves. To live in the moment, to dance in the winds of combat."

Varik nodded slowly. Silas handed him the final intact enhancement from the case, the light orb. The sphere pulsed with hidden power, some Bit-Minder programmed photo array primed to take neural root and form new martial programming.

"If a Grievar is ever truly to be free, he must fight for nothing but himself," Silas whispered. "For that is why we are here. For ourselves. For our own kin. Not for them."

Silas stood above Varik. "Break it," he commanded.

Varik obediently squeezed the light orb. It first shuddered before it shattered. The shards cut his hand and the boy's blood dripped down into the pile of broken enhancements.

"When you are truly free," Silas said, "that is when you will have it all. Strength, speed, agility, endurance, awareness. You will have what you were created for. You will not need this." Silas gestured to the pile on the floor.

"And, soon, we will not need them," Silas said.

The System speaker came online, the announcer employing his loudest voice for the main event.

"And for tonight's main dispute, two nations straddling the western front, Kiroth and Desovi. This match will decide the fate of the long-disputed rubellium reserves, just north along the Bydal Mountain Range. The winning nation will be bestowed full rights to the invaluable fifty-mile span of mines, which have provided the primary source of ore to the empire for the past two decades."

The announcer took a long breath, before bringing his voice up another decibel. "And, first, representing our visiting nation's interests, the Desovian champion, the Knight who has taken more than one hundred heads over the span of his decorated career, the Grievar feared from the Northlands to the southern Isles, known by all as the Giant of Gaspari. I introduce to you, Gylshtak Toliat!"

Silas and Varik heard the roar of the Desovian crowd, booming the name Toliat over and over throughout the stadium, shaking the floorboards of the storeroom they stood in. Silas watched Varik carefully; the boy's eyes flicked from side to side, his breath rapid.

Was he worried for Silas?

"And, representing the empire of Kiroth. Our champion. The man who needs no introduction. The Grievar who has never lost a match in the Circle. The silent one. The Slayer himself, Silas!"

Silas gathered his cloak around himself and headed for the storeroom door. It was then he heard the voice he'd been awaiting, reverberating in his skull like a sharp-struck musical note.

He turned back toward Varik, a shadowed silhouette against the exterior hall's light.

"If you are to be my squire, I have orders for you."

"Yes, of course," Varik replied breathlessly.

"First, never lie to me again," Silas said.

"No, never," Varik replied.

"Second," Silas said, "I want you to walk out with me into this arena today. And I want you to play your lute."

"Wh-what?" Varik stuttered. "Play? What for? What would I play?"

Silas beckoned the boy forward. "Come, grab your instrument. Play a song from your heart again. One that the people will remember and pass on."

*   *   *

They come from frost of north,
With frigid wind and storm.
They come from isles of lore,
With emerald shores beyond.
They tread in shadow and time,
With fists shrouded in light.
They feel no fire and follow no lord,
With darkness they dance to fight.
They come to fields of gold,
With harvest grown to thresh.
They come from stories of old,
With beast and shadow they rest.

The normally raucous crowd housed within the dome of Nonrespar was quiet as they listened to Varik's song. The squire walked a pace behind Silas with his lute in hand, letting his fingers flow across the instrument's taut strings. The boy kept his eyes on the ground as the two found the center of the stadium.

The silence of the crowd was shattered when the Desovian opponent emerged from his stall. Gylshtak Toliat was nearly eight feet tall and bounded with neuro-enhanced muscles. The crowd poured their voices down from all angles, Kirothians and Desovians set on either side of the arena, screaming the names of their champions.

Silas watched his squire walk to the sidelines, the boy clutching his lute. He wished he could hear Varik's ballad just a little bit longer instead of the noise spewing from the crowd.

Silas stepped into the Circle with his waiting opponent.

Toliat raised his thick arms in the air as his section cheered maniacally for him. His shoulders flexed like two rippling slabs of meat as he clenched his fists and displayed the heavy flux work etched on his back. The man let out a roar as he leapt into the air several times, easily clearing Silas's head with each bound to billow clouds of sand into the air.

Silas narrowed his eyes, watching his opponent through the cloud of dust that had enveloped the ring. He knelt to the ground and lifted a handful of sand in his fist, letting the grains flow out in a stream.

This man was no Grievar.

Once, this man had been a child, much like Varik. Like Cego or Sam. Silas could see his opponent's life coming and going, like the grains of sand falling through his hand. Toliat had grown up in a small village surrounded by blackwood pines. He'd wrestled with his kin, smiled and laughed in the kicked-up dirt, licked blood off his lips.

This Grievar boy had learned to hunt with his pa, tasting the meat fresh off a grown tusker after his first kill. He'd learned to fish in the river with his ma, crouching over the stones and knocking the leaping trout to shore with open-handed slaps.

Toliat had been free as a boy: dodging through the pines, diving into the ice-cold river and shivering on the shore, laughing in the spring rains and huddling by roaring bonfires on winter nights. This boy had been free to fight once.

This man standing across from Silas was not free any longer. Toliat was bound by Daimyo chains, fighting for their petty disputes, his blood running thick with their enhancements.

This man was no Grievar.

And so, Silas would not give him the honor, the respect, he would bestow upon one of his own. He would give this man no bow, no acknowledgment of shared combat roots. He would give this man no fist held to the air, no Grievar salute to say: *We possess these same tools for violence; let us use them skillfully so that our ancestors would be proud.*

Nor would Silas give this man a proper death, quick and noble, to send him to the afterlife.

Silas advanced, even-paced as if he were out on a morning stroll.

Toliat roared, such a bellow that quieted his own fans in the crowd, one that seemed to give pause to the crows circling overhead as if the birds wondered whether they were in danger even from such a distance. And then the giant charged, his legs rippling as he took wide bounds across the Circle.

Silas watched him as he approached. He saw the berserk look in the man's eyes showing lust for the kill. He saw the strain in the man's muscled frame, how his lower back arched slightly beneath his weight. He saw how Toliat favored his right leg, how his left knee quivered slightly on the impact of each of his strides.

Every creature had a shatter point, where the rest of the body gave way like a storm wall crumbling to the waves. In experienced opponents, the shatter point could be difficult to locate; it was masked with skill. With this brute, though, the shatter point was a gleaming gem laid out on fresh snow.

The crowd seemed to hush as Toliat closed in on Silas, swinging his tree-trunk arm in an arcing blow. Silas ducked, Toliat's fist grazing his head. He held back an easy counter to the body.

"Why do you fight?" Silas asked as the two exchanged positions.

Toliat met Silas's eyes before roaring and coming in again, this time with a spring-loaded front kick meant to shatter his midsection. Silas slightly shifted his weight and let the kick pass him by a hair's length. This time, he held back a foot sweep that would have toppled the brute.

"Why do you fight?" Silas asked again as he stood statue-still at the center of the Circle.

Toliat seemed unsure of how to respond, and so instead he dove at Silas, attempting to wrap him up in his enormous wingspan. Silas felt Toliat's hand grasping at his ankle like a gnarled steel vise, but he ripped his foot away. He restrained the counter knee that could have easily caught the big man on the chin.

"Why do you fight?" Silas repeated. Toliat was starting to breathe heavily.

Muscle was good but it required oxygen to feed it.

"I fight to smash shitstains like you!" Toliat replied this time in a guttural yell. The giant came in with a barrage of punches, surprisingly fast for a man of his size, yet in slow motion for Silas, who turned his chin at the last second for each strike, letting the man's fist graze his face.

Ah, there it was. The fear.

Silas could now detect it faintly in the form of the giant's heavy breathing, sweat droplets starting to dot the dirt, the widening of his pupils. A question was beginning to form in Toliat's head: *Why is this man standing across from me so calm? How can he be so stoic in the face of my violence, which would bring most men to their knees?*

"Why do you fight?" Silas asked again, watching his opponent's eyes become wide as anger flooded them.

Anger, one of fear's brothers, a useful tool when applied properly but in most cases a distraction.

"Shut your mouth!" Toliat roared as he came in again, attempting to clinch with Silas, throwing a cutting elbow followed by a body shot.

Silas smiled. At least the brute had changed his strategy. This was what Toliat should have been doing from the start: entrenching Silas in a fight of elbows and knees, head butts and body shots.

Silas casually glanced up around the arena. The crowd had quieted, especially the Desovians, who had come to expect the treat of Toliat providing a grisly finish at the start of a bout. The Kirothians knew what was to come, though. Silas could feel the home crowd's collective breath held in their chest.

They waited for the shatter point.

Silas felt the rage start to rise in his stomach on command, boiling up from the deep, a swelling of urgency, a force waiting to be unleashed. Silas knew how to use his anger; he knew how to direct it, electrify it into the speed of his limbs. Silas's eyes glowed and

Toliat nearly stopped in his tracks as he sensed the sudden change in demeanor.

"I know why you fight," Silas said. "You fight because you are afraid of them."

Toliat didn't respond. The giant already seemed defeated, with his shoulders slumped and heaving for breath.

Silas felt the energy rise to his skin. The blacklight. It was a part of him, it always had been, even after he'd been released from the cocoon of darkness, from the Cradle of his birth. The blacklight had stayed within him, dormant until Silas had learned to release it with anger. He could unleash it through the rage for those who had chained his people, those Daimyo who would try to enslave him. Steam began to lift from Silas's shoulders like a ghostly mist curling toward the sky.

"You shouldn't be afraid of them, those Daimyo up in the boxes," Silas growled. "You should be afraid of me. I am the Slayer."

As the words left his mouth, Silas moved. Not as he'd been moving before, dodging Toliat's lumbering attacks. This time, Silas moved with predatory intention. Just as a great cat springs to sink its teeth into the neck of a hind, Silas launched forward, feinting his hands high in a flurry of movement but striking low with a lightning-fast kick to Toliat's right kneecap. The shatter point.

Silas kept his eyes on Toliat's face as the giant's knee exploded. He wanted to see the moment in the man's eyes where pride turned to pain and anger turned to fear.

Toliat's leg buckled as he stumbled backward, attempting to create space and regroup, but Silas was already on him, a whirlwind of violence touching down on the giant. Toliat's nose exploded as a fist caught it at the perfect angle, breaking the bone and driving it inward. The giant's orbital was next, cratering as Silas lanced a knee into it.

The giant was on the floor then, curled up into a ball with his hands over his face, waiting for the onslaught of kicks. They didn't come, though.

Silas stood over him, waiting silently.

Toliat struggled back to his feet, thick blood hanging from his shattered nose. Silas again feinted high, a cross that would have gotten through and finished the job of pulverizing the giant's face, but his fist stopped short, the precursor to a low kick that smashed into Toliat's good leg.

The giant fell to both knees, no longer able to support his weight.

"Why are you doing this?" Toliat blubbered, spitting several broken teeth to the ground.

"Because you are no Grievar," Silas replied. "I want the world to see the abominations the Daimyo have created."

Silas grabbed the giant's head and snapped it down, before quickly swiveling around to Toliat's back. He didn't want the strangle. No, that would be an easy way out. Instead, Silas slammed his fist into the curled-up man's rib cage, finding the floating rib that jutted out and breaking it, driving the splintered point deep into the lungs. Silas rammed his fist down again and again like a jackhammer, delighting as more ribs splintered.

Toliat lay on his stomach, laboring for breath like a beached whale.

Silas was not finished. He slammed his heel down on the man's exposed shoulder blade, a smile curving his face as he felt another deep foundation in the giant's body crack. Toliat groaned as he turned onto his back. He feebly swung his intact arm at the air.

"I am the Slayer," Silas said as he leaned his knee into the giant's crushed ribs. "Look at me."

He knelt in front of Toliat and reached down to peel the man's swollen eyelids open.

"Look at me." Silas burrowed his fingers deep into each of Toliat's eye sockets and ripped, pulling the man's eyeballs from their homes, like sea jellies trailing stringy tentacles.

Toliat screamed. No longer the roar of a warrior, of a man ready to fight. He screamed like a man ready to die.

He would not have that honor, though. Silas would not put him out of his misery. Silas turned toward Varik, who watched wide-eyed from the sidelines, before walking away from his prey. He left the man lying in the Circle, broken and blind.

The crowd at Nonrespar Arena watched in horror and fascination. They listened to Toliat's screams, the once-great warrior pleading to be put out of his misery. But no such mercy came.

"Play your song again, my squire," the Slayer said as he walked from the Circle. "Play it again for those who remain."

*   *   *

The roc traveled the same treacherous path downward as dusk fell. The sun dipped behind the black pines and splashed reds and oranges across the shadowed crags of the mountainside. When this land became dark, the predators of the night would emerge, great cats and gar bears searching for their next meal.

Silas didn't mind. Perhaps one of them would get to him, rip him off his mount, and devour him as its nightly feast. A fine death; he'd be sure to put up a good fight.

Varik did seem to mind, though. Silas could feel the boy shaking in his seat behind Silas, saddled on the roc together.

Though Silas certainly did not need a squire, he'd grown fond of the boy. Perhaps it was because he reminded him of his brother Sam, the way he looked at the world in such an innocent manner. Or perhaps it was Cego the boy reminded him of, possessing the doggedness that always let Silas's brother stand up each time he'd been knocked down.

"Fear is only fearful if it is uncontrolled," Silas said over his shoulder. The words of the old master were always at the tip of his tongue.

The boy stayed silent. Perhaps what he'd seen Silas do in Nonrespar Arena had quieted him.

The night singers were in full force, the insects swarming the pines and cheering the coming darkness.

"Do you hesitate now on your path to become the next great Knight of the empire?" Silas asked. "After you've seen with your eyes what it means? What real combat can be?"

The boy remained quiet, though Silas could still feel him trembling.

He remembered once when Sam had been scared too. The old master had sent the youngest brother into the night to collect herbs for one of his culinary concoctions. Maybe it had been another of Farmer's tests, or maybe such plants really did only grow among the thickest brambles of ironwood trees all the way on the dark side of the island.

Silas had seen Sam before he left for the journey, the boy's pack slung over his shoulder. His brother had looked so small, frozen to the path in front of him.

"Why did you not finish Toliat?" Varik's faint voice broke through the din of night singers. "Why did you let him suffer like that?"

Silas breathed deeply as he steered the roc over a particularly treacherous part of the mountain's downgrade.

"Toliat suffered for the good of all Grievar," Silas responded.

"What do you mean?"

"They needed to see," Silas whispered. "See that the heroes they've built of our kin are not what they think. They are not gilded champions to be heralded and paraded down city streets. These so-called heroes are mere bodies, sacks filled with blood and bone that can be spilled and feasted upon by crows."

That had been Cego's problem too. His brother had believed in heroes. From the very beginning, training together on the island, Cego had always possessed some code, some wiring that he thought told him right from wrong. And he'd not been afraid to act on it.

Some wild beast roared as the day's last light fled and darkness fully engulfed the mountainside. Karo's footing stayed sure, her eyes glowing in the night.

"The Grievar hero is part of the story, the lie that the Daimyo spread. They are characters in this world they've built made to play a very specific part. And if the Grievar plays their part, fights in their arenas, settles their disputes, wins accolades and honors and promotions, if they garner the praise of fans, the Daimyo world can continue as it is. With them, looking down on us from above, watching us fight and bleed and get buried, all to serve at their pleasure."

The roc paused the descent for a moment, perking her head to listen to the sounds of the night.

"This is why I made him suffer," Silas said. "This is why I spilled his guts and let the light shine on his exposed bones. They needed to see Toliat was no hero. Nor am I. Nor are any of us. That is part of the Daimyo story, the one that they want us to tell. But I will not tell their story. I will not spread their lie."

Silas felt that the boy had stopped trembling. They rode on through the blackness, broken only by the pinpricks of stars above and the dull glow emanating from far-off Tolensk.

"But if there are no heroes, then what is there?" Varik asked.

"There is you," Silas said. "And there is me. And there is the blood that flows through our veins. Pure, not tainted with their stims and their cultures and their laws. We are Grievar-kin and our deep roots must keep growing. These roots have not yet died, but they are withering."

"Roots," Varik repeated softly. "How do we keep them growing? How do we stop our roots from dying?"

The roc finally emerged off the steep mountain grade onto the level ground of the Grievar Road. Silas urged Karo and she broke into a gallop back toward the light of Tolensk. The wind caught Silas's cloak and it drifted behind him like a billowing ghost in the night.

"We break the world they've built," Silas answered.

CHAPTER 24

The Ghost and the Sentinel

When crossing a coursing river, one must swim against the current to reach a fixed destination directly on the other side. The same is true in combat: One must anticipate and move against an opponent's technique in order to overcome it.

Passage Three, Ninety-Sixth Precept
of the Combat Codes

The blackshift seeped through the silk skin windows of Maharu's tearoom.

Murray could sense the blacklight touching his mind. He saw his father, felt the calloused slap of the man's hand. He was blanketed in the warmth of his mother's embrace. He relived his Knighthood, working his way up in the arenas and fighting for the Citadel.

The blacklight spoke of his old master; it whispered to Murray of Coach's tutelage. It told him of the honor Farmer had lived by and the Codes he'd imparted.

But now, on his knees in the tearoom with his hands manacled behind his back, Murray had nothing but pure hatred for the old man. Farmer stood casually beside his employer on the raised step, his hands folded in front of him in his robe.

"Look at him," Maharu said, striding across the room, the black Sentinel his shadow. "Look at his rage...and for who?"

Farmer replied only with the hacking cough, wiping the sleeve of his robe across his face.

Maharu stood in front of Murray, the little man utterly confident with the obsidian mech looming beside him. Murray spat blood at the lord's feet. One of the nastier guards named Din had been given license to use Murray as a heavy bag through the past several days he'd spent as a captive in the lord's prison. Now the darkin' soap-eater had finally had Murray dragged out to bleed across the tearoom floor to answer for his crime.

"You know well now, working here, that I never force those in my service to break their Codes," Maharu said. "I give my Grievar a place to find their path, to find what comes natural to them."

Murray trembled with rage, staring directly at Farmer. "Is it so natural for you to turn on your own kind?"

"I wish you had listened to me, Murray," Farmer said softly.

Murray strained against the manacles and abruptly sprang to his feet, making a run for the frail old man. If he was to die there today, he'd take Farmer with him.

The Sentinel's steel arm smashed into Murray's chest, sending him sprawling several feet across the floor. Murray heaved for breath, felt the familiar shooting pain of broken ribs. He spat blood again and looked up at Farmer's blurred form.

"Why?" Murray whispered between labored breaths.

"Perhaps this is my fault," Maharu interjected. "I put my trust in you, despite seeing the signs. They told me you were crazy, addled and addicted, and I saw it. I've seen it in your twitching manner, your constant babbling. But still, I believed the great Murray

Pearson showing up at my step was a sign. A sign that you had come to redeem yourself in my service. To rehabilitate your life and become the man you once were. I never wronged you, Murray Pearson. And yet you sought to put a knife in my back, to steal from me."

Despite the pain, Murray was able to sit up, the adrenaline fueling him. "Steal from you? What you have below are not your things. Those are darkin' kids, innocent Grievar that never asked to be stored within your basement."

Murray looked back to Farmer. "Those kids... their blood is on your hands. You're a living stain, a traitor to your kind. You're a monster."

"Sometimes, one must be a monster to follow the path," Farmer said. "It is better to realize what you are and live the truth in the light than to creep in the shadows of uncertainty."

Murray clenched his teeth and tried to take another racking breath.

"Despite all I've done to bridge the gap between our kinds, there are some things that seem to always elude you Grievar," Maharu said. "What I purchased at fair price, legally, that lies in my basement now, is my property. What it stores does not matter—"

"I'm darkin' done listening to speeches like these. Get on with it, then," Murray growled. "I stole from you and we know the price. So put me down. I'm ready to go."

Murray slowly rose to his feet and stared at the Daimyo pilot within the Sentinel's frame, set behind a thick glass shield. The blue-veined creature smirked, ready to take on the task.

"As you wish," Maharu said. "But what sort of example would I be to Din and Yahalo here if I didn't at least provide you a proper death, by the Codes?"

Murray let out a labored breath. "And will you make me fight with my hands behind my back?"

Maharu nodded and Yahalo stepped forward to unlock the

manacles. The kid looked at Murray for a moment and mouthed a word. *Sorry.*

Murray nodded. It wasn't the kid's fault. But if he had to go through Yahalo, so be it.

He circled his wrists in front of him, eyeing the two guards. "So, which of you will it be?"

"Neither of them," Maharu said. "Don't take any hope, old Knight. You'll die fighting here; of that I'm certain. You will face Trial by Combat against my Sentinel."

*   *   *

Murray had often dreamed about smashing his hand through the glass of a mech and reaching within the inner sanctum to the Daimyo pilot within. Those smug soap-eaters, thinking they had all the protection in the world behind their tech, thinking they could trample the rest beneath their greed and lust for power.

And so, Murray channeled that deep-seated rage into his arm, diving forward with a leaping cross aimed to spear the pilot in front of him.

His hand shattered against the Sentinel, the small bones in his fist fracturing and sending bolts of pain coursing up his shoulder.

"A worthy attempt!" Maharu laughed from a seated position across the room. The Daimyo lord sipped a glass of Hiberian amber as he spectated the Trial by Combat beside Farmer and his two guards.

Murray saw the Sentinel pilot smirk through the blood his fist had smeared on the capsule's window. The man blinked and the Sentinel's steel arm shot out in response, impossibly fast. Murray dove back, but the thing's hand still grazed him. The force of the glancing blow spun his body to the ground.

How could he fight such a beast with no vulnerabilities?

Murray stood again, his head swimming, as the Sentinel stepped forward and threw its arm at him. His years of experience in the Circle still served him. Murray anticipated the attack, ducking it and throwing a kick to the knee joint of the beast.

Murray's foot met the joint and bounced off, stinging but not broken. He'd held back his attack; it was useless to throw full force and incur damage to himself every time.

He shoulder-rolled as the Sentinel threw a front kick that blasted through the folding screen at the center of the tearoom.

"Let's not destroy my house altogether," Maharu said.

Murray ducked another looping roundhouse, lowering himself to a crouch and shooting past the Sentinel toward its back. He grabbed around its waist with a double-handed clinch.

Murray grunted as he attempted to lift the thing, but the Sentinel didn't budge. He was like a child fighting a full-grown Knight. Murray thought back to when he'd first seen Cego fighting in the slave Circles, against a boy nearly twice his size. The kid had climbed onto the large boy's back, out of harm's way, and strangled him unconscious.

Murray jumped and threw a hand over the Sentinel's neck, hefting himself up onto its shoulder.

Though he couldn't move the beast, he could hold on to it. He threw a sharp elbow down to its blocky head, meeting the enforced steel encasing. Electric pain jolted up Murray's arm each time he attacked, and he could feel the skin shearing off his elbow, but he drove it down again and again as the Sentinel spun around to try to dislodge him.

"Impressive!" Yahalo let out a shout of enthusiasm.

"Shut up," the Daimyo lord said to his guard.

Murray's elbow became a weapon, the skin completely gone now. He could see the gleam of his bone protruding from the bloody mess. Murray screamed as he continued to hack his bone into the back of the mech's head.

"Stop playing with him!" Maharu yelled.

The Sentinel abruptly stopped spinning. The mech bent its legs and threw itself backward, Murray still clinging to its back. The Sentinel blasted through the weapon's rack at the far side of the room, throwing spectral rods and staves as Murray was crushed beneath the creature's weight.

Something sharp punctured Murray's side. He could barely make out the Sentinel standing above him. It placed a steel boot against his chest and started to press down. Murray's rib cage crumpled inward.

"What a mess you've made of my tearoom." Maharu shook his head at the Sentinel. "But you've done the job, though it certainly took more than I'd expect against an old, crazy Knight. Now let's finish it."

The looming black figure above Murray increased the pressure to his chest. His organs squeezed inward and rings of darkness closed around his vision.

"Stand down."

The Sentinel immediately released the pressure, removed its boot from Murray's chest.

A figure stood between him and the Sentinel, a frail arm set on the steel creature's waist.

Farmer.

Murray attempted to stand but fell back to his knees. He coughed a thick spray of blood onto the floor and started to shuffle backward, away from the mech. Away from the old master.

Lord Maharu yelled from across the room. "What do you think you're doing? Did you not hear me? I said finish him!"

Farmer stared at Murray. The man was as pale as ever, nearly ethereal beneath his hood.

"Farmer..." Murray sputtered. "What the dark do you think you're doing...?"

The Sentinel's frame shivered with effort. The mech was straining toward Murray, attempting to obey its master's commands and crush him, and yet Farmer's lithe hand against the Sentinel's waist was somehow preventing it from moving.

"Now is your moment, Murray," Farmer whispered.

"How...how are you doing this...?" Murray shook his head in disbelief.

Maharu stalked to the Sentinel's other side and slammed his little fist against the glass of the pilot's encasing. "What do you think you're doing? Why are we watching this insane Grievar talk to ghosts when he should be pulp on my tearoom floor by now?"

The Daimyo pilot's voice replied through the Sentinel's speaker. "Lord...I'm trying. Something is wrong with my mech; it won't obey my motions." The little man was frantically waving his hands within the cockpit, and yet the steel frame around him still did not respond.

Farmer spoke again. "I can control the beast momentarily, but I cannot destroy it. You must do that, Murray."

The old master waved a hand and one of the fallen spectral staves from the broken weapon's rack suddenly flared to life not far from Murray. But something else caught Murray's attention as he bled out on the floor. Even as the Daimyo pilot continued to try to drive the mech toward him, even as Maharu screamed obscenities, Murray's eyes widened at Farmer in sudden realization.

"You can't see him..." Murray spoke to Maharu. The lord hadn't even seemed to notice that Farmer was standing beside the mech, somehow holding it back. "Farmer...you can't see or hear him, can you?"

"Enough of this," Maharu growled. "Enough of your blathering. I told you, I've put up with your addled nonsense, your conversations with your dead master since you walked through my doors because I thought you would still be of use to me, because I thought your service would outweigh your lunacy. But now you've done more than steal from me. You've inconvenienced me by not dying quickly enough. You've leeched my valuable time. If my Sentinel can't finish the job, my men will. Din, Yahalo, put this miserable man down."

Murray stared at Farmer as the old man's ethereal hand suddenly passed through the mech's armor as if it were an optical illusion. Murray's ragged breathing became quicker.

"Who...what are you?"

"There must be a balance, Murray," Farmer said as his entire form disappeared into the mech's body.

Murray managed to pull his gaze from the mech to see Din advancing on him from across the room.

"Always wanted to put a Grievar Knight down," the merc sneered. Murray could barely stand, let alone take on a trained fighter half his size, so he threw his body at the spectral staff in a desperate attempt to grab the fallen weapon. But he fell short, helplessly sprawled on the floor as Din approached.

The merc's head suddenly erupted in a fountain of blood, the Sentinel's hand outstretched after the lethal punch. Din's lifeless body dropped to the floor.

"What are you doing, you tin-plated fool?" Maharu screamed at the Sentinel, the veins across the lord's face bulging with rage. "He wasn't the enemy; you killed my own man!"

The Sentinel abruptly turned on Maharu. The mech took a menacing step toward the lord.

"I can't control it!" the pilot screeched from within the cockpit.

Sudden fear creased the lord's face as he fell backward and shuffled away from the giant Sentinel. Maharu picked up a rod that had been tossed from the weapon's rack and held it in front of him, a blue charge sparking at its steel head.

"Protect me, you idiot!" the lord screamed at Yahalo, his only remaining guard, who was staring at the entire scene in astonishment.

But the Sentinel didn't pursue the fleeing lord. The mech turned back toward Murray.

"I can't control it much longer, Murray. You must destroy it," Farmer's voice seemed to come from directly within the Sentinel.

"Why are you doing this?" Murray struggled to get on his knees. "Is it really you in there?"

"It's always been me, Murray," Farmer said. "Go get Sam."

The Sentinel strained, as if fighting some sort of internal war, before hurtling toward Murray like an onyx meteor.

Murray felt his hand grasp the cold shaft of the fallen spectral staff as the mech launched itself to the air to crush him on impact.

As the Sentinel descended, Murray braced the staff against the floor and lanced it into the Sentinel's belly with all his strength. The spectral weapon plunged through the casing into the pilot's compartment. The end of the staff found the Daimyo's head, bludgeoning it into the back of the capsule and rupturing it like a vatgrown grape.

The Sentinel hung lifelessly above Murray, still propped up against the staff that had impaled it. Murray rolled backward from beneath the mech's shadow.

He coughed blood again and managed to push himself to his feet. Murray grabbed the staff, pulled it hard, and the Sentinel dropped to the floor, splintering the ironwood planks beneath it.

Murray tested the weight of the long spectral weapon in one hand. Blue blood and brain matter smeared the staff's head. Murray turned his eyes on Maharu, who was still backing away.

Murray limped forward to cut off the Daimyo's advance to the tearoom's exit.

"Protect me, please..." Maharu pleaded, turning to Yahalo, who was staring at the broken Sentinel's form. "You'll be promoted. You'll be captain of my guard. Just stop this insane man."

Murray paused his advance to meet Yahalo's gaze. "I've got no problems with you, kid."

Yahalo nodded, looked once more at the scene, and left the tearoom.

"Wait now...Knight Pearson, I'm sure we can work something out." Maharu trembled as Murray cornered him.

The lord started to raise his rod in defense, but his eyes widened as Murray swung his spectral staff in an arc in front of him.

The lord threw his weapon to the floor and bent to his knees. "Please! You can't do this. You...you're a man of the Codes. They forbid you from hurting a defenseless opponent."

Murray looked into the Daimyo's black eyes.

"Codes also say not to use darkin' weapons."

He swung the onyx staff full force, taking the lord in the head and tossing his body across the room like a doll.

Murray threw the weapon to the side and limped over to kneel beside the Sentinel's broken form.

"Are you...are you in there still?" Murray searched for the pale form of the old master in the wreckage of the mech. "Farmer, where are you?"

There was no response. Farmer was gone, he could feel it. But the old master's final words echoed in Murray's skull.

Go get Sam.

Murray stood slowly, stared at the bodies strewn across the tearoom, and limped out.

CHAPTER 25

A Single Move

A Grievar shall breed only with fellow fighting kin. Doing so will fortify the martial bloodline. Breeding outside of kin will not only taint the strength of blood but can disrupt the peaceful balance of power between all peoples.

Passage One, Seventeenth Precept of the Combat Codes

Just like she'd done every morning for the past month, Sol walked across the hall from her room, making a habit of touching two fingers to the Kova stone before knocking on N'auri's door.

They hadn't spoken a word of Lord Cantino's museum tour during their training camp. The Emeraldi girl kept her head down and did the work that was required. Something had shifted in N'auri, though. Not that she didn't train hard. Sol still had trouble matching N'auri's frenetic pace in the Circle or keeping up with her on their arduous runs up the floating stairs.

N'auri opened the door, not with the sharp-toothed smile Sol remembered.

"'Lo, Sayana." N'auri nodded as the two hastened out of the

living quarters to the first-floor facilities. The instructors there were even stricter than they'd been at the Lyceum. The one day the girls had been late to practice, they'd had to run the floating stairs three times in a row.

Today, they barely made it in time; all their teammates had already paired up in the training Circles. N'auri quickly paired with Gull, leaving just one unpartnered Grievar: Wraith.

So far, Sol had managed to avoid Wraith during their sparring practice. Not that she didn't want to learn from him, but he was notorious for hurting his partners, not holding back even during training. After experiencing what the man could do at Aquarius, Sol would rather remain in one piece.

Wraith didn't look particularly enthusiastic that Sol was his partner either, with that same blank expression he always had etched on his face. "Standing only first" was all he said as Sol stepped into the Circle. No banter or friendly hello like she'd exchange with Gull or Nayassa.

She squared up with Wraith. They were about the same height and build. He also didn't appear to be the quickest in the stable, from what Sol had seen; N'auri took that mantle. And yet every time Sol watched Wraith spar with someone, he bested them. She couldn't quite place why he won; it was almost like the man wielded some invisible power.

Wraith methodically approached Sol with his hands up, expressionless, as if he'd just gotten out of bed. Sol clenched her jaw and breathed out as she waited for him to make the first move. She'd done well playing her counterattack game so far against the other stablemates.

Sol circled on the outside, moving away from the power of Wraith's left kick, the one he'd put her out with. Wraith threw several probing jabs, not to make contact but just to test Sol's reaction. Sol didn't give him anything. She kept circling and bobbing her head.

Wraith threw another jab and probed deeper with a reaching front kick. Sol reacted accordingly, throwing her own counters that Wraith easily dodged.

The two played this game for a few minutes, neither making any significant contact. It was clear Wraith was waiting for Sol to take a risk, throw a significant strike so that he could time a counter and gain the advantage.

Sol gritted her teeth and kept to her plan, trying not to overthink her opponent's strategy. Her father's words were still fresh in her head:

Fight your fight, Solara. Not your opponent's fight. Not the spectators' fight. Your fight.

Suddenly, Wraith switched. Something changed in how he carried himself. He no longer appeared calm, smooth, and relaxed. His body tensed and he moved in toward Sol with a flurry of punches, wide, looping shots to the head and body. Sol easily evaded them, ducked and wove while keeping her guard tight to her body.

Had she figured Wraith out? Simply outlasted the counter game and made him impatient enough to come in haphazardly like that?

Wraith came in several more times with the same wild rhythm, swinging with wide, looping shots, his body tense as if he'd forgotten his fight game from a minute ago.

Sol saw an opening: a punch thrown with power but evadable and ripe to counter. She ducked and felt her body go into autopilot, launching a body shot that blasted through Wraith's defenses. She felt her hand connect with his rib cage. He turned as it landed, the punch glancing across him, and suddenly he was spinning, his elbow coming across the other side and slamming into the side of Sol's head.

Sol stumbled forward. How had Wraith gotten through so easily? She'd seen spinning elbows before; it was a technique she herself employed.

"Again," he said.

Sol shakily stood and squared up with the man again. Wraith turned to his side this time, only showing Sol a sliver of his body as he started to rapidly circle her on the balls of his feet as if he were dancing. Sol had seen this style before; he'd likely throw long side kicks from a distance.

Sol turned to keep even with Wraith as he moved around her. He leapt in with a high side kick just as she'd predicted, connecting with her raised hands and shoving her backward. He seamlessly followed the attack with a spinning back kick from even farther away, this time catching Sol square in the midsection.

Sol doubled over, gasping for air.

"Again," Wraith said without inflection.

Sol slowly stood, eyeing her opponent. Who was he? What was his fighting style? Sol had no idea what to expect.

This time, Wraith stayed still, his arms down at his sides, not showing any aggression. Sol tried to predict what the strange Grievar would do.

Fight your fight, Solara.

Sol inched toward Wraith, keeping her hands up. She'd seen Wraith's wingspan and she believed hers was equivalent. She'd inherited her father's long arms. Sol turned to her side, angling her body as she closed in.

She stopped just outside range and started to circle Wraith, slowly. She made him turn on his heel, forced him to face her. She needed to be patient. She needed to fight her fight; it didn't matter what he was doing.

Minutes passed and Sol continued to circle. She heard N'auri yell in triumph from the training Circle to her side. The whirring of the fans droned overhead. A flock of birds passed outside, cawing in chorus. Somewhere in the distance, a Flyer jetted away from the compound.

She met Wraith's eyes. Sol realized that, until now, Wraith had never directly looked at her; his gaze was always slightly down, looking at the collarbone of whoever was across from him, whether in the Circle or at the dinner table. The man's eyes were a brilliant yellow, like little fireballs.

And then Sol was on the floor again, her nose bent sideways and spewing blood.

Wraith stood above her. This time, he offered a gloved hand, which Sol accepted. He hefted her to a seated position.

"Here," the man said, handing Sol a towel to stopper the blood streaming from her nose.

Wraith sat beside her. "You did well that last time."

Sol chuckled. "You call that doing well against you? I'd hate to see... Well, actually, I did see what it was to not do well against you at Aquarius."

"You did well then too," Wraith said. "Considering you weren't used to the darkness."

"You said I did well in the last exchange, but not the first few," Sol said. "What did I do better?"

"You know already," Wraith said. "You don't need someone to tell you that."

Sol thought about the few bouts she'd just had with Wraith. She'd tried to stick to her strategy of counterattacking. But it was only the last round that she'd felt she had any sort of slight advantage, for a split second. But she had not capitalized on it.

"I underestimated your reach, your speed," Sol said. "I thought I could get in range and move faster, wait to counter."

"Yes," Wraith said. "But you forced me to act. You made me attack by coming within range and circling. Yes, you miscalculated my speed and range, but if not for that, you would have been successful."

That made sense. She had forced Wraith to suddenly strike out at her. He'd been cornered, limited to one specific technique out of many. In each of the other exchanges, he had a wide range of techniques to choose from; he'd been free to take his pick.

"Just like Bythardi," Wraith said.

Sol was familiar with the game. Her father had played it with her on occasion when they weren't training; a turn-based board game of strategy with the goal of capturing all of an opponent's pieces.

"A good Bythardi player sets his pieces so that his opponent is limited to several moves, and he can then properly set traps for each of those options," Wraith said. "A master Bythardi player limits his opponent to a single move that he can predict far ahead, one that he can capitalize on with a finishing strike."

Sol nodded.

Wraith met her eyes again.

"Have you limited the options? Are you ready to capitalize on your plan for a finishing strike?"

Sol's heart nearly stopped at Wraith's words. Was he speaking about her fighting strategy? Or something else? The words *capitalize on your plan* rang too close to Sol's reason for being there at House Cantino.

"I don't think so, not yet," Sol replied awkwardly as she slowly got to her feet. "Thank you for the training, and...the lesson."

Wraith nodded and was quiet again. She realized that the training room was empty. They'd worked for far longer than the other stablemates, who were likely running the floating stairs by now.

"Thanks again," Sol said as she handed the bloody cloth back to the man. "See you soon."

Sol turned and walked from the training room, feeling Wraith's penetrating gaze at her back.

*   *   *

Sol's boot sank with each step up the floating stairs.

Despite having climbed the stairs every day since she'd joined House Cantino, Sol still felt off-balance on the strange machinery.

The near mile-long stretch of stairs was suspended in the air, spanning from the shores of Lake Kava to the mouth of Cantino's floating compound. Gull had tried to explain the tech to her; it was the same mechanism that enabled the entire compound to float effortlessly above the hillside. Some force within each metal stair propelled it to defy gravity.

Sol didn't care how it worked. All she knew was she felt like she was never on solid ground, sinking each time she tried to take a step upward. She wasn't able to gain momentum as she did running Kalabasas Hill back at the Lyceum, where she'd often place near the head of the pack of students.

Somehow, N'auri floated up these stairs like they were nothing. Her Emeraldi friend was about twenty steps ahead of Sol and gaining distance. N'auri bounced lightly on each stair.

Just like fighting in the mud! N'auri had shouted when they first attempted the floating stairs. *You need to keep from sinking down, keep your knees high, never plant your feet!*

Easier said than done, Sol thought as she breathed heavily, attempting to keep up with her feather-footed friend.

It was just the two girls running the stairs today. Sol had insisted that she make the run at least twice per day to improve, and N'auri had decided to join her to give her someone to chase after.

Though Sol certainly wanted to improve her conditioning, she had other reasons for making the climb so often. She'd decided these stairs were her only potential exit from House Cantino after she acquired her father's body. She'd explored several exit strategies, including the far-fetched idea of hijacking and learning to pilot a Flyer.

All the plans involved incredible risk. Success seemed doubtful any way Sol approached getting her father out, but the floating stairs seemed to have the fewest potential downfalls. Wraith's words had stuck with her.

Limit the options of her opponent.

Her opponent was Lord Cantino himself, his guards, time, gravity, and what seemed like all the other forces of the world, working against her.

"What you doing, taking a break?" N'auri yelled from above, stopping to look down at Sol in the distance.

Sol tried to push her pace, but her plan sat within her head, as if it were weighing her down physically.

Cantino's guards would be another problem. They were posted everywhere across the compound: at the entryways and exits to the floating stairs, at the entrance to the museum. And those brutes patrolled the gardens in shifts.

Sol knew she needed a diversion, but what could possibly draw the attention of the entire force of guards and let her stroll down the stairs with one of Cantino's most prized possessions?

Sol gasped for air as she finally made it to the top, collapsing to her knees on the compound's soft entryway.

"For how many times you been running these stairs, you still seem pretty tired up top." N'auri stood above her, barely breathing hard at all. "Want to go again?"

"No!" Sol exclaimed. She needed to plan, that was certain, but she couldn't handle another ascent. "I think I'll be ready."

"Right," N'auri said. "One week out, so you don't want to push it."

Her friend was referring to their first fight under Cantino's banner at Aquarius. That was what the team had been preparing for over the past several weeks, building their skills, endurance, and strategy. Sol's attention had been divided, though. She needed to be prepared to fight and prove her worth to Lord Cantino, but she also needed to plan her escape. She needed to plan her betrayal.

Given what she'd seen of Lord Cantino, Sol didn't have the slightest regret for betraying his trust, leaving in the dead of night with his so-called property. But she did feel a pang of guilt for having to leave her team. Gull and Nayassa had proven to be valuable mentors as well as loyal team members, often sacrificing their own personal time to provide guidance to the younger Grievar.

Wraith, of course, had also turned out to be a top-notch training partner and wise teacher. Sol didn't think the quiet man would mind her leaving, though; he still barely seemed to notice her.

Most of all, Sol felt an ongoing onslaught of regret for having to leave N'auri behind. The two had developed a real friendship as training partners and kindred spirits. Sol was worried that her sudden departure would leave her friend isolated and alone in the service of the man she hated. And knowing N'auri, Sol thought anger would be the first emotion to rise in the girl when she learned of Sol's escape.

"Come on!" N'auri broke Sol from her thoughts as she urged her to pick up the pace. Even on a cooldown walk, the Emeraldi was constantly forging ahead.

As was their habit, the two girls walked through the expansive gardens, passing below the shadows of giant hedges and letting the spray from the fountains cool them off. They rarely had free time apart from training, and so even a few minutes to catch their breath felt like an eternity.

They stopped in front of the aviary, which, aside from the museum beneath the gardens, was Cantino's pride. The lord had nearly as many trainers working with the rocs throughout the day as he did instructors working with his Grievar.

The two leaned up against the steel fencing as one of the trainers led an orange-hued fledgling across the aviary grass. He tapped a thin spectral rod to the bird's flank every so often to urge it in the right direction. The bird didn't seem to mind the flash of pain; it changed its path as directed.

"Strange that they actually do work, for these birds," said N'auri.

"What do you mean?"

"The Daimyo," N'auri whispered, nodding at the veiny youth leading the fledgling. "I never see them do any work, except for the clerics in medward. But here, he's doing something…something real, training these rocs. Not trading slaves or bits or lording over others."

"Right," Sol said as she watched the young Daimyo. She thought perhaps he was around her age, fourteen or fifteen, but she could never quite tell with the Daimyo, who often lived several hundred years. She recognized the boy, though. He was one of Lord Cantino's many offspring. A prince at home in his castle.

"It's because even doing this, training this beast, they enslave it," N'auri whispered. "Cantino says they give it what it's been bred to do. Direct it on its true path. But these animals are wild. Elders still pass down stories of a time when the rocs roamed forests, hunted and bred as they wanted. They once were free."

The boy snapped his fingers, prompting a Grunt servicer to rush to him. He said a word and the Grunt knelt on all fours, enabling the boy to step onto his back with sharp riding boots and climb onto the saddled roc.

Sol saw N'auri's jaw clench, her teeth grinding together.

The boy dispensed a burst of energy from his rod to bring the roc to a trot across the grass. The young prince caught their eye as he rode, his pupils jet-black like his father's. He smirked as he grasped the spectral rod harder and laid the metal against the beast's neck, sending it into a full-on sprint across the aviary.

N'auri turned away. "I can't watch this. Don't care if they can't feel it; it's still not right."

Sol followed her friend back through the gardens toward the Grievar stables, passing beneath the fountain to feel the cool spray once more. Sol watched sunbeams pass through the water, refracting in a medley of light and color.

N'auri shook her head, clearly still thinking about the scene at the aviary. She met Sol's eyes. "Wish those rocs were free. Not only do they deserve freedom, but imagine the chaos if they got out. Nice diversion."

Sol's breath caught in her chest as N'auri began walking again. *It is the perfect diversion.* The piece of Sol's plan she'd been missing. But the way N'auri had looked at her just now, speaking about a diversion. The Emeraldi knew.

N'auri stopped on her heels and turned back. "What?"

"Um..." Sol hesitated, knowing she needed to still play the game. She thought of Wraith's words on Bythardi. Whatever N'auri knew, this was Sol's *only* move.

"I was just thinking you're right," Sol finally responded.

"You crazy?" N'auri asked, that sharp-tooth smile emerging on her face. "Right about what?"

Sol smiled back.

"You're right that those rocs should be free."

CHAPTER 26

Bite of the Frost

Attempting newly learned techniques must be accomplished with a clear mind. Often, a novice will become frustrated at their inability to execute new movements in the heat of combat. The novice will repeatedly make attempts without success and soon give up on the technique. This path is like throwing rocks into a pool of water to help the mud settle. A Grievar must wait and let the water fully settle to see clearly.

Passage Two, Thirteenth Precept of the Combat Codes

D arkin' amazing."

Varik watched Devana spit on the ground. The liquid froze the second it left her mouth to shatter beside her heavy boots.

"Never gets old." The marshal smirked as she paced atop the bluff. Devana stared out at the vast expanse of icy tundra that stretched into the distance.

"Why don't you try it, boy." The Grievar woman eyed Varik disdainfully as she spat again. "Certainly would be more use than all else you've been doing."

Varik shifted his feet uncomfortably on the ice. Devana didn't respect him. Perhaps she even hated him since he'd started his surveillance of Silas.

"Varik is doing exactly what he's been told to, which is more than can be said of most," Vlador remarked. "And you best save your spit for the arena, Devana. Myrkonians say they'll have us wiping their asses by sundown, and from the look of most of them, we'll need some extra help."

Devana laughed, her heavily furred shoulders heaving up and down. "You still got some humor to you after all, Vlador," she said. "Thought it had all dried up soon as the bluebloods got to you."

The brief smile left Marshal Vlador's face as he kicked at an outcropping of icy stalagmites jutting from the ground. "You know why I keep them close. You know better than anyone."

The Grievar lady breathed out frosty mist as she stared into the expanse. She suddenly turned her gaze back toward Varik. "You want to know something, boy? When I was young, I knew another boy, just about your age. He was more than you, though. He followed the Codes. He fought a village chieftain, my own father, and brought him to his knees. I was just a wee shit too at the time, but I can still feel my blood pumping as I watched that boy become a man, saw the fire in his eyes, how much it meant for him to fight for his people, to uphold the Codes."

Vlador's cheeks flushed, and Varik knew it wasn't the cold. Devana was speaking of the marshal.

Vlador shook his head stubbornly. "Don't pretend to be some naïve highlands girl still, Devana. You know as well as I what the empire does for us. The resources, the facilities they provide our teams. And you know what happens if we fall out of step. You've seen what they can do."

"And for what?" Devana's voice became fiery. She turned and pointed to the sky at the floating airship, the bloated behemoth of a mech with space enough to house a village and the firepower to incinerate one in an instant. "So the bluebloods can sit warming themselves in their luxury suites up there while we Grievar freeze our asses to death out here?"

Varik cast his eyes back to the ground. He'd left Silas's side to report to these two, and though the Slayer knew where he'd gone, Varik still felt uncomfortable staying too long. Certainly not to hear these two marshals argue about their old love life.

"You're welcome to go up there and warm yourself alongside them, Devana," Vlador said. "The empire provides for us all."

"I don't give a deepshit about sitting in a darkin' airship," Devana said. "I'm talking about more than that. More than us. We represent Grievar-kin, Vlador. We were elected to be marshals by our people, to make sure they're getting the fair end of the tusker bone. Way I see it, those Daimyo sitting up there have done nothing but try to take from us. First lessening the rations going out to highlands training ops. Then the decree to pull the top-ranked kid from each village without even getting local consent, acting like darkin' Desovians all a sudden."

She spat on the ground again, smashing the ice with her boot.

"What's the alternative, Devana?" Vlador asked. "This is the way it's been. Since before we were both naïve kids. We Grievar are strong, but they have the power."

Vlador stared up at the airship casting its massive shadow over them.

"Not here in the Northlands, they don't," Devana retorted. "Most Flyers go down in this cold. That airship can barely move. They ain't so tough. That's why the Myrkonians are independent, the only real sovereign Grievar."

"Not for long," Vlador whispered.

"What'd you say?" Devana asked.

"Not for long," Vlador said again. "You know why we're up here. At least, if you tried to fulfill your role on the council, you'd know. We're not here for any normal diplomacy with the Myrkonians, Devana. This one's bigger."

"I know what your lords are cookin'," Devana said. "It's not going to work. They won't bow to no Daimyo. Nor will I."

"They will," Vlador said confidently. "We have Bertoth himself stepping in the Circle. The only man to unite the eight Ice Tribes in centuries. They worship him, Devana, like a god."

"You've tried it before," Devana said. "The last two of our champions, corpsed out here in the frozen North. Bertoth didn't break a sweat."

"Now's different," Vlador said. The marshal stepped to Varik's side and placed a hand on the boy's shoulder. "Now we have Silas."

Devana was silent. "Silas agreed to fight Bertoth?"

"Yes," Vlador said.

"Silas respects the ice-tribers," Devana said. "How did you get him to agree?"

Vlador looked down at Varik. "Varik has done well. He's provided us with valuable information. Leverage on the Slayer."

Varik shivered, not because the icy wind was picking up again but at the thought of the many lies he'd spoken to the Slayer.

Devana shook her head in disgust.

"You're blackmailing our own champion?"

"No," Vlador said. "But with a lone wolf, an unpredictable Grievar like Silas, we need some leverage to make sure he stays on track. Otherwise, what's to prevent him from simply jumping ship to fight for another nation? Perhaps one day he decides to head south and step onto Memnon's team?"

"Even if Silas does fight and manages to beat Bertoth, what makes you think that will change anything? Suddenly, every tribe on this ice hunk decides they'll bend the knee to the empire?"

"No," Vlador said. "We don't expect that. They can stay sovereign. But they will follow the man that defeats Bertoth. They will follow the man that can best the unifier of tribes. And Silas is ours. So, when we need Myrkonian strength to shore up our defenses against the Desovians, or to make another run against Ezo on the Spine, we'll have it."

Devana's braids flailed in the frost wind. "That boy from the highlands. The one I remember. He really is gone, isn't he?" she said sadly.

Vlador didn't respond; he stared out into the expanse.

Devana finally looked back down at Varik.

"You think you're doing this to be a Knight someday, boy? You think this is the way to win honor?"

Varik's gaze dropped back to the ice.

"So be it," Devana said as she turned and walked away.

*   *   *

Silas watched the squire tend to his roc.

Varik squatted, carefully filing at Karo's long talons. Though the bird needed her claws sharp, the creature's running stability was compromised if they grew too long. In the wild, rocs would rake their talons against a boulder to wear them down, but that wasn't nearly as precise as the boy's work with the iron file. One of the many useful tasks Silas had put his squire to over the past months.

"It's all right; hold still, my friend," Varik whispered to Karo.

The roc deserved the respite. She'd ably carried both Silas and Varik on her back over the Caravini Range, no easy task. The start of the journey north had been fast enough, following the river on the flat plateaus, but then they'd spent nearly three weeks climbing a particularly precipitous stretch of the rising mountains that fed through to the Northlands.

The three huddled in a small ironwood grove as night fell and the frost wind began to blow in earnest.

"Done with the nails, my friend," Varik said as he began to carefully brush the bird's feathers. Silas had noticed a growing bond between his squire and mount as they'd traveled the span of Kiroth.

The squire had proved useful beyond care of his roc. The boy prepared equipment for their journeys, procured rations when they didn't have time to hunt. He always secured a private training room for Silas in the crowded towns and a quiet space for ki-breath practice in the noisiest arenas. And the boy could run messages to Vlador so that Silas needn't speak a word to that man and his bureaucrats.

Silas watched quietly as Varik finished brushing Karo's feathers and then silently set to collecting kindling around the grove, searching for sticks that hadn't been touched by the permafrost. The boy shivered beneath his cloak as the wind cut through the trees.

Silas turned and walked to the edge of the grove, uncaring as frost pummeled his face, dressed his eyelashes with white crystals.

He looked out at the vast northern tundra: The pregnant moon rose like a spotlight to reveal icy desolation spanning in all directions. Below the bluff he stood upon, Silas saw the multitude of fires from the Kirothian camp, burning like embers in the night. The whole of the battalion had arrived just yesterday, a week after Silas. They'd set up camp in the valley, where they could find shelter from the frost wind.

The empire's arrival had dispelled the northern tranquility Silas had savored, rumbling tanks and walkers tromping on the ice. The battalion had brought what mech power they could by way of the eastern plateau that cut through the lower foothills.

And the airship crew, stationed there long before Silas arrived— Grunt builders and construction mechs sent to preemptively create the docking station, all frozen corpses and broken-down machinery by now. Silas sneered as he eyed the airship floating at the edge of the valley, set in front of the great ice expanse.

Even the greatest of mechs looked small against the backdrop of the tundra. They brought the airship as a symbol of their power. They wanted to feel like lords even in the face of the unconquered northern reaches. Vlador and the rest of the Grievar council were likely blanketed beside those Daimyo up there, hiding.

The cold blasted Silas's face again. He didn't mind it. There was a time when all he could remember was the cold, the frost wind cutting him as he trudged through the endless snow of this very tundra that lay before him.

The cold had made Silas strong then, just as it had made the Myrkonian people strong for centuries. The cold was why the Myrkonians still retained their sovereignty.

Silas stared into the distance toward Starkguard Arena, like some ancient behemoth rising from the tundra, carved from the very granite of the mountain. Starkguard was said to be the most frigid spot in the entire Northlands. There, the weak froze before they even stepped into the Circle. It was at Starkguard that the Myrkonians had turned back champions from every corner of the world, seeking to plant their nation's flag on the northern ice.

Vlador and his Daimyo lords thought they had commanded Silas to come to Starkguard. But it was not they he'd listened to. It was not their cowardly voices that commanded him.

Silas looked toward the grove to see Varik had already set the fire, burning hot below an iron pot of simmering stew. Another skill his squire had proved capable of: Varik was a fine cook, satiating Silas on the road with meals such as spiced and stewed elk and flame-braised tusker thigh.

His squire had set his back against a large ironwood with his lute cradled in his arms. The boy's fingers moved masterfully across the strings, like spider legs weaving a web. Varik played the same tune he'd practiced on the road so often. He played the same song that Silas had heard hummed by village children and knitting wives and aspiring Knights across the empire.

Varik's breath steamed as his serene voice carried on the night wind.

> *They come from frost of north,*
> *With frigid wind and storm.*
> *They come from isles of lore,*

With emerald shores beyond.
They tread in shadow and time,
With fists shrouded in light.
They feel no fire and follow no lord—

"Tell me why you've lied to me," said Silas, interrupting the song, the fire flickering red in his eyes.

The boy stopped abruptly, setting the lute down and staring wide-eyed back at Silas. Even now, after Varik had been by his side for nearly a half year, Silas saw his little brother's freckled face and sparkling eyes looking back at him.

"What...what do you mean, sir?" the boy stammered.

The wind howled through the ironwoods.

"You've learned much, traveling with me," Silas said. "Why is it you still believe their story? The tales they've weaved. The lies they tell."

"I don't know—"

"Do you want to know something I've not told you?" Silas stepped toward Varik and knelt in front of him.

"Yes, sir. Yes, that would be fine," Varik whispered timidly.

"You remind me of my brothers," Silas said. "You're curious like Sam, stubborn like Cego. Perhaps that's why I've kept you by my side for so long."

"Oh..." Varik huddled into his cloak as the fire flickered with another gust of wind.

"I needed to leave my brothers behind, though I loved them," Silas said. "Sometimes, even those we love we need to leave behind so we can push forward."

"I understand," Varik said, some confidence returning to his small voice.

"After I left them..." Silas said. "I was here. Walking this great northern tundra below us, stumbling in the winter wilds for days, months. I was so cold. So hungry."

"Why?" the squire asked.

"Because it was my path," Silas answered. "I was meant to feel the pain. I was meant to grow strong in the cold. I needed to follow the voice on the frost wind."

"Voice?"

"Yes," Silas replied. "He told me of my kind, trapped, enslaved, tortured by the Daimyo on every forsaken corner of this world. He told me of Grievar children ripped from their mothers' arms, elders thrown to the burning fires. He's spoken to me since, given me truths, told me to come here to the Ice."

"Who is it... that speaks to you?" Varik's voice broke.

"It matters not who speaks, but how we respond," Silas said. "Do you know how I responded, my squire?"

"No, s-sir." Varik shivered.

"I called back," Silas whispered. "I howled into the wind and told him I would seek out and punish those who hurt my kind."

A spray of frost suddenly covered and extinguished the fire as the wind shrieked through the trees. Karo let out a screech as she pulled against the oak she was tethered to.

The embers glowed in the near pitch-black.

"Sir, should I t-try and get the fire—"

"There were fires that first night," Silas said. "Torches in their windows. I came down from the mountains, the very hills we climbed on the journey here. I saw their light. I felt their comfort. I heard their laughter. And I knew it was all built on my people's backs. They laughed and played and ate while my own toiled and died."

"Sir, I r-really think we need some w-warmth..." Varik said through clattering teeth.

Silas didn't seem to hear his squire; he stared into the embers. "I went to their home that night and I took their comfort. I took their smiles and laughter. I took their warmth. I took their light."

Silas suddenly turned his glowing eyes on Varik. The boy

desperately tried to wrap the cloak around himself as a shield against the incoming wind.

"You lied to me," Silas repeated as he stood.

"I didn't, I p-promise...I didn't." Varik squirmed his back against the oak.

Silas shot forward like a cat, punching his gloved hand out to pin the boy's neck against the tree. Silas squeezed as he looked into those bright eyes.

Varik's arms flailed as he attempted to speak. His voice came out a desperate gurgle.

"It is *they* that tell the lies, my squire," Silas whispered, gently this time. "There is no place in the coming world for those who've been infected with their lies."

The frost wind blew harder as the embers cooled and extinguished.

CHAPTER 27

Fight to Be Free

A Grievar must not stray from home for more than sixteen days of the full year. A Grievar's home is their source of vital energy, where they can best learn, grow, and repair. Just as a tree's roots grow deepest at its base, a Grievar's spirit holds strongest at home.

Passage Three, Sixty-First Precept of the Combat Codes

Sol slowly opened the door to her room, making sure the hinges didn't creak as usual.

Circles ringed her eyes and she felt a deep weariness in her bones; several sleepless nights mixed with hard training days were an ill-fitting combination. She was used to it, though, preparing fastidiously for the tests at the Lyceum, staying up all night with Cego and Abel to make sure they had every technique prepared to perfection.

Sol certainly shouldn't be thinking about her home at the Lyceum now, of all times. But as she crept out the door into the darkness of the hall, the Lyceum was all she could think about.

How was Cego doing? Did he figure out anything about the

strange flux on his arm? Did Abel finally work up the courage to talk to the lithe Level Three girl he'd awkwardly stare at every visit to the dining hall? What boneheaded trouble had Dozer gotten himself into this semester? And did big Joba still have that everlasting smile crossing his face?

Her thoughts drifted to N'auri as she passed by the girl's closed door. She would be sleeping now, snoring like a tusker, from what Sol had heard back at her home in the forest. Sol almost stopped out of habit to knock on the door.

Where is it?

Sol squinted her eyes in the dark and ran her hand along the wooden frame. *Nothing.* N'auri's Kova stone was gone. Sol had seen it just yesterday evening. N'auri would be livid if the family heirloom were lost. But Sol knew it was no coincidence. The Emeraldi knew something—she'd goaded Sol to free the rocs.

But it didn't matter, Sol didn't have time to deal with this, not now. She had to keep moving forward.

She crept light-footed down the hall, and descended the stairs to the main practice room. The space was dead quiet at this hour, the Circles empty, the heavy bags motionless. Even Wraith needed to rest sometime, apparently, though Sol half expected the pale Grievar to emerge from the shadows.

She snuck into the warm night air, measuring her breathing as she navigated the gardens. Sol had never seen the grounds at night. Empty fountains and stone-faced statues were bathed in pearly moonlight. The stars were radiant in the sky, so luminous that they seemed within arm's reach.

Sol flinched at the shadow of a garden hedge bristling in the night wind. She breathed deeply again. Her execution needed to be flawless. No room for error there.

Cutting toward the aviary, she made sure to avoid the dry leaves that dotted the grass. She circled the high steel fence, passed the locked gate, and crept to the northern edge of the perimeter.

Through the grates of the fence, Sol could see the shadowed exterior of the roost where the rocs slept. A tall bythelwood tree rooted outside the perimeter reached in to bristle against the building's thatched roof.

Sol dug into her rucksack and produced a pair of black leather gloves, light mitts she'd taken from the training facility a day earlier. She stood at the base of the tree, looking up at a near thirty-foot climb as she pulled the gloves on.

If the movement is in your body, if you are ready, thinking will only hinder you. Don't think, just go.

Her father's words spurred her on as she leapt onto the wooden core of the tree and began to climb. She pushed branches out of the way as she ascended the trunk, thankful for the cover from aerial patrols, the reason she'd decided against scaling the fence itself.

A sharp branch gouged Sol's face like talons, gashing her just above the eyebrow. She kept climbing. Just as in the Circle, she needed to execute her game plan without hesitation.

She neared the top of the tree and scuttled across the outlying branch that reached over the fence. The end of the branch would not support her weight. This was where Sol needed to make the leap. The roof of the roost was not an option for a soft landing; she'd crash through the thatched material.

Sol needed to make it back to ground level.

The moonlight caught Sol's shadow as she hurtled from the branch over the fence, face-first. Sol had been practicing her front rolls since she was a toddler, since before she'd learned to walk. She'd been thrown by her father, by numerous instructors, by her training partners and friends. The act of flying through the air with the earth rushing to meet her was commonplace to Sol. And so, she landed with grace thirty feet down. She rolled and distributed the impact, sprang to her feet, and escaped into the shadows beside the building.

No time to hesitate.

Sol shimmied along the wall of the roost until she reached a corner and peered out to check on her target. Even from a distance, the guard looked big, larger than he'd seemed standing in front of the museum. She recognized the dent on the man's helmet.

Digging into her rucksack again, she found what she was looking for, round and smooth. A timer. One of many from the training facility used to measure the length of sparring rounds. She clicked the device on and tossed it across the aviary into a small patch of high grass.

Sol waited, steadying her breath, coiling her body for action.

The guard yawned beneath his black visor as he stretched his hands in the air. He checked the spectral rod at his belt, scratched himself, and returned to his statue-like position.

The timer went off like a strange bird chirping in the night. The guard's head cocked toward the sound immediately. He didn't move yet, just turned and listened cautiously.

She was on him already, springing out of the shadows and wrenching her arm around his neck. Sol found the slight gap beneath his helmet with her forearm and used her full weight to pull him backward onto the ground.

The guard reached frantically for whatever demonic creature had landed on him. He gurgled and gasped for air, kicked his feet so hard that he pulled the grass up.

But Sol's strangle was cinched. The guard was out in ten seconds, his eyes rolling into his head to take in the full moon above. Sol didn't need this man waking up. She listened to the chorus of chirping night singers as she kept her strangle tight.

Sol released the man and gently laid him down on the grass. She removed the visor. He was a young Grievar, perhaps only a few years older than Sol, with curly brown hair matting his still-sweaty brow.

How did you end up here?

Sol closed the boy's eyes before unfastening the spectral rod at his belt. She tucked the cold steel weapon into her rucksack and knelt to heft the guard's lifeless body over her shoulder. Kata guruma.

She took his listless hand and held it to the lightpad set at the roost's door. It slid open.

Sol walked within, smelling the musk of feathers and bird droppings. Twelve roc pens surrounded her, each with a pair of taloned feet visible beneath the stalls. The birds breathed deeply in their sleep.

A high stack of hay bales was piled at the center of the roost.

Sol crept to the closest stall and slowly unlatched the door, revealing the shadowed form of a tall bird, its crested head hanging at its heaving breast. Sol moved to each pen and did the same. Some of the rocs stirred but didn't wake. She counted her lucky punches that they seemed to be sleeping as soundly as N'auri.

Sol arrived at the final pen, the twelfth, this one with Cantino's gilded crest embedded in the wood. Sol slowly opened the door to reveal the lord's personal mount. *Firenze.* She admired the creature, having never seen him this close before. The beast stood more than twice her height, a male with a beak like a golden curved dagger, a strong wiry neck, and thick, muscled legs ending in razor-sharp talons. The roc's sleek red plumage glistened like embers in the darkness.

Suddenly, the roc's eyes sprang to life, two piercing orbs staring back at Sol from only an arm's distance. The creature did not move. He cocked his head to the side and kept his gaze on Sol, sniffing at the air.

Sol held her breath. If the bird wanted to rend her, he could do so easily, no matter her fighting prowess. She'd seen a roc tear a tusker apart like a silk screen when she was a child.

Sol extended her hand, palm up, and knelt in the soft hay. She bowed her head and closed her eyes.

"Right here," Father said as he patted Sol's belly. *"That's where the fear begins to form."*

Sol was standing in the peaceful Grove outside her house. The place where she remembered Father best, where the two had spent most of their hours together.

"Then the fear will move up to here," he said in his baritone, patting her back, between the shoulder blades. *"If the fear gets too high up, here in your chest, you won't be able to breathe, think, act.*

"Keep your fear down here," her father said as he patted Sol's belly again. *"Here, you can use your fear. Here, it is your friend."*

Sol kept her head bent and breathed deeply. She let the fear in, flowing through her lungs and sinking into her gut. She felt the fear swim toward her back, circling the base of her spine like a razor shark.

She could hear the roc step toward her, his talons piercing the hay and drawing across the wooden floorboards. He sniffed at her again; she could smell his musty breath as a gust of hot air from his nostrils tossed her hair to the side. His cold beak shoved her, nearly throwing her off-balance to the ground.

Sol stayed kneeling, quietly.

This would be an honorable end, despite not being in the Circle. She was fighting. This was her path.

Sol opened her eyes. The roc was right beside her, his giant head peering at her with a fist-sized eyeball.

"I'm here to help," Sol said quietly, calmly. "I'm here to free you, Firenze."

The roc reared up suddenly, as if he were about to take her head off with a snap of his enormous beak. But instead, the bird lay down with his belly flat across the floor.

Sol had seen this behavior before. He was inviting her to mount. She sighed in relief.

"We won't need this anymore," Sol whispered as she carefully unfastened the buckles on the roc's saddle. She tucked the hard leather beneath the hay before gingerly climbing onto the beast. His feathers were soft and slippery, so she clasped her legs to his back and encircled her arms around his neck as he stood.

"Let's finish this," Sol said as she urged the roc forward with a gentle squeeze, guiding him out the pen door and into the center of the roost. Sol reached back into her rucksack and produced the guard's spectral rod. She'd never used one before, but she'd seen them in action enough to know the basics.

She squeezed the handle, and as expected, a spark lit at the rod's base and began to circle upward, traversing the length of the weapon before returning to the base again. The spark began to move faster across the steel as Sol squeezed harder, illuminating the darkness of the roost.

She heard one of the penned rocs squawk in alarm as it clawed at the wood with its talons. And then another roc screamed, louder this time, bursting through a stall door into the center of the room. Sol held the rod into the air above her head, dispelling every shadow in the roost.

Her own mount reared, but she calmed him with a gentle touch while still holding up the brilliant weapon. Another roc emerged from its pen, fear in its eyes as it pecked at the air frantically.

Soon, all the birds were out of their pens, eleven of them peering at their alpha, who was mounted by a strange Grievar girl.

"Go, be free," Sol said. She tossed the fully powered spectral rod into the pile of hay at the center of the room. The bales burst into flame and chaos erupted.

*   *   *

In their frantic escape from the roost, the rocs managed to kick and carry some of the burning hay onto the grass outside. The flaming piles of hay around the field further perturbed the birds. They frantically sprinted the perimeter of the aviary to get away from the fires.

Sol guided her roc to the steel gate and dismounted, sliding from the bird's feathered back onto the grass. She slid the long bolt aside and put all her weight against the heavy door. It barely budged; she'd witnessed two full-grown Grievar put their strength into closing the thing two evenings before.

Suddenly, the gate was opening rapidly, Firenze pushing his head against the steel frame above her.

"Thank you," Sol said as she climbed onto the bird's back.

He does want to be free. He knows this is the way.

The other eleven rocs screeched and sprinted toward the exit as they watched their alpha head out. Sol could now hear security sirens sounding across the compound, accompanied by yelling guards. She goaded her mount into a gallop, sending him across the garden toward the museum. She didn't bother following the path; her roc easily sailed over a hedge and scrambled across a raised flower bed.

It would only be a few minutes before the Flyers were on them, shadows from above that meant certain death.

Sol expected to see the standard guard posted at the entrance to the museum. If her roc couldn't dispatch him, she'd prepared herself to leap from her mount to take him down. But the guard wasn't there; the post was empty.

The sirens wailed louder and the shouts became a chorus. Firenze waited for his next command.

Sol could see the aviary clearly from the elevated position. The entire roost was now a brilliant conflagration in the night. Several guards were standing at the edge of the fire, blasting it with frost sprays, which only seemed to enrage it. And the blaze was spreading outside the aviary now, flames rippling at the edge of the gardens and building at the base of one of the large guard barracks.

She'd wanted an ample distraction and she'd gotten one. But would the fire last long enough?

Sol heard a whirring noise overhead. Perhaps it was the wind picking up and catching the hedges, but she didn't even bother to look up and check. She urged her roc directly down the bone stairs of the museum, the bird obeying and scrambling down on the uneven footing, nearly falling the entire length of steps but somehow keeping his balance to the bottom.

She caught the eye of a surprised Grunt servicer mopping the floor as they sprinted at full speed down the wide hallway, the roc's talons desperately trying to grip the slippery marble floor.

They dashed below the suspended skeletal behemoths and raced past the dead eyes of ancient beasts staring back at them. Sol gripped the left side of the roc's breast, making sure not to rip his feathers as they skittered past a hallway, retreated several steps, and then sprinted down a new path. *The Hall of the Grievar.*

She didn't slow the bird. They streaked passed the ancient Grievar skeletons and the modern heroes, approaching the shadowed end of the hall that Sol hadn't yet seen. She slowed Firenze to a trot as they approached the exhibit's end, where one torch flickered above a display case set on a marble slab.

There he lay.

Sol peered down from atop the roc at the face of Artemis Halberd. He was lying flat, his eyes open but colorless, not the brilliant yellow that had stared back at Sol throughout her childhood. His long, muscled arms were crossed over his chest.

She slid off the roc and looked down at her father, trying to breathe, trying to keep the fear from overtaking her. Wires were running from his naked body into the walls of the display case, no doubt feeding into some invisible system.

Even in death, the Daimyo use us.

This wasn't Sol's father. Artemis Halberd was gone. This was merely the vessel that carried him, one that had served him well. A body that had served the nation, won lands and resources and pride for two decades. This was the body that had built Ezo.

Sol couldn't hesitate, not now. She kicked the case holding her father's body, hard. The synthetic shell shuddered but didn't give.

She kicked it again, several times in the exact same spot, where a small spiderweb of cracks formed.

Sol breathed deeply, stepped back and twirled around, putting her full rotational force into a side kick that landed on the mark, shattering the case in a spray of shards.

She grabbed her father's body. His skin had a strange leathery feel, like the hide of her boot, and seemed to rapidly wither as the exterior environment touched it. The smell of rot came on fast, hitting Sol like a body shot. Without the preservation case, the body accelerated on its natural path toward decay.

It's not him. Just a vessel.

She kept her eyes from his face as she knelt to rip the wires out from his head, armpits, and spine. No blood spilled as she tore the decaying skin.

Sol reached into her rucksack and unraveled a long thin sheet she'd taken from her room. She began to wrap Artemis Halberd in it, grunting as she had to turn him over to bring the sheet beneath him and then around several times again, before tying off a tight knot.

Sol looked at her father once more before she put the last of the wrap around his head. The skin of his face had almost fully decayed, exposing the white of his cheekbones. His eyes were gone, two empty sockets in a skull. He was not so different now from one of the ancient specimens down the hall. She covered his face.

Her roc was already lying flat, ready to take the new cargo. Sol rolled the body onto the bird's lower back, making sure to try to distribute the weight equally. She then reached into her sack and removed the last item within, a coil of rope that she tightly looped around the body and the bird.

Finally, Sol took her spot on Firenze's upper back. He stood shakily with the extra weight.

"Thank you," Sol whispered again, gently touching the bird's feathered head.

He cawed loudly and took off down the hall in a sprint.

Sol's mind raced along with her mount as they retraced their frantic steps, back toward the museum staircase to the garden level. She'd looked for another exit to the museum, some back door that would allow them to escape undetected. But the bone stairs were the only way in and out.

Though their daring robbery had been quick, that didn't mean Lord Cantino's full entourage wouldn't be waiting for them outside. Sol expected to stare into the muzzle of an Enforcer's cannon on ascending the stairs. There was no turning back now, though; she'd just have to push through any defenses, make a mad dash for the floating stairs, and hope her roc wasn't taken down on the way.

She stopped Firenze short at the bottom of the stairway, peering up into the night. Sol listened carefully. It was eerily quiet. The sirens had stopped. She didn't even hear the shouts of the guards.

"Let's go," Sol whispered as she pushed her roc into a sprint up the stairs. She felt the humid night air greet her, saw the light of the constellations above. She waited for a death blow, some incinerating blast of energy to put a quick end to this quest of hers.

Nothing. The night sky, the stars above, a gust of wind rustling the hedges.

Sol looked down to the aviary in the distance. The smoldering embers of the roost pushed a cloud of hot steam skyward. No one was down there. No guards, no servicers, no mechs.

She nearly jumped off the bird as a thunderclap burst overhead. Several sleek Flyers careened past them, hurtling toward the city below.

What is happening?

Sol had to keep moving. She urged her roc toward the floating stairs at a trot, trying to keep quiet in the darkness.

Where did everyone go?

She passed through the gardens on the same moonlit path, trotting by the empty fountains and elaborate topiaries. She looked toward the Grievar stables. The rooms were unlit, the training studio's windows shuttered.

Firenze suddenly stopped in his tracks, jolting Sol forward, her father's corpse shoving up against her back.

A shadow stood in the path ahead, a stationary form centered between two large hedges. The person blocked the only path to the floating stairs. She urged her roc forward.

Let's blast through this guard; we can't stop now.

The bird didn't move, though. Its head was slightly bowed as it clawed at the dirt.

Was it Lord Cantino himself? Who else would have such sway over the roc? Sol dismounted and stepped toward the twin hedges. The shadow stood firm.

"I won't stop," Sol announced herself. "I'm going down those stairs, even if it means going through you."

"I know," a voice replied. Wraith stepped from the shadows.

"What's going on?" Sol asked. "Where is everyone?"

"I would think you know what's going on," Wraith said, nodding to the wrapped body draped across her roc's back.

"He's mine," Sol said as she took a step toward Wraith. She raised her fists, ready to meet him. "You can't take him away from me. Not again."

"I know," Wraith said. "You finally have your father back, Solara Halberd."

"How…how do you know?" Sol stuttered. But she knew how already. *N'auri.*

Wraith stepped toward her.

"If you knew, why didn't you tell Cantino that I was hiding my identity?" Sol narrowed her eyes.

"The fire was necessary," Wraith answered stoically.

"What?" Sol asked, nearly shouting in frustration. "Necessary for what?"

Wraith looked up at the moon overhead, letting the soft light illuminate his face. "We took the opportunity you gave us, something we had been waiting for."

"Who is *we*?" Sol did shout this time. "You and N'auri? Why would you want me to set the fire as a distraction?"

"*We*," Wraith replied. "We who are not bound by the world they've built."

He took another step toward Sol.

"We who do not fight in the service of lord or noble, politik or Governance. We who are free to fight."

Wraith closed in, his yellow eyes gleaming beneath his cowl.

"We who will fight to be free."

Wraith stood within striking distance of Sol. They'd been there before. In Aquarius Arena. In the training hall. Both times, Sol had lost the exchange, ending up with her head bouncing off the floor.

She breathed and prepared herself.

She wouldn't stop. This was her path.

Wraith's hand came forward, but slowly, not in the blinding flash of one of his punches. His palm was extended. Sol met his eyes and reached forward to grasp his wrist.

"You need to leave now, daughter of Halberd," Wraith said, squeezing her wrist and releasing it. He stepped off the path and swept his arm forward in a gesture for her to pass. "It won't be much longer that the Flyers follow the false trail. No more questions, not now."

"And the guards?" Sol asked. He was right; she didn't have time to ask more questions, even the ones burning on her tongue.

"The guards that are still living are also following that false trail. Avoid the markets; they'll be searching there. Follow the hilled terrain; your roc will be able to handle that and Cantino's men don't have any birds to follow anymore. Go to the dockyard. We will have someone there, waiting for you."

Wraith smiled then. It was strange.

Sol mounted her roc and sent him toward the floating stairs

just beyond the twin hedges. In the moonlight, the metallic steps looked like links on a long silver chain draped to the lakeside far below.

She looked down at Wraith as they trotted past him. *Just one more question.*

"You say you fight for yourself," Sol said. "That you don't fight for any lord. But what about Cantino?"

Wraith smiled again. A new trend.

"No one fights for Cantino anymore," he answered. "The lord is dead."

CHAPTER 28

The Path Home

Strategy is the preparation of technique that will best serve to defeat a specific opponent. Strategy is the key to unlocking an opponent's weakness. However, too much preparation for any single opponent can confine a Grievar's mind and cage the variety of technique that should be available.

Passage Three, Fifteenth Precept of the Combat Codes

Y ou're looking green, boy." Marshal Vlador eyed Varik wearily.

Varik couldn't even open his mouth to reply, in fear that he'd lose his breakfast. The airship lurched again and Varik braced himself against the wall.

"You get used to it," Vlador said. The man's voice quieted as he stared at an empty seat beside him in the airship's viewing room. "I suppose we can get used to anything."

Varik had not seen Marshal Devana since the conversation on the edge of the tundra, and he suspected Vlador hadn't seen the Grievar woman since then either.

Of course, Devana wasn't aboard this craft. She followed the Codes strictly enough to avoid boarding an airship to watch today's fights from a comfortable distance, shielded from the frost wind. Varik would have also rather faced the bitter cold than sit in the belly of this flying beast, feeling sick and so far from the action below. So far from Silas.

Varik slowly looked up from the floor to the massive curved windshield set in front of him, facing down toward the granite heart of Starkguard Arena. He sat over a thousand feet in the air, suspended in a glass bubble, defying the forces of gravity with the humming elemental engine of the airship.

"Look at them," Mansher Ik Tathrain, the viceroy of Karbrok, chortled from his seat beside Vlador. "Uncivilized brutes."

Below their bubble in the sky, hundreds of Myrkonians crowded the arena, standing wherever the stone allowed them: on cliff faces, atop abutments, against cragged granite walls. Children hung from stone handholds, climbing and jostling for a better view of the action.

Within the arena, all eight Ice Tribes were represented, though to the Daimyo viceroys sitting beside Varik in the airship's posh viewing bubble, the Myrkonians all looked the same: nearly naked, wild-eyed, drunk to the gills, lunatic berserkers screaming to the wind.

"Brutes they may be, my dear, but soon they will be our brutes. And that is a good thing." Millisand Ak Nathra, the viceroy of Zytoc Province, crossed her legs as she sipped a flute of bubbled wine.

Two such Northmen fought at the center of Starkguard, within a simple Circle of rocks. Varik watched through the airship's magnified windshield as the two Grievar grabbed each other from the onset of the fight and smashed their heads together, repeatedly, until one fell to the ice in a heap. A pissing match with no technique, yet Varik was still impressed both had managed to stand for so long. The Grievar boy felt his breakfast rising in his gut again and quickly looked away from the vast spectacle.

"You, of course, are no brute, Vlador," Millisand reassured the marshal as she placed her veined hand on the man's arm. "You're different from many of your kind. You understand the subtleties of governance. Bridges need to be crossed to make headway. The old ways cannot hold back the new, else we're to lose the civilization we've worked so hard to build."

Vlador shifted uncomfortably in his seat.

"Yes, yes," Mansher chimed in as he peered down at the fights. "Though as much as I love civilization, how incredibly entertaining it is to watch these barbarians smash their heads in."

Millisand sipped at her bubbles again. "I've had enough head-smashing for today, Mansher. I look forward to seeing our champion finalize the diplomacy we've been working so hard at for the past decade. Silas is the final piece to put in place."

Varik looked to Vlador; he could see the man was stifling his laughter. Even Varik, a boy, a squire, knew the truth of the situation more than these Daimyo lords. Though Varik didn't believe he was skilled at many things, he had become a good listener.

It was true the Kirothian Empire had been seeking to gain a foothold in the Northlands for a decade. They'd offered to trade resources, lands, even mechs to the Myrkonians in exchange for a swipe at the abundant elemental mines that filled these mountains. Of course, the Myrkonians had rejected it all—they didn't care for any of that; they were sovereign and intended to stay that way.

Even Varik knew that it had been Marshal Vlador who had recognized the Ice Tribes had all united behind one man: Tharsis Bertoth. Vlador had sent champion after champion to travel north and face Bertoth, not for diplomacy but because he knew defeating the Myrkonian champion would earn the honor of the Ice Tribes. And that was all that mattered to the Northmen. Honor.

Of course, Marshal Vlador let the empire think they'd set the wheels in motion for the historic event today. The man let them think that they'd cultivated Silas the Slayer, established the rules and place of combat, facilitated the eight tribes to attend. Varik knew it didn't matter to Vlador if he got credit. All the man cared about was a win there.

Which was why he had used Varik. Made him a squire, a spy, a whisperer in the ear of the Slayer. Varik shivered as he thought of the night Silas had spared his life.

Leave me. Go down to the camp, with the rest of the officials, those who lust after comforts and warmth, those who like to wag their tongues, those who send spies to do their dirty work. Go to Vlador, tell him your mission is complete. Tell him you've convinced me to fight Tharsis Bertoth.

"Here we go!" Millisand clapped her hands, breaking Varik from his reverie. "It has begun."

Varik peered through the windshield below to see throngs of Myrkonians raising their hands to the air. A crowd parted and a beast of a Grievar stepped forward into the stone Circle. Tharsis Bertoth.

The Myrkonian champion paced the Circle as the crowd waited for his challenger to appear.

"Don't think your Silas had a change of mind, do you?" a familiar voice said from behind the watchers.

Devana casually walked into the airship's viewing bubble and took the empty seat beside Vlador, putting her feet up against the glass window.

Vlador watched her with his jaw hanging.

"Glad you could make it to this historic event, Marshal Devana," Mansher remarked from his seat. "Can we offer you any appropriate refreshments for the occasion?"

"Naw, can't stomach that bubbly shit bluebloods sip," Devana said as she produced a small steel flask from her leather jerkin and took a swig. She met Varik's wide eyes on her. "Got some real drink if you want any, boy."

"Perhaps I'll even agree to that swill," Mansher said as he pointed down to the Circle, "if we've something to celebrate in a few moments. There he is. Silas has arrived."

*   *   *

Silas had been told of this moment since he'd arrived in this world.

Since he'd emerged from the Cradle of darkness, the simulation created by the Bit-Minders. Since he'd crawled from the cave concealed in the Myrkonian mountains. Since he'd first felt the frost wind cut his naked body as he stared out at the vast expanse of the tundra, Silas had seen this moment.

And Silas savored it now. He threw his black cloak to the ice and walked into the stony embrace of Starkguard Arena. The roar of the Northmen echoed on the towering mountain walls. He felt familiar electric heat rising in his body, the blacklight like an old friend excited to greet him. As he stepped toward the Circle, a steaming mist rose like a ghost from his black leathers toward the blue sky above.

Silas peered up at the airship hanging over the mountain like some bloated bird, out of place on the pure landscape. He knew the Daimyo lords sat above in their luxurious bubbles, watching and anticipating the outcome of his fight. He knew what was at stake.

He breathed the frigid mountain air deeply, letting it burn his lungs as it had long before. He took a step toward the Circle.

These steps in Starkguard were preordained. He was destined to be there.

Silas crossed into the stone circumference of the Circle and looked across to Tharsis Bertoth. The Myrkonian was thick as an ice bear, wild and scarred. A real Grievar. A man with no lord standing above him. A man who had kept his people free from their control.

The wind howled and flew across Starkguard like an ice serpent, snaking through the ranks of cheering Northmen and rattling the steel frames of the mech Enforcers that stood among them like silent sentinels.

Silas felt the eyes of the world on him as he stood in the Circle. He felt the eyes of his kin, the Grievar of the highlands and the Northlands, the Isles and the Underground. He felt the eyes of his brothers, lost for so long and yet still close to his heart.

Most of all, Silas felt *his* eyes on him, watching. He was always watching.

This world they've built, it is not for us.

Soon, this storm will come to them.

Soon, we will find our path home.

Silas stepped toward Tharsis Bertoth, his body now engulfed in a steaming mist as long-dormant energy flowed freely through his body, bubbling against his skin.

Tharsis showed no fear as he strode toward Silas like a frost giant, his beard and chest layered with ice crystals.

Neither Grievar backed down. They would meet on a collision course at the Circle's center.

*   *   *

Varik held his breath along with other viewers in the airship as they watched Silas and Tharsis Bertoth charge each other in the arena below.

This was the moment of impact. The reason why Vlador and the Kirothian Empire had massed resources to cultivate Silas, standing fast behind him even when the man remained insubordinate. This was why they'd made Varik don a squire's clothes, become a spy, forsaking his honor and his path to becoming a Knight. Varik knew this was the moment when Vlador's name would be written into the histories—*the man who tamed the North*—while Varik remained unsung and invisible to the world.

But then the combatants stopped.

Silas and Bertoth stood within the Circle, nearly an arm's length from one another. They both held their ground.

"What is Silas waiting for?" Viceroy Mansher whined. "Why isn't he attacking?"

"Just wait for it," Vlador responded measuredly. "This is how Silas fights. He's different from most. He's waiting for the Northman to make the first move. He wants to counterattack."

"Well, they both look imbecilic, standing there, doing nothing," Mansher said, peering through his monocle.

But Varik knew Silas. He'd traveled with the man for months, rode beside him, shared meals in silence, watched him fight in a multitude of arenas across the lands. Varik knew Silas the Slayer did not wait to go for the kill, not unless he was playing, toying with an opponent.

"For once, I agree with you, Mansher," Viceroy Millisand said. "If they plan on standing there for much longer, perhaps I'll have the time to refill my glass of—urk!"

Varik swiveled his head, hearing the sudden gasp from the Daimyo viceroy.

Devana was gone from her seat. Instead, the marshal was standing behind Millisand, grasping her neck. She lifted the frail lady from her seat like a child and made eye contact with Vlador.

Devana violently torqued Millisand's neck and then dropped her limp form to the ground.

"What in the—" Mansher stood, staring in shock at his downed companion.

Before the viceroy could react, Devana threw a heavy-booted kick into his chest, launching the small man against the glass wall of the viewing bubble, right beside Varik.

Barely comprehending what was happening, Vlador threw himself between Devana and the broken Mansher, who gasped for air through a shattered rib cage.

"What in the darkin' depths are you doing?" Vlador yelled, wild-eyed.

Devana put her hands on her hips calmly. "Are you going to get out of my way, or am I going to have to kill you too?"

"Are you insane? Their Enforcers will be here in five seconds—"

"Those tin cans are taken care of, Vlador," Devana said. "Do you think I'm stupid? Or that I act alone here?"

"We're on a darkin' airship!" Vlador screamed. "Thousands of feet in the air. How the dark do you think you'll escape?"

Devana's lips curved into a smile.

"I don't plan on no escape," she said softly. "Now, turn around and help me put this miserable creature down or stand and do what you were born to do, fight."

"I won't—"

The airship lurched heavily, catching Vlador off-balance. Devana took full advantage of the opportunity. She careened toward him, catching him full on the chin with a powerful cross. Vlador fell back in a heap against the viewing bubble beside the broken Viceroy Mansher.

Varik stood frozen beside the glass. Devana stood over Viceroy Mansher with her boot pressed against the man's chest. The airship jolted again and Varik felt his stomach drop. Sirens wailed across the craft's loudspeakers.

"And you, boy?" Devana said calmly despite the chaos. "Will you stand up against me as well? Will you fight against the tide, against the coming Flux?"

Varik suddenly felt more worn than a boy his age should ever feel. He looked down in a daze at the arena below, which seemed to be getting closer. He caught a curious sight within the Circle. Silas and Bertoth were grasping hands in brotherhood.

"Down there, they're all in on this?" Varik asked in resignation. "Silas..."

"What did you think?" Devana laughed wildly as she held on to a bolted chair to keep herself from toppling. "The Myrkonians were just going to let these bluebloods lord over them? Without a fight? Did you think Vlador's plan, your spying, would really turn back the tide?"

Devana pressed harder into Mansher's chest, smiling as she listened to the *crunch* beneath her boot.

"The Flux is coming," Devana yelled over the wailing of the sirens. "We who fight will be free again."

Varik didn't hear the lady's words. He was too busy staring through the glass, watching the ground rapidly approach as the airship fell from the sky.

*   *   *

Tharsis Bertoth extended his gnarled hand toward Silas, and Silas reached forward, grasping the Northman's wrist to hold it firmly.

Tharsis met Silas's eyes and nodded. And then the Northman bellowed. The giant produced a single, powerful note, deep and trembling, like a call of the wild.

The bellow was matched by every Myrkonian in the arena: man, woman, and child joining into a chorus, vibrating and resonating with the surrounding mountain walls.

The Northmen across the arena broke into a melody, their voices harmonizing and carrying on the wind. The song they sang was ancient, like the stones and the ice, passed down over generations. Embedded within the song was a message.

Silas knew this message; he felt it in his bones, in his beating heart, in the heat rising rapidly in his body. The melody repeated one thing, loud and clear:

Now is the time to fight back.

Just as abruptly as it had begun, the chorus ended, giving way to an eruption of chaos around the arena.

The airship above spiraled from the sky like some massive felled behemoth, smoke trailing it and the blue fire of its engines sparking and dying.

The Northmen, screaming like berserkers, swarmed the mech Enforcers in their ranks.

In one section of the arena, a mass of Myrkonians brought a thousand-pound Enforcer to the ground. They smashed at the heart of the mech, dozens of repeated bone-handed strikes against the protective glass to finally rip out the pilot within. They fought for the prize like wolves on downed prey, one particularly large Northman claiming the wide-eyed Daimyo, grabbing both of the frail man's arms with a roar and ripping the body in two in a spray of dark blue blood.

A spectral cannon exploded from the arm of another Enforcer across the arena. A mass of Grievar were eviscerated, blood and bone becoming a crimson cloud polluting the air. More screaming Northmen replaced their fallen companions, throwing their bodies at the Enforcer, trying to cripple its heavy steel legs.

Silas watched from the Circle as the Enforcer tossed aside incoming Grievar like playthings. It swung hydraulic arms as heavy as tree trunks, crushing skulls and imploding rib cages like kindling. Still, the Northmen kept coming, undaunted by death and hurling their bodies at the steel creature with wild abandon. Finally, they buckled one of its steel joints to bring the Enforcer to a knee and swarmed across its shoulders.

Suddenly, the entire arena quaked as the airship crashed into the side of the mountain, exploding into a brilliant fireball. Clouds of black birds, unsettled from their caves, swarmed to the air in alarm. The Northmen didn't even give pause; they continued their assault on the trapped Enforcers.

Silas noticed that Tharsis Bertoth was no longer within the Circle with him. The leader of the Ice Tribes had sprinted into the fray and now stood over one of the downed mechs like an avenging force of nature. Tharsis bellowed as he slammed his naked heel down into the pilot's protective casing repeatedly, while a dozen of his men controlled the Enforcer's arms and legs.

Finally, the shell cracked. Tharsis's foot leaked a stream of blood onto the terrified Daimyo within. The frost giant reached in and pulled the pilot out. Tharsis stared her in the eye and roared as she screamed back in terror, and then he slammed his massive forehead into her face, pulping it like a ripe fruit.

The last standing Enforcer blasted through a throng of Northmen with its cannon and set to a fifty-mile-per-hour sprint, rag-dolling bodies off its steel frame as it cut through the arena.

Silas watched the Enforcer abruptly stop and cock its head, as if it were listening to some unheard noise. Orders from above.

The Enforcer swiveled its head toward the Circle, toward Silas. The mech broke into a sprint again, meeting rushing Northmen head-on like a bull before it leapt into the air. It careened thirty feet upward and unleashed its spectral cannon into the crowd of Northmen below, pulverizing all caught in the blast and rending a canyon in the stone.

The Enforcer landed across the Circle from Silas, sending a cloud of stone dust into the air on impact. The mech's black visor tilted toward him. Silas could hear the hum of the spectral cannon regaining its charge.

A grating mechanical voice pushed though the steel beast's speakers.

"You are ordered to stand down, empire ordinance ten twelve. Flyers are incoming; all participants in the insurrection will be executed on sight. You are empire property and so will be spared. I repeat, you are ordered to stand down."

Silas took a step toward the Enforcer, slowly, steadily, just as he'd walked his path from the start. And the voice spoke to him, as clear as ever.

This world they've built, it is not for us.

The blue glow of the spectral cannon pulsed menacingly, now at full charge. The Enforcer pointed the weapon at Silas.

"I repeat, you are ordered to stand down or you will be executed. Now is your last chance."

Soon, this storm will come to them.

Silas stepped forward again. He could not stop. His destiny lay before him.

Soon, we will find our path home.

The Enforcer raised its spectral cannon and discharged it. An expanse of blue fire engulfed Silas.

CHAPTER 29

Blood of the Grievar

The gar bear is the master of the forest, while the leviathan lords over the waters. Neither beast attempts to intrude on the domain of the other; to do so would disrupt the natural balance. The same is so with the Grievar and the Daimyo. The Grievar fights so the rest shall not have to. The Daimyo rules so that chaos does not.

Passage One, Eighth Precept of the Combat Codes

Sol watched the sunrise over the sea, sitting atop her roc.

The night seemed a blur of mad sprints in the dark: scrambling down the floating stairs on Firenze's back, climbing into the rocky foothills surrounding Lake Kava, and finally arriving at the edge of the shipyard, now with her roc's talons firmly planted in the grainy sand beneath the wooden docks.

The waves gently lapped at the shore, and Sol planted a hard slap to her own cheek to keep herself awake.

She'd caught sight of Lord Cantino's guards several times, swarming at the edge of the marketplace and even starting to venture into the foothills. Just as Wraith had said, they were following some false trail, clearly thinking the culprit had escaped into the city.

Now, beneath the docks, Sol waited for the mysterious confidant that Wraith had said would meet her there. She didn't trust Wraith, especially after finding out that he'd known her identity for months and had used her for his own purposes.

Assassinating Lord Cantino.

Sol still could not believe the man was dead. Such power accumulated over centuries: riches and slaves, land and tech. All gone in a moment. Lord or not, the man couldn't take the bits with him beneath the ground.

She'd assumed Wraith had done the deed himself, although she had no idea how he'd pulled it off. Sol had deduced some key facts on her journey to the shipyard, though. The fire she set must have been the perfect distraction for the assassin to get to Cantino's quarters with the fewest obstacles in the way. Though Cantino likely had maintained some of his personal guard, most of his forces would have been dealing with the flames, escaped rocs, and the hunt for the arsonist.

Sol touched the empty spot behind her on the roc, feeling for the bulk of her father's body, as if it might have all been a dream: her journey to the Isles, winning her way into Cantino's stables, stealing into the night.

The body wasn't beside her any longer. Artemis Halberd was now on board the *Erah Confligare*, set belowdecks and ready for the return voyage. The captain of the ship, Diam, had personally loaded up Sol's newfound cargo with a raised eyebrow but hadn't asked any questions.

Her father was heading home for a proper burial. Sol was finally going home. She gently rested her head against the roc, his soft feathers like a pillow beneath her cheek. She closed her eyes.

"You two look good together," a voice came from above, on the docks.

N'auri.

Sol straightened her back, sensing the danger she was in. She didn't even know who this girl was. Everything she'd learned about her supposed friend was now suspect.

"Wraith told me you'd come," Sol said, deciding to cut through the deepshit. She dismounted and stood on the shore, looking up at the girl. "Cantino is dead."

N'auri leapt from the dock, landing and kneeling in the sand beside Sol.

"I know," N'auri said as she reached down to touch the sand, just as the girl had done when she and Sol had first fought. Sol knew what was coming next.

She was ahead of N'auri this time, though, dodging to the left as the girl sprayed a handful of sand at her. Sol put her fists in the air.

"Good!" N'auri flashed her sharp-toothed smile. "Making sure you are learning, Ezonian."

"I'm not here to play games with you," Sol responded, not returning the smile. "You betrayed me. You and Wraith, you used me."

"Yes, we did," N'auri said. "And I'm sorry. But, to be fair, you also used us."

"How?" Sol asked angrily.

"Sayana?" N'auri laughed. "You could at least pick a better name. You used us the entire time. You never wanted to be on Cantino's team. All those times you brought me to walk the garden or visit the birds or go to the museum, you were scouting your big heist. You lied to me."

Sol gritted her teeth. The girl did have a point. Sol had lied to them from the start, about who she was, about why she was there.

"But, even so...you knew I was lying!" Sol protested.

"Yeah," N'auri said as she plopped down in the sand. "So, I guess we're even, right?"

Sol couldn't help but chuckle. And then, as if some dam broke within her, she began to laugh loudly, wildly. She fell to the sand, looking toward the sky and laughing until tears streaked her cheeks.

"You crazier than me," N'auri said.

"I guess so," Sol replied, trying to catch her breath. She looked across at N'auri. "The truth, then, from now on."

N'auri inclined her head. "The truth."

"Who are you?"

"I'm N'auri," the girl replied.

"I know you are N'auri," Sol said. "But who are you really? Who are you and Wraith?"

"I am who I said I am," N'auri said. "Everything I told you about myself is the truth. Where I'm from, about my mafé—"

Sol interrupted. "I also didn't lie about my father dying."

"I know." N'auri smiled. "I know who you are, Solara Halberd. Daughter of Artemis."

Sol nodded. If they'd known enough to see through her disguise, they clearly knew about her famous bloodline. Half of it, at least.

N'auri rose to her feet. She offered Sol her hand and yanked her up. "Wraith and I, we are part of the Flux."

"The Flux?"

"We who are not bound by the world they built," N'auri whispered. "We who do not fight in the service of lord or noble, politik or Governance."

Sol recognized the words. They were the same that Wraith had said to her last night.

"We who are free to fight." N'auri stood tall as she spoke. "We who will fight to be free."

"Free from the Daimyo?" Sol asked.

"Yes," N'auri said. "The winds of change are blowing, Solara. In Kiroth, the fight has already started. In the far north frostlands,

Grievar rise up as we speak. We will no longer be ruled by them, used by them. We will be free people again."

"But how?" Sol asked. "How can we stand against such power? Their weapons, their mechs..."

"Lord Cantino was powerful, no?" N'auri asked. "One of the greatest lords of the Isles. Three hundred seventy-five years old. And his life was ended as easy as any other. A strangle, held tight...just long enough."

Sol's eyes widened. "You? You killed Lord Cantino?"

N'auri met Sol's stare. "Yes, that is why I was recruited. Wraith was already embedded at Cantino's for years. After my mafé died, he approached me in secret. He told me about the resistance, what they would do. He recruited me so that I could do my part. We just needed to wait until the perfect moment. *You* were that moment, Solara Halberd."

Sol shook her head in disbelief. This whole time, training in the pits, fighting in the arenas, spending every waking hour together at the compound, N'auri had been preparing to assassinate Lord Cantino.

"But even so...even though you were able to kill him," Sol whispered, "it took you and Wraith years to plan just to take one of them down. And he's just a lord. He's not Governance. Ezo, Kiroth, Desovi, they run the world. They are unstoppable. No matter how many Grievar rise, we wouldn't make a dent..."

"I said the same thing to Wraith," N'auri said. "I thought the same as you. But then I heard the stories, I heard word from the North. There is one who will lead us. One who will guide the Flux. One who can fight back against the power, against such weapons that the Daimyo wield. He will lead the Grievar back to their rightful place in this world. Even if it means the start of war again, giving up our own lives. Even if it means removing the stain that is their kind, wiping every last one of their bloodlines clean."

Sol's stomach sank. The blood that ran through her own veins was the blood N'auri was talking about wiping out. Another secret she must keep. Another lie she must continue to tell.

"Who?" Sol whispered. "Who can do such things?"

N'auri looked to the horizon and then back at Sol. "They call him the Slayer."

CHAPTER 30

Wet Earth and Dry Leaves

Ki-breath is an effective technique to focus the mind. The act of concentration serves to shield a Grievar from the distraction of passing thought. But concentration is not enough. A Grievar must dispel the self that concentrates and only be the present action within the Circle.

Passage Three, Fortieth Precept of the Combat Codes

Wet earth and dry leaves.

High Commander Memnon stared out the shield window set on the south wall of his private quarters. Though climbing the long stairwell had grown tiresome since he'd cut the neuros, Memnon still enjoyed the solitude of his room's thick oaken walls. He didn't have much, just his frayed heavy bag, the tatami mat to sleep on, and this view of the Black Forest, with the ridge of Kalabasas Hill running down its center.

Memnon could remember running Kalabasas when he'd first entered the Lyceum as a bright-eyed kid. He could still smell the pines, taste the river water he'd scoop up between strides down the trail. Albion Jonquil Memnon, Level One, born and raised of the privileged purelight houses and groomed to be high commander of the Citadel.

Memnon's brow furrowed as he looked up to Kalabasas's high bluff, where he'd sprinted to the finish so many times during conditioning class, always vying for first spot against his best friend, Farmer.

Not long ago, he'd watched a group of students standing up on the bluff, within the grove of tall pines. Cego's team had stood up there, the Whelps. Cego's friends: the little Desovian kid and the boy with the scar. The thickheaded one from the Deep and the new female recruit from the Isles.

The team had stood around a burial mound, grieving together. Memnon had watched the young Grievar spend an entire day covering the body of their fallen companion.

Wet earth and dry leaves.

Even though the massive boy's frame had a gaping hole in the middle of it, his team had given him a proper Grievar burial. They had collected the moist streamside dirt and fallen leaves from the sparse faola trees. They had covered the boy three feet high with the muddy mixture, without speaking, just setting to work to get the task done. They'd given him proper passage to the next realm.

Joba.

Memnon would never forget the giant boy's name. Joba had done more than Memnon ever had during his years at the Citadel. Joba had protected his friend when he needed it most. Joba had died for a real cause, not some Daimyo-ordained path.

Joba.

Memnon turned from the window as the sun began to sink into the Black Forest. He found his heavy bag and set it swinging with a hard round kick. He grimaced as he felt the familiar nerve pain course up his hip.

He grabbed behind the bag and threw his knee to the leather, following up with a left hook that made his wrist buckle.

Memnon was falling apart, but at least his mind was clear, outside the cloud of neuros. He'd grown weak trying to make his Knights' team strong.

He tested his left again, this time with a hard jab. He gritted his teeth and threw it again.

He couldn't stop thinking about Cego, even months after the boy's trial. The high commander had attempted to make contact; he'd spoken with the Governance to determine where they'd taken him. But the bastards had stonewalled. Said it was above Memnon's clearance.

Memnon breathed hard as he slammed his jutting forehead into the heavy bag, sending it reeling backward, and then caught it high with a side kick that rattled the chain.

"O Toh!" Memnon barked, his deep voice echoing in the empty room.

He'd always known they were corrupt. He'd always known they looked down on him even though he held the highest Grievar post in the land. But Memnon had still worked with the Daimyo because he knew it was the only way. *Change happens from the inside*, he'd told himself.

The big Grievar threw a series of wide, looping hooks and then a cross right up the middle. He let combat flow through his veins, trying to dispel the uncertainty with sweat and blood.

The job had given him pride for so many years: high commander of the Citadel. The highest-ranking Knight in Ezo, tasked with leading an elite Grievar Knight force that molded the world through combat diplomacy. A team that paved the way for the Grievar of Ezo, provided them shining examples to strive for.

But after that sham of a trial, Memnon had seen through the curtain. The Codes were an instrument of the Governance. Honor and patriotism were virtues made to enslave the Grievar, keep them on task. Only one thing mattered to the Daimyo—power.

"Ahh!" Memnon bellowed as he slammed his fist into the heavy bag repeatedly. He fell to his knees. Everything he'd worked for, all that he'd sacrificed. It was for nothing.

"You're lookin' tired, old man."

Memnon looked up to see a thick Grievar standing at the entrance to his quarters.

"Murray...Murray Pearson?" Memnon panted. "You're alive?"

"I guess you could call it that," Murray muttered as he stepped forward. "I'm breathing. Though sometimes I ask myself that same thing. Perhaps this is all some Sim. Would we darkin' know the difference anyway?"

Memnon stood and stared at Murray as if he were a ghost. Pearson usually looked banged up, but now the man appeared truly battered, his face a mess of welts and bruises, and one of his arms bandaged tight to his side.

"Where have you been?"

"Gone Deep," Murray replied, moving to the heavy bag to test a few jabs with his good arm.

"I had our Scouts looking for you down there," Memnon said. "Told them to search every bar in the Underground."

"Can't say honestly I didn't spend some time drinkin'," Murray said. "Though I was mostly on the streets...tried to stay far from the Circles."

Memnon met Murray's single eye. They'd fought together, served together, and worked together for nearly two decades. Pearson knew something was off.

"What's going on?" Murray stopped the swinging bag and turned toward the high commander.

"Your boy...Cego." Memnon felt the guilt rising in his chest. "They've taken him."

"Who the dark has taken him?" Murray growled.

"The Daimyo," Memnon said.

"What do the bluebloods need with him?" Murray closed in on

Memnon. "They already built the kid for their purpose. Why take him back?"

"Something happened," Memnon said. "Cego was accused of breaking the Codes. Sent to trial and charged. But he survived. Cego won his Trial by Combat, against the Goliath."

Murray's lips trembled as he stepped closer. "The kid fought the darkin' Goliath?!"

"Murray," Memnon whispered, holding his hands up. "You should have seen it. Your boy, he…changed. The Goliath was no match for him. But after he won his freedom, the Enforcers grabbed him, loaded him onto a Flyer. Dakar believes they've taken him to Arklight."

"Mother of the Deep…" Murray whispered before suddenly grabbing Memnon by the shoulders, shoving him backward.

"And you've done what about it, High Commander?" Murray spat. "Sat on your ass, pretended it's all for the greater good again?"

Memnon backpedaled as Murray shoved him again, the burly Grievar's brow creased in anger.

"Do you expect those bluebloods to suddenly drop a Flyer in the yard with Cego returned, unharmed?" Murray shouted, pushing Memnon up against the padded wall.

Memnon stayed silent.

"Exactly what I darkin' thought!" Murray screamed as he raised his trembling fist.

Memnon wasn't afraid. He wanted Murray to put that fist into his face. He'd at least feel it, after not feeling anything for so long.

"Murray…" Memnon trailed off. "While you've been gone, I've finally gotten off the neuros. They were clouding my mind for so long."

Murray stared at Memnon, his jaw still clenched. He lowered his fist and stepped back, breathing hard. "You deserve it. But you're as useless as the lot I busted up down below."

"You what?" Memnon asked.

Murray muttered as he pulled a flask from his side pouch and swigged at it. "Had to smash some faces to get some answers. To find what I was lookin' for."

"What were you doing in the Underground, Murray?" Memnon questioned. "Why did you leave?"

Murray crouched into a squat and looked toward the room's open door. "Kid! Come on out."

Memnon watched as a small boy, perhaps ten years old, emerged. The boy cautiously stepped into the quarters.

"High Commander, I'd like you to meet my friend Sam."

Memnon looked down at the boy, whose eyes were oddly familiar.

"You seem to have lost Cego," Murray said. "But I've gone Deep and found his brother."

CHAPTER 31

Shadows and Light

There is an order to our planet, to our society. Some will serve and some will rule. Some will toil and some will rest. Some will fight and some will die. There is a path that must be followed for each, a purpose for the greater good. Without such order, all shall fall to chaos and war. Without such purpose, all shall perish.

Passage One, Second Precept of the Combat Codes

Cego longed for the darkness.

Just one moment, one break in the bombardment of light and pain.

One moment of darkness so that he might somehow forget the shackles that had become a part of him, pinning his arms and legs and neck to the steel wall.

So that he might be distracted from the wires that writhed across his body like eels, plunging their heads into his skin and burrowing inside him. So that he might disregard the thick feeding tube rammed through his navel to keep him alive.

Cego desperately wanted to close his eyes and forget the thing atop his shoulders, a throbbing cold steel helmet compressing his skull with tubes spiking into both his ears.

Just a moment of darkness and he might remember the world outside this prison. Some faraway vision of a boy attending school at the Lyceum among his friends, whose faces were fast fading from his memory.

If Cego could close his eyes, he might even fall back further. To his home before the Lyceum. The sun-swept island. The cool black sand between his toes. The salty brine that dried on his face after swimming the warm waters.

But they did not let Cego close his eyes and find sweet reprieve. His eyelids were stapled open, forced to gape and gasp like sea clams pried apart.

Perhaps they knew if Cego closed his eyes, he'd slip away, escape to the darkness, far from the pain and their prying eyes. They'd kept Cego alive and awake so they could observe him, experiment on him, torture him.

These clerics, on the other side of the glass, were not like his friend Xenalia.

They did not work to repair, to heal. These clerics probed him with sharp steel, electricity, and light, watching his response on their data feeds while dispassionately communicating among themselves.

Cego could do nothing but helplessly watch the clerics in their room, bright and sterile, as they scurried from machine to machine. He tried to look past the experimentation room to the long corridor that ended in a giant steel door, where an Enforcer stood guard.

An electric jolt screamed up Cego's spine as one of the clerics pressed a button. Cego cried in pain, though no noise escaped his parched lips, no tears wet his face.

Another cleric glanced at a lightboard feed and casually lifted his hand. Cego knew what the gesture meant. More charge. More pain.

Another blast of electricity coursed through Cego's body,

lighting every nerve on fire. He'd grown used to the smell of his own burning flesh.

The two clerics stood and walked toward the back of the room, reporting whatever they found to another, an old man with skin like parchment paper who almost never left his chair. The old cleric sat in front of a lightboard like an egret waiting for a fish, hunting with his beady eyes for some secret on-screen.

This man was the head of this endless operation of torture. They sought to understand Cego. They wanted to know how a year two student at the Lyceum had destroyed the Goliath during his Trial by Combat. They sent electricity coursing through Cego's body to somehow activate the dormant energy they knew lay within. These men sought Cego's secrets. They sought his power.

But Cego hadn't felt any power, only pain and bone-deep weariness since he'd arrived, since the Enforcers wrenched him from the Flyer and carried him down the mute prison halls.

The two subordinate clerics returned to their seats, one stationed again at the lever of pain. He reached toward it, ready to raise the charge once again.

The cleric stayed his hand as the lights planted atop the ceiling suddenly flashed red. Cego watched all three clerics jump from their seats in alarm, looking up at the flashes.

Though Cego couldn't hear the alarm, he could see the lead cleric's annoyance. The old man yelled down the hall toward the Enforcer, who moved forward and pointed his giant steel arm up toward the flashing lights.

And then Cego got his wish. Though his eyes were still stapled open, a sudden darkness fell on his cell and down the long corridor.

One of the clerics rushed to his frozen data feed and furiously pressed the board, while another continued to yell at the Enforcer, pointing at the large steel door at the end of the corridor.

The Enforcer spun away from the frothing cleric, his giant frame stomping toward the door.

Cego couldn't hear anything beyond the glass, but he saw the way everyone reacted. All three clerics stared at the steel door at the end of the corridor.

Cego recognized the rising blue pulse on the Enforcer's arm. He was charging his spectral cannon. Cego could suddenly smell burning flesh, Joba's burning flesh. He could see the gaping hole in his friend's body left by the cannon's blast, the ever-present smile suddenly absent from the big boy's face. Though many memories from outside this prison were hazy, Joba's death was still visceral. Cego would not forget.

Why was the Enforcer charging his cannon in a secure prison?

The steel door suddenly curved inward at its center, a seemingly impossible shape for something that appeared so thick and heavy.

The Enforcer took a wary step away from the door and waved the clerics back. The little men scurried into the experimentation room while keeping their wide eyes on the end of the corridor.

Another section of the door bubbled inward. What could cause such force? Another mech, trying to get in?

The Enforcer took another step backward and raised his cannon, which now glowed the angry blue of a full charge. The clerics hid and huddled behind desks and chairs.

The center of the door cratered, the metal fraying and wrapping inward like the open maw of some beast. A thick white smoke seeped through the hole.

Cego watched as an alien form, small compared to the Enforcer but with strange light pulsing across its naked body, stepped through the newly formed opening. It was a man, masked in the mist that swirled around him. He stepped toward the Enforcer.

The Enforcer's arm jerked back and released the spectral charge, a pulse of energy that enveloped the approaching man in a brilliant blue explosion.

Cego felt it. Though he was behind the glass within his cell, strapped to the metal wall, Cego felt the energy race through his body. Radiance rose and tingled against his skin. One of the clerics turned and pointed at Cego, yelling something, while the others stared at the blast zone of the Enforcer's cannon, where the floor and walls had melted.

The naked man stepped from the smoking crater, still moving toward the Enforcer. The mech retreated while frantically attempting to recharge his cannon.

Strange energy coursed through the man's limbs, and Cego could feel his own body reacting, his muscles tensing and straining against his shackles. He felt the steel straps clasping his forearms and the collar on his neck melt away, as if they'd never really been holding him down.

Cego kicked his legs free and fell to the floor of the cell in a crouch, keeping his eyes on the alien form as it suddenly darted to the side and launched itself at the Enforcer with impossible speed.

The Enforcer raised a mechanical arm in defense, but he was not fast enough. The man raised a glowing fist and punched through the mech's protective casing. His hand found the inner sanctum housing the pilot and painted the compartment with an explosion of azure blood.

The mech toppled. The man, white mist pouring off his radiant body, walked toward the experimentation room where the clerics huddled.

Cego could suddenly feel the fear of those clerics. It seeped off their huddled bodies like a fragrance and Cego drank it in. Their fear was sweet nectar.

Cego looked down at his own body, shivering and wilted but glowing, the entire thing. Trails of energy coursed up and down his legs, across his abdomen, and around his shoulders and arms. The energy was awake and speaking to him, whispering secrets to Cego.

He knew who approached.

Cego looked away from his transformed body. Death was

everywhere in the experimentation room. Fist-sized holes punctured two bodies crumpled on the floor, their blue blood splattered across the lab's equipment. Smashed against the glass like an insect, the lead cleric was looking back at Cego, terror etched on his lifeless face.

The glass shattered and the old Daimyo fell forward to the cell's floor. The killer stepped in, standing above Cego's crouched form.

"Hello, brother."

Cego looked up at Silas. His brother's naked body pulsed with coursing energy.

Cego tried to speak, but his voice eluded him; only a parched rasp escaped. "H-how?"

"I'm here now, brother," Silas whispered gently, still offering his hand. "There's nothing to fear."

Cego grabbed the hand and shakily rose to his feet, looking into Silas's eyes. His brother flashed his curved smile. That same smile Cego remembered from the island. A chiding smile that told him Silas knew some secret that he did not.

"It has begun," Silas said.

Cego held Silas's hand tightly as energy pulsed between the two brothers.

"What has?" Cego asked.

"The Flux," Silas said. "Our war against the Daimyo has begun."

The story continues in...

Blacklight Born

Book Three of The Combat Codes

Keep reading for a sneak peek!

ACKNOWLEDGMENTS

I know we often hear of "middle book syndrome," where the second book in a trilogy serves to do nothing but move the characters and world pieces around to prepare for a satisfying finale.

At least when writing *Grievar's Blood*, I felt no such robotic inclination; I sincerely loved taking each character on their new journey and developing the world of the Combat Codes to be a more realized place. Of course, the pieces had to be set for the final book, but *Grievar's Blood* was more than a stepping stone—it was to be enjoyed equally as much as beginning and end.

In fact, middles are often my favorites. On this book's publication date, I'll be forty years old, which is most often considered the beginning of "middle age." Those words might seem dreadful to some, but I feel like I'm just starting to feel comfortable in my shoes. I think the same goes for many stories: The middle book is one where the characters are fully formed, comfortable in many ways. So it's the perfect opportunity to take them on their most important journeys, the adventures that will break their comfort and define their lives.

In the practice of Brazilian jiu jitsu, we often say, "Find comfort in the discomfort." I hope this middle book had made you, my reader, uncomfortable at times, perhaps feeling the pain of the characters or the merciless nature of the world. But at the same time, I hope this book has given you much comfort: in knowing the strength of determination, grit, and friendship.

As an author, writing this book has certainly given me comfort as well, mostly in realizing the massive support network behind me. My stalwart agent, Ed Wilson, standing as my cornerman in this bludgeoning arena of publishing, providing both tactical and inspirational words throughout. My editor, Bradley Englert, holding mitts for me to strike daily, with questions on craft and industry, all the while ensuring my stories find their best conditioning. The entire PR and marketing team at Orbit, especially Angela Man, who have likely lost their voices shouting about these stories as they prepare to enter the fray. The Orbit art department, led by Lauren Panepinto, who have dressed the books to look the part so that the crowd might stop and peer beneath the surface. And to the team at Orbit UK, Jenni Hill and Nazia Khatun, for ensuring that Combat Codes could put up a fight overseas.

And of course, thank you to my endlessly supportive family. Katie, Natalie, Jane, and Claire. Without you, I'd have no one to come home to, no one to celebrate the wins and weather the losses. Mom and Dad, you gave me the will and the way to follow my path.

And most of all, thank you, intrepid reader, for again spending your time in the world of the Combat Codes, and finding comfort and discomfort along with me.

extras

orbit

meet the author

Jeanette Fuller

ALEXANDER DARWIN is a second-generation Vietnamese Jewish American author living in Boston with his wife and three daughters. Outside of writing, he teaches and trains in martial arts (Brazilian jiu jitsu). He's inspired by old-school Hong Kong action flicks, JRPGs, underdog stories, and bibimbap bowls.

Find out more about Alexander Darwin and other Orbit authors by registering for the free monthly newsletter at orbitbooks.net.

if you enjoyed
GRIEVAR'S BLOOD
look out for

BLACKLIGHT BORN
The Combat Codes: Book Three

by

Alexander Darwin

The third book in an action-packed science fiction trilogy set on a far-future world where the fate of nations is determined by single combat at the hands of famed warriors. Perfect for readers of **Red Rising** *and* **Jade City**.

The Grievar War has engulfed the empire of Kiroth, and Silas the Slayer has given voice to his warrior kin, igniting a revolution within a people once bound by a thousand years of servitude.

Cego is released into a war-torn world where the lines between shadow and light are blurred. He must decide which path to follow: the one of his brother's righteous rebellion or the one that leads to the family he's finally found.

Once-famed Knight Murray Pearson leads a group of Lyceum students on an adventure across Kiroth to follow the path of combat mastery. But Murray seeks something more on this long road: redemption.

In this explosive conclusion to the Combat Codes saga, the truth will be revealed and one final question must be answered as they step back into the Circle:

What is the cost of losing the fight?

"Darkin' Bird."

Murray Pearson shifted uncomfortably in the saddle atop his mount. Maybe it was the back injury he'd sustained years before, or maybe this roc was purposely sloping its long neck toward the road to unbalance Murray.

"Ku, you should probably call his proper name if you want him to ride better," a dark-haired girl said from beside Murray, astride her own, smaller roc. The girl stroked the midnight feather plumes on her bird's head and pressed a foot against its hindquarters. "Let's go, Akari!" The roc burst forward in a show of speed and the girl turned back toward Murray and smirked.

"I've given mine a name," Murray muttered. "Let's go, Bird!"

Instead of this prompting his ruffled grey roc to speed up, Murray's mount reared and jolted its head forward, tossing him onto the dusty path. Laughter erupted from Murray's traveling companions, all stopping to witness the burly Grievar's fall.

"How about some darkin' respect?" Murray shouted from the ground. "Four decades your elder, and your professor too. I could have all your Level Three asses held back until you've got grey in your beards."

A lanky boy with a wicked scar crossing his face dismounted his roc to help Murray up with a firm wrist-to-wrist grasp. "We know you won't be doing that, Coach. You'd hate to go all that ways back south to be writing reports to Callen Albright."

Murray accepted the helping hand as familiar pain shot up his back. "You're too sharp for your own good, Knees."

A burly kid, shirtless and thick with muscle, joined Knees beside Murray. "Plus, we know you're having good fun out here with us on pilgrimage."

"It's because of your fun we're pressing to make the next challenge, Dozer," Murray responded.

"Hold on," Dozer protested. "That girl back in Mirstok was giving me eyes; I'm sure of it."

The dark-haired girl dismounted her black roc and slapped Dozer on the shoulder. "Right, so is that why you ended up with your bit-purse gone, your rations eaten by her friends, and no action to show for it?"

Knees nodded. "Brynn's got a point there."

Dozer's face reddened. "I did have something to show, just not enough time to work it. She even said she'd make me her ma's stew when I come back—"

"Enough idling here," Murray said as he dusted himself off. "If we're to make the Tanri challenge, we need to move now; we're still two days out at this pace. Plus, I need to stop in Wazari Market to resupply."

"Are you sure that's a good idea?" Brynn Mykili asked. "Those harvesters we passed a few hours back said patrols have been constant off the Grievar Road. Spirits be asked, if we were detained, we'd certainly not make the next challenge."

Murray's face darkened. "They find us and they'll see exactly what we're here for: pilgrimage. It's been Lyceum tradition for the past fifteen decades, even while Kiroth and Ezo have been tearing at each other's throats. A little rebellion shouldn't change nothing."

"Little rebellion?" Knees said incredulously as he deftly leapt onto the back of the large brown roc he shared with Dozer. "From what we heard, this be more than little. They say the Slayer took down the biggest stim depot east of Karstock few days ago."

"I don't want to hear another darkin' word about that one," Murray said. He vainly tried to cajole his grey roc toward him, making a clucking sound. The bird sauntered away, pecking at some worms in the mud. "I've heard this story before, someone stands up and says they'll change the way things have always been. Thinks he'll move against the Daimyo. Want to know the end of that story?"

"What's that?" Dozer said from behind Knees atop their roc.

"They get ground into the dust by the mechs, then folk keep going on about their business," Murray said. He tried to grab at his roc's saddle, only to have the bird scramble out of range again.

"But Silas took down the entire northern front!" Dozer exclaimed. "He united the Ice Tribes behind Bertoth; he's got thousands of Grievar backing him up and he's got some special powers like—"

"Enough," Murray growled with frustration as he unsuccessfully attempted to grab his roc. "Bird, get back here before I decide we'll be having poultry over the campfire tonight!"

"But they said Silas broke into Arklight. He destroyed a battalion of Enforcers on his way to getting his brother. Cego might be with him!" Dozer protested. Murray shook his head.

"Those are stories, Dozer, the sort that grow like weeds." The old Grievar Knight looked pleadingly at Brynn. "Some help?"

The girl urged her mount forward and pulled up beside Murray's roc. She gently whispered in its ear and stroked its grey feathers. Bird clucked, as if letting out a sigh, before hopping over to Murray to lower his head.

"Thanks," Murray muttered, finally climbing onto the roc and breathing deeply. He turned to Dozer. "And that story about Cego, that's the worst to be repeating. That story will be giving you hope. And that's not what we're out here for. You're here on pilgrimage. You've got matches to fight across the whole of Kiroth along the Grievar Road. You do good here, you'll be adding to your scores back at the Lyceum as Level Threes, so keep focus."

Dozer quieted down, awkwardly wrapping his big arms around Knees from up on their Roc.

"Time to be on our way, Boko," Knees said to his bird as they set pace on the road snaking through the green plains ahead.

"Let's go, Akari!" Brynn yelled.

Murray watched the Jadean shoot past the boys on her sleek black roc, kicking up a cloud of dust behind her. The Kavel mountain range sprawled like a pale slumbering giant in the distance, set beneath the cloudless blue sky. Murray shifted uncomfortably from atop his roc. He could have sworn the bird was purposely tilting forward.

"Bird's a fine darkin' name," Murray muttered as he followed behind in the dust.

*   *   *

Murray was accustomed to the street-stalled markets of the Underground; the clamor of Markspar Row; hawkers screaming at the top of their lungs in front of their rusted carts, selling imported lightdecks and illicit neurotech. But Wazari Market, the sprawling tent city that sprang up in the Kirothian highlands every summer, made Markspar seem an organized affair. Murray sucked his stomach in as a wooden cart nearly ran him off the path through the market. A trio of rocs pulled the cart at breakneck speed, and the driver screamed back at him in some dialect he couldn't understand. Murray had visited Wazari only once before, during his own pilgrimage through Kiroth. The giant market sprang up alongside the influx of traveling students. Pilgrims from every nation came through, and the local hawkers did not discriminate as long as you had a full bit-purse.

"Maybe I'll replace you," Murray muttered, thinking of his own rebellious mount, as he passed a tent full of squawking rocs cooped up in cages.

"You want?" A hawker caught Murray eyeing the scrawny birds. "Guarantee you fill bit-purse many times over if you bring one of my roc to the ring! They bred for fighting, like you."

Murray shook his head and pushed on toward the central stalls farther in. Dusk cast the market in a crimson hue, the colorful tent awnings like a field of wildflowers set on the Kirothian plains. One could purchase not only a new mount at Wazari but any sort of wild beast. Murray passed iron cages with pacing gar bears and penned-up wild tuskers from the northern forests. He even saw a hawker pawning a giant boa snake from the Besaydian jungles. As a student, Murray hadn't paid attention to how chaotic Wazari was; he'd probably had his mind on his next fight, or maybe, like Dozer, he had been focused on some blushing highland girl he'd seen at the last village along the Grievar Road. Murray's memory of Wazari was likely as naïve as the rest of his youthful thoughts, right up there with the notion that he'd been fighting for honor, for his nation, for the Codes. He passed a section of purple awnings with the heavily perfumed scent of night flowers wafting from them. A veiled woman draped in silk peered out seductively and waved Murray toward her.

The kids would have enjoyed this, Murray thought. Dozer would likely have tried to steal off for a peek into these courtesan tents. And he could imagine the Jadean girl, Brynn, looking wide-eyed at the assortment of animals. If he'd only come for rations, like he'd told the Whelps, he probably would have brought them into the market.

But that was not why Murray had come to Wazari.

He weaved his way through several stalls selling colorful silk robes and emerged in front of a red tent with a six-fingered hand symbol on the awning. Murray pushed the thick curtain aside and walked through the dimly lit tent. The goods sold here were not up on display like in the rest of the market, and buyers looked over their shoulders as they took wrapped bundles under their arms. He ducked his head as he passed into a short stall set against the tent's back wall. Murray pulled his cowl back and looked down at a little man in a steel chair wearing a strange pair of bifocals that magnified his eyes.

"Stims or neurotech?" the hawker said nonchalantly as he fiddled with a broken deck.

"Neither," Murray replied.

"Then you're wasting my time," the man responded. "Get out of here."

"Thaloo said I could come to you for something else."

The man looked up from his work, pushing back his chair.

"How is that fat bastard doing now?"

"Same as always; he's a piece of shit," Murray replied.

The man nodded. "So, what now did Thaloo say I might be providing you?"

"Information," Murray said. "I'm looking for someone's whereabouts."

"There are many someones who I used to know the whereabouts of," the man responded. "But strangely, my memory is foggy right now."

Murray laid three midnight onyx pieces on the table and waited.

"Ah, yes," the hawker whispered. "I remember where some of these folk are. Who in particular are you looking for?"

"The one known as Silas," Murray said.

The man burst out into laughter. "You think I'm crazy?! You want to know where the Slayer is at? I do not have a death wish." Murray sighed. He reached into his pocket and pulled out six more bits and laid them on the table.

"There are Enforcers at all way-stops on the road, and even some patrolling this market, asking the very same question as you," the hawker said.

Murray emptied the rest of his bit-purse onto the table. The man's eyes gleamed, as if he were salivating, but he shook his head as he pushed the pile of onyx back.

"I can't do it. I don't know shit. Why don't you get out of here before you get us both buried?"

Murray didn't back down. "I need to know where Silas is."

The man turned away, grabbing a piece of neurotech off the shelf.

"I told you, I don't know anyone by that name."

Murray reached over the table and grabbed the man by the shoulders. He lifted the little hawker like a doll and wrapped a thick arm around his neck. Murray squeezed for a moment to constrict the man's arteries. "Now, it'll be a few seconds of me squeezing and you'll be out," Murray whispered. "And while you're out, you know what I'm going to do? I'll take all the darkin' stim in this shop and give it out to those hungry-looking Grievar mulling about outside."

The man tried to struggle but could not move an inch. Murray squeezed again, sensing darkness was closing in on the man.

"Wait!" The hawker managed to get the word out, and Murray loosened his grip.

"Last I heard, Slayer had taken a stim production depot to the west," the hawker said.

"I already knew that," Murray growled. He began to ratchet the strangle up again.

"And!" the man yelped. "And there's been word he's close to the capital. Clerics been ending up dead in and around Karstock."

"Are you lying to me?" Murray felt the man's pulse against his arm. "Why in the dark would the Flux leader put himself in the seat of the empire?"

"I swear, I'm telling you the truth," the hawker pleaded. "Let me be."

Murray threw the man back over the table and onto the floor of the little stall. He slid the onyx pile back into his purse, all but one coin that he tossed onto the floor beside the hawker.

"One more question," Murray said. "And I need you to think carefully before you answer."

The man glared back at him with his beady eyes.

"Is the Slayer with anyone else?"

"What do you mean, *with anyone else*?" the hawker yelled. "He's leader of the darkin' Flux; he's got an army of rebels with him!"

"With anyone in particular, though," Murray said. "Someone close by him most of the time."

"Yeah." The hawker stood and dusted himself off. "I heard he's got a kid with him. Some boy that doesn't leave his side."

Murray stared hard at the man before turning and ducking back beneath the low entry.

"And tell Thaloo he owes me!" Murray heard the hawker scream as he went back the way he came.

if you enjoyed
GRIEVAR'S BLOOD

look out for

INFINITY GATE
The Pandominion

by

M. R. Carey

From bestselling author M. R. Carey comes a brilliant genre-defying story of humanity's expansion across millions of dimensions—and the AI technology that might see it all come to an end.

INFINITY IS ONLY THE BEGINNING.

The Pandominion: a political and trading alliance of a million worlds. Except that they're really just one world, Earth, in many different realities. And when an AI threat arises that

*could destroy everything the Pandominion has built, they'll
eradicate it by whatever means necessary.*

*Scientist Hadiz Tambuwal is looking for a solution to her
own Earth's environmental collapse when she stumbles across
the secret of interdimensional travel, a secret that could
save everyone on her dying planet. It leads her into the middle
of a war on a scale she never dreamed of. And she needs to
choose a side before every reality pays the price.*

0

They say that children born in wartime are likely to have problems throughout their lives; to struggle both with the uncertainties of the world and with their own emotions and to search in vain for happiness.

This has not been true for me. I was born in one of the biggest conflicts this universe has ever seen, the war between the vast empire called the Pandominion and the machine hegemony (which may have been greater still), and what I remember most of all is the moment when I was suddenly able to reflect on my own existence. I had been a thing but now I was a sentient, a *self* in the language of the Pandominion. It was a miraculous thing and I cried out loud at the sheer joy of it.

But you can probably see from this the problem I face when I set out to tell you the story of my life – which is my goal here, however indirectly I may seem to come at it. My case is not typical. I existed for a long time *before* I was born, and there was nothing inevitable about my becoming self-aware. It depended on the efforts of three individuals, three selves, and not one of them had any conscious intention to deliver me.

One of the three was a scientist, who came to be famous across a thousand thousand continua of reality but remained uncelebrated in the universe into which she was born. Her name was Hadiz Tambuwal. She was a genius, but only in a small way. Her greatest discovery was made almost completely by accident, and it had been made before by others in a great many elsewheres. In fact Hadiz's contribution to history is marked throughout by things done casually or without intention. She changed the Pandominion forever more or less by tripping over it. But she left gifts for the people who came after her to find, and she came to be an instigator of outcomes much bigger than she had ever aimed at.

The second of the three, Essien Nkanika, was a rogue – but generally speaking no more exceptional a rogue than Tambuwal was a scientist. He was born in the gutters and he felt this justified every cruel and callous thing he did to claw his way out of them. Determined to serve only himself, he fell very readily into the service of others who were cleverer than him and more ruthless. He did unspeakable things for them, much worse than anything he ever did on his own account, but he had one great thing in him too. It is for this that I remember him.

And that third self? At the outset she was the least remarkable of all. She was Topaz Tourmaline FiveHills, a rabbit of the Pandominion, from the city of Canoplex-Under-Heaven in Ut. She was a bad fit in some ways for the society in which she grew, independent to the point of recklessness in a culture that prized emotional restraint and caution above all. But she was also clever and brave and curious, and sheer chance put her at the nexus of huge, seismic movements that drew in uncountable worlds. She learned, and grew, and made decisions. What she ultimately achieved was of greater significance and wider reach than any diplomat or leader of her time.

I will come to all these stories in their place, ending – inevitably and without apology – with my own story. My awakening, which was the end of history. The end of empire. The end, you might say, of an uncountable infinity – the biggest kind of infinity there is.

I meant no harm to anyone. I would even argue that what I did was for the best. Nobody had ever attempted before to perform surgery on entire universes. For such a task, you need a knife of immense, all but incalculable size.

Me. I am that knife.

1

Hadiz Tambuwal saw Armageddon coming from a long way off.

At first she was fairly philosophical about the whole thing. The sources of the impending cataclysm seemed to lie firmly in the nature of humanity as a species, so she didn't see much point in anguishing about them. To wish for the world to be in a better state was to wish for the entire history of life to have played out differently. It was a pretty big ask.

Hadiz had been accused – by her mother, among others – of being cold-blooded and unfeeling. She resented the allegation at the time but later came to see some truth in it. Certainly she was aloof. Cerebral. Difficult to get close to, and disinclined to meet people halfway when they tried. She lived alone by choice, and did her best to stay out of the massive web of connections and obligations that made up her extended family. She loved her aunts, uncles and cousins, some of them very much, but that stuff got complicated. It was much easier to love them from a distance.

She avoided friendships too, because of the complications that came with them; because they forced her to try to intuit other people's motives and desires, which always seemed much more opaque and muddled than her own. She satisfied her sexual needs in brief, transactional encounters: with her near-black skin, thorn-thicket curls, rudder nose and commanding height she was more striking than beautiful, but even so she never had any trouble finding a casual partner for a day or a night. She just preferred her own company, which she didn't see as a character flaw or a handicap. In her discipline, which was particle physics, you got your fair share of introverts.

But as the droughts and famines intensified, the air curdled and the resource wars burned, Hadiz found her customary detachment harder and harder to keep up. From a purely personal point of view, she preferred a world that had art and music and literature (and people who could appreciate those things) to one that didn't. From another perspective, she saw the disappearance of a richly diverse and complex ecosystem as a scandalous waste. More than either of those things, she loved her work and hated to leave it unfinished. The ruin of civilisation had come at a very inconvenient time.

It has to be said, though, that she had a good vantage point from which to view it. Hadiz lived and worked at Campus Cross, the most richly endowed research facility not just in Nigeria but on the entire African continent and most likely in the world. She was surrounded by geophysicists, biochemists and engineers who were trying to think their way out of the box their species had put itself in. She knew from the news media and from conversations with her extremely well-informed colleagues exactly how bad things were getting on a planetary scale and which longshot solutions were being attempted. She kept her own tally of the interventions that had already failed.

Campus Cross was a small side project jointly owned by the Catholic Church and by three billionaires who had all separately decided that the world was now so badly screwed that their individual fortunes might not be enough to unscrew it. They had pooled their resources, or at least some of their resources, creating a blind trust to administer the eye-watering sums of money they were pouring into this Hail Mary play. They had managed to lure in many very fine minds, although some had refused them outright because of the stringent terms of the contract. In exchange for a stratospheric salary the researchers ceded all rights in their work, the fruits of which belonged exclusively to the four founders, or – as they were mostly referred to on campus – to God and the Fates.

Hadiz had come to Campus Cross for the same reason that most of her peers had: it seemed to her that any work not directly related to the problem of saving the world was something of a waste of time. She had no illusions about her employers. She knew that the billionaires had eggs in other baskets, not the least of which were off-Earth colonies and generation ships. They would stay if they could, but they were ready to run if they had to.

The fact that Hadiz *lived* at the campus was a well-kept secret. As far as anyone else knew she had an apartment halfway across Lagos in a district called Ikoyi. But the campus was a long way outside the city's main urban cluster, and getting in by public transport had become an increasingly unpredictable and stressful experience. Ikoyi's water supply had recently been contaminated with human growth hormones. Then there were the blackouts, caused by systemic failures at the Shiroro dam which supplied hydroelectric power to the eastern half of the city. Blackouts had always been a daily fact of life in Lagos, but they were becoming longer and more frequent as the Kaduna River shrank to a half-hearted trickle. When enough was finally enough, Hadiz had packed a few clothes and quietly decamped, without telling anyone or asking anyone's permission.

In the smallest of her lab building's storerooms she set up a foldaway bed and a stack of three plastic crates to serve as a wardrobe. There was a toilet right next door and a shower in the gym block a short walk away. The building had its own generator, and steel security shutters which came down an hour after sunset to shut out the world. Hadiz was undisturbed there for the most part, especially after her four assistants, one by one, stopped coming into work. They were not the only ones. In the staff commissary she saw colleagues whose projects were more labour intensive than her own brought to tears as they were forced to scale back or even abandon research programmes into which they had poured years of their lives. She was glad that her own work required no mind or muscle other than her own. She kept her counsel and continued with her research, head down and shoulders hunched as an entire global civilisation tilted wildly, its centre of gravity now way outside its tottering base.

The world is a solid thing but we experience it in the abstract. Once Hadiz moved into Campus Cross she almost never ventured down into Lagos proper, so apart from the TV news and a few polemical websites her measures of how things were changing were small and local. The fires in Lekki and Victoria Island turned the sky bright orange and filled the air with ash for three weeks. That was followed by a photochemical smog that was appallingly toxic, full of aldehydes and carboxylic acids.

The campus's board of governance temporised for a while, issuing masks and air quality monitors, but eventually they yielded to the inevitable. They offered double wages to any support staff who continued to turn up for their shifts, but allowed the rest to remain at home on indefinite leave. It was assumed that the scientists themselves would somehow make shift and would not abandon their work in progress. But as Hadiz worked late into the evening she counted the lights in the windows of adjoining buildings. There were fewer each time. Some nights there were none at all: hers was the only candle lit to curse the dark.

The tremors came next, and they came as a shock. Sitting on a single tectonic plate, Nigeria had long been thought to be immune to seismic shock. Even when those estimates were revised in the early twenty-first century the prevailing opinion was that only the south-west of the country was at significant risk. The tremors came anyway, toppling the Oba palace and the cathedral. At Campus Cross fissures opened in the ground and cracks proliferated across the walls of the main buildings. Part of the admin block collapsed, but nobody was hurt. The offices there had been deserted for weeks.

Increased geothermal activity not just in Africa but across the world degraded the air quality to new and more alarming levels. Thick clouds veiled the sun, so mornings were as dark as evenings. Wild dogs roamed across the campus and nobody chased them away. Hadiz found an inland route to the commissary that took her through three neighbouring departments and avoided the need to step outside. She served herself these days, leaving a signed chit each time for the food she'd taken.

The chits piled up. Dust drifted across them, as it did across everything else.